Copyright © 2023 by Sherilee Gray

Edited by Karen Grove

Proofread by Judys proofreading

& Shelley Charlton

Cover Designed by Natasha Snow Designs

www.natashasnowdesigns.com

An Oath at Midnight - Sherilee Gray - 2nd ed.

ISBN:

978-1-99-118062-9 (Epub)

978-1-7386194-5-0 (Print)

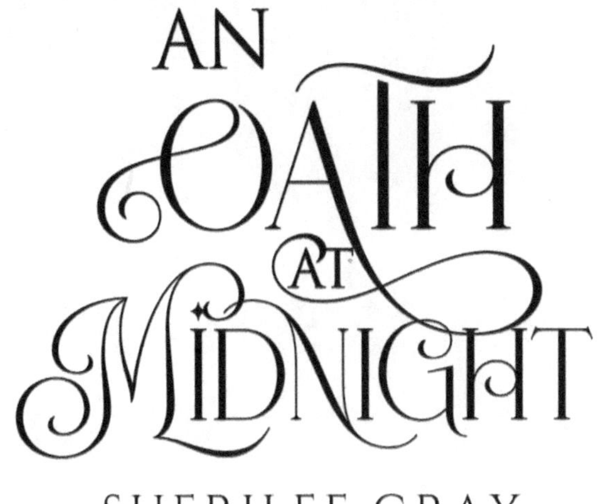

AN OATH AT MIDNIGHT

SHERILEE GRAY

Play List

- FIND ME - Sigma, Birdy *(I listened to this on repeat while I wrote Bram's scene in Chapter 19)*
- THE DEATH OF PEACE OF MIND - Bad Omens
- WORSHIP - Amber Run
- SOMEWHERE ONLY WE KNOW - Keane
- JUST PRETEND - Bad Omens
- I WANNA BE YOURS - Arctic Monkeys
- SWAY - Bic Runga
- I WANT TO – Rosenfeld
- RUNNING UP THAT HILL - Kate Bush
- WILDEST MOMENTS - Jessie Ware

For Vaughan,

The wind beneath myyyyy winnngs!

Prologue

Magnolia

My heart raced so fast, I felt dizzy.

He was back.

It was *really* freaking hard, but I sat as still as I could and stopped myself from turning to look at him again. The sly glances I'd managed his way; there was no missing how utterly magnificent he was. Goddess, he was living, breathing midnight. Every part of him, from his pointed beak to his vicious-looking talons was black. His feathers, so shiny, I was desperate to feel how silky they'd be against my fingertips.

He was beautiful.

I'd spotted him for the first time a month ago. He'd been perched in the huge oak tree that bordered our cemetery, and every day since he'd come closer. I wanted to talk to him, badly, but I had to wait. He needed to approach me, that's what Willow and Iris said.

He needed to come to the realization that he was my familiar on his own. If I tried to force the connection, I could freak him out and he might leave. But it was *so hard* to wait. So hard not to run over to tell him that he was mine. That we'd be best friends forever, and that no matter what happened to either of us, we'd always have each other. Butterflies went wild in my belly, and I forced myself to breathe through them.

I couldn't take it. I had to peek at him one more time, and I glanced over my shoulder.

Coal-black eyes locked with mine, and something invisible, but *huge,* hit me so hard that I rocked back, sucking in a startled breath. Happiness, the kind I never knew existed, filled me, and it was so vast there was no stopping the smile from spreading across my face.

The big black crow's wings extended, and with a *caw,* he dove from the tree branch and flew away.

I jumped off my seat. "Don't go! Come back! Please, come back!"

What had I done? What if he never came back? What if I'd ruined everything? I wanted to run after him, but I'd never be able to catch up to him...and if he didn't want to be found, I'd never see him again.

I couldn't remember the last time I cried, but tears welled in my eyes now.

My head jerked back, a cry bursting from me. I touched my forehead, and my fingers came away coated in blood. A rock lay at my feet.

I looked up at the sound of laughter. Amelia and her best friends Leah and Claire watched me. Each holding rocks in their hands. Amelia smirked, and her familiar, Scott, a feline shifter at her side, puffed out his chest with a smirk.

I straightened. They hated me, all of them. I wasn't sure why, but it'd been that way since we met on my first day of elementary school. Amelia had taken one look at me and decided I was a threat to her, that's what Wills said, anyway. She said that jealousy made people act like assholes.

Scott tilted his head to the side, his green, feline eyes moving over me. "You get uglier every time I see you."

Amelia threw her head back laughing as Scott took the stone from her hand.

"Start running." He grinned. "We're just trying to help you. Look at yourself, you could use the exercise."

I stood there in shock, blood still dripping down the side of my face. "Aren't you a little old for this playground bully bullshit?" I said, pleased when my voice came out strong and not as shaken as I felt.

"Run," he said again with more force, throwing the rock in the air and catching it. "Or I'll open up the other side of your face."

"Run, you stupid bitch," Amelia said, then snatched the rock back from her familiar and threw it.

I covered my head with my hands, ducking.

The rock was snatched out of the air, followed by a thud as black boots hit the ground in front of me.

It was him—my crow.

But there were no feathers this time. No, this time, he was in his human form. I straightened, taking in the boy in front of me. He was tall, towering over me, and thin. He wore black jeans and no shirt, and through his dirt-streaked skin I could see several tattoos on his back and arms.

The witches across from us stared at him in shock. Scott flexed his biceps, hands fisted at his sides, and took a step forward. I couldn't see my crow's face, and he said nothing, just shook his head, making his glossy black hair move in a way I knew it'd feel as silky as his wings would.

Scott stopped in his tracks. He was still scowling, trying to look tough, but there was real fear in his eyes. "I'm finished with these fucking losers," he announced, then spat on the ground and strode away, Amelia and her friends rushing after him.

I stood still and silent behind my crow, waiting for him to turn around, and prayed to the mother that he wouldn't shift and fly away again. The muscles in his back flexed, and I held my breath, but he didn't change forms and fly away, he turned.

When his black eyes met mine, he jolted, and his lids slammed down. The fan of his thick, black lashes quivered against his cheeks for several seconds, before they slowly opened and he looked at me again.

I had no idea what he was thinking, so I swiped my tears away and smiled tentatively. "Thank you for stopping them." His head was dipped, his glossy black hair hanging forward, obscuring some of his face, but there was no missing how beautiful he was in this form as well. His brow was broad, his jaw square but a little pointed. His nose was prominent but refined, and his cheeks were sharp. I wanted to brush his hair out of the way and get a better look at him.

He said nothing, just studied me with those obsidian eyes.

"You've been watching me," I said.

He nodded.

My hands trembled with excitement, with fear that he'd leave again. "Why didn't you say hello?"

Still, he said nothing, but his chest rose and fell faster, his eyes searching mine.

"You don't need to be afraid of me or hide." I smiled gently and took a small step closer. "I'd never hurt you. Not ever."

His feet shifted, his head still dipped.

"My name's Magnolia, what's yours?"

His chest expanded and a shaky breath rushed past his perfectly formed lips. "Bram."

Goose bumps lifted all over me at the sound of his voice. It was impossibly deep, deeper than I expected, yet soft as well somehow.

He didn't move, didn't look as if he were going to try to leave again, and I couldn't hold it in any longer. "I've been waiting for you," I said. "For so long...my whole life."

His head jerked back, his hair falling away from his face, and his gaze grew impossibly intense.

"You know, don't you? What we are to each other? That we belong together?"

His fingers curled and uncurled at his side, and his nostrils flared. "Yes," he said, and something changed in the way he stood, in the look in his eyes. It was understanding. Relief. And the wall he held between us dropped and crumbled to dust.

I needed to get closer to him. I let the feeling fill me, guide me, and closed the space between us. He didn't step away as I wrapped my arms around his waist and pressed my cheek to his chest. "You're finally here. I finally have my familiar." His arms tentatively wrapped around me as well. "We'll be together forever, and nothing will ever tear us apart."

Chapter One

Six years later

I laughed as Bram dipped low, spinning as we flew above the forest canopy.

His low chuckle rumbled through his chest, and I couldn't wipe the smile off my face. He'd partially shifted, so instead of going full crow, he was wings only. He looked like a dark angel in this form, a deadly, tattooed, obsidian-eyed, goth angel.

He tightened his arms around me and did another wide loop. I cackled again, and he flashed me a grin.

How long had it been since we'd done this? Hung out, laughed, just...had fun. Too long. Things had been strained between us for so long, but today we'd both called an unspoken truce, and I refused to be the one to break it and dredge back up all the hurt that had been simmering between us—or let my anger get the better of me. Today he was here, we were together, and I *would* bank the inferno constantly blazing in my gut and enjoy every damn moment.

Bram pointed to the forest floor through the trees. A group of demons looked up at us, pointed teeth bared, running to try and keep up, as if they had a hope in hell at getting anywhere near us. This part of the forest was infested with demons and other creatures. The hounds had killed and driven most of them from their territory, and a lot had settled here. This area had always been infested with monsters, though, and they all wanted to take a bite out of you.

We were on the outskirts of the Roxburgh State Forest and far from civilization. The area had been left to run wild a long time ago, and Bram's people, who also lived out here, and the bat shifter colony not far from it, used it to their advantage.

If you didn't have wings, getting anywhere near them was impossible.

They used the deadly forest as a first line of defense, and it had worked for them both for a very long time.

A cluster of tree houses appeared in the distance, and Bram changed direction. My hair whipped around my face, and I shoved it back so I could take it all in. The tree houses in Bram's village were all different shapes and sizes, eclectic and beautiful in their own way, and were joined by intricate swing bridge-like walkways high in the trees. The village was fairly spread out, and their warriors set up their places on the outer edges, protecting those more vulnerable from attack—if anyone managed to make it through the first line of defense, that is. Bones, demon mainly, hung from the branches and swing bridges like macabre wind chimes, skulls mounted on every post and above every tree house door, a final warning to any enemies that might come too close.

The demons heeded that warning and avoided the crows' territory. They'd learned long ago that getting too close would cost them their heads. Crow shifters were a rare breed, dark and deadly and preferring their own company. Most of the people here barely left the area or ventured to the city.

We landed on the deck of one of the larger tree houses. It belonged to Payne, Bram's older brother, and he had not one but three demon skulls nailed above his door. It flew open now, and Maeve, Bram's niece, ran out, her long, glossy black hair streaming out behind her.

Bram lowered me to my feet and lifted her into his arms, pressing his face against her little throat. "Happy birthday, Maeve," he said low.

She hugged him tightly back. Maeve was sweet and shy, watchful of strangers, and she'd warmed up to me a little the last couple years.

Maeve was Payne's only child. I had no idea what happened to her mother. I did know she was a witch named Farah, but she'd been gone when I met Bram and Payne refused to talk about it with anyone, even his family.

Uma, Bram's aunt, walked out, wiping her hands on her apron and grinned. "You're here, finally."

Uma was a small female, her black hair streaked with gray, and she had sharp eyes. Like most shifters, crows were long-lived. I had no idea how old she was, but she looked as if she were only in her late forties.

"Glad you're home," she said to Bram, giving him a tight hug.

She released him, then held her arms out to me. I let her pull me in for a hug as well and somehow managed to stop myself from pulling away or flinching. I was having a good day, but my scars often made it hard to forget they were there. Sometimes, it was as if they were alive, crawling all over my body—making me feel as if the people who put them there were right there as well.

I fought my shudder as she released me, and I stepped back. I was short, but even I had to look down at Uma. The older female had only recently come home from England. She'd lived with her mate, at one of the crow villages there, for seventy years. After Uma's mate died, she came home. Bram said she couldn't be there anymore, the reminders of her female were too painful.

Maeve only had eyes for the gift in my hand and looked ready to burst out of her skin. Laughing, I handed the little crow the gift Bram and I had for her.

She sat on the ground, tore away the paper, and gasped. Her eyes flew to Bram. "I love it!" The art set we'd gotten her was in a cool wooden case with all the paints, brushes, and markers a kid could need.

Bram pulled the other gift he had for her from his pocket and placed it on her lap.

"Another one?" She tore that paper off as well, and gasped. "Wings! Did you make them, Uncle Bram?"

He nodded, looking uncomfortable. Bram didn't like a lot of attention, even from his own family.

"He spent hours carving it," I said, admiring the wings Bram had labored over for his niece. Each feather was incredibly detailed and utterly beautiful.

She turned it over and saw the little space Bram had carved out. It had a small cork in it. Her gaze shot up to us.

"I added some herbs, a spell for protection and good health," I said. I didn't know if Maeve would develop magic abilities from her mother's side, but I wanted her to know what was possible, and to feel comfortable asking me anything if she ever had questions.

"Thank you, Magnolia." She smiled wide.

It'd taken us a while to get to this point. Bram's family had struggled to understand our relationship. Like why he'd moved away from his people, or why he had trouble leaving my side. Crows didn't trust easily, and it didn't help that I was a witch. For years, his brothers thought I'd cast a spell over him, that I was controlling him somehow.

They seemed to have accepted me a little more now, but I

knew they still resented me for keeping him from them. It didn't matter that neither of us had any control over our connection. And honestly, I didn't blame them. I hated being parted from Bram as well.

Talon dropped out of the sky, landing in a crouch in front of Bram. "You're needed."

Bram raised a brow.

"Secret birthday shit," Talon said. "Let's go."

They both shifted and exploded into the air. Bram was the youngest, then Talon, Rook next, and the oldest was Payne. Payne was the exception to the whole acceptance thing, he didn't just resent me, he didn't trust me, and sometimes I thought he might actually hate me. I watched Bram disappear over the treetops above us, until I couldn't see him anymore. Uma covered my hand with hers, startling me, and drawing my attention back to her.

"How have you been, honey?" she asked, and there was concern in her eyes.

"I'm good," I said, lying. She continued to stare, seeing right through my lie. "Bram's talked to you?"

Uma shook her head. "No, my nephew keeps his own counsel, but I know things must be difficult for you at the moment."

"So you know what he's doing? What this new job is that takes him away all the time?" He'd started a new job eighteen months ago, leaving at all times of the day and night, a job he said he'd had to sign an NDA for and couldn't share with me. His "job" had been taking him away more and more frequently, and I had no idea where he was going, what he was doing while he was gone, or why, when he came home, he was often injured.

She didn't answer, which was answer itself. Cool, everyone knew but me. Flames licked my insides, my anger trying to rear its head. I forced it back down.

"You don't need to know," a deep voice said behind me.

I turned to see Payne materializing from a dark corner, shifting into his human form. Crow shifters had several forms: human, shadow, bird, and wings only, and Payne took full advantage of the shadows, looming in dark corners, silently watching...judging. His dark eyes locked on me, his lashes so thick and dark, it looked like he had coal around his eyes.

All four brothers had those lashes. They were all similar in appearance. Black hair and eyes, tall, tattooed, but Bram and Payne were the most alike. Bram wore his hair differently than his brothers, though. They wore theirs tied back and had one or both sides shaved, and all three had a series of lines inked there. I'd asked Bram what it meant, and he'd just shrugged and said it was what their warriors did, that it was tradition.

"Be nice," Uma said to him.

Payne's wide chest expanded. "Of course."

Uma's eyes narrowed. "I need to check on the meal. If you upset Magnolia while I'm gone, we'll be having words."

He inclined his head, and his aunt bustled off. His dark gaze slid from his aunt, and he smiled down at his daughter. "Go help your aunt, little feather."

Maeve jumped up, doing as he asked, and Payne scooped up the wings Bram had carved, turned it over, pulled out the cork, and dumped the tiny leather pouch filled with herbs and other ingredients for the spell I'd put in it for his daughter over the side of the deck, then put it back. "She doesn't need your spells. She doesn't need anything from you."

Yeah, that hurt, but I wasn't surprised by it, and I refused to let him see how shitty he'd just made me feel. My anger rose again, and I blew out a breath as I jammed it back down, though I knew from experience, that would only work so long. "You said I don't need to know about Bram? Why?" I said instead of telling him what a giant asshole he was. I knew Payne wasn't my biggest fan, he'd never bothered hiding it. I'd never really cared, but for some reason, right then, I kind of hated the resentment I saw in his eyes when he looked at me.

"Because it's none of your business."

"Bram's my best friend, my familiar. We share everything," I said, and this time there was no controlling the bite of anger in my voice.

"Obviously not," he said and eyed me for several long, uncomfortable seconds. I'd always had a kind of sixth sense. It had never developed into anything more than that, but I'd always just known things—not like a psychic, but at a gut level. I'd lost touch with that side of myself the last couple of years, but I was slowly getting it back—and there was something wrong about Payne, something off. No, he wasn't a danger to me, not physically, but looking into his eyes sent a shiver down my spine, always. "You've seen the picture of our mother?" he asked cryptically.

"Yes." I'd seen it many times. Bram had a framed photo of his parents in his room at home.

"Do you know how she got the jagged scars down the side of her face?"

"Fighting with a demon." Bram didn't like to talk about his parents. They'd died when he was young, and eighteen-year-old Payne had taken responsibility of his brothers. Things had been tough for all of them. "But I'm not sure what that's got to do with anything. I want to know what's going on with Bram..."

The coldness in his black eyes intensified, shutting me up.

He angled his head to the side of the house, telling me without words to follow. He led me around to the other side of the deck and stopped at the railing, his rough, scarred, and inked hands gripping it as he stared out at the large clearing in front of us.

I'd seen it many times, of course, and right now it was covered with wildflowers, a riot of color and sweet perfume. It was beautiful, but I didn't know why he'd brought me around here.

"She was younger than you are now when it happened." He pointed to a spot in the distance, on the other side of the clearing. "My father told me that was where she burst from the trees, a hoard of demons behind her. One tackled her, taking her down. She fought and killed it, then kept on running."

I stared at him stunned. "Why didn't she fly away? Why didn't anyone help her?"

He turned to me, and I forced myself to stand my ground and not retreat when his black eyes locked on mine. "Because she was determined to pass the test, to win our father. She'd known he was hers since she was fifteen. My father knew it as well, but he had to wait until she was old enough, and because of who he was, he waited for her to make the first move. She needed to decide what she was willing to risk to be with him. But she'd decided as soon as she realized he was fated to be hers. My mother trained hard, and when she turned eighteen, she was finally ready to claim my father, to become his mate. She went to him and told him she was leaving, and that she'd be back in two days."

I frowned. "I don't understand. What test? Ready for what?"

"She told him to wait for her right there," he said, ignoring my questions, and motioned to the edge of the clearing below us, to the chain-link fence across it. "He knew what she was about to do, what she had to do if they were going to be together. He also knew there was a chance she wouldn't make it, but there was no stopping her. He told me he'd never been more terrified in his life or more proud. When she broke through the trees that day, he was waiting, like she'd asked him to." Payne's Adam's apple slid up and down. "It killed him to stand by while she fought, but if he'd helped her, she would've failed. Our people would've seen her as weak, someone in need of rescuing, and not a fitting mate for their future leader."

I stared out toward the forest filled with demons and other creatures. *Holy shit.* "I had no idea."

He gripped the railing tighter. "It's called the demon run."

"Jesus," I muttered. "Why would anyone do that?"

His nostrils flared, his knuckles turning white. "Our people are strong. Fierce. There's a reason others avoid us and why we keep to ourselves. We are predators, without mercy or remorse. It's in our blood, it's the way we're made." He looked down at me. "We don't have kings and queens, but my father led and protected his people until the day he died. They look to me and my brothers to lead them now. And whoever my brothers mate, will need to be just as strong as our mother was. They'll need to be resilient, courageous...merciless. They need to be willing to risk everything to be with us."

The way he was looking at me—an uneasy feeling settled in my belly. I quickly looked away. "Does every mated couple do the demon run?"

"Only those who want to mate a warrior. Not many can handle a male with that kind of strength. We may try to fight our true natures..." I felt his gaze burning into me now. "But it always comes to the fore. Being with a male like that is not for the faint of heart. Our mates need to be as strong as us, and the demon run is how they prove it."

Bram called my name from the other side of the tree house, and there was an edge to his voice. He hated when he didn't know where I was, and no matter how irrational it was, there was no missing his concern. Pretty ironic, since he did the same to me all the time.

I turned to go, but Payne stopped me. I turned back and he stared at me for several uncomfortable seconds. Whatever he was going to say, I wasn't going to like it.

"Do you understand what I'm telling you?"

"Not in the least, so instead of scowling, how about you enlighten me?"

He crossed his inked arms. "Bram will meet a female one day, a female the fates have chosen for him, one worthy of him, one who is willing to prove to him and his people that she's strong enough for him."

Pain shot through me like a barbed dagger, followed by pure undiluted rage. "Why are you telling me this?"

His hand shot out and he gripped my shoulder, his hold firm, unforgiving. Pain speared through the scar beneath his palm. I gritted my teeth.

"I don't give a fuck that he's your familiar. When that day comes, you *will* step aside. You'll let him go," he said, no, demanded, his voice sending shards of ice through me.

I stared at him in shock.

Bram called again.

"I need to get back." I pulled away, dislodging his hold on me and rushed off.

As soon as I rounded the corner, Bram closed the distance between us, reassuring himself the same way I did after he'd been gone, and pulled me close, his face pressed to my throat. Bram liked to touch me, to be close, it'd always been that way since we found each other. He was the only person I could tolerate touching me most of the time, but sometimes, even that was too much, and now, under the weight of his brother's stare and after the conversation we'd just had, I eased away in the guise of checking out the cake Talon and Rook were placing on the table.

"Is this what you were doing?" I asked Bram.

His lips twitched. "I'm the best with frosting."

He was.

Payne joined us. I felt his gaze on me, and I did my best to ignore him.

Rook lit the seven purple candles, the flames glinting off his necklace made of fangs, demon mostly, but others as well, then Talon nudged Bram and we all sang happy birthday to a beaming Maeve.

I tried to relax after that, to enjoy the rest of the evening, but after what Payne said, it was impossible, and the anger stayed, no matter how hard I tried to shove it down again.

No matter how hard I tried not to think about why I felt this way.

~

"Land here," I said to Bram when we flew over my family's two-story, Victorian house.

He frowned but did as I asked. "You need something from your room?"

"I need some time on my own," I said, shoving my hands in my pockets and balling them into fists.

Bram rocked back like I'd backhanded him. It fucking stung, knowing that I'd hurt him, but I was hurting as well, and with all this anger inside me, I didn't want to take it out on him—and I would if I didn't get away from him right now. His family knew what he was doing, where he was going, but not me. *We* were family, closer than family, yet he refused to tell me anything. The cut of that, after talking to his aunt, was deeper tonight, and I couldn't hide it from him or hold it in any longer. If I didn't get some distance between us, we'd fight. I'd say shit I'd regret, we'd hurt each other, and I didn't want tonight to end that way.

He knew it as well, which was why he didn't say anything, why he stood there with pain in his eyes, with a look that said he didn't recognize me anymore. Well, he wasn't the only one. His Adam's apple slid up and down his throat, and he took a step back. "Whatever you need."

"Night, B," I said and rushed inside, shutting the door behind me.

"Drink?" Else asked from the kitchen counter, startling me. She was in her favorite fluffy pink robe and her soft, silver hair was still damp from her shower. She looked tiny tonight, and fragile. I wanted to wrap my arms around her and hold her tight, to let her comfort me and to beg her to never ever leave me, but my scars were alive, the pain more than I could stand. I didn't know why, but I could barely stand my own arms against my sides, let alone someone else touching me.

I did my best to hide the way I was feeling when I turned to her, but I couldn't hide shit from Elswyth Thornheart. No one could. I shook my head. "I'm fine."

My great-aunt was seventy-four years old, and looked like a sweet, little old lady, but she was smart, sarcastic, and a powerful healer. She and I were alike in a lot of ways. We both had an aptitude for potion making, and though I was nowhere near the healer she was, my talent for it had finally shown up several months ago and was steadily growing.

"You look like you could use some cocoa," she said, her brown eyes softening.

I forced a smile. "I just need a good night's sleep."

"Okay, pumpkin." She shuffled past with her steaming mug. "See you in the morning."

"Night."

A good night's sleep was what I desperately needed, but I didn't have a whole lot of them anymore, especially when Bram was away, or we slept apart.

I waited for Else's door to close and slipped back outside. I quickly glanced up at the tree house. The lights were on. Bram was inside.

Spinning around, I raced down the road to our cemetery, opened the iron gates and ran through, then I yanked off my jacket, shoved it against my face, and screamed into it, releasing all the pent-up rage inside me. Rage that wouldn't leave me alone, that had only grown with every passing month. That anger had lived inside me for two and a half years. I knew when it started, but I had no fucking clue how to control it. Or stop it.

Lying on the ground beside Gran's grave, I stuffed my jacket under my head and stared up at the stars, trying to fucking breathe. Sometimes I felt as if I were truly losing my mind.

I kicked off my shoes and pressed my bare feet and palms to the earth, relishing the texture of soft grass beneath me. I couldn't be with Bram right then, so this place was the next best thing.

The power from our cemetery danced over me, reaching through my hands and feet, and I felt it filter through me. Even after death, witches exuded magic; it poured from our bones into the earth. Everything in this place was useful and held power. The dirt, plants, the grass. Mom and Art tended gardens here, so Else and I always had a supply of ingredients for the tonics and potions we made for the store, and it was strongly warded, for the same reason.

Breathing deep, I bathed in the light of the moon and worked at calming myself.

It was a long time before my eyes finally grew heavy. I tried to fight it, knowing what would come, but the way I felt tonight, it was inevitable. Then I couldn't fight it anymore.

I shivered, wrapping my arms around myself, naked in every way a person could be. Clayton's cold blue eyes slid over my bare skin, and I whimpered, wanting to recoil, but I couldn't move. He gripped my throat, pumping more of his magic into me, causing me to tumble more and more out of control. I was lost, here, but also in the world he was spinning in my mind. His hand slid over my breast, squeezing roughly, a look of disgust on his face.

"You are utterly repulsive. You make me sick, Magnolia." He closed the space between us, his hand going lower, shoving between my thighs, the other taking my forearm in a bruising grip. "Your family is in agony. They're bleeding because of you. Do you see them? Can you hear their screams?"

More of his magic pulsed through me and I screamed, I screamed with them.

He smashed his cold lips against mine in a hateful kiss, biting me before he lifted his head, a twisted smile on his face.

"Kill me," I choked out. "Please, kill me."

My eyes flew open, and I sat up with a gasp.

The images were still there, in my mind, and I gripped both sides of my head. *It's over. He's dead.* The images he fed me, the sounds, they weren't real. Bram, my sisters, Mom, Else, Arthur, they're okay. Everyone's okay.

Snatching up my shoes and jacket, I ran from the cemetery, sprinting along the dirt road back to the yard and across the damp grass. I raced up the ladder to the tree house and through the door. Only then could I breathe, only then did the racing of my heart and the terror in my gut begin to calm.

I walked into Bram's room. He was on his side, the sheet at his hips, revealing an expanse of smooth, golden skin. I craved the warmth of it, of him. I tiptoed to the side of the bed, eased the covers back, and tried to get in without waking him.

"Come here," he said in his sleep-roughened voice.

My scars had calmed for now, the pain was gone, so I let him pull me into his strong, warm arms, let him hold me in that comforting, familiar embrace, soothing me the way only Bram could.

Chapter Two

Bram

I woke to the rustle of leaves, and the creak of the tree house. That sound always soothed something inside me.

The clouds were thick, the room washed in muted gray. I looked down at Magnolia again, curled against my side. We'd gotten home late after visiting my family. I studied the familiar curve of her cheek, the bow of her upper lip. She'd seemed distracted most of the night, then she'd gone straight up to her room when we'd gotten home. She'd been angry and trying to hide it from me, but I didn't miss it. I knew exactly why she was angry, and I deserved it.

I'd come to my tree house in the backyard and tossed and turned until I finally went to sleep. I'd woken again around three a.m. to Magnolia crawling into my bed.

I brushed the hair away from her face. Even in sleep she looked tired. My beautiful, wild, tortured, brave, maddening-as-fuck, little witch.

I swiped my thumb over the scar on her forehead, the one she'd gotten the day we first met.

One of many scars Magnolia had on her body now.

Scars she'd gotten when a sick, twisted monster had used magic to carve slices into her skin. I'd held her thrashing, bleeding body in my arms while she screamed in agony and fear. I'd been utterly helpless, unable to fight an invisible enemy attacking my reason to live.

That was two and a half years ago. The monsters were gone. One locked up, the others dead—one at my hand. That day still fucked with me, though. It felt like yesterday. I dreamed about it most nights. Sometimes about a different outcome, one that I couldn't bear to contemplate in the waking hours, one that took Magnolia from me. And other times, I dreamed of their screams, of their blood on my hands, of making the ones who hurt her pay again and again.

The anger she carried now, it started then, the kind of anger born from hopelessness, but it had grown into something more. Something she struggled to contain every single day, and I didn't know how to help her.

What the fuck would have become of me if we'd never found each other? My entire life, something had been missing, there'd been this feeling, this gaping nothingness inside me. It'd gotten worse after my parents' deaths—then I found my Magnolia, and I was whole for the first time. She'd been my world since.

You know, don't you? What we are to each other? That we belong together?

Her words filled my head, the ones a fifteen-year-old Mags had said to me that day. Yes, I'd known. After I found her, it was all I knew. I'd been sixteen, nearly seventeen, and maybe, if I'd been younger when we met, the truth of what we were to each other would have grown more gradually. But I hadn't been, and along with a deep knowing that Magnolia was my witch and I was her familiar, came the undeniable truth—that she was also my mate.

Something I never imagined would happen for me, and definitely not when I was so young. It wasn't something I'd ever wanted. I'd seen what loss and pain looked like when my father died, when my mother died soon after of a broken heart. I'd wanted none of it.

Then I'd seen Mags. She'd been at her family's cemetery. I'd been drawn there, pulled to that spot by a force deep inside me, unable to resist. I'd seen her hair first, black and thick and wavy—then she'd tilted her face up to the moonlight.

I'd stopped breathing.

She'd been perfect to me in every way. Everything my secret teenage heart had dreamed up had been sitting right there. She'd been too young for me then, and I'd been prepared to wait, for as long as she needed. To wait for her to come to the same realization as me.

It never happened, though.

My best friend, my mate, didn't want me the way I wanted her. She didn't recognize that part of the bond between us and thought of me only as family—maybe even a brother.

She was my everything, and being by her side the last six years had been a privilege and an honor, it was what I'd been born to do, but the last couple of years, after someone tried to take her from me during her sister Willow's trial, everything had changed.

I'd changed.

And so had Mags.

My gaze slid lower. While she slept, her shirt had slipped off one of her shoulders, revealing more silvery scars. She hated them. I hated how they got there, and how that day, and the ones leading up to it, irrevocably altered everything between us.

I looked at her face again. Her lips were full and deep crimson. Her dark lashes rested on her pink cheeks, her beautiful amber eyes locked behind closed lids. My crow's song built in my chest, like it often did at times like this, but I swallowed it back down and willed her eyes to open. I craved the way she looked at me, the same way I craved the wind on my feathers. Those eyes, they'd never hidden anything from me. The day we met, there'd been no lies when she'd looked at me, only truth.

We'll be together forever and nothing will ever tear us apart.

She'd said it and meant it. I'd believed it with everything in me.

I wasn't so sure anymore.

When she looked at me now, there were secrets.

She blinked, waking, and immediately gave me a sleepy smile, cracking my heart right down the fucking middle—because I had secrets of my own. Secrets I was forbidden to share. Secrets, that even if she did want me the way I did her, made it impossible for us to ever be anything more than we were.

"Hey," she said.

"Hey."

Rolling into me automatically, she curled her arm around my middle. I lay back and she rested her head against my chest.

She yawned. "So what're we doing today."

I opened my mouth to answer, but the thud of boots hitting the deck outside reached us.

A throaty *caw* followed. Rook. He liked talking even less than me.

Mags pulled away from me, sitting up, her gaze instantly growing distant. "I guess that answers that."

The peace between us shattered. "Mags..."

She climbed out of bed, shoved on her boots, and walked out of the room.

I tugged on my jeans and followed her out as Rook walked in.

He greeted Mags with a chin lift, and she forced a smile in response as she strode past.

I went after her, jumping off the deck and landing on the ground before she could get down the ladder. I stood in front of her before she could storm off. "Wait."

I expected fire, her anger, because that's what we did now, snapped and snarled at each other out of fear and desperation.

Instead, when she looked up at me, that tiredness was back in her eyes. "It's fine. Go."

That look, the defeat in her voice, it fucking terrified me. "Mags—"

"Whatever it is you're doing, just be safe, okay?"

I studied her expression, hating what I saw. Distance yawning wider between us. Every time I left her, every time I kept another secret from her, the canyon between us grew deeper, wider. "I want to tell you," I said, but giving her that small amount was all I could.

"But you can't, right?" Her gaze slid from me to the house on the other side of the yard, already checking out, already gone.

I'd taken the kind of oath that was binding for a lifetime. Only family, mates, could be told more. And though Mags meant more to me than anyone on this earth, she wasn't family, not in the blood sense, and we weren't mated. There was one other way—if she found out on her own. But the idea of her finding out that way? No, I couldn't fucking stomach it. That'd be the worst thing that could happen.

What would she think if you did tell her? Would she still look at you the same if she knew the things you'd done? If she knew what you truly were? How deep your darkness truly went?

She pressed her hands to my chest, and at the innocent contact, my heart smacked hard against the back of my ribs. I wanted to pull her close, my instincts screaming for me to press my face to her throat, nuzzle her smooth skin, to breathe her into my lungs.

"Be safe," she said and smiled up at me. It was forced, false. "I'll see you when you get back."

Then she dropped her hands and strode away, back to the house.

Rook dropped to the ground beside me. "Tell her how you feel or move the fuck on."

My brothers had picked up I had feelings for her, but they didn't know she was my mate, and I wasn't in a hurry to tell them.

I ignored him, watching until Mags disappeared inside. If I told her how I felt, I'd destroy what we had now. Yes, it was volatile and shaky, but she still cared, she still wanted me around.

After what Clayton did to her, she'd closed off completely when it came to any kind of romantic relationships. They made her uncomfortable, even in movies. She'd turn off the TV if anything even remotely sexual happened.

Telling her the truth was the worst thing I could do.

I used to hope that one day she'd see it, feel it for herself. That I'd wait forever if I had to.

I didn't wish for that anymore. I hoped like fuck she never felt it. I never wanted her to see the dark corners inside me, the twisted things in my mind, the things I needed to do just to stay sane. No, she could never see what I truly was, and if we were mated, there'd be no hiding it.

"Let's get the fuck out of here," I said.

Rook shifted, and took flight.

I did the same, following my brother.

What was another black mark on my soul?

Magnolia

The road to the keep was bumpy as hell. I gripped the steering wheel and tried to breathe through all the anger and pain. It wasn't working. Only one thing would help me.

I parked, and as I walked up the steep track to the keep, a wolf howled in the distance, alerting everyone of my arrival. Since Iris moved here with her mate, Draven, she'd become familiar with the different howls the wolves made, different pitches and lengths, and she was walking out of the keep to greet me as I strode across the clearing.

Iris was the second oldest out of the four of us, she could talk to animals, take on their traits and also did this weird thing that wasn't exactly shifting into an animal, but also kind of was.

She grinned. "I wasn't expecting you. This is a nice surprise."

I let her hug me, the coolness of her cheek brushing mine. The damage from her ex-boyfriend, Brody's, attempt to kill my sister had left a permanent black mark on her face. I squeezed her in return, though it was hard today. When I was like this, full of banked rage, I didn't want to be touched. I felt every scar as if it were a fresh slice, heard every twisted word that'd been muttered in my ear on repeat. The monsters were only in my head, but they were as real to me now as they were back then—when I'd made the biggest mistake of my life, breaking a blood oath and almost causing the death of my entire family.

My soul had been damaged that day, a fissure of darkness creeping through. It grew wider by the day, settling deeper, and there was no stopping it.

"Maybe we could visit later?" I said to Iris. "I'm actually here to train. Is Ash around?"

She gave me a look, one I didn't like, one that said she saw way too much of what I was trying to hide. "She's getting ready to leave on patrol, so you may as well hang out with me—"

"Thanks." I rushed off before she could finish, dashing around the side of the keep. I spotted Asher with several other wolves, including Draven.

Asher and I had gotten off to a pretty rocky start, and when she offered to train me six months ago, to help me deal with my anger, I'd turned her down flat. But my anger had continued to grow, had become so overpowering, the darkness inside me digging so deep, I'd scared myself, but worse, I was scaring everyone around me.

So much so that I shoved down my pride and asked her to train me.

Asher was cool, I could admit that now, and it turned out fighting the wolf, focusing my anger outward, helped me a lot. She wasn't family. She didn't give me a pass or go easy on me. She pushed me to my limits, forcing me to get a handle on my anger, and to work through what I was feeling. I learned quickly that using anger to fuel you, at least my brand of wild and uncontrollable anger, was the fastest way of getting your ass kicked.

She spotted me and strode over. "Can't train today, feisty. I'm rostered on patrol."

"Let me come with you."

She snorted, her golden eyes sparkling. "You think you're ready to take on a real live demon, little witch?"

I gritted my teeth. "Yeah, I do. We've been training for nearly six months. I can hold my own. You know I can."

Her expression grew serious. "This isn't playtime, Mags. One of those fuckers gets hold of you, it'll tear you to pieces."

Draven strode over. "What's going on?"

"She wants to come with us."

He didn't spare me a glance. "No."

I planted my hands on my hips. "You didn't even think about it."

"Don't need to," he said in his deep, growly voice.

"I'm ready, you know I am," I said, working really hard at not letting my anger get the better of me and firing attitude at him. Draven was not the kind of male to be talked into anything. He'd tell me to fuck off if he thought I wasn't in the right headspace. We'd talked about the possibility of this, when I was ready, and I was. More than ready.

He crossed his arms, looking down at me, his vibrant green eyes deadly serious. "My mate would fuck me up if you got hurt, you know that, right? And I won't be very fucking happy either if I have to carry you back in pieces."

"You've seen me train. And I'm going to need to know how to fight on my own, the mother will call me soon…"

"You still have time," he said.

I bit back a curse. So far, she'd called my sisters, one year apart. Going by that timeline, I had another six months. "The more practice I get, though, the better my chances. I want to do this, Draven."

"What you want and what you're ready for are two different things," he said.

"I am ready."

He turned to Asher. "You've been training her. You think she's ready to go out in the field? Keep in mind, it's your head on the chopping block if anything happens to her."

I bit back another curse.

"Physically, she's up to it. But what about in here, feisty." She tapped the side of my head, and I shoved her hand away. "You let your anger get the better of you out there, you'll wake up to the horrific sound of demons singing 'Kumbaya,' an apple jammed in your mouth, while they roast you over an open fire."

Draven's lips twitched. I ignored him, curled my fingers tight to control my temper, and nodded. "I've got it under control."

She flicked my forehead. "You sure?"

"Ash—"

She did it again. "Yeah?"

"Yes, I'm sure."

She gave me a shove. "Positive?"

I gritted my teeth. "Asher—"

She grabbed my forearm, a trigger spot for me, which she well knew, and tugged me forward. I snapped and swung at her instantly. Ash grabbed my fist midair and shoved me back. "You're not ready for shit. Get your ass inside before you get hurt."

Fuck. "Ash, come on."

She shook her head. "You came to the keep 'cause you're pissed off. That's more than fine when we're training. But that won't fly when we're on patrol."

"Asher, please—"

"You heard her," Draven said. "Get inside."

Then they turned their backs on me and ran into the surrounding forest, leaving me behind. I stood there breathing hard, fury exploding through me as I spun away and strode back across the clearing.

Iris called my name.

"I need to leave," I said, not looking back, and jogged to my car.

A minute later, I sped away. Not sure where I was going, or what I was going to do. The tree house was empty. Bram was gone.

Nothing made sense anymore.

My life fucking sucked, and I didn't know what the hell I was going to do about it.

Chapter Three

Magnolia

I grabbed a sprig of rosemary and plucked several yarrow flowers from the dried herbs hanging above me, then added them to the bubbling pot of healing elixir I was currently standing over. If I stopped stirring before it was done, the batch would spoil, and I'd have to start over again. Stock for several of our elixirs was low at The Cauldron, the shop owned by my oldest sister, Willow, and Else and I were busy trying to replenish them.

Else limped in. Her prosthesis gave her trouble in the morning and her limp was always more pronounced.

"Almost done, pumpkin?" she asked as she dumped a bunch of lavender on the worn wooden counter.

"Yeah." I lifted it off the burner, finally able to stop stirring, and put the brew aside to cool.

She came over and eyeballed it. "Should fill about forty bottles, I reckon." She ran a gnarled finger down the list in our order book. "That'll do for now. We'll start on the rest of these in the morning." She patted my shoulder, and I forced myself not to flinch. "Go do what young people do. I'll clean up."

I snorted. "Oh no, you don't. Connor will be here any minute. You're not getting out of your CEA meeting by using me and a messy workshop as an excuse." Else had recently been roped into joining the Coven Elders Assembly. They'd been trying to get her to join for years. I was pretty sure Connor had been the reason she'd finally caved.

She scowled. "I wasn't doing that."

"Yes, you were. Now, go pretty yourself up for your gentleman caller. I'll clean up here."

"You're a smart-ass, you know that?" she muttered as she headed across the room.

"I take after you."

She flipped me the bird, and I laughed as she walked out. Connor was her *very* good friend, though she hadn't confirmed or denied that they were dating. The male was a saint, though, always calm and steady. It also helped that he thought Else's grumbling was totally adorable.

I pulled my phone from my pocket and checked it again, and my smile slipped away. Still no word from Bram. It'd been thirty-six hours. I was worried. Goddess, I felt sick all the time when he was gone. When he was away, everything was just...worse.

I forced myself to focus on cleaning, putting things away, but my inner demons were in full swing without Bram here to distract me, and they were pushing in from all sides. I rubbed my forearm. Phantom pain throbbing below my skin, where the bruise had been, a perfect outline of Clayton's hand. It'd been visible for two weeks after.

He was dead, but when Bram was gone, my fucked-up mind brought him back to life. The darkness let him creep back in, reminding me of how stupid I'd been, how naive, how I'd let him use me to get to the people I loved most in this world, and no matter how hard I tried to force him back out, I failed every damn time.

Voices traveled in from the hall. Else and Connor, and there was no missing the alarm in their voices. I strode out, and as soon as I spotted Else, I knew something was wrong.

"What's going on?"

She turned to me and all color had drained from her face. "There's been another one," she whispered, her hands shaking. "I knew there would be, I goddamn knew the council was trying to downplay it. Idiots."

"Another murder?" A rock settled in the pit of my stomach.

"Another execution." Else sat heavily in the seat behind her, a look on her face I'd never seen before.

I gripped the doorframe. "Who?"

Pain filled her eyes. "Margot Huxley."

Margot was my age. We'd gone to school together. She and I and another guy named Jamie had been kind of friends. We'd all been loners, preferring our own company, but we'd hung out sometimes, occasionally ate lunch together if we were in the cafeteria at the same time. If we were forced to do an assignment with someone else, or some other group activity, they were my first choice and I was theirs. I hadn't seen her in a while, but whenever we ran across each other, we made time to catch up. "Is there a chance it could be unrelated?" I asked, my heart a lump in my chest.

She shook her head. "They carved judgment into her skin, Mags..." Her shrewd brown eyes locked on mine. "You need to be careful. Don't go anywhere on your own, not until this animal is found. Promise me."

I nodded and walked woodenly back into the workroom, still in shock. The first victim, Clara Hope, had been older than Margot, and the same word had been carved into her when they found her. I hadn't known Clara. She was Willow's age, but their deaths had to be by the same psycho.

Roxburgh already had its fair share of monsters. We didn't need another one.

Images flashed through my mind—of my own monster.

The way he'd touched me, making my skin crawl from the utter wrongness of it, of the images he'd projected into my mind. Images so horrific and real—

Gasping, I grabbed on to the edge of the counter as more of them filled my head, one after the other.

Blood, gore, flaying skin, dismembered limbs—the screams. Oh goddess, the screams of my family, of Bram.

I squeezed my eyes closed and tried to fight it.

For hours Clayton had filled my head with horror, until something had broken inside me, until I believed what I saw and heard. Until my screams were just as loud as the ones in my head.

And now I heard Margot as well—I heard her screams of terror and pain. As though the darkness in me was on the same frequency, broadcasting that horror right into my mind.

Opening the small box on my workbench, I slid the false bottom aside, took out the key, and rushed to the old dresser across the room. I quickly opened the heavy wooden doors and crouched, moving the stack of old recipe books out of the way. I'd found the key over a year ago and had no idea what it was for. Then several months ago, I'd discovered the drawer. I unlocked it now, taking out the small, black leather book I found there, and ran my hand over it. It had belonged to my grandmother and was half full of spells she'd created, spells I knew without doubt she'd kept hidden. Because Gran had been like me—more than I'd ever known.

A sense of calm washed over me immediately.

I'd put hours of work into the contents of this book. Hours alone in this workshop while Else was out and about, while Bram was gone, hours deep in my fear, in my rage, in my terror that history would one day repeat itself—of Clayton gripping my arm, pumping me full of dark magic while he whispered in my ear, reminding me of the horrors he'd made me see, of what could happen if I wasn't vigilant, if I wasn't strong enough—turning words into a twisted reality in my head.

This little book full of spells and recipes, of potions and elixirs, was my safety net. This was how I slept at night. When I channeled my anger into the spells I wrote in it, the same book Gran had used, it calmed me, it banked the inferno in my gut like nothing else could.

If anyone came for my family again, I could destroy them with what was written in this book, with my words, my magic.

Flipping to the back, I lifted out the small business cards there. One from Rose, the name of a counselor she wanted me to speak with. I don't know why I'd kept it, probably because it'd seemed so important to her. The last thing I wanted was to dredge up my pain to a complete stranger.

I put it back and studied the second—Umbra Sanitarium. It was an institution, a place for witches who skimmed too close to the dark side, those who dabbled in dark magic and got burned or needed help back to the light.

It was touted as a place of healing. But Umbra was also a prison. We recently found out that was where Cora had been sent. The evil bitch was Else and Gran's cousin. She was being held in a separate area, a place for those who couldn't be saved, who didn't want to be. I clenched my teeth. Two and a half years ago, Cora and her grandson Brody had plotted against our family, and with the help of Clayton Whitlock, they'd made their move. Cora had murdered the previous Keeper of our coven in the hopes the position would pass to her grandson, but instead of her branch of the family, it went to ours—and she'd almost succeeded in killing us all to get what she wanted.

Willow was Keeper of our coven now, but after she passed her tasks and trial, the mother had thrown us a curveball. Because the position of Keeper had moved to a new branch of the family, each of us—me, Rose, and Iris—had to pass a task and trial of our own to prove our line was worthy of keeping the magical gifts she'd bestowed on our coven over the centuries. To lose those gifts would be devastating. A coven that couldn't hold on to its power became a target for those who could.

My sisters had all gone through their trials and passed. It was now down to me.

The ritual was nonnegotiable and included a demon-infested forest and some up-close-and-personal time with a giant serpent possessed by Mother Nature. I wasn't looking forward to her inevitable bite, which would pump me full of her magical venom, leaving behind a permanent tattoo-like mark. The black tattoo would eventually become colorful, if I passed the ultimate task she gave me. But that wasn't all. A magical combat trial was the final piece of her twisted puzzle. If I didn't win that? Bye-bye magical gifts.

I stared at the nondescript card again before sliding it back into the book. My darkness nudged me, pushing again. I didn't know if I could hold it back indefinitely, but if I ever got really bad, I'd do what I had to so no one got hurt.

The moment I broke a blood oath, one I'd made to my family, by going to Clayton for help—the trajectory of my life had changed. I didn't know how exactly, I just knew it had.

After that day, after we battled Cora, Brody, and Clayton at our cemetery, everything had fallen apart.

Bram had started going away, leaving me, and I'd felt the darkness crawling closer.

I became someone else, someone full of anger, who lacked any kind of control—someone I didn't like very much at all.

It'd been two and a half years and I still hadn't worked out how to live in my own skin again. I was lost, and I wasn't sure I'd ever find my way back.

I slid the book into the drawer and closed it. But maybe that was a good thing. The old Magnolia had messed everything up, had almost gotten herself and her family killed.

That wasn't who I was anymore, but I did know, if this new monster came for any of us, I'd destroy it.

~

"Come by the clubhouse Friday night. We're having a party," Willow said as she grabbed her bag and strode toward me.

I often helped Willow out at The Cauldron, and today I was working the afternoon for her since she had some appointment she needed to get to. Wills was an earth witch, she could manipulate wind and the plants and trees, move boulders, and could cause a fairly decent earthquake if she wanted to. She also had a magical blade that warned her of danger.

"Whose birthday is it?"

She chuckled. "Lothar."

The hounds had taken to celebrating birthdays recently. It started when Willow threw a party for Warrick, and now they all wanted one. It was getting out of hand, but the hounds loved to party hard and were taking full advantage. "What kind of party are we talking about?"

"Nothing too wild," she said, reading my mind and giving me a nudge. "You know you want to. Everyone will be there."

Everyone except Bram. When he vanished like this, he could be gone days. My belly gripped. I really hated how we'd left things before he left. I hadn't even said goodbye. I rubbed my chest, the ache there wouldn't subside. "Maybe."

"I want us to hang out. I feel like we haven't talked in ages. Come, okay? It's important."

I opened the door for her. "I'll try."

As she passed, she gave me a look that said I'd better be there, and then she strode out. I pulled my phone from my pocket, checking it again. Still no word from Bram.

I'd dreamed about Margot all night, and I was exhausted today. To keep my mind off everything, off Bram, and Margot, I needed a menial task, something that forced me to concentrate. Grabbing a notepad and pen, I got to work taking stock of our inventory in the storeroom. Willow didn't do it nearly often enough. Then she'd run out of something, and Else and I would be left scrambling to make more.

My and Else's tonics and potions were stored in the back for safety, only the harmless stuff was displayed out front. I was working my way along the shelves by the register when the door opened and three witches walked in. My spine straightened, but I didn't let what I was feeling show on my face. I wouldn't give them the satisfaction.

Amelia, as always, was in front, with Leah and Claire following. Always following. It was seriously pathetic.

"Oh, look who it is, ladies!" Amelia said. "I haven't seen you in so long, Magnolia. What have you been doing with yourself?"

No, we hadn't seen each other in a while, we'd barely had any interaction since we finished high school, which was the way I liked it. "Working," I said. "Is there something you need?"

She grabbed a basket. "Just a few bits and pieces for my new place, you can't be too careful. I plan on strengthening my wards." She leaned in. "We heard about Margot." She screwed up her face, eyes wide. "Sounds like she was *tortured*...they carved into her before they finally...you know..."

My fingers curled into fists, and I turned away before I swung at her.

There was silence behind me, my disgust in her gossiping over Margot's horrific death was received loud and clear. I ignored them and got on with what I was doing while they made their way around the store, talking under their breath but loud enough for me to hear, like we were still in fucking high school.

What I wanted to do was kick their asses out, but again, I wouldn't give those bitches the satisfaction.

Leah finally walked over and peered at me through the shelf I was standing behind, her familiar, a small dog named Biscuit, tucked under her arm. "Sorry, we didn't realize you and Margot were friends," she said, a ridiculous, overly innocent look on her face that said she did in fact know.

"Do you have everything you need?" I said, ignoring what she'd said completely.

"Oh, um…almost." She smiled in a way that had my hair standing on end. "So…how's Bram?"

Amelia laughed, giving her friend a little shove. "I knew you couldn't help yourself."

Leah blushed.

Just hearing Bram's name from her mouth had fire shooting through my veins. "What are you talking about?" I moved out from behind the shelf.

"Oh nothing," Leah said. "I just saw him out last night. He was at The Bank with another guy I assume was his brother. The hair color, and those eyes. The two of them together…" She bit her lip and grinned. "They were a whole lot of eye candy, and I wasn't the only one who thought so. They were surrounded by females."

Bram was at The Bank? What the fuck was going on? Why was he at a club? I locked down my emotions, which was hard, but I refused to let her see me react.

"Bram can do what he wants," I said, even as the pain in my chest became almost unbearable.

Leah leaned on the shelf beside me. "I'm really glad to hear that because I got his number from a friend of a friend and was thinking of asking him out."

It took every ounce of willpower not to slam my fist into her smug face. Over my rotting corpse would I let this grasping bitch anywhere near Bram.

"You guys definitely aren't, you know, together?" she asked, watching me like a hawk ready to tear its prey's eyes out, while she stroked her familiar like a comic book supervillain.

I shook my head, finding it impossible to speak without firing a whole lot of verbal poison at her. The urge to pull my knife and make her bleed was there as well, and that was even harder to resist —which should worry me, but I wasn't thinking rationally right then.

"Did you hear me and Scott bought a new place?" Amelia said, hating that the attention was off her for even a moment. "That's why I'm here. I want to make sure the apartment has a strong ward. I like to be ready for anything."

"Awesome," I said. "You truly are perfect for each other." Her familiar, Scott, was a narcissistic creep.

Her gaze sliced to me, and I could tell she wasn't sure how to read my tone. I didn't give a shit. She could read it however she liked. We may be adults now, but I had a long memory, and I was petty as shit. I had no plans on letting go of the way they'd treated me.

"Yes, we are," she said, her eyes locking on mine as she handed me her basket. "Maybe you'll find out for yourself what that's like, Magnolia. I'm sure your mate will turn up...someday." She smiled, and it was full of spiteful glee.

I refused to engage. If I opened my mouth now, I'd tell her what an asshole I truly thought she was. And honestly, I didn't trust myself to stop there. My fingers curled into a fist at my side as I finished ringing her up. Shoving everything into a paper bag, I slid it to her.

She opened her mouth to say something else—

"Bye," I said before she could.

She shut her trap and, with a snotty look, turned and headed for the door.

"Tell Bram to expect my call," Leah said before she walked out after her friends.

I gripped the edge of the counter to keep from launching over it. I wasn't okay. Not at all. Bram had apparently been out partying with one of his brothers yet wasn't able to call or text me?

Cool. That didn't feel like being kicked in the gut multiple times *at all*.

So many thoughts, dark ones, flew through my mind. I shoved them down. This was Bram, *my* Bram. He didn't like partying, he barely spoke to anyone but me and his brothers. I needed to calm the fuck down. Until I spoke to him, I wasn't going to jump to any wild assumptions.

Somehow, I managed to keep a lid on everything I was feeling the rest of the afternoon. Just after I closed up the shop and was heading to my car, my phone chimed.

When I checked it, my relief was so strong, my legs actually went weak.

Bram. Finally.

Be home tonight.

~

Mom and Arthur were setting themselves up in front of the TV to watch their favorite gardening show when I got home.

"Another cushion, my sweet Daisy?" Art said.

I smiled. I loved the way he always called her *his*.

"You're back," Mom said when she saw me. "I was getting worried. Grab some dinner and come watch TV with us."

I plonked down in the chair by Art. "Bram's coming home tonight. I'm going to wait at the tree house. I'll eat when he gets here."

"I made apple sponge pudding," Art said.

It was Bram's favorite and one of Arthur's specialties. "I hope you used the big dish?"

He flashed me a smile. "Sure did."

Arthur was middle-aged with dark brown skin and kind eyes. He was an owl shifter, but preferred his human form, and Mom's familiar. He'd been in love with her from the moment they found each other. It took Mom a little longer to work it out, but they were now deeply in love, and we were all thrilled about it.

Art was loving and protective and the closest thing any of us had to a father, since our own sperm donors were either absent, wastes of space, or in Rose's case, a psychotic, power-hungry piece of shit. We all adored Art.

Both Mom and Art had also welcomed Bram into the fold when he showed up and promptly built himself a tree house in our backyard. They were the best, and I'd do anything to protect them...and to make up for what I'd done. If I could only give them back half of what they'd given me...

I stood. "Enjoy your show. I'm gonna take some food to the tree house."

"Okay, baby," Mom said, squeezing my hand as I walked past, then stopped me by holding fast. "Promise me you'll be safe. After what happened to Margot... I can't think why anyone would want to hurt her." Her hand trembled around mine. "Promise me, Magnolia."

"I promise." I kissed the top of her head. "Besides, Bram will be here." Though as I said it, I wasn't sure it was the truth. It used to be, but not anymore.

I shut those thoughts down and loaded a basket with food, getting double helpings of dessert, and headed out the back door. It was dark, but it was still hot. I hated summer. The last thing I wanted was my skin and all my scars on display. People mostly just stared, but there were always others who didn't think there was anything wrong with asking how I got them.

I reached the tree house, attached the basket to the pulley, winching it up to the deck, then locked it in place. I climbed up after it, and grabbed the basket. Bram had built this place when he was seventeen, and he'd lived here since.

I walked into the tree house and switched on the light.

It was beautiful, a work of art, and even better than his tree house back at the village. The living space was fairly big, with enough room for a kitchenette and a short breakfast bar on one side, a decent-sized couch and flat-screen TV on the other. The windows in this room were all different shapes and sizes. He had designed and made each one with different colored glass that bathed the room in a rainbow of colors during the day. His bedroom was off the living room, and only a bit smaller, and there was an ensuite as well. The entire tree house was bigger than a lot of apartments in the city.

It was my favorite place in the entire world.

I put the food in the fridge and tidied up the living room, then stripped the sheets from the bed and put on fresh ones for him. I always liked fresh sheets after I'd been away, even if it was only after a night or two.

Then I opened the reading app on my phone, so my mind didn't wander back to Margot, and lay down to wait.

Chapter Four

Magnolia

My eyes snapped open, and I sat up, blinking into the dark room. "Bram?"

"Yeah." The bathroom door opened. "Go back to sleep." He shut himself in and the water turned on.

I stared through the darkness. It'd been too dark to see him, but something wasn't right.

The door finally opened again, and I flicked on the light and gasped.

Bram stilled, his jaw tightening, his gaze dropping to the floor. "I'm okay."

I flew out of bed. "What the hell happened to you?"

His wet hair had fallen forward, covering his face. My hand shook as I lifted it to his bruised stomach and chest, to the bloody slices scattered across his smooth, inked skin. He'd pulled on shorts, but the rest of him was bare, and I took inventory of every mark on his lean, muscled body.

"Please," I whispered. "I can't take this anymore. I can't bear it. You're hurt, you keep getting hurt, and I'm terrified that one of these times you'll leave me...and you won't come back." I finally said it, the thing that terrified me the most. I couldn't survive without him. I just...I couldn't. I wouldn't want to.

He reached for me, and I pushed his hands away, scared and angry as hell. I couldn't be hugged by him then; I couldn't hear how much he cared about me when he wasn't being honest with me. I knew he loved me, I was his best friend, but that didn't make the secrets any less painful.

I wouldn't let him touch me, but the need to touch him, to heal him, was overwhelming. Brushing his hair back, I took his chin and tilted his head to the side. There was a bruise on his jaw, a cut by his eye.

"It's nothing serious." His voice was full of grit and lifted goose bumps all over my body.

"Lie on the bed so I can tend your wounds."

"Maggie—"

"Please," I said, my heart squeezing at the use of his nickname for me, one he used rarely and only when we were alone. I had trouble meeting his eyes all of a sudden, something else that was new. More distance, more pain.

He did as I asked. We'd done this several times now, but he'd never been this badly hurt before.

I grabbed my basket of healing supplies from the bathroom. I'd taken to leaving one here since he'd needed them more often. "Can you at least tell me what kind of creature did this so I know the best treatment to use?"

He didn't answer, just shook his head.

I muttered a curse and pulled out a generic poultice and the herbs and balm I'd need, then started cleaning the cuts...or scratches. I wasn't completely sure what they were.

"I'm okay," he said into the quiet room.

"Bullshit."

He didn't contradict me, lying still as I slowly and methodically cleaned out his wounds and smeared them with Else's healing balm to get the regeneration of tissue started. Then, laying the poultice over the top, I closed my eyes, held my hand over it, and muttered the spell that would go one step further. "Blood and bone. Flesh torn, skin bruised. Return what was broken...again to what was." Warmth radiated from my palm as I said the rest of the spell, a spell that was unique to me. Like all healing witches, the spells needed to be of our own making, since no two witches had the exact same healing power. Mine had come to me in a dream, at least part of it, and I'd developed the rest from there.

I checked under the poultice and the bruise beneath hadn't healed completely, but it'd lost some of the angry purple and the slice in his skin had thinned, the deeper tissue beginning to heal already. I moved to the next. A slice across the rigid muscle of his abs, and repeated my spell, doing it over and over again, until I was shaking and exhausted from all the magic I'd drained working on him.

I moved to the next—

Bram grabbed my hand, stopping me. I looked up.

"No more. Bed, Magnolia. Now."

I'd gotten the worst of them, but I couldn't bear to think he was in pain. "I'm fine, let me finish—"

"I don't need it. Bed," he said in that incredibly deep, velvety voice of his. It'd surprised me the first time I'd heard it. I loved his voice. I could listen to him talk all day, if he was the kind of male to talk nonstop, which he was not. His voice had only grown deeper, grittier as he'd gotten older. But that wasn't the only thing that'd changed. The way he spoke, the things he said.

The last couple of years another side of Bram had come out, a more demanding, blunt, forceful side. Gone was the shy boy I'd met that first day. He still didn't like to talk much, not to anyone besides me and his brothers, but a dominance radiated from him now that he hadn't had when he was sixteen, but it'd sure as hell grown over the years. He'd always been protective, but he could also be seriously possessive.

I'd tell him to stop being so goddamn bossy now, if I wasn't so exhausted. I stood on shaky legs. I'd expended a lot more of my power than I'd realized—

My legs gave out, and Bram cursed, jackknifing up. He hooked me around the waist and planted me in the bed beside him.

"I should be the one cursing right now," I muttered, giving his shoulder a pathetically weak shove.

He pulled me close, ignoring my pitiful struggles, and pressed a kiss to the top of my head. "Rest."

I should resist, ask him about The Bank and what he'd been doing there. I could say a lot of things, but I didn't want to fight. He wasn't going to tell me no matter how angry I got anyway.

And honestly, I didn't have a fight in me. So I let him manhandle me to where he wanted me, wrapped in his arms, his face to my throat, because I was just glad he was home.

Then I closed my heavy eyes and let the heat of his body soak through me.

When I woke again, Bram was dressed and in the middle of lacing up his boots.

"What's going on?" I sat up.

His jaw clenched.

"You're leaving again." My stomach tightened into a painful knot.

"One night. I'll be back sooner, if I can."

"Right." I jerked back the covers and shoved my feet in my boots. "Cool." Deja vu hit. I was living my own personal *Groundhog Day*. I said my lines, then he said his. Nothing changed.

He grabbed my hand when I tried to walk past. "Mags..."

I looked up at him. "What? What could you possibly say that will make this okay?"

His hand around mine tightened, and he tugged me closer before his other arm hooked around my waist and held me tight, so tight I struggled to breathe. "I'm sorry," he said roughly.

Tears sprang to my eyes, but I fought them back and pushed away from him. "Yep, you've said that already, I don't know, like three thousand times." I stared up at him, waiting, hoping he'd say something more. He didn't. I shook my head and walked past him. "See you later, I guess."

Then I strode out of the tree house.

~

"Come on, maybe it'll be fun." I grabbed Jasmine's hand and pulled her along after me.

"I don't feel like going to a party," she grumbled, while several butterflies fluttered around her head. Like Rose, who didn't have just one familiar but instead countless—in Rose's case, bats, she could call and control—Jazzy had butterflies.

I wasn't sure how it worked, and she hadn't elaborated yet. We didn't like to push because Jasmine wasn't one to share unless she needed to. She liked to sort through things on her own first. She'd had a lot to sort through lately, not only with her sister gone so often but with learning to deal with her gift. She was a medium, like Zinnia, and could communicate with the dead, something that had once terrified her. Else and Mom were trying to help her, but it was tough.

"Willow said we all have to be here. It'll take your mind off everything." Jasmine was nineteen and our cousin. She was living with us while Zinnia, her older sister, was living in Limbo—with Death, as his consort. It was all pretty complicated and fucked up, but Zinnia had no other choice. She had, however, negotiated the terms of her time there. She stayed with Death every other month until Jasmine turned twenty-one, after that she would have to stay there permanently.

Well, that wasn't fucking happening. We had two years to figure something out, and we wouldn't rest until we'd found a way to get her out of the bargain. Zinnia wasn't as hopeful as us, and she didn't talk about her time there when she came home. This was her month to be away, and Jasmine desperately needed a distraction, and I did as well.

We got out of the car and strode toward the clubhouse. There was a huge garage to the right of it, and both had the Devil Dogs logo painted on the side of the building.

The clubhouse was in Linville, a thirty-minute drive from Roxburgh, and the hellhounds who lived there looked and acted like a human motorcycle club, for the sake of the humans in this town. They lived all together in the den they'd dug out below the main building, and Willow lived here with Warrick, her mate and alpha of the hounds.

Jazzy and I walked in and were hit by a wall of sound and pure undiluted testosterone. The latter so thick you almost needed a shovel to get through it. Leather, motor oil, bulging muscle, and lots of hair. The hounds were huge, all close to seven feet, and had lived the majority of their extremely long lives in Hell.

Tonight, they were partying. Mom and Arthur had just walked in ahead of us, and everyone else was already here.

I turned to Jazzy. She looked cute in shorts and a baggy, black T-shirt. She was no stranger to the hounds and hung here with Willow a lot. She also liked to draw, and Roman, the hounds' tattoo artist, had gotten her to work with him a few times. Jazzy had asked for payment in ink, and now her arms and hands were decorated with a bunch of small tattoos. Flora and fauna, animals and insects. They were pretty and delicate and suited her. "Let's go get a drink."

Jasmine nodded, but she was still taking in the room with wide eyes, and I knew the moment she spotted Ren because she froze.

Ren was a fox shifter, and Willow's familiar. He was the same age as Bram, twenty-two and model handsome. Add in the scars he'd collected over the last couple of years living in the wild, demon-infested woods...well, he was a lot rougher around the edges than he used to be. He had females throwing themselves at him left and right.

Ren had embraced partying and lots of sex as his coping mechanism, after all he'd been through. It was concerning, but at least he was back with us.

"Jazzy?" My cousin had a mega crush on him, and right now there was a female, a wolf shifter from Draven's pack, running her fingers through Ren's auburn hair with one hand, while the other slid across his stomach.

"I'm not really in the mood for this," Jazz said, though I had to read her lips over the loud music.

Willow strode over with a huge smile on her face, but her eyes gentled as they slid to Jasmine and who she was watching. "Come and hang with me and Warrick."

Jazzy sucked in a breath and dragged her gaze from Ren, who was now making out with the wolf, and she smiled, though it was more a baring of teeth. "Yeah, I'm just...I need a Coke." She strode off across the room, toward the bar.

Willow looked over at Ren and worry shifted across her features before she turned back to me. "Try to have fun, okay?" Then she followed Jasmine.

The hounds could get wild, but this was a bit more relaxed than some of their parties, despite the making-out sessions here and there. I spotted the birthday hound and strode over.

"Hey, Lothar. Happy birthday."

He glanced down at me and gave me a chin lift.

"So how old are you?" I asked.

"Stopped counting a few hundred years ago."

I smirked. "Damn, that old?" He didn't look old. He looked like a male in his early thirties. He was hot and broody and at times scary as hell. But you could say that about all of the hounds, honestly.

He shifted, his whole body turning to face me. "You ever come so hard you lose consciousness, Magnolia?" His deep voice resonated right through me.

I blinked up at him. "Uh..."

He flashed his teeth, white and sharp, and it was sexy and terrifying all at once. "You ever want to, you know where to find me."

I laughed. The brazenness of these hounds was unmatched. Not surprising, considering they were created by Lucifer and were emotionally deficient. They understood loyalty, they knew anger and lust well, but that was about as far as their emotional range went—the rest was beyond their grasp. Warrick and the other mated males were the exception—after they mated, their emotions developed, to different degrees. "Warrick might have a problem with that, don't you think?" I said. My bother-in-law was extremely protective.

Lothar shrugged. "I was at your twenty-first birthday party, sweetheart. You're a female, old enough to decide who she fucks." Then he waited, watching me for a response, I assumed.

I didn't have one. "That I am. So, I'm just gonna...go over there."

"I'll be here all night, you change your mind."

"Noted," I said and hustled across the room to the table Ren and his wolf were leaning against, along with several other hounds and their females, well, the ones they'd chosen for that night, at least. One of the males handed me a beer, and I settled in. Ren was too busy to talk, so I chatted with one of the wolves.

But slowly, over the next hour, they all drifted off in pairs to find a room and some privacy, no doubt.

I ended up at the table alone, watching everyone around me.

Draven had his arm hooked around Iris's neck, and they were sucking face every few minutes. Rose and Ronan were here as well. She was on her mate's lap, and every now and then, he'd tug her down for a kiss. Six months ago, Rose discovered who her biological father was, and the reason she'd been sick most of her life—now she had these amazing white wings and could fly. She was also a seer and, through scrying, received messages and visions.

I glanced across the room. Willow and Warrick were just as bad with the PDA. She stood leaning against the bar, Warrick behind her, one hand resting on her belly, the other resting on the bar in front of her. And yep, every so often he'd lean in to kiss the side of her neck, telling her without words what he wanted, and she'd turn to him and give him the kiss he was silently asking for.

What would that be like? To have that? To be wanted like that?

An image of Bram filled my mind, of how he'd looked last night. Bruised and cut. After I'd healed him, I'd drifted off, but I'd woken again a couple of hours later. He'd been asleep, lying on his back, his muscled body defined by the moonlight filtering through the room. His face had been relaxed, his thick, black lashes resting on his cheeks, and his lips, full and deep burgundy, had looked so incredibly soft.

For a split second, goddess, for just a moment, I'd actually had the insane urge to lean in, and—

I swallowed hard.

Then Clayton's hateful face had filled my head, like it did now, and had turned the soft feeling that had filled me into something jagged and awful. As if he were standing in front of me, blocking what lay ahead, stopping me from seeing anything good, or real. He was here with me now. I saw his cold blue eyes staring back, mocking me, making me feel sick to my stomach.

But worse, I felt his lips on me, cold and hard. He'd been my first kiss, my only kiss. My hand lifted to my mouth, and I rubbed at my lips, trying to take away that cold, awful feeling.

Suddenly, I couldn't breathe. I was suffocating. I rushed across the room, plugged the code into the keypad by the door, and ran down the stairs to the den, and the coolness and silence it offered. The stone walls made it soundproof, and the wall sconces offered a soothing, warm glow. I strode along the wide cavern, not knowing where I was going, only that I needed a moment alone. The hounds slept down here. They each had their own quarters, and there was also a common area, a gym, a fighting pit, and cells for locking up and torturing their enemies—and I'm sure a lot more I didn't know about.

A deep thumping sound echoed down the cavern, rapid and repetitive. It was coming from the gym. I made my way there on autopilot and opened the door. It was Relic. He was in a pair of shorts and nothing else, his long hair tied back in a knot, his body straining as he smashed his bare fists into the stone wall over and over again. I guess when you were immortal and impossibly strong, a normal leather punching bag didn't quite cut it.

He stopped and turned, sensing me as soon as I walked in. He was panting, but not as much as he should be, not after trying to punch through a cave wall in the name of fitness. Relic planted his hands on his hips. "Mags, hey, what's up?"

I'm freaked out and lonely as hell. How about you?

"Why are you down here and not up there with the others?" I said instead.

He shrugged a massive shoulder. "Felt like punching shit."

The male was a bit of a mystery. Relic was one of the next generation of hounds, only hundreds of years old instead of thousands. I assumed he was as emotionless as the others, though he definitely hid it better. After leaving Hell, the hounds taught themselves to imitate emotion to fit in, and Relic had mastered the skill. He was also Lothar's son, which was extremely weird since Relic looked only slightly younger, like a guy in his mid-to-late twenties.

"Your dad seems to be enjoying himself," I said.

He shook his head. "It's fucking weird when you say shit like that."

"You don't call him dad?"

"Never." Relic flexed his scarred fingers. "We're brothers, all of us, doesn't matter how we were created or by who."

I skirted a pile of free weights. "Why?"

"Because we're fucking old. Shit gets blurred when you've lived as long as us." He ran a hand over his hair. "So why are you here and not upstairs?" he said, asking me the same question.

"It was getting a bit much." My gaze slid to his mouth. He had nice lips. He was also extremely hot and loved to flirt shamelessly with my sisters and me whenever he came by the house. I should be attracted to him, I should welcome his attention, right? That would be normal. A normal response to a male like him.

Clayton flashed through my mind again and nausea gripped my belly. I rubbed my forearm when that phantom ache below my skin throbbed harder. "Kiss me," I blurted, surprising myself. Whether or not Relic was surprised, I couldn't tell. I should take it back, but I didn't.

He tilted his head to the side. "Why?"

I huffed out a laugh. "I ask you to kiss me, and you ask why?"

"Yeah, I'm asking why. You're sure as fuck not into me. And Willow would slit my throat if I laid a finger on her baby sister."

When Clayton kissed me, it'd been hard, punishing. His teeth had scraped against mine, his taste had turned my stomach, his fingers had dug into my flesh so hard he'd left bruises.

I needed him gone. I needed Clayton gone.

A weird desperation filled me, and I had to curl my fingers into fists so Relic didn't see them shaking. "What does it matter? Just fucking kiss me. What's the big deal?"

He crossed his arms. "Talk to me."

"I don't want to talk." I crossed my arms as well, feeling so incredibly vulnerable. I hated it. "You literally suck face with anyone who throws themselves at you, but I'm the exception?"

"Mags—"

"Forget it." Humiliation burned my cheeks. What the hell was wrong with me? I spun to leave, but he moved fast, stopping me.

"Wait," he rumbled in his impossibly deep, barely human voice.

"It's fine. I just want to go."

He growled a little and held me fast. "You're definitely not into me?"

"I'm definitely not," I said, giving him the truth. He didn't look offended in the slightest.

"But you want me to kiss you and you won't tell me why?"

"That's right."

He ran his hand over his hair again. "The females in your family have been sent to fuck with me, I'm sure of it." Then he cursed under his breath, took my face in his hands, dipped low, and planted one on me.

His lips were warm and soft, but also firm. They brushed over mine softly once, twice, then he took my chin in his hand and opened my mouth, swiping his tongue inside. I touched his in return. He tasted nice, mint and a hint of bourbon. He made a growly sound and sucked my lower lip gently, then lifted his head.

His otherworldly golden eyes were glowing brighter. "Well?" he said roughly.

I stared back.

I felt—

Nothing.

His face seemed to morph, change. It was all in my mind, but there was no stopping it, his gold eyes flashing to frigid blue. The nausea rocketed back, twisting my gut, and I threw a hand over my mouth, gagging.

"The fuck?" Relic said, jerking back. "Are you gonna hurl?"

I lifted a hand and shook my head. "It's...it's not you," I said through my fingers. I was definitely close to hurling, though, and my scars burned, pain radiating through me. I wanted to fucking scream.

"You just gagged, right after my mouth was on yours. I'd say that sure as fuck has something to do with me." I took a step back, and he grabbed my arm, stopping me. "Talk to me. What the fuck is going on here?"

The pain heightened under his grip, and my fingers curled into a fist all on their own. Instead of lashing out, though, I yanked my arm free, and he let me. Still the look in his eyes said he wasn't going to let me leave without some kind of explanation, not after that little display. He knew about Willow's trial, because the hounds had been a part of it. He also knew what had happened to me, some of it, anyway.

So I gave him what he needed and hoped he didn't ask more questions, because I sure as hell wasn't in the frame of mind to answer them. I tugged down the collar of my shirt, flashing him some of my scars. "Just dealing with some old demons," I said and held his bright gaze, silently asking him to drop it.

His gaze moved over the scars, then came back to mine. "Babe," he said gruffly, somehow conveying a whole lot of feeling in that one word, and again making me think he felt a lot more than a lot of his brothers.

"It's fine. I'm fine. I need to go." I took a step back, and he let me walk away this time.

I strode out into the cavern and guilt hit me, along with a sense of wrongness over that kiss that made me feel sick all over again. I wasn't sure why.

Bram's face filled my mind, and I forced it back out.

Shoving down the feeling inside me, I rushed back upstairs.

Chapter Five

I pushed open the door, back into the noise, laughter, and chatter of the clubhouse. I was heading toward the door and freedom when Warrick whistled loudly, silencing the entire room.

I forced myself to stop and turn to him and Willow, who was now pressed into his side. His arm was around her, tucking her in close under his arm—and my big sister was, goddess, she was beaming, glowing with joy. Willow was gorgeous, but I don't think she'd ever looked as beautiful as she did in that moment.

"Ready, dove?" Warrick said to her.

She smiled up at him and nodded.

Warrick looked out to the room full of family and friends and flashed his vicious-looking white teeth. I'd never seen him smile like that, and I stilled along with everyone else in the room.

"It's not just Lothar's birthday. There's another reason we brought you all here tonight 'cause we've been through a lot of shit the last few years and for once we've got something good…" He shook his head. "Something...fucking awesome to share with you." His arm tightened around Wills.

"I'm pregnant!" Willow cried.

Mom shot to her feet with a cry and ran to Willow—Iris, Jasmine, and Rose following—the hounds howled their approval. There was no stopping my own smile. I shoved down my own crap and walked toward them—

The door to the clubhouse flew open, and several members of the witches council along with their enforcers walked in, magic swirling around them. The hounds closed ranks immediately, blocking their way. Calvin Adler stood in front, eyes wild. He'd taken Cesare Sartori's place on the council when Sartori resigned a few months ago. I didn't know much about him, except he'd quickly grown a reputation as a hothead.

There'd been two other resignations. Sapphire Eldridge and Sara Hayashi, and of course they'd both endorsed their own children as their successors. Which was why Sapphire's asshole son, Isaac, was standing with Calvin, and Asuka Hayashi was at his side.

"You better have a fucking good reason for walking in here," Warrick said, voice cold. "She told you already she's not fucking selling," he said, pointing at Isaac. "Bringing your council buddies here won't change her mind."

A couple months ago, a company approached Willow, offering to buy her store for some development project. Willow rejected their offer. A few weeks later, someone tried to torch the store next to hers. She did some digging and found out the company was headed by Isaac, and he didn't just want her store but the whole block.

Willow pulled away from Mom and pushed her way to the front, stepping out beside Warrick, who was staring them down. "Is that what this is about? What's going on, Nathan? Why are you here? This place is warded, how did you get through?"

Nathan Trotman had always been someone we could trust, for a lot of years the only one we could trust on the witches council, and right now he looked seriously rattled. "We broke it under the dangerous witch clause in the council's code of conduct."

The room went silent. There were three ways to break a ward: the first, a spell that literally judged your intentions and only worked if they were good; the second was known only to council members and they were forbidden to use it unless it was a matter of life and death; the third, the worst kind of dark magic.

Willow jerked back, as shocked as the rest of us. "What?"

"Willow Thornheart, you are required to come with us for questioning in relation to the murder of three witches—"

"What the hell are you talking about?" she said, her confusion obvious.

"You're not taking my mate anywhere," Warrick snarled.

Willow put her hand on his arm to calm him because her male was about to start tearing the council members to shreds. "There's been another murder?"

Calvin stepped forward. "Yes, there's been another murder."

"Who?" Willow asked, paling.

His jaw tightened, fury in his eyes. "As if you don't know! You fucking murdered Katana!" His hand shot out, magic buzzing from him.

Warrick stepped in front of him, grabbing his fist, and got in his face. "She did nothing. You aim your magic at her again, and I'll turn you inside out."

"Katana's dead?" Willow asked, moving around Warrick again. He locked his arm around her, pulling her back. "Why the hell would you think I did it?"

Isaac Eldridge placed his hand on Calvin's shoulder, and there was a smug-as-fuck look on his face. "Justice will be done, Cal, I promise you that." His gaze slid to Willow. "This was inevitable, wasn't it? You wanted everyone to know how powerful you were during your trial, and you took pleasure in defeating my family, in watching your mate kill my brother, but you let that power go to your head, you let it corrupt you." His eyes darkened, filling with hatred. "You let it turn you into a monster."

Willow's gaze sliced to Asuka. They were friends, had been since school. No, they weren't as close anymore, but Asuka had to know Willow wasn't capable of this. "I didn't do it. You know me. You know I'm not capable of what they're accusing me of."

Asuka looked pained. "They found Katana in your shop, Willow, in your bedroom in the back. She was tortured and killed, like the others."

Willow said, her spine stiff, "My shop is warded. Did the council break that one as well?"

"It was already down."

"And that's not a fucking red flag to you?" Willow bit out. "We keep the store warded at all times. Somehow, someone broke it. They're trying to set me up."

"Or that's what you want us to think," Asuka said, without heat.

Willow stared at her friend, stunned. "This is insane, you have to see that?"

"Time to go, Willow," Isaac said, fucking glee dancing in his eyes as he motioned their enforcers forward.

They weren't listening to her, to reason.

Warrick roared, the sound rattling the windows, his canines extended. Willow grabbed his arm and shook her head. Warrick and the hounds slaughtering the council would only make this worse.

Warrick's furious stare slid to me, then toward the door to the den. I knew what he wanted, and I eased my way back through the crowd of people. They truly thought Willow had murdered those females and bringing enforcers here, onto the hound's territory rather than waiting to get her on her own, said how desperate they were to bring her in, and just how guilty they believed she was. I quickly plugged in the code right as the room erupted into chaos. The hounds ran forward, getting between

Warrick and Willow and the council as magic snapped through the room.

Warrick snatched Willow off the ground and ran toward me, I opened the door and slammed it shut, the locks clicking into place behind them.

Calvin strode over, grabbed me, and shoved me back. "Open the fucking door."

"Can't, sorry, I don't know the code," I said.

He gripped my wrist tight, so tight I knew he'd leave a bruise. "Yes, you can, you lying, little bitch." He forced my hand over to the keypad. "Enter the fucking code. Now."

Warrick and Willow needed more time. I assumed there was a secret exit, but I needed to buy them as much time as I could.

Draven closed in, baring his teeth. "Let go of her or I'll take off your fucking head."

Calvin spun around. "She needs to open the door, or we'll be taking her in as well for her interference."

I yanked my hand from his. "It's fine, I'll do it."

I pushed a bunch of numbers, then tried the door. A red light flashed, and it remained locked. "Hang on. Let me try again."

Calvin hissed behind me.

I did it again, punching in some random numbers. Again, it flashed red. He was an asshole, but his cousin was dead, had been murdered brutally, so I understood his anger, but he was directing all that rage at the wrong people.

He spun me around and slammed me into the door, the handle digging into my spine, making me wince. "My cousin is dead, and your sister murdered her. I'm not in the mood for your bullshit. Open the fucking door. Now!"

Draven threw him back and stepped in front of me. "She doesn't know the code. Maybe you should ask one of the hounds."

The door opened behind me, and Relic stepped through, stopping me from falling through with his body, and closed the door behind him, tight.

Calvin's nostrils flared. "Let me through, hound."

"Your council holds no authority here. You're trespassing. Leave, or you'll be slaughtered where you stand," he said, his barely human voice resonating through the room.

Calvin roared, then turned back to me.

"Touch her again, and see what happens," Relic said and flashed his wicked-looking canines.

Isaac strode forward and grabbed Calvin's arm. "They can't hide forever, we'll get her," he said, his sharp gaze slicing to Relic, then to me. I felt his hatred down to my bones.

Calvin stormed off, and Iris and Rose rushed over to me.

Relic, Ronan, and the rest of the hounds strode after the councilors, seeing them off the property.

"Good work, Mags," Iris said.

"They got away. Willow's safe," Mom said, but there was fear in her eyes.

"Warrick won't let anything happen to her or the baby," Rose said, wrapping her arm around Mom's shoulders.

Ronan strode back inside and over to us. "The hounds are leaving tonight, they're following Warrick."

"Where are they going? Where would War have taken Willow?" Draven asked.

"Home," Ronan said before anyone else could.

Warrick was taking Willow to Hell, where no one could reach her, not even us.

Bram

Magnolia wasn't in the tree house.

I shoved down the panic, jumped from the deck to the yard below, and strode toward the house.

Coming home and finding Mags in my bed was the fucking

highlight of my day. She slept in my bed more often than her own, and always after I'd been away. The fact she wasn't there, waiting for me now, stung.

She didn't owe me anything. She'd given to me, constantly, and without expectation of anything in return. She'd been there for me since the day we found each other, even with all the shit I was putting her through, still she gave. She was pissed off, yes, but she put that aside to care for me. She made sure I had food in the fridge, that my wounds were tended, my place was clean, and I always came home to fresh sheets.

She constantly fucking worried about me.

All I'd done lately was take and cause her pain.

Acid churned in my gut.

Had she finally given up on me? Was this the day she finally told me to fuck off and never come back?

The house was dark. I used my key and quickly let myself in, taking the stairs two at a time to her room. Mags had moved to Willow's bedroom when she'd left. It was on the top floor, the tower, and far enough from everyone else in the house that she could make noise, play her music, and not bother anyone else.

Light glowed from under her door. She was here and awake, which meant she was avoiding me. I gripped the handle, tapped on the door, and eased it open.

She stood by her dresser, and when her gaze met mine, there was something in her eyes that had me gripping the door handle tighter. "Why are you still up?" It was two in the morning.

"Couldn't sleep. It's been an...eventful night."

She didn't run to me and throw her arms around me like she usually did. No, she stayed back, and I felt the distance acutely between us. I took her in. She was wearing her favorite jeans and the boots she'd bought last week. Her red shirt had a neckline that dipped way too fucking low and hugged her little, curvy frame far too fucking close. "Did you go out?"

"A party, at the clubhouse." She stood and grabbed her robe.

"We need to talk, but not now. Tomorrow," she said and started toward the bathroom.

I shoved my fingers through my hair. "Will you come to the tree house when you're done?" I tried to keep the desperation from my voice.

She crossed her arms. "Not tonight."

"Why?" Jesus, it felt like a dagger in the chest.

"I just...my head's all over the place. I just wanna sleep in my own bed."

She was pulling away. She'd needed to be alone after Maeve's party as well. We didn't do alone. We were better together, always. "Bullshit."

She released a wary breath. "I'm tired. I don't want to argue. You have no idea how messed up tonight was." The "because you weren't there" went unsaid. Her hands went to her hips, and her amber eyes locked on mine. "So, if you're around tomorrow, and you still want to talk, or argue, we can do it then."

"Don't be like that." The adrenaline pumping through my veins hadn't calmed from earlier that night, and every muscle in my body tightened. I had to stop myself from grabbing her and tugging her closer.

Her eyes never left mine. "Like what?"

Fuck. I felt as if my world was falling apart, slipping away beneath my feet, and I didn't know how to stop myself from falling with it. "You're pissed off. So let me have it." I deserved her anger. I needed it. This indifference she was giving me, I fucking hated it.

"Go to the tree house, Bram. I can't do this with you right now." She walked past and reached for the door handle. A scent hit me like a wet fucking rag to the face and possessive fury exploded through me.

My hand shot out, grabbing her arm, stopping her. "You smell like hound." The words were out, hard and accusatory, before I could stop them.

"Like I said, I was at the clubhouse," she said, not looking at me.

My other hand snaked out and caught the side of her throat. I tugged her closer, struggling to contain the possessiveness, the rage at what I was positive I could smell on her. I dipped my head, dragging my nose along her throat to the corner of her mouth, and a series of hoarse, rhythmic *clicks* rumbled from deep in my chest. My crow right there.

"Bram?"

"Relic," I snarled. "His mouth was on yours."

She was mine, my mate, whether she knew it or not, whether she ever acknowledged it or not, and another male had put his fucking mouth on her.

I lifted my head and stared down at her. "He kissed you."

Her eyes were wide. "I asked him to...but none of that matters—"

"You want him?" I barely stopped myself from rocking back. The effect of her words, a physical blow.

"No." She trembled slightly. "I wanted Clayton gone, and Relic was there."

My eyes slid shut, and my vision filled with blood, with death, with agonizing screams. Clayton's. Warrick had torn him to pieces that day at the cemetery, but as far as I was concerned, he'd died too easy. When I opened them again, Mags was staring up at me, her breathing erratic. I wanted to claim her mouth. I wanted to be the one to wash Clayton from her lips. That wasn't Relic's to take. It was mine, it should have been mine.

"Bram—"

"Don't," I said harshly, unable to control all I was feeling. "Don't ever kiss him again, understand? You kiss him again and I'll kill him, Magnolia. I'll fucking end him."

Our eyes locked, and we stared at each other as seconds ticked by. I waited for her to tell me I was out of line. To ask me why I'd said what I just had. She didn't, like every time I veered too close to possessive or all but declared her mine, she broke eye contact first and pulled away. I wanted to grab her and shake her, to roar at her to see me—*to fucking see me.*

Somehow, I had to contain what was flaring up inside me—a male staring down at his female and wanting, needing, so badly to wash away the stain of another male's kiss from her lips.

But if I did that, I risked fucking up everything. I risked losing her completely. So no, I wouldn't kiss her, but I also couldn't pretend I didn't need her. Especially after being away from her. "You're sleeping with me in the tree house," I said, a demand leaving no room for argument. "You can shower there."

For once, Magnolia didn't argue. Deep down was she afraid of what I'd say if she resisted?

Fucked if I knew, but something was seriously wrong, and the sooner I had her in my bed, in my arms, the better. She let me take her hand and lead her back down the stairs, out of the house and across the yard. When she reached for the ladder, I stopped her, yanked off my shirt, and partially shifted. My wings exploded from my back, and I scooped her up and flew to the deck and carried her inside. As soon as I put her down, she walked into the bedroom, grabbed one of my shirts, then strode into the bathroom, shutting herself in—or maybe me out?

Fuck.

I stood there, staring at the door for long seconds, then finally sat heavily on the bed. Every time I left, every time I did what I had to, I felt myself slipping deeper into the shadows, into the role of monster. I became something, someone else without Mags to hold me steady, and it was leaking into my life here, it was ruining what she and I had.

But the truth was—I'd never felt more myself.

Because I was a monster.

Because that was exactly what I was meant to be.

Chapter Six

Magnolia

I looked over my shoulder, checking out my back in the mirror. There was a dark bruise low on my spine and another around my wrist. I grabbed the balm from the cabinet and smeared it across my skin before tugging on Bram's oversized shirt.

Bram was in bed when I walked out, his arm propped up behind his pillow, dark eyes on me.

My belly churned, my heart and mind rioting. Usually just being in the same room as Bram calmed me, not tonight. My belly hadn't stopped churning over what happened at the party. When would I see Willow again? How the hell were we going to prove she was innocent? And my heart was still beating hard after what happened in my room. I studied Bram now. There was something in his dark eyes I didn't recognize. I'd tried to pretend I never saw it, but I did, more and more often lately. The realization that he'd kept pieces of himself from me, that there were parts of him that I didn't know, unsettled me. Wounded me.

I tugged back the covers and got in, and he immediately pulled me in close.

Neither of us said anything.

Bram was protective to the extreme, but tonight he'd threatened to kill Relic if I ever kissed him again. And the look in his eyes, so cold, so devoid of all emotion except rage when he said it—he'd been deadly serious.

It was a giant step over the line, but I didn't call him out. Something in me said not to. No, it screamed it.

His arms tightened around me, and I willed the tension from my body, relaxing into him. If anyone walked in here now, they'd think we were a couple—that we were lovers. Was it weird to other people, how close we were? I'd never really thought about it too hard. I'd just done what felt right, and being with Bram as often as possible was what felt right. That's the way it'd always been. I guess that's why his unexplained absences were so painful.

I was the most important person in his life, and he was mine. And once upon a time, we'd told each other everything.

I rested my head on his chest and slid my arm across his stomach.

He dipped his head and breathed deep, scenting me. It was subtle, but I felt it, heard it. Thankfully, I'd washed all traces of Relic away. Whenever he'd gotten possessive in the past, this was the part where he'd apologize for overreacting. He'd say he was just worried about me, or only wanted the best for me. As the silence dragged out, I realized that wasn't going to happen. Not this time.

A weird feeling slid through me.

His hand traveled over my back, and I jerked.

He froze. "You're injured."

I needed to tell him what happened, but I'd been prepared to completely avoid it until morning because saying it out loud meant it was true. That my pregnant sister was in hiding, that she was most likely in Hell, and I had no idea when I'd see her again.

"Magnolia?"

"A lot's happened the last few days." My hand was on his chest, and his slid to my wrist, lifting it. Every one of his muscles beneath me tightened.

"Who the fuck did this?" he snarled and rolled me off him so I was on my back. "What the fuck is going on?"

Pain stabbed at me, as everything that had happened while he was away hit me again. I ignored it. I'd gotten good at that. "There was another murder, a couple days ago...Margot. She was tortured, carved up and killed," I said woodenly. He didn't move, his black eyes locked on mine. "Then there was another one tonight. The witches council came for Willow, they think she did it." Art had talked to councilor Trotman and he'd shared, probably more than he should. "The evidence against her is overwhelming. The witch killed tonight was found at The Cauldron. There was no break-in, no sign of forced entry. The body was found in Willow's old bedroom in the back."

Wills had lived in the shop for years before she moved home during her trial. There was a small apartment behind the store, but we didn't use it anymore. The door between the back room and the storeroom had been closed and locked. No one could remember the last time we'd actually been in there.

"There were traces of blood and hair, but not just the latest murder, the other two as well."

Bram cursed viciously. "Where's Willow now?"

"They got away. The rest of the hounds are with them. Willow's pregnant...we were there to celebrate, then..." My voice cracked.

Bram pressed a kiss to my forehead. "War will keep her safe until we can figure this out."

"I know," I said, fighting back angry tears.

He ran his thumb over my bruised wrist. "Who did this to you?"

"One of the new councilmen. I got in his way so he couldn't go after Willow and Warrick. His anger got the better of him. If I hadn't, he'd be dead. Warrick would have torn him to shreds. He should've thanked me, not shoved me against a door."

Bram's jaw clenched, and his eyes turned frigidly cold. "He'll pay for that."

"It was his cousin who was murdered tonight. He's an asshole, but I think he deserves a pass on this one." Bram didn't look as if he agreed. I blew out a breath. "Isaac Eldridge was there as well, the smug bastard."

"That prick's overdue for an ass kicking."

Bram wasn't wrong.

"You know where War took Willow?"

"We don't know for sure, but we're guessing they're in Hell. It's the safest place for them right now." Saying that out loud seemed insane, but besides Lucifer himself, the hounds were one of the most feared creatures down there. No one and nothing would get near Willow.

"It's going to be okay," he said. "We'll get through this."

I nodded and hoped he was right.

His arm tightened around me. "You think you'll be able to sleep?"

"I don't know." I glanced up at him. "If I do, will you be here when I wake up?" There was bitterness in my voice. I hadn't meant for it to come out like that, but the hurt was impossible to hold in anymore. I shouldn't have said anything. The storm was over, and those words had the power to open the floodgates again.

His eyes slid to mine. He'd heard it as well. "I'd never leave without telling you. You fucking know that."

I studied him. Bram had changed so much. For a long time, when we were around others, he'd preferred his bird form, to hide and go unnoticed. He didn't do that anymore. There'd always been a darkness to him, but it had deepened in ways I couldn't describe. There was also a hardness to him that had never been there before. It'd happened slowly, but there was no missing it now. "I thought I knew a lot of things. Turns out I was wrong."

Don't say it. Do not say it.

I didn't want another confrontation, I'd had enough emotional turmoil for one night, but I couldn't not say something. Not when it was eating at me. "Amelia was in the shop yesterday; Leah and Claire were with her. They saw you at The Bank with one of your brothers."

He stilled against me.

I slipped my arms from his waist and hugged myself. "It's true, then."

"Mags—"

"Leah said you and your brother were surrounded my fawning females... Oh, and she also said she had your number and planned to ask you out."

"That's not what happened—"

"How about you explain it to me, then? So I can understand." I'm the one who said I didn't want to fight, and here I was, starting one. "So you're, what? Going out with your brothers to pick up females, then lying to me about it for some fucked-up reason?" As I said the words, my anger grew. "Or maybe you're fucking demons? That would at least explain why you're coming home so messed up?" I shifted farther away from him. "I'm not one to judge. If fucking monsters is your thing, then just tell me—"

"I'm not fucking demons," he said, his obsidian gaze unwavering. "I'm not fucking anyone."

He reached for me, and I swiped his hand away and sat up. "You could. You could go out with Leah, fuck her, let her scratch up your chest. I'm sure she'd be into it. You can do whatever the fuck you like, you already are, right? Just don't come to me and expect me to heal you afterward."

"Mags—"

"Christ, I'm not even an afterthought, anymore, am I?"

"Magnolia," he all but snarled.

I shoved off the covers, fully worked up now. "No, you go off and do whatever it is you do, go out and party with your brothers, or whatever. I honestly don't give a fuck anymore." I stood, heart pounding, feeling sick to my stomach.

He shoved back the covers and stood as well, taking a step toward me.

I lifted a hand, warning him to stay back. "I can't do this." The words escaped before I knew they were coming, but I didn't try to take them back, because I meant it. "I can't wait around at home for you, scared out of my mind, not knowing if you'll ever come back. You've checked out. You're my best friend, and I'm losing you." I was shaking, my emotions rioting through me. "You were mine. I was yours. We were inseparable, now we're—"

One moment I was standing there, the next he was in front of me, lifting me off my feet and planting me back in bed.

"Stop," he bit out and loomed over me. "You haven't lost me. You will never lose me." His nostrils flared, his big body shaking. "I need you to trust me, Magnolia. I need...I need you to tell me you know I would never do anything to hurt you. Ever. I'd fucking die before I purposely caused you even a moment of pain." One of his big, rough-skinned hands took hold of my jaw, his coal-black eyes on mine. "I would tell you everything, fuck...everything, if I were able to, but I can't. I want to tell you what I'm doing, where I'm—"

He made a choking sound.

"Bram."

He gasped for breath. "I would...I'd—" He choked again, then again tried to speak, and it was like some invisible force had him in a choke hold and was squeezing.

I slammed my hand over his mouth. "Stop. Stop trying to talk."

Oh goddess. He couldn't tell me, not because he didn't want to but because he was physically unable to. "You're being gagged by a silencing oath, aren't you?"

He said nothing. But he didn't deny it. He just continued to stare deep into my eyes, silently asking me to see the truth as his breathing slowly evened out. He was bound so tightly that he'd choke, most likely to death, if he even tried to tell me. Which meant whoever he was answering to was extremely powerful. Silencing oaths were rarely used. They were forbidden by everyone —except those in the highest of high-level positions.

"You really can't tell me, can you?"

He continued to hold my gaze, saying nothing.

No. He couldn't.

~

"Magnolia," Bram's voice was low, insistent.

My hair was brushed back from my face, and I struggled to open my eyes.

"Mags. Wake up."

My mind was fuzzy, then everything snapped back into focus —the murders, what happened with Willow, what I'd learned about Bram—and my eyes flew open. I groggily tried to sit up. "What's wrong?"

I expected it to be morning, or that I'd slept in. But it was still dark outside, the moon high in the sky.

"I have to go," Bram said, tucking my hair behind my ear. "Something's come up."

Disappointment washed through me. It still hurt, but at least now I knew he'd tell me where he was going if he could. "When will you be back?"

"Tomorrow. This shouldn't take long," he said.

I nodded and covered his hand still lingering at the side of my face. "Be safe. I'll be here when you get back."

He was watching me, his body incredibly still.

His gaze dipped to my lips.

I found it hard to breathe all of a sudden, and tension stretched out between us. The kind that I tried to pretend didn't exist, the kind that had panic firing through me. I quickly looked down, breaking eye contact, while my heart hammered behind my ribs, so hard and fast, I felt dizzy.

He slid his hand from under mine and stood. "Go back to sleep," he said as if nothing had just happened, as if he hadn't felt that tension as well.

I nodded, but there was no chance of me going back to sleep now.

He planted a kiss on the top of my head and walked out, and I lay there for a while, listening to the leaves rustling. But it was hot, and my mind was all over the place. Places I didn't want it to go. So I got up, wandered into the living room, and turned on the TV.

Not that I paid much attention to what was on. Goddess, where was Wills now? Was she already in Hell? Or had Warrick taken her somewhere else? Who and what had called Bram away in the middle of the night? Honestly, if it wasn't for the fact he could fly and I couldn't, I would've followed him by now.

My mind was so busy, it took me a moment to realize my voice wasn't the only one in my head.

Come to me, daughter of Coven Thornheart, echoed through my mind.

I stilled. That's what I thought I heard. I shot to my feet.

Oh fuck.

The mother—she was calling me.

This wasn't supposed to happen yet. I had another six months. And this sure as hell wasn't supposed to happen without Bram.

I couldn't wait for him to come home, though. When the mother called, you went, no matter what. I couldn't even ask Relic to go with me because he'd left with the other hounds. There was Asher, but her loyalty was with Draven and Iris, and I didn't want my family knowing about this, not yet, and she'd definitely tell them. My family couldn't help me, or come with me, it wasn't permitted, and they'd want to. Badly. Telling them would only cause them worry, when there was absolutely nothing they could do to help me, and I was convinced if they knew, they'd try to find a way even though it was forbidden.

I couldn't risk it, not after everything my sisters had been through to get us this far.

I called Bram as I shoved on my shoes. When he didn't answer, I left a message asking him to call me back. I didn't want to tell him over the phone. I didn't want him distracted if he was doing something dangerous. He'd call back as soon as he could. I took the ladder to the yard below and ran for the house. I didn't believe in coincidences. And being called on the night my sister was accused of murder—yeah, that sure as hell wasn't one. I quickly let myself in, changed into something more suitable for running—and fighting—grabbed my knife, loaded a backpack with a few things I'd been working on, grabbed my car keys and slipped out of the house.

Oldwood Forest was twenty minutes away, and I gripped the wheel for dear life the whole drive, running through everything I knew about the meeting place, about what would happen when the mother came, what could happen afterward, over and over again. I still had to make it to the meeting spot in one piece, but the most dangerous part was afterward.

All three of my sisters could have lost their lives if they hadn't had help after the mother was done with them. I needed a plan, one that would mean me getting out of the forest alive. I didn't love the idea of becoming the main dish at some demon dinner party.

The clearing loomed up ahead, the forest opening so dark I couldn't see anything beyond it. It was creepy as hell, but I had no choice, this was happening and I had to be ready for anything.

Pulling over, I checked my knife again, pulled on the dark hoodie I'd swiped from Bram's room to help me blend into the shadows, tugged on my backpack, and walked into the forest.

Chapter Seven

Magnolia

Something was following me.

I hadn't seen it yet, but it'd clocked me fifteen minutes ago and had been on my tail since. Its smell gave it away first. It was disgusting, like rot and manure, but also perfect for my needs.

Other than my new friend tailing me, I'd managed to go unnoticed. I'd heard demons in the distance—voices, calls and whoops and growls, and what sounded like some kind of party in full swing in the opposite direction—but the darkness had provided excellent cover.

And Asher had trained me well. She'd taught me how to move soundlessly through the forest, where to walk, what to avoid. And what I was about to do? She herself had done once, and it'd gotten her out of a tough spot when she'd been a young wolf and found herself alone in a forest full of hungry demons. I was close to the meeting spot, so close, I could feel the humming of it, calling me.

The demon tracking me darted to the other side of the path,

getting closer. I'd only seen him in my peripheral vision, but the demon looked smaller in size, a similar height to me, which made sense or it would've attacked already, possibly one of the smaller scavenger breeds.

Just a little farther. I was only a few feet from the clearing now. Gripping my knife, I pretended to trip and stumble, dropping to the ground—and waited.

As expected, as soon as it thought I was wounded, it struck.

I spun just as it reached me and buried my knife in its throat, then jerked the blade to the side. Spinning, I swept its feet out from under it, flipped it over, and sliced through the tendons on each leg, then across its wrists so it couldn't run or fight.

It roared and thrashed while I covered its mouth with my hand, pulled a piece of string and a large needle from my pocket, and curled it tightly in my fist. "Thread the needle with this twine, seal your mouth shut for all of time." It was a variation of a spell Willow used once, and it had left an impression. Hers used invisible magical thread, mine on the other hand did not. I'd need to be conscious to maintain a spell like that, but I wasn't sure I would be after this, so real thread was best this time.

Gripping the demon's ankle, I dragged him after me. He was small but heavy, and he struggled as I towed him into the middle of the clearing. He stared up at me with wide, furious eyes, a stare that said he wanted to tear me into tiny pieces.

"You were about to eat me, asshole, you deserve what you got. So keep your mouth shut, or you'll tear your lips off along with your stitches." I pulled my top over my head and tossed it aside.

Getting naked in front of this creep wasn't my idea of a good time, but I had no choice and quickly removed the rest of my clothes. Stripped down to nothing, I strode to the squirming demon and made a couple more holes in him, then covered myself in his blood, disguising my scent with its seriously nasty one. The demon was finally too low on blood to fight, and thankfully passed out.

There was a circle of stones in the middle of the clearing, and I whispered a simple spell, igniting a blazing fire inside it. All that was left was to let the mother know I was here. Pulling from my pocket the small jewel-handled knife Mom had given me when I was thirteen, I made a slice in the side of my thigh. Blood slipped from the slice instantly.

Dropping my knife, I closed my eyes and recited the words. "Guide me, old ones. I am your servant, the Keeper's sister chosen to fulfill the rite of Coven Thornheart." A gust of wind hit me, whipping around me out of nowhere, it swirled faster and faster, blasting against my naked body. "I'm here to accept my task. Whatever you ask, I will undertake."

The wind grew stronger, so fierce it was hard to draw breath.

Then finally, a rattling sound reached me, followed by a hiss.

She was coming.

The mother wasn't all goodness and light. She wasn't all evil and darkness either. She was both, she was everything, and I felt that now. It danced through me, over my skin, lifting goose bumps all over me.

I had to fight my fear to hold my ground. She had no corporal form, so when the mother did need to make an appearance, she inhabited the body of her massive pet serpent.

My heart thundered in my ears as the rattling grew louder, closer. There was a hiss by my ear, then hot breath brushing my skin before I felt a raspy, tickling sensation against my thigh. She was tasting my blood, making sure I was exactly who she'd called to her.

Open your eyes, daughter of Coven Thornheart.

Her voice echoed through my mind, and I made myself do as she bid—then bit back my gasp at the sight of her. She was massive, her huge head swaying, black eyes looking through me, as if she could peer right into my soul.

You've come alone. Brave or stupid?

"Probably a little of both," I said.

She hissed, her head jerking forward, and I slammed my mouth shut.

There is greatness in you, child, if you choose to take hold of it, but it's volatile. Your sisters, they were full of light. Not you. You have shadows, so many of them, and you are blind to so very much.

I stayed silent, her words sending a chill down my spine and terror through my heart.

You must complete the task I give you by the time the vines meet. If you fail, you will be unworthy of trial, and gifts past will be returned to the mother. If you complete your task yet fail to win your trial, again, your coven's gifts will be returned to the mother.

"I understand," I said.

Her massive head swung my way, her black eyes meeting mine. *Your inner rage is a gag, a blindfold, it's the heavy cloak you hide behind. If you can't find a way to best it, child, you will fail this test. You will lose everything.*

"I'll do whatever it takes to pass this task," I said, a knot in my stomach.

We shall see.

Her head jerked back suddenly. I didn't have time to suck in a breath or brace before she struck. Her massive jaw wrapped around my torso, and she sunk her fangs into my body, my stomach and lower back. I knew it was coming, but still I stood there in shock as fire blazed through me, suspending me there for what felt like forever when it must have only been seconds.

Finally, she released me. I swayed, stumbling to the side, fighting desperately to stay on my feet as she spun and slithered back into the forest. Her venom pumped through me now, hard and fast, and my legs gave out from under me. I fell to the ground, naked and alone in the middle of the woods.

Darkness creeped in at the edges of my eyes...I grabbed for my bag.

But it was too late.

I passed out.

~

Groaning, I forced my eyes open. It wasn't easy.

It was still dark.

And somehow, I was still alive. The demon blood had worked.

The fire had gone out, and thankfully, the demon I'd captured was still unconscious. I couldn't see much of anything as I felt around for my clothes. The weakness was so strong, I ignored everything but Bram's oversized hoodie and my boots. It was a struggle, but I finally pulled them on. Then grabbing my knife and pack, I fought to stand. It wasn't easy, and it took almost all my energy, but I did it.

I stumbled back toward the trees, muttering a protection spell as I went, calling on my ancestors to protect and guide me, since I had no one else.

I tried as hard as I could, but with how unsteady I was, there was no way I could be quiet. I sounded like a goddamn elephant stomping through the forest. I stumbled over my own feet again and hit the ground hard. Darkness tried to creep into the edges of my sight—a rustling came from the trees to the right of me.

More demons. And I was about to pass out again. *Fuck.*

With the last of my strength, I jerked off my pack and pulled out several of the glass vials I'd put in there, crushing them in my hands. The glass cut through my skin, but that was the least of my worries.

The potions in these vials would disorient anyone they came in contact with, causing hallucinations, delirium, blindness, and a constant ringing in their ears. It seriously fucked you up. It was only temporary, the effects usually lasting about thirty minutes. I'd just surrounded myself with it, which meant I'd unfortunately be getting a dose as well. The darkness around me grew heavier. I didn't know if it was the potion or from my meeting with the mother at this point.

I just hoped it kept me safe until I woke up.

Then everything went dark again.

~

I didn't know how many hours had passed, but I woke with a gasp, the horrors of my hallucinations dissipating like smoke.

That was the third time I'd used the potion.

There were several demons wandering around, their hands over their ears, staring blindly into the distance—I looked down at myself—still in one piece.

I left the clearing...it had to be hours ago, but I'd been falling in and out of consciousness and lost track of time completely.

The walk in had only taken me twenty minutes, walking out had taken me a hell of a lot longer. I stumbled to my feet as a disoriented demon crashed through the trees toward me. It was foaming at the mouth, eyes dilated, staring blindly ahead, following the sounds I was making.

With a cry of desperation and exhaustion, I stumbled to the side, spun, and slashed its throat. It didn't stop, too lost in its own hallucination to even feel it. It swiped at me, and I spun again. Approaching from behind it, I wrenched back its head and hacked it off. The last thing I needed was it wandering out onto the road and terrifying some human driving by.

It turned to ash, and I pushed on, one shaky step at a time, toward my car.

My vision was blurring again by the time I reached it. I yanked the door open quickly and locked myself in before I passed out again.

~

I woke just before dawn. Orange streaked the still-dark sky, the first rays of sunlight struggling to break through the darkness. With trembling hands, I shoved the key into the ignition and started the car, then pulled out onto the road.

I'd done it, on my own.

And I'd survived.

~

Bram

Pulling off my shirt, I tossed it aside and sat.

I'd put this off as long as I could, but it was time. The markers were building up, I couldn't delay it anymore.

I was a warrior of our people. This was the way our father, our grandfather, his before that, had worn their hair. This was a rite of passage, letting everyone know what I was.

A warrior and provider for my people.

Resting my elbows on my knees, I dipped my head, while Talon sectioned off a thick strip of hair down the middle and tied it back. Payne got down on his knees beside me, pulled his knife from its sheath, and began slicing away the hair at the sides. It fell to the wooden deck as Payne muttered the ancient words of our people, the vow of our warriors.

Talon stood back, leaning against the railing, watching, while Rook prepared the ink he'd be adding to my skin.

The blade was scraped against my scalp, taking it back to skin.

What would Mags think when she saw me? How would I explain it? I couldn't. It was one more thing I couldn't share with her. Something important that I had to keep from her.

I'd brought her here, she'd met my brothers, my people, but she didn't know what we were at our core. I'd made sure of it.

Crows were true predators.

She knew we were deadly hunters, but she didn't know the

extent of it, because I'd never shared it with her—no, I'd actively kept it from her, afraid of what she'd think if she knew my true nature. I'd also spent a lot of years trying to suppress my desire to hunt. But after what happened in the cemetery that day, stopping that fucker from hurting Magnolia, there was no suppressing it. Not anymore.

And letting that side of myself, my dark urges, free, had felt so right.

Just as a wolf was compelled to howl at the moon, a crow was compelled to hunt—and kill.

This was who I was, what I was born to be.

I was a crow.

A warrior.

A killer.

Which meant my job was perfect for me and my brothers. We fulfilled a necessary service, and we fed the dark need inside us.

Rook came forward, taking Payne's place. He gripped the top of my head, tilting it to the side and pressed his tattoo gun to my skin. "Say their name," Rook growled low.

The ink loaded in Rook's gun was laced with blood. Every soul I sent to the afterlife, a piece of them would stay with me in the markers I'd carry on my skin, that was my burden.

It was the price we paid for embracing what we were, but this one, I wanted it. He deserved that disgrace, and I hoped his soul burned for eternity.

My lips peeled back from the hatred filling me before his name could pass my lips. "Brody," I snarled.

No, tonight wasn't my first kill, that was in the Thornheart cemetery two and a half years ago—when I killed the male holding a knife to Magnolia's throat.

When the fighting ended that day, before his body had been taken, I'd collected Brody's blood because deep down I knew this day would come. I wished I could add a marker for Clayton Whitlock as well, and hated that Warrick had killed him before I could.

The buzz of the gun, the bite against my skull, had me breathing hard. Not from the pain—no, I welcomed the pain—it was from the fucking rightness of it. Payne's hand came down on my shoulder and squeezed.

Again, I wondered what Mags would think if she knew the truth. I wasn't afraid she'd hate me or fear me because I killed, I was more worried about her looking into my eyes—and seeing how much I liked it.

Rook finished and quickly cleaned the gun and loaded the new ink laced with the blood of another of my kills.

I said the next name, and the next, and I kept on saying names until I had eight markers on the side of my head.

Maeve had come out to watch and was sitting on Talon's shoulders.

"What do you think?" he asked her.

She pressed her hand against the shaved side of Talon's head, something she often did to Payne as well, since she was a baby. "I like it. I'm gonna be a warrior too when I'm a grownup, like Daddy," she said and wrapped her arms around Talon's neck, resting her chin on top of his head and grinning. "I'll have more markers than all of you."

Payne muttered a curse.

Talon gave her leg a squeeze. "Yeah, you will, little feather."

Rook chuckled low as he wiped the side of my head with a damp cloth.

Payne strode over and held out his hand. "How do you feel?"

I took it, and he pulled me to my feet. "Good. Right."

He nodded. "Stay and have a drink with us to celebrate."

"Yeah, maybe." I checked my phone, I'd forgotten to turn the sound back on after we'd been hunting. There was a message from Mags. I listened to it, then called her back. No answer. She was probably asleep. "Another time," I said to Payne. "I need to get back." Mags had no idea what just happened here, what it all meant, but I needed to be close to her, now more than ever.

I needed to be close to my mate.

The only female I wanted—that I would ever want.

I ran my fingers over my hair, nerves firing inside my gut.

The need to be close to Magnolia pumped hotly through my veins.

After last night, finding out all she'd been through—Margot's death, the shit at the clubhouse, seeing the bruises that fucking prick Adler had given her, the way she blew up at me—I needed to smooth things over with her, and that wasn't going to happen if I was never here. I needed to be here for her more. I just didn't know how I was going to make it all work.

All I knew was I couldn't lose her.

I knew loss.

And Magnolia was a loss that would fucking end me.

Darkness swirled around me, through me. There wasn't one thing I wouldn't do to make sure that never happened. To make sure I never lost her. I'd tear it all down before I let that happen. I'd snatch her from her world, and I'd make a new one, just her and me.

I'd fly away with her and never come back.

She wasn't expecting me home so soon, and my need to see her was a deep, relentless ache inside me now. I quickly headed across the yard toward the house.

The sound of a car pulling up out front reached me. Magnolia's car. I detoured and jogged around the side of the house.

The driver's door was open. Mags was struggling to get out—and she was covered in blood.

I sprinted to her, scooped her into my arms, and frantically searched her, trying to find where the blood was coming from. "Where're you hurt? Where's the blood coming from?"

That's when I smelled it, not just Magnolia's blood—demon as well.

"Take me...t-to the tree house. I don't want anyone else to s-see me like this," she said.

My wings exploded from my back, tearing my shirt to ribbons. Clutching her to me, I flew over the house and landed on the deck of the tree house. Shoving the door open, I strode to the bathroom.

"Where're you hurt?" I asked again as I lowered her to her feet and, still supporting her, helped her out of her boots.

"I'm not s-sure," she said and swayed to the side, her eyes rolling into the back of her head, almost blacking out.

Fuck. I pulled her against me and carefully pulled up my hoodie that she was wearing. She was completely fucking naked underneath, her small curvy frame covered in dried blood and mud. I needed to wash all this off to see the damage. I turned on the shower and carefully lifted the hoodie over her head, tossing it aside.

"I'm n-naked," she slurred.

"I don't give a fuck. I need to see what we're dealing with."

I kicked off my boots and scooped her up, stepping into the shower still in my jeans, and held her under the water. I let it wash away the worst of it, not wanting to rub at her skin in case I made something worse.

"What happened? Why are you naked? Did someone force you...did they..."

She groggily shook her head. "N-no one...t-touched me." She went limp then, blacking out for a moment before jolting back to consciousness.

I grabbed a washcloth and carefully cleaned the rest of the mud and blood away. The more of her skin I revealed, the more relieved I became. There were some superficial scrapes and grazes, her hands were all cut up, but nothing life threatening.

What the fuck was going on? "Why are you having trouble talking? Who did this? Did you run into Adler–"

"I was...at Oldwood," she rasped.

"What? Why?" I swiped the washcloth over her stomach, taking away the last of the dried blood.

And froze.

Fuck.

Markings, ones that I'd seen before, on each of her sisters. My gaze shot to hers. "No," the word burst from me.

Her lids were heavy as she struggled to stay conscious. "Y-yes. After you left. I called you, but..." Then her eyes drifted shut, and she went limp in my arms again.

"Maggie? Magnolia?" Her breathing was slow and even. She'd passed out again.

Fuck, I'd called her back a couple more times on the way home, but when she hadn't answered, I was positive she was asleep, tucked up safe in bed.

I made sure I got all of the blood off her and quickly shut off the water. Wrapping her in a towel, I carried her into the bedroom and laid her on my bed to carefully dry her off. I rolled her to her side to make sure I hadn't missed any injuries. A few more scrapes, but nothing deep, nothing that needed stitches or for me to get Else.

The black thorny vine markings on her skin swirled low on her stomach, around her belly button, and there was a mirror image in the middle of her lower back. They looked like tattoos, only these, I knew, would move and grow. The vine from her stomach and one on her back would reach out until both vines touched. If she hadn't passed the task the mother had given to her by the time that happened, she'd fail.

I stared at those markings and tried to fucking breathe. We knew this was coming, that the mother would call on her, but we thought we had another six months. I thought *I* had six months.

When Mags's turn came, I was supposed to be there with her,

to protect her from the demons that infested the forest. I planned to be there with her every step of the way. Instead, she'd gone alone. She'd been alone and vulnerable.

The only explanation I could come up with for all the demon blood on her skin was that Mags had covered herself in it to disguise her scent. She'd killed a demon.

Magnolia had met with the mother. She'd fought at least one fucking demon, then she'd walked back, all by herself.

She could've been killed.

I could have lost her.

Breathing heavily, I tore my eyes from her, then rushed to grab the basket filled with her healing supplies, the one she kept here for me, and pulled out Else's balm. I carefully applied it to every scratch, scrape, and bruise on her smooth, pale skin. When I was done, I grabbed one of my shirts and carefully pulled it over her head, working her arms through the sleeves.

I wanted to keep her as she was, I wanted to hold her close to me, her bare skin against mine, so I could feel her alive and breathing and warm. But she wouldn't be cool with that. Mags wasn't shy about her body, at least not in front of her sisters, some spells required the witch to be naked. I made myself scarce during those times. Yes, I'd accidentally walked in on her during a spell once or twice, but best friends didn't sleep together naked.

It didn't matter that she was so much more than that to me.

I quickly yanked off my wet jeans, pulled on some dry shorts, and got under the covers with her, carefully pulling her into my arms.

"Bram?" she said suddenly, startling awake.

There was no missing the fear in her voice. "I'm here." She was so used to me being gone, so used to doing it all on her own now, when that was never how it was meant to be.

She sighed, relaxing against me, and fell back to sleep—or losing consciousness, I wasn't sure which.

After the mother bit a witch, her potent venom pumping

through their veins, it took them out for at least a day, and staying conscious was damn near impossible. "How the fuck did you get out of that forest?" I said against her damp hair, talking to myself, not expecting her to respond.

"My potion," she muttered. "Th-the one I've been working on."

I dragged in a ragged breath, every muscle in my body locking tight. "The one that causes hallucinations?"

She nodded against me. "I c-covered myself in it."

So anything that came close to her while she was unconscious got a dose, which meant, she would have as well. Fuck. *Fuck.* "What if one of them had attacked you while they were still out of it?"

"They didn't," she said.

What else could either of us say? She'd done all she could to protect herself, because her familiar hadn't been there to do it for her.

This wasn't how it was fucking supposed to be.

I pressed my nose to her hair and breathed deep, the monster in me needing reassurance, needing her in my fucking lungs. I was born to walk beside her, to protect her, to make sure she was always safe. And I'd failed.

I'd failed her.

I'd been failing her for the last couple of years.

I pressed my mouth to the top of her head again. No more. "I'm not going anywhere, Mags. I promise, I'm staying right here."

She didn't answer, not this time.

I didn't know if she'd passed out again—or if she didn't answer because she didn't believe me.

Chapter Eight

Magnolia

My eyes snapped open when something cool touched my stomach.

It was morning, light filling the room, and Bram was sitting on the mattress beside me. His hair had fallen forward, covering most of his face, and he was so focused on what he was doing he hadn't noticed I'd woken up. I looked down as he smeared healing balm across a scrape low on my belly.

I was wearing one of his T-shirts and a pair of his boxers. They were low on my hips, and there was more balm on a scrape on my ribs, and another beside my belly button, right over the new markings the mother had given me.

"Hey," I said, my voice croaky as hell.

His gaze shot to mine. "Fuck, finally."

"Why am I dressed as your female alter ego?"

His gaze darted down my body and back, and the tendons in his muscled forearms popped. "You don't remember?"

I remembered a lot of last night, and the rest was slowly coming back. "The drive home's still a bit fuzzy. I got here, then you...appeared, and you..." He'd lifted me into his arms, flown to the tree house, stripped me naked and cleaned the blood and mud off me before he'd tended my wounds. I looked up at him again and wanted to squirm as the memories flooded me. But this was Bram, my best friend. So I was naked, so what, right? "Yeah, I remember. Thanks for taking care of me."

He sucked in a sharp breath and shook his head. "You're thanking me now?" His jaw clenched. "I know I've been doing a shitty fucking job of taking care of you, of being there for you, I know that, and I promise, I'll be here from now on. When you need me, I'll be here."

He meant it, but he was lying to me, and to himself. It wasn't intentional. He was deep in denial. Seeing me messed up last night had scared him, and he wasn't thinking logically. "You can't promise that, Bram, and I don't expect you to. I know you can't tell me where you go and what you do, but you're bound by a silencing oath, which means you're working for the kind of people who don't like to be ignored."

The muscle in his jaw jumped. "Let me worry about that."

"You want to protect me? I feel the same way about you. If something happened to you because you ignored an oath? I'd never forgive myself. I've done that, remember? Trust me, you don't want that."

His expression didn't change, and he didn't agree with me or argue his point, because he was going to do whatever the hell he liked.

"Bram—"

"How are you feeling? You were out of it last night."

Okay, he wasn't going to talk about it now. Fine. But if he thought I'd just drop it completely, he was mistaken. "I'm fine." I slid my legs out of bed and stood. Not as shaky as I thought, and my hands that had been cut up were already healing. I walked to the bathroom and lifted the shirt to take a closer look at the markings on my stomach. "Shit." Thorny vines swirled around my belly button and spread a little out to the sides.

"Check your back," Bram said, leaning against the doorframe.

"Seriously?" I turned and looked over my shoulder. Okay, that was excessive. "The mother obviously decided less wasn't more where I was concerned. The belly design wasn't enough, noooo, she thought I needed a tramp stamp as well?"

"They suit you," Bram said.

I glanced his way, and his gaze was moving over my exposed skin, lingering on my belly. Warmth curled right under the design, stealing my breath, and I dropped the shirt. "You're just saying that so I don't freak out." The shirt was way too big and had slipped down over one of my shoulders, uncovering more of my scarred skin. "I guess I should thank her. At least they cover a few of my ugly scars." He made a strange sound, and I glanced up at him again.

He shook his head, making his glossy black hair shift in a way that, if I was close, I'd reach up and touch it. I loved his hair. I'd told him a million times over the years how jealous I was of it.

"There's not one fucking part of you that's ugly," he said.

I stilled. The way he'd said it lifted goose bumps all over me. We stared at each other for several tense seconds, and my heart slammed into the back of my ribs, so hard I lost my breath for a moment.

I tore my gaze from his and busied myself by washing my hands, even though I didn't actually need to wash my hands, but the weird tension between us was too much. "I haven't felt the call to my task, but I don't need it, I already know what it is," I said drying them off.

"You do?"

"Willow gets accused of murder, then the same night the mother calls me, six months ahead of schedule." I strode toward him, and for a moment I didn't think he was going to move, he kind of paused, staring down at me with a look I couldn't decipher, but then he tucked his hair behind his ear and stepped back.

My breath was knocked from me and I blinked up at him. "What have you done?"

He tensed.

"Your hair." I reached up, and he held still as I brushed it back on one side, then the other. "You shaved it."

"It's how our warriors wear it," he said roughly.

Like his bothers. "And you're a warrior now?"

"Yes."

There was new ink on the side of his head, eight lines, something else the warriors in his village had. "And these?" I said as I ran my fingers over them. "Can you tell me what they are?"

"A warrior's markers," he said but didn't elaborate.

It was all he could or would tell me, which was nothing at all.

I dropped my hand. "It suits you."

His gaze searched mine. "Yeah?"

I nodded, then turned away and strode out to the living room, my heart in my throat. It was only hair, but something inside told me that it was a lot more than that, not just one more secret between us.

"So you're looking for a murderer," he said, following and picking up the conversation about my task where we'd left off.

"Looks that way." Now I just had to figure out where the hell to start.

I'd showered and changed, and Bram and I were making a late breakfast. He was wearing his usual black jeans, boots, and worn tee, the fabric straining around his biceps in a way it never used to. He'd tied the wide strip of his black hair back, and I kept sneaking glances his way. He looked so different. He was still my Bram, but also...not—though then that went deeper than just his appearance.

The front door opened and closed, and I couldn't see them, but I heard Iris and Rose talking as they walked in. We were having a family meeting this morning to discuss what we were going to do about Willow, and though it was terrible timing, I needed to tell them I'd visited the mother last night, and my suspicions about my task before they started looking into it. The mother would see it as interference. A witch couldn't get help from her coven when her task had been set, and knowing my sisters, they'd already formed a plan.

"I can't believe she's calling her favor in now," Rose was saying. "The timing couldn't be worse."

Iris made a sound of agreement. "Have you heard from her at all since you and Ronan went to her cottage?"

"No, and I'd kind of hoped she'd forgotten about our bargain."

"What will you do?" Iris asked.

Rose let out a frustrated breath. "What I won't be doing is asking her. It's too dangerous."

"Our baby sister is twenty-one years old. She doesn't need us to protect her from everything, not anymore. Is she still struggling with some things? Yes, but don't write her off. When Bram started vanishing, it crushed her, but she's been getting better, controlling her anger, she's grown so much stronger, become a lot more independent. And she's been training her ass off with Ash."

Well, fuck. Thanks a lot, Iris. I felt Bram's eyes on me, and I couldn't bring myself to look at him.

"I thought you were just hanging out with Ash, learning a few moves?" he said softly, so he didn't blow our cover.

I don't know why I hadn't told him the extent of my training. Maybe it was me being petty. He was keeping something from me, so I was from him.

"What do you think Agatheena will do if you break your bargain?" Iris asked Rose before I could answer him.

I lowered my butter knife, and Bram tensed beside me at the mention of that witch's name.

"It's fine. I'll just take her what she wants," Rose said.

"But she asked for Magnolia, not you."

Rose cursed. "She asked me for the favor, no one else was mentioned."

"What exactly did she say? What words did she use?" Iris asked.

Rose was silent for several seconds. "A favor, at a date and time of her choosing."

"There was no mention of who," Iris said. "She's a powerful witch who dabbles in dark magic. You think pissing her off is a good idea?"

Okay, that was enough skulking in the kitchen.

"This is my mess. I'm not asking Mags to clean it up for me," Rose said, her startled gaze slicing to me when I walked out into the hall, Bram right behind me. "You're here," my sister said, guilt written all over her face.

"Yep, and I heard every word."

Rose paled. "Mags—"

"What does Agatheena want me to do?" I said and felt Bram close in behind me, volatile energy radiating from him.

"I don't want you involved with this." Rose crossed her arms. "Just forget you heard anything."

I snorted. "Well, that's not going to happen."

"Tell her," Iris said.

I could have hugged her but was having one of those days when touch wasn't something I could tolerate.

Rose sighed and pulled something from her pocket. "She wants you to take this to her." She held up a small vial.

"Why me? And what is it?"

"It's blood from a very powerful vampire. Another debt apparently. Ronan collected it." Rose chewed her lip. "I have no idea why she asked for you. It makes no sense. She and I made the bargain. If I'd known she'd do this, I would have told her to shove it." Rose cursed, looking worried. "I don't like this. She's half demon and extremely powerful."

"She wants me to deliver it, I'll deliver it. Everything'll be fine." I shoved my hands in my pockets as a tremor moved through them for some unknown reason. "And I'll even keep my attitude in check so she doesn't eat me."

"Don't even joke about it. I'm not actually a hundred percent sure that she doesn't eat people."

"Awesome." Shit was just getting better and better. Yesterday, I woke up and it was like any other day. Within forty-eight hours, I learned Bram was bound by a silencing oath, my sister was accused of murder and was in hiding, the mother called me, and now I had to visit a witch who may or may not be a cannibal. I'd obviously pissed the fates off somehow. "There has to be a reason she's asking for me." I took a steadying breath. "Maybe it has something to do with my task?"

Iris sucked in a sharp breath, and Rose's eyes went huge.

"Your task?" Iris said. "What do you mean, your task?"

"Magnolia?" Rose whispered.

"How did I not see it," Iris bit out, not letting me answer either of them. "Look at her," she said to Rose, "She's barely recovered. Show me," my sister said.

I knew what she was asking and lifted my shirt, showing her the vine markings on my stomach and back.

"Holy shit," Rose said.

I dropped my shirt. "My words exactly."

"It's too soon." Iris planted her hands on her hips. "What the hell is going on?"

"My guess? My trial has something to do with this mess with Willow."

Rose blinked rapidly, then yanked me into her arms, hugging me tight. I had to fight my wince and the urge to pull away. She needed it, and I had to let her. When she pulled back, she looked up at Bram. "Thank the goddess you have wings, at least you didn't have to fight your way there and back."

Bram's entire body went rock solid beside me.

Rose frowned, not missing his reaction. "You were...there, weren't you?"

"He didn't know," I said quickly. "It's fine, I'm fine."

"You went alone?" Iris yelled.

"Keep your damn voice down. I don't want Mom knowing, not yet. She'll only worry, and there's nothing she can do to help me."

Iris bared her teeth like one of the wolves she lived with. "How the fuck did you survive it?"

"It doesn't matter, I did. It's over and done with. Let's move on," I said, the tension around us so thick I couldn't bear it. It wasn't Bram's fault, and I hated the way they were looking at him.

"Do you have someone to go with you to Agatheena's?" Iris asked, not looking at Bram.

Rose appeared even more pissed, her eyes flashing to her bat's, turning black for a second before returning to blue. "Relic would. Maybe we can get a message to him somehow? What about—"

"I'm standing right here," Bram said, and that volatile energy grew, swirling around us both.

Bram never usually said boo, but that had changed, especially the last year.

Iris stared up at him, and her head tilted to the side. "You can't blame us for asking, Bram. You've not exactly been around lately. Magnolia literally fought her way in and out of Oldwood Forest *alone*, something I can't even fucking bear to think about."

"You have been *extremely* busy," Rose said, and the look in her eyes as she stared up at him gave me pause.

"Magnolia comes first," he said, and there was a whole lot of grit in his voice.

"Does she?" Rose's stare was utterly frigid. "She didn't last night."

Whoa. What the hell? I knew they were pissed off on my behalf and hated seeing me upset when he left, but my sweet sister looked ready to go into battle. "Rose, there are things you don't know—"

"Did you tell her you visited The Vault a couple nights ago?" Rose asked, not looking away from him. "Is that where you were last night instead of protecting Magnolia?"

"No," he ground out.

I spun to face him. "The Vault?" I thought he was at The Bank, the club above it. Apparently, that was only half of the story. The Vault was below the popular nightclub and a place where blood drinkers went to feed and fuck willing donors. Bram wasn't a blood drinker, which meant the only reason he would be down there was to—

His eyes clashed with mine, but he said nothing. Not one fucking thing. I spun away and snatched the vial from Rose's hand. "I've got this. I'll let you know when I'm back."

"Mags, hang on. You can't go alone—"

Bram growled behind us, like a wolf or a freaking hellhound. "She won't fucking be going alone."

At his tone, both my sisters jolted in surprise. He'd never spoken to them like that, and they'd been too caught up in their own stuff, with living their own lives, to notice how much he'd changed. They noticed now.

"No," I said. "I won't. I'll ask Asher."

"Like fuck you will," Bram said, grabbing my hand and gripping it tight. "You're pissed at me. I deserve it, but I can't do anything about that. I will be going with you, though. So it's your choice. Either be pissed off all day, or get the fuck over it, because I'm your familiar and no one protects you but me. Understand?"

The room went utterly silent. Rose was blinking up at him stunned. Iris was wide-eyed, and going by her expression, she couldn't decide if she was angry or impressed.

I knew what I was. Yanking my hand from his, I spun away and stormed from the room, Bram hot on my heels.

"Call when you get back, or we're coming after you," Rose called after us.

I strode out the door, and Bram grabbed my arm before I could get in the car.

"Stop it," he said. "We're not doing this. Do you hear me? We're not fighting about this. Whatever you're thinking, it's wrong. So completely fucking wrong."

"I'm thinking you went to The Vault to feed and fuck a vamp," I said.

He did that thing where he locked eyes with me and said fucking nothing, like he wanted me to read his damn mind. The oath. He was there because he had to be. But he couldn't tell me why, or what happened. I pulled my arm free of his hold and dragged in a steadying breath.

I was acting like a jealous girlfriend. I needed to rein it the hell in. Whatever the details were, he couldn't tell me, and getting pissed at him for something he had no control over wasn't very constructive.

"I'm sorry," I said, and it wasn't easy to gather control of my anger, but I managed to bring it down from inferno to simmer. "Let's just focus on what we need to do, okay?"

He nodded, but his jaw was tight as hell. "We'll drive to the edge of the forest, then fly. It's dangerous. There're creatures there that make the demons we're used to look like kittens."

"Fantastic."

Bram bared his teeth. "They come anywhere near you, I'll tear them to fucking shreds."

A weird swirly sensation spiraled through my lower belly. "Noted."

<h1 style="text-align:center">Chapter Nine</h1>

Magnolia

I tried really hard to clear my head and focus on what I needed to do as we headed for the forest—and not on what Bram might or might not have done while he was at The Vault. I was failing.

The forest ahead thinned, and I pulled over on the side of the dirt road. The track that would lead us to Agatheena's cottage was just ahead. I slid my smaller knife in my pocket, the one I used for spelling, then reached under the seat and pulled out my bigger one.

Bram watched me. "Where'd you get that?"

"It was a gift." I got out of the car.

He did the same and rounded the hood. Slipping the knife from my fingers, he tested its balance and weight. His fingers curled around the hilt, gripping it tight, so tight his knuckles turned white. "From who? Relic?"

"What? No."

I frowned and took it back, strapping it to my thigh. "Asher. She gave it to me two months ago." I glanced up at him. "The first time I managed to take her down to the mat."

His brows shot up. "You took Asher down?"

"I've taken her down several times now," I said and grabbed my pack, pulling it on.

His dark eyes searched mine. "So, what Iris said, about you training?"

"It's true. And I'm good. Really good. I can take care of myself now. So you don't need to worry about me." It wasn't the reason I'd gone to Asher in the first place, ignoring my pride and with my tail between my legs, it had been about an outlet for my anger. But the more Bram was away, the more I realized I'd need to take care of myself, that Bram wouldn't always be there to look out for me like he used to be.

His nostrils flared, the muscle in his jaw twitching before he looked away.

"Bram?"

"We better get going." He tugged off his shirt, tucking it into the back of his jeans, then scooped me into his arms.

His wings unfurled, beating hard, and we lifted off. A moment later we were above the forest, looking down at the treetops.

"You don't like that I can fight?" I asked when the silence stretched out.

He shook his head. "I don't like that you had to learn because of me."

"I didn't do it because of you, I learned for me." I tightened my arms around his neck and pressed my forehead to his cheek. Goddess, my heart couldn't take much more of this, all this animosity and hurt, and just plan weirdness, between us.

"And the other thing Iris said about when I started leaving all the time?" I felt his throat working and his voice had grown incredibly deep. "I crushed you?"

"Don't," I said instead of answering, because we both knew the truth and there was nothing either of us could do about it now.

My world was in a spin, and he'd always been my steadying force, I needed that from him again now. I needed that more than anything right then. "Can we just be us. For today, can we just be Mags and Bram again, the way we used to be?"

His chest expanded, and he turned his head, pressing his lips to my forehead. "Yeah," he said against my skin before he turned back and focused on where we were going.

The farther we flew, the darker and denser the forest became. Strange sounds, cries and calls and growls, echoed up from below. Bram said there were creatures here that I'd never seen before, that the demons who lived out here had no choice because there was no way they could pass for human like the ones who lived in the city. And when Bram pointed to one below us, I understood what he meant. It was tall and skinny, gray in color with a greenish tinge at its joints. It also had pointed ears and holes where its nose should be.

The roof of a cottage appeared in the distance, peeking through the trees. "There."

I felt Agatheena's power then, like a dense fog wrapping around us.

Bram circled the area a few times, making sure there weren't any demons or other creatures right below us, then landed. His wings folded in and disappeared, but he didn't release me as he scanned the trees surrounding us.

With how dense the forest was here, the sun could barely break through. It made the air damp and heavy.

I pulled the knife from the sheath strapped to my thigh as Bram and I listened for anything approaching. "I can't believe she lives out here on her own."

"Not entirely on her own," Bram said when a demon roared in the distance.

I turned to the cottage. Rose was right, it looked like something from a Grimm's fairy tale, where a child-eating witch lived, or one working on evil spells and plotting revenge.

Smoke drifted lazily out of the chimney, even though it was the middle of summer, and the cottage itself looked almost part of the forest—its moss-covered stone walls butting up against thick tree trunks, a couple growing right through the thatched roof.

Her wards would be impenetrable, they'd have to be out here.

"What now?" Bram asked, his gaze sliding to the thick pines that stood on either side of the worn dirt path, and what hung from them.

Bones, some clean, some still covered in blood and gore dangled from thick twine. Skulls from different breeds of demon, and other creatures I had no chance of identifying. There were jars filled with bits of fabric, floating eyeballs, fingernails, and several others with organs of some kind stuffed into them. Another was half filled with a multitude of different colored hair all matted together.

The path led to the cottage's front door and branches arched over the top, forming a leafy canopy, also covered in Agatheena's macabre decoration.

"Now we let her know we're here." Rose had shared what happened when she came here, so I was prepared.

I reached out, and her ward sent fire coursing through my veins. Cursing, I yanked my hand back, clenching my fingers and shaking them out.

"Didn't tickle, then?" Bram asked.

"No, smart-ass. And I'd say that was just the warning." I walked to one of the pines. "Rose said Agatheena needed her blood, for confirmation of who she was. She said to look for a smooth patch on the side of the tree. It'll be darker in color."

Bram nodded and searched with me.

"Got it," he said a minute later.

I took a closer look. In the middle of a knot was a smooth,

indented patch. The tree was lighter wood, but this spot was a deep mahogany color.

"Yeah, that's it." I slipped my big knife back in its sheath and pulled out my small one, the one Mom had given me on my thirteenth birthday. Every witch in our coven had one, since we often used blood magic, and unlike my other knife, this one wasn't big enough to take my hand off.

Bram scanned the trees again as I made a slice in the tip of my finger. Blood bubbled to the surface, and I pressed it to the center of the darker patch in the tree.

Bram took my hand as soon as I was done, some of Else's balm already on his finger. "Now what?" he said distractedly as he smeared it over the cut, something he'd been doing since I first cut myself in front of him six years ago.

A low creak echoed from the cottage, the door swinging open slowly a moment before a very old and tiny, hunched-over female walked out with a raven perched on her shoulder.

"Now I go visit with Agatheena, and you wait here for me," I said, not taking my eyes off the old witch shuffling toward us.

"Like fuck," he snapped. "Where you go, I go."

"Magnolia Thornheart," Agatheena said as she drew closer. "I wasn't sure your sister would let you come." She smiled, briefly flashing red demonic eyes and yellow, pointed teeth, reminding me of her demon blood. As if I could forget.

"She wasn't either," I said. "But I convinced her."

Agatheena chuckled.

I took a step forward, and Bram hooked an arm around my waist, not letting me go any farther. "Rose said you asked for me specifically, why?"

"I like you," she said, stopping in front of us. "I knew I would."

Her skin was wrinkled, and her gray hair was wild and wiry. I had no idea how old she was, but I'd say *very*. The only thing between us was her ward, and my heart banged a little harder when her now piercing green eyes locked with mine. The raven on her shoulder looked up at Bram and bobbed, making a high-pitched *caw*.

Bram replied, a gritty sound coming from low in his chest.

"Why am I here, Agatheena?" I asked again.

"You'll find out, but first." She waved toward one of the jars hanging on the tree. "It needs a lock of your hair before it'll let you past," she said.

I wasn't sure what *it* referred to, the ward or the tree. Either way, I needed to add some hair to her collection. I guess I should be grateful she didn't demand an organ.

"I'll be waiting, so get a move on," Agatheena said, then headed back up the path and into her cottage.

"I'm coming with you," Bram said as I pulled a piece of hair forward from underneath and sliced off a small section.

I glanced up at the cottage and back at him. "Ronan wasn't allowed past her wards, but she didn't say you couldn't. Maybe it'll be okay?"

"I don't give a fuck if it's not. I'm coming." He unscrewed the lid of the jar and held it out.

I shoved my hair in, and he did it back up, letting the jar hang.

"Let's get this over with," he said and curled his fingers around mine.

I lifted my hand, and the buzz of power that had zapped through me was gone. "The ward's dropped. Let's go." I stepped through, turning back when Bram pulled on my hand—

He snarled as his fingers were ripped from mine and he was tossed backward, landing hard on the forest floor. He shot to his feet and bolted toward me but was thrown back a second time. He jumped to his feet again and stormed forward, his black eyes filled with rage. "This isn't happening. You are not going in there without me."

He was afraid for me, but I had no choice. "I have to do this. I'll be okay."

"Don't you dare walk in there," he said through gritted teeth.

I was already stepping away. "I have to. Rose owes her, and she called me here for a reason. Maybe she can tell me something about Willow, or my task."

"No," he bit out and stepped forward, reaching for me without thinking—and was tossed back a third time.

Agatheena obviously got sick of waiting, because her magic suddenly coiled around me and dragged me right up the path and to the front door before Bram could storm back to the path entrance.

The door opened, and I was thrust inside before it slammed shut again.

I looked around. There were more...*things* hanging all over the cottage, from the walls and ceiling. Things that would turn anyone's stomach.

Agatheena walked out of a room to the side, the kitchen. She was sucking on a pipe, blowing out blue smoke.

She held it up. "You gonna throw a hissy fit? Or are we all good?"

"I'm good."

She grinned, showing me those pointed teeth of hers again. "You tell me if you change your mind. I'll give you a dose of my blue smoke and all your stresses will melt away."

Bram yelled my name.

"Your male might need it, though. If he's anything like your sister's mate, he'll caterwaul until you're back."

"He's not my mate. He's my familiar."

The kettle whistled, and she lifted it off the stove, put some basil, chamomile, lemon balm, and lavender in a couple of mugs, then poured water over them—a mix used to help with relaxation. I didn't see her add anything else, but there could've been something already in the mug. Her familiar flew from the living room, cawing, and landed on her shoulder. She chuckled. "You see it, too, Dolores?"

The bird bobbed its head.

"The eyes are useless when the mind is blind," she said, and pulled something from her pocket and held it up, seed. The bird ate it from her hand.

Bram roared my name again, his panic coming through loud and clear.

Agatheena ignored him and carried the mugs over to the table, putting one in front of me. "Sit."

I did as she said.

"First things first." She held out her hand.

I stared at it, wrinkled, fingernails more like claws.

"The blood," she added.

"Oh, right, shit." I fished it out of my pack and handed it to her. "One vial of powerful vampire blood, as requested."

She took it from me and slid it into her pocket.

This female was terrifying, no doubt, Rose was right about that. There was a darkness that flowed from her that sent a shiver through me, but I didn't feel in any immediate danger.

She dabbled in dark magic, I was sure of it. This little, old female did what she wanted, and that piqued my curiosity. "Can I ask what it's for?"

"No," she said, then studied me, closely.

I struggled not to squirm in my seat.

"You feel it, don't you, child? The line I walk?" she finally asked, like she could read my mind.

"Yes." There was no reason to lie. "How do you do it? How do you stop from falling into total darkness, from letting it overtake you?"

"Some of us are born with a little darkness in us already. Only those witches can do what we do," she said, her piercing gaze not leaving me.

"We?" I straightened in my seat, preparing to stand. Now I was afraid, but not of her.

"If you stand, I will make you sit, understand?"

I nodded and forced myself to stay put.

Bram had lost it completely outside. Roaring my name, cursing, and trying to break through the ward over and over again, going by the thud of his body hitting the ground repeatedly as he tried to get in, when he knew better, when he knew it was impossible.

"Can I tell him I'm okay?" I asked, lifting out of my seat again.

"No."

An invisible force shoved me back down.

"You'll be back to him soon enough. And you saying it won't appease him. I doubt he'd believe you. He knows too much about magic."

The raven on her shoulder *cawed* again and shook out its feathers.

There was no point arguing, her mind was made up. "You still haven't told me why I'm here," I said, an uneasy feeling flowing through me.

"A message, obviously." She gave me an exasperated look. "Why the hell else?" She motioned to my drink. "Drink your tea, and I'll give it to you."

I looked down at it. "Are you going to read the leaves?"

"No, I just don't want good herbs going to waste. And I don't get much company, so we're going to drink tea together first, then I'll give you your message."

I sniffed the drink, then took a sip. "It's good."

"Of course, it is." She chuckled. "You're not nearly as jumpy as your sister."

"You met her after being sheltered and sick for most of her life. You wouldn't recognize her now," I said, giving more information than I should to this witch, but I truly didn't think she was as bad as everyone thought, the possible cannibalism aside.

Bram roared my name again, and goose bumps lifted all over me.

"You know why the fates chose a crow as your familiar, don't you?" she asked.

"No, but I'm glad they did." Her gaze remained steady on me. "Is this the part where you tell me?"

"You already know, Magnolia, but whatever, I'll humor you." Her gaze sharpened. "They chose a crow because they have an innate darkness in them. They're born with it, and so were you. Your own darkness grew, though, and changed, after whatever it was that caused those scars all over your body. And your male?" She chuckled. "Well, there's a reason a group of crows is called a murder."

I stilled. "What do you mean?"

She motioned to my tea, and I quickly took another sip.

"The mother called you," Agatheena said, ignoring my question and changing the subject.

I forced myself to meet her shrewd gaze. "How do you know that?"

Her lips curled up, and those sharp teeth had me biting back my next words.

"I know a lot of things," she said. "You're very impertinent for someone so much weaker than me. You're lucky I like you, Magnolia Thornheart."

There was a tone to her voice that said she was humoring me, that if I pissed her off, she'd cut out my tongue, or some other part, going by her choice of home decor. "According to my sisters, I have a death wish and anger issues," I said, gripping my mug tighter.

"Are they right?" she asked.

"Probably."

She laughed again, and I guessed as long as she found me amusing, I'd be okay. Bram roared, so loud my scalp prickled. I needed to get out of here. I took another sip of my tea, and she nodded her approval. This whole thing was so freaking weird.

"Your task, it'll be a test of strength—magical, physical, but mostly..." She tapped the side of her head. "But mostly a test of what's in here. Are you mentally strong, Magnolia? Because you'll need to be." She shot out of her seat and pressed a finger against the center of my chest. "And in here. Your heart will need to be sure, true."

What did that even mean? I blinked up at her when she stayed where she was, standing over me. This close she was even more terrifying, especially when one of her pointed claw-like nails was digging into my chest. I assumed she was waiting for a response. So I nodded.

She pulled her hand back and sat. "If you're not, and you fail, you'll not only hurt your coven but you'll lose everything and everyone you care about." Her green eyes burned into me. "Including the crow."

Fear filled me, so frigid it chilled me to the bone. "What do I need to do?"

"That darkness inside you, Magnolia, you can't deny it, not anymore. You couldn't even if you wanted to. It's too late." She didn't look away. "If you accept it, if you loosen the binding you have around it, it can help you control that rage burning inside you that's been burning for so long. But you need to be very careful. The spells you've created, they're potent, but you already know that. Do you know why?"

I shook my head.

"Because they were created with hate in your heart, with rage and thoughts of vengeance burned into your soul. That's the quickest way into darkness."

She was right. That's exactly how I'd created my spells and potions, every one of them in my book, I'd written in a frenzy of emotion, usually anger, and always pain.

She covered my hand with hers. "The darkness can be your friend...or it can be your enemy. But like any new acquaintance, you must be on your guard. Don't trust it easily. It'll lie to you, flatter you, try to bring you closer, to tip the scales. Only the strongest can walk the path between dark and light. Only the strongest can dip their toe into a pool of terrors and walk away only missing that one toe."

"And the others, those not strong enough?" I held my breath.

"They become one of the terrors."

Chapter Ten

I walked out of the cottage, my mind racing as Agatheena's words, her warnings, flew through my head.

I glanced up and saw Bram, and my breath caught.

He stood at the end of the path, waiting just beyond the ward. He looked...wild. His shirt was in tatters on the ground, his tattooed chest and arms glistened with sweat, his wings extended, his face contorted with fear and rage.

I rushed down the steps, breaking into a run.

His black gaze was locked on me as he gripped one of the tree trunks bordering the path, holding himself back. He bared his teeth, his chest heaving, struggling for control, no doubt afraid Agatheena would suddenly snatch me back.

"I'm okay," I called when I was almost to him. Then finally, I was there, and I closed the space between us, running through the ward to reach him.

Bram snatched me off my feet with a feral snarl, clutching me to him, and shot into the sky.

"Bram?"

He tucked me closer and shook his head.

"I'm okay," I said again.

His arm was banded around me, holding me tightly to his front and his long, thick fingers dug into my waist, not giving me an inch of space. I didn't fight it. I needed him close as much as he did me. It'd always been this way between us. Physical closeness was something we both seemed to need from each other. Even on my worst days, when I couldn't stand to be touched, Bram was usually the exception. Being close to him calmed the storm inside me.

I rested my head on his shoulder. "I'm okay," I whispered once more, because he needed to hear it. I'd say it a hundred times if I had to.

We flew over the treetops, past the demons and other creatures below us, back to the edge of the forest. Bram kept his arms locked around me the entire time, every muscle in his lean body rock solid.

His arms flexed around me as we landed by the car, then his hold loosened, but he didn't let me go. His chest was pumping when he looked down at me, his midnight eyes moving over my face.

"Bram—"

"I thought I'd lost you. I thought she was hurting you and I couldn't get to you..."

I took his face in my hands, silencing him, with my fingers brushing over the newly shaved sides of his hair. He trembled, and a shiver moved through me as well at the look on his face. I knew there was more to the fear in his eyes, the desperation. It wasn't just about today, it was about the past few months, the last couple of years, of us growing more and more distant.

Losing me was his biggest fear, just like the thought of losing him was mine. What happened at the cottage had just brought that into sharper focus.

"You didn't lose me." I brushed my thumb over his jaw, feeling the stubble there.

He was no longer the boy who'd rescued me from a group of bullies; he was a full-grown male. We were both so different, had gone through so much, and if that wasn't enough for us to navigate, it felt as if there were a whole lot of outside forces trying to tear us apart.

This energy between us had always been there but had steadily grown more intense, more volatile over time and swirled around us now. I didn't know what it meant, but sometimes it scared me. I did my best to ignore it now. "No matter what happens in the future, you will never lose me. I promise I won't let anything tear us apart."

His dark gaze was intense, and I dipped mine, finding it hard to look into his eyes all of a sudden, and landed on his beautifully sculpted mouth. It was darker than usual—

His fingers slid into my hair, and he fisted it in a way he never had before, sending electricity zapping across my scalp and shooting through my belly. My gaze flew to his, and he tugged me forward as he dipped his head, and for a moment I thought he was going to...that he was—

He pressed his lips to my forehead, then released a shuddering breath before finally letting me go.

My heart was thundering in my chest for some stupid reason. "L-let's go home," I said and stepped back.

He nodded, and I walked around the car, opened the door and tossed my pack in the back. Bram got in on the passenger side.

I opened the driver's door and, as I did, a snarl came from behind me.

I spun as a demon burst from the tree line. Bram exploded out of the car, but I'd already delivered a flying kick to its face. Its head jerked back, and it lost its balance, falling to the ground. I advanced, bringing my boot down hard in its ribs, then dropping to my knee, I slammed my knife into its throat, thrusting the blade to the side and semi decapitating it. I jerked the blade the other way, then dropped the knife, spun around, gripped the sides of its head, planted my feet against its shoulders, and, grunting, yanked its head off the rest of the way.

I fell back as the demon turned to ash. *Gross.* I was covered in it. Panting, I dusted my hands off on my jeans and jumped to my feet.

"What the fuck, Mags?" Bram stood watching me, his shock obvious.

"Told you I could take care of myself," I said and got in the car, and yeah, I was secretly pleased he'd seen that. That Bram had seen with his own two eyes what I could do.

He got in as well and stared over at me. "But that...that was..."

"Impressive?"

He thrust his fingers through his hair. "Yeah, that...and fucking terrifying."

I grinned, and he blew out a shaky breath. I gave his hand a squeeze and started the car. "You'll get used to it."

He didn't look convinced.

Later that afternoon, we headed to the city. I needed specialty supplies, and even if The Cauldron hadn't been off-limits while the witches council investigated, they were things we didn't stock and never had.

It was getting dark, and Bram was silent beside me, so deep in thought that a heavy energy rolled off him. I'd shared some of what Agatheena had said to me, and his fists had been clenched ever since. Seeing me take down that demon wasn't helping the situation.

Nerves curled in my gut, but I refused to let the fear take hold.

The things Agatheena had said about me, yes, they'd scared the shit out of me, but they were also true.

That darkness inside you, Magnolia, you can't deny it, not anymore. You couldn't even if you wanted to. It's too late.

I'd known what I was doing when I made those potions and came up with those spells. I'd felt the darkness while I did it, and instead of retreating from it, I'd embraced it. I'd been too filled with anger to do anything else. Knowing that it had always been part of me was actually kind of reassuring, and finding Gran's book, knowing that she'd been the same as me and kept control of it, helped me as well.

If I was going to survive my task, and the trial that followed, I needed to embrace who I was. I needed to walk the path between darkness and light, like Agatheena said, like Gran obviously had.

I just had to make sure I didn't slip too far into the shadows.

"It's too dangerous," Bram said into the silence.

I glanced over at him. "What is?"

"Everything, all of it," he said roughly.

"You know there's nothing I can do to stop this, that I have to pass this task."

He ran his fingers through his hair. "Yeah, I know."

His hair was down and fell to one side. It suited him, but it was still taking some getting used to.

I made a turn and the energy around us immediately grew thick, lifting the hair on the back of my neck.

Bram stiffened beside me. "You're sure about this?"

"Yes." And I was, but I still had to get my head around the shift. All my life I'd been told dark magic was wrong, that witches who practiced it were evil. I'd never considered there was a space in between. I'd been fighting it so long, embracing it—the shadows swirling inside me—was frightening but also a relief.

I scanned the street ahead. This part of Roxburgh was known to humans as "the wrong side of the tracks" where the "bad guys" hung out, and they actively avoided it. Good thing, too, because this was a demon neighborhood. Those still living here had once been ruled by a powerful female named Vorena. Willow had bartered with her in the past, and by all accounts, she'd been utterly terrifying, but she had kept her demons in line. Then she'd been killed, and the demons who wanted to hurt humans had run free. The knights of Hell had done their job, had taken them out, and the demons who were allowed to remain here were the ones who had controlled themselves and continued to follow the knights' rules. They were watched closely, and as long as they kept to their end of the bargain, they kept their heads.

The new demon in charge was named Rune and, word had it, he was placed here by Lucifer himself to keep those still here in line. I'd never met him, didn't know what kind of demon he was, and after the things I'd heard about him, I wasn't in a hurry to get acquainted. He lived in what had once been known as the Sunnydale Insane Asylum back in the 1800s. The building had long ago been abandoned and decommissioned, and before he moved in, teenagers used to dare one another to spend the night in the creepy, haunted building.

Coming here was a risk, but with Bram able to get us out quickly, if need be, I wasn't overly worried.

We got out of the car and headed up the street. Bram tied his hair back as we strode along the pavement. It definitely made him appear more intimidating, though I wasn't sure if that was his intention or not.

The street was lined with shops, demon-run cafes and clothing stores, bars and supermarkets. This was their world, where the demons who were humanoid in appearance, and didn't have a driving desire to kill or torture or eat humans, were allowed to reside.

As we walked by, heads turned, some openly staring at us with otherworldly eyes, some sniffing the air to find out what we were, others scowling with open hostility. Two male demons walked out of a bar in front of us and turned our way. They stilled, one tilting his head back as he stared directly at me and scented the air.

It was—unnerving.

Bram's hand was suddenly gripping the back of my neck, pulling me closer, in a hold that was utterly possessive. It was for the demon's benefit, of course, they'd be less likely to try anything if they thought I was claimed—it didn't matter that I could kick both of their asses on my own.

Bram touched me all the time. I had no idea why my heart was suddenly racing again, or why I couldn't stop myself from sucking in a sharp breath.

What the hell was wrong with me?

We carried on, passing them, and both demons eyed Bram, their gazes sliding up to his face, his head. Their eyes widened, and they quickly looked away.

I shot a glance at Bram and did a double take. He was baring his teeth in their direction, his smile so sinister, so full of promise, of the most horrific kind, it sent cold chills shooting up my spine.

His fingers squeezed the back of my neck a little more firmly, and he pulled me in closer. I let him. I wanted to walk back out of here in one piece, and if Bram somehow made the demons here uneasy, I wasn't going to complain. I also wasn't going to think about it too hard or ask him all the questions now firing through my head, because I got the feeling he wouldn't be able to give me the answers I wanted.

I spotted the shop up ahead. *Malicious Brew* was scrawled on a sign swinging in the summer breeze.

Bram strode up to it and opened the door. We walked in, and a whole lot of different smells assaulted us, potent, not entirely unpleasant, but different than what I was used to. A mix of herbs and roots, of plants and elixirs and other things we didn't stock at The Cauldron or use at home.

The demons here catered to those with darker desires and tastes, and I guess that included me now.

The sound of door hinges creaking in the back of the shop echoed through the room, and I turned as a demon walked out. A stunning female with peridot eyes, wide and tilted up in the corners. Her small nose was slightly upturned, and her mouth was full and lush. Her hair hung to her waist in blood-red waves, and she had several tiny plaits hanging down each side of her face.

She strode forward, her gaze moving over me before sliding the length of Bram, then her spine stiffened. Her gaze darted to me, then back to him.

Bram shook his head for some unknown reason, and the female in front of us seemed to understand because her posture lost some of its rigidness.

"What do you want?" she said, her pale, yellow-green eyes still on him.

"It's me you'll be dealing with," I said, stepping forward.

She tore her eyes from Bram, and they narrowed. "You're not one of my regular witches."

"Will that be a problem?"

She shrugged. "No, as long as you and your...shadow..." Her gaze darted to Bram and back. "Don't try anything that we'll both regret."

"I just want my supplies, then we'll go."

She nodded, but her gaze kept darting to Bram, like she expected him to pounce at any moment. "Well?" she said impatiently. "What do you want?"

I slid the list from my pocket and handed it to her. In the past, I'd made a lot of my potions by foraging, in safer parts of the forest, usually around the keep after I'd trained with Asher, and by mixing a few things together that witches were strongly advised not to.

She looked down at the list. "You got money? 'Cause you'll need plenty of it."

Well, shit, that tone said I'd probably need a lot more than I had.

Bram pulled a roll of cash from his pocket. "Get her what she wants."

I'd seen more rolls of cash like it in his tree house. His "employer" paid well.

She laughed huskily, her gaze coming back to me. "Ahhh, now I get it. I guess the cash is worth the risk, huh?"

I frowned. "What?"

"The risk of lying down next to him at night and not waking up?"

"What the hell are you talking about?" I asked, looking between her and Bram.

"Your boyfriend, he's a crow." She gave me a look that said she thought I was missing several brain cells.

"Just get what she asked for," Bram bit out, cutting her off.

Her eyes flashed at his demand, but she didn't bite back. She spun and strode off, presumably to do what he said.

I turned to him. "What the hell was that? What was she talking about?"

"No idea," he said, crossing his arms. "She's a demon."

He said it as if that explained everything. "What does she mean, risk not waking up?"

His gaze hit mine. "How the fuck would I know?"

The bite to his voice, his obvious overreaction to my question, told me he was lying, and I hated the feeling.

The demon strode back, stepping in behind the counter, and dumped my supplies on top. I walked over as she rang everything up.

"I'm out of belladonna, but I have rosary pea. It's more potent, you'll need less. It's heavy-duty shit, and I'd advise you to leave it here if you don't know what you're doing with it."

"I'll take it." Abrus precatorius, or rosary pea as it was more commonly known, was deadly. No, I'd never used it before. Like belladonna, it was forbidden by the council to grow ourselves, but I knew how to handle plants and herbs, deadly or not.

She smirked. "If you say so. As for the vamp blood, leave a number and I'll call if I get some in."

"You have any idea when?"

"Could be days, could be weeks. Harvesting that shit isn't like plucking a bunch of herbs from your back garden, sweetie."

I ignored her attempt to get a rise out of me, and it wasn't easy. "So you have a lot of regular witches coming here?"

"Yep," she said as she wrapped the rosary pea and slid it in the bag with my other supplies.

"From here or out of town?"

"Both." She grinned, and I realized she had sharp, elongated fangs, not vampire or shifter, these were all demon.

Were these other witches like me, like Agatheena? Did they carry darkness inside them along with light? Or were they pure darkness? Did I know them?

The other female slid the bag toward me, and Bram handed her a wad of cash.

She grinned. "I'll call if we get some blood in."

I nodded, and we walked out. The street was fairly busy, and I could hardly believe everyone around us were demons. The knights always said not all demons were created equally, and I finally understood what that meant. Those around us were nothing like the monsters we encountered in the forests.

Not everyone here was harmless, of course, but if they wanted a life outside Hell, they had to obey the rules, and, apparently, most of them had been.

As we headed back the way we came, several questions were on the tip of my tongue, like, what the hell was the demon in that store talking about when we walked in?

I dropped my keys and stopped to scoop them up. Bram kept walking, not realizing I'd stopped. I straightened, about to jog to catch up, when someone hooked me around the neck and jerked me in close to their side.

"Hey, gorgeous," a roughened voice said against my ear. "Wanna party?"

"Not even a little bit." I clenched my fist, about to dislodge him the way Asher had taught me, when a dark shadow materialized behind him.

One moment Bram was a shadow, the next he stood behind the demon, one hand gripping his chin, the other pressed to the side of his head, and that vicious, sinister look was back on his face, his features distorted by rage.

"Release her, or die," he said in a voice I barely recognized, a voice that projected pure hatred and violence.

The demon released me instantly, but Bram didn't let go. No, his arms tensed, his muscles flexing. He was going to break the demon's neck anyway.

"B," I said, gripping his forearm, "he let me go. Let's walk away."

The demon nodded. "Listen to your female. I was just messing. Didn't mean any disrespect. Saw a pretty girl on her own, thought I'd take a shot. My bad."

"Bram," I said again.

His nostrils flared and his bicep bulged.

"Bram," I said more forcefully.

His black eyes shot to me and locked on.

"Let go. I'm okay. No harm done," I said, keeping my voice as calm as I could.

Finally, he released a slow breath, dropped his hands and stepped back. The demon instantly took off.

Bram and I stared at each other for long seconds, that weird tension growing between us again, and I suddenly found it hard to breathe normally.

Then I felt it—so strong, I jolted.

"What is it?" Bram said, closing the space between us.

"I'm being called somewhere." A terrible feeling filled me, gripping me behind the ribs. "Something awful's happened."

Chapter Eleven

Bram

Mags sat in the passenger seat, staring blindly ahead. "Turn left," she said as a great shudder moved through her small frame.

I'd seen a lot of things since we found each other. I'd been with her while she spelled, performed rituals, and used potions. I'd seen her cut herself more times than I could count. I'd also been around during her sisters' own tasks and trials. I thought I'd seen it all, was prepared for what was coming—I sure as hell never expected this feeling growing inside me right now, now that it was finally Mags's turn. I felt fucking helpless, powerless, and I didn't know how to deal with the feeling.

I wanted to take this from her, all of it, but I couldn't. When she'd walked out of that fucking cottage, after what felt like forever, I was so close to saying something—to *doing* something I could never take back.

I'd never wanted to kiss her more than in that moment, and I'd barely resisted the urge.

Then that female demon had almost told Mags what I was. That wasn't fucking done. You talk about us, about what we are, you die. She'd need to be dealt with. Then the fucker on the street had put his filthy hands on Mags. I'd almost snapped his neck. I still wanted to go back, find him, and end him.

Throughout the day, the ever-present darkness inside me had gone from a low hum to a silent roar. I thought I could keep my shit tight, but that was easier said than done. And the closer I got to that darkness, the deeper it pulled me in, the more the crow, the predator, the male who craved his mate, roared along with it.

"Take the next right," she said, her voice lost, distant.

I dragged in a steadying breath, forcing myself to focus. We had no idea where we were going and what we were about to walk into. Fuck, the thought of her doing this without me turned my insides to stone. As much as I craved the hunt, needed it, being by her side, making sure she was safe, surpassed it all.

I'd called Rook, and he was going to try to cover for me, but that wouldn't work forever. Ignoring an assignment wouldn't be tolerated, and sooner rather than later, I'd need to go for my own sanity.

"We're close," she said, gripping the door so tight it had to hurt. "There."

She pointed to an old garage. The faded sign above it hung on an angle. SID'S GARAGE. The building was covered in graffiti, and weeds had burst through the cracked concrete in front of a rusted roller door.

Magnolia continued to stare out the window, her big amber eyes wide. She bit her lower lip.

"Mags?"

"I don't want to go in there," she said, her voice barely more than a whisper.

Neither did I. What I wanted to do was drive away and never

come back. To take Mags away from the danger that she was about to face, away from the mother and her fucking sadistic test of strength, away from everyone—to a place where no one or nothing could come between us. Where she'd be mine alone. Just her and me.

But I couldn't, because nothing was that easy, and the shit swirling around us was way more complicated than that—and I couldn't see a way through it.

"Let's go," she said and shoved her door open.

I grabbed a flashlight from the glove box and rounded the car as she strapped that massive fucking knife to her thigh. A knife she more than knew how to use, thanks to Asher.

Taking her hand, we did a quick scan of our surroundings, then moved through the shadows, walking down the narrow alley between the garage's concrete wall and the decrepit building beside it.

It was quiet back here. Silent.

"Can you scent anyone nearby?" she asked.

"No." But I tilted my head back and scented the air again just to be sure.

Fuck.

"What is it?"

"Blood. A lot of it."

Magnolia stared up at me, her gorgeous eyes wide. "It's another murder, isn't it?"

She wasn't actually asking, she already knew. We didn't need to go in there to know what we were about to find, but we had to anyway. The door was locked, so I quickly picked it. As soon as it opened, the scent of death hit us, sweet and sickly.

I turned on the flashlight and shone it around the room. It was the old workshop and mainly empty besides a few tires and a car completely stripped of anything worth anything.

The scent grew stronger as we walked deeper into the wide space.

The door to what I assumed was the office, was ajar. Mags motioned to it before I could.

I walked ahead and pushed the door open, Mags right behind me. *Fuck.*

The room smelled like fear and decay, and the scene before us was something I'd never seen before. I tried to stop Magnolia from walking in, but she wasn't having it. This was her task, and no matter how gruesome this was, she had to see it for herself. I kept my arm around her middle, holding her close to me, and good thing because her knees gave out when she saw it for herself.

People killed for different reasons: a sense of justice, or a need for revenge, or to feel powerful. Some killed because it turned them on, giving them some kind of sadistic pleasure. Some just couldn't deny their predator's nature, no matter how hard they tried.

And some killed out of raw anger, or hatred. That's what we were looking at here.

Mags's hand flew to her mouth and she retched. "Who would do something like this?"

I didn't move any closer, not wanting to disturb the scene, and shone the flashlight at the dead witch. Their eyelids were swollen mostly shut, but I could tell there weren't any eyeballs behind them. Their mouth had been sewn shut, and I was pretty sure their teeth had been pulled out first. "Someone who wanted to make a point." I trailed the light lower. The face would be impossible to ID, since it was barely more than pulp. "Someone filled with rage." The witch wore blood-soaked trousers, and his shirt was in tatters on the floor. There was bloody wire dangling from the ceiling, where I could only assume their hands had been strung up above their head on an iron hook, before both arms had been cut off, and taken. "The witch is male." They'd been sliced open, their organs spilling out.

"A wallet," Mags said, motioning to the floor.

Leaving that behind was no mistake. "They want to make it easy for the body to be identified."

Mags grabbed an old rag from the desk and crouched to pick it up. She flicked it open. "Fuck." She looked back up at the body again. "That's Calvin Adler."

Well, fuck. "And with Willow missing—"

"They'll pin this on her as well," Mags said.

"He's from a prominent family. They have money, influence, power," I said, eyeing the scene, searching for any clues as to who would have done this. I stepped closer, carefully so I could check his back. "They carved Judgment into his flesh."

"Like the others," Mags said.

"He's missing his heart as well," I said and took a closer look. "Maybe some other organs too. And those slices around his shoulder, they're clean. His arms weren't just hacked off, care was taken there." It was the only part of him that showed any control.

"Why? What the hell does that mean?"

I did another quick search of the room. "We need information on the other killings, what was done, if any limbs or organs were taken."

Mags put the wallet back on the floor where she found it. "We need to get out of here. There might be cameras?"

"There aren't."

She looked up at me. "How do you know?"

Because I knew all the places around this city where you could go undetected. "This part of the city, people don't like to be watched. Most of the cameras have been destroyed."

She nodded, believing me, trusting me. I kept my arm around her middle, keeping her close as we backed out of the office. She was trembling hard against me. Mags was tough as hell and incredibly brave, but this horror show was too much for anyone.

She'd been trying so hard to keep it together, so when her legs gave out again and I held her up, I pressed my face in the crook of her neck, so she felt me right there, skin on skin. "I've got you. We're nearly out, just a little bit more."

She nodded again. "W-who would do this? W-what kind of a

monster would torture someone like this?" Her breath hitched. "No one deserves to die this way. No one."

"I know," I said as I got her through the next door and finally back outside.

She sucked in fresh air and, getting her legs back under her, pulled out of my arms. Pacing away on shaky legs, she bent at the waist, her hands on her knees, and breathed deep. I stayed quiet, letting her get it together.

Finally, she looked up at me. "What he must have suffered. What they all must have suffered. Margot..." Tears sprung to her eyes, and she squeezed them shut, shaking her head as if she was trying to shake the images out of it. "Goddess, she must have been so scared."

I took a step toward her, but she straightened and took a step back. At times of high emotion especially, Mags couldn't tolerate touch, but I was usually the exception. "Mags..." I wanted to pull her back into my arms so fucking badly.

"What kind of a person can just...take someone's life like that, goddess, *enjoy* it, without remorse? How can they live with themselves? Who the hell do they think they are playing God? They don't get to choose. They don't have the fucking right."

My gut tightened, twisted. Would she see me the same way? A monster playing God? If she knew the things I'd done, that I wanted to do? What I needed to do to stay sane?

I'd lose her forever.

Yes, the circumstances were different. Very. But it still amounted to the same thing. Me taking lives and feeling zero remorse afterward. Feeling nothing but relief.

"We need to go," I said.

She let me take her hand, and I released a relieved breath. Touching her, feeling her warmth, the silky texture of her skin against mine, calmed me. She often sought out my touch as well, because it was the same for her. The reason for that was the same for both of us, even if she didn't know what that reason was.

But I did.

No, I couldn't make her mine, but as long as I had this, as long as I could hold her close, breathe in her scent, have her near, I'd be okay. It was ironic that it was her calming touch, her presence, that kept the violent need I constantly had for her swirling inside me, under control. Her touch made not being able to make her mine in truth bearable.

As long as I still had her, I'd be okay.

I just had to make sure she never gave up on me—that she never let go.

Chapter Twelve

Magnolia

Foxglove Funeral Home was owned by Ren's parents, and the only mortician the witches in Roxburgh used. If there was a magic-related death, they took care of it. The last thing we needed was to draw the attention of the human police.

Ren lived in a small apartment in the basement, and his parents had a house just down the street. Taking the steps, I opened the main door and we walked inside. Low classical music drifted out from hidden speakers, and it smelled of orchids, and the vanilla perfume Ren's mom, Sally, always wore.

She walked out of her office then and smiled brightly when she saw us. "It's so nice to see you both."

"Hi, Sally." Bram and I used to pop over often and hang with Ren if he wasn't at our place already, but not so much the last couple years. "Is Ren around?"

"He's in the basement." The phone started ringing. "Head on down," she said and rushed back to her office.

I hadn't seen Ren since the party at the clubhouse. He'd walked in with the female he'd left with earlier, after the mess with the council was over. We'd had to tell him Willow and the hounds had gone, that they'd had to leave him behind. The look on his face, before he'd shut all emotion down, had hurt to look at.

Bram opened the door for me and we took the stairs. Music drifted up, telling us exactly where Ren was. The mortuary door was open, and Ren was sliding one of the cold cabinets closed. I knocked.

He turned and his brows lifted. "Hey."

"You got a minute?"

"Sure." He was in jeans and a T-shirt and wore a black rubber apron over the top. "What's up?" He undid the apron, lifted it over his head and hung it up.

"I was hoping you could tell us about the murdered witches, they were brought here, right?"

He crossed his arms. "So it's true? You're hunting their murderer?"

"Yeah, and so far, we're hitting a bunch of dead ends."

Ren strode to the small desk in the corner, opened up the laptop, and tapped a few keys. "Dad was called to a house in Cicada Drive. He said the place was empty. No one had been living there."

"This was Clara Hope?"

"Yeah. The witches council had taken her down, but she'd been strung up with wire around her wrists, but only one arm." He turned to me, and the shutters came down, like something had switched off inside him. "I looked after her when she came in. The other arm had been removed, the cut clean, done with precision. It was odd. Some of the cuts were like that, done with purpose, with control. Like the one down her midsection, when they'd removed her internal organs. Her other injuries...yeah, not so much. Her mouth had been sewn shut as well."

I took a steadying breath, my stomach churning. "And Margot?"

Ren's eyes gentled. "The same. She was missing an arm, mouth sewn shut. Her eyes had been taken as well."

I forced myself to focus on why we were here and not let images of my friend like that overtake me. "Where was she found?"

"Like Clara, Margot was in a vacant house, but this one was a new build in some up-and-coming neighborhood."

"Anything else you can think of?"

He shook his head. "Sorry. That's all I've got."

"No, that's really helpful. Thanks, Ren." He slid his hands in his pockets, suddenly looking uncomfortable. I hated it, that he still had walls up between us and him.

"How you doing?" Bram asked him.

Ren met his gaze and something passed between them, a knowing. And I felt like crap for not thinking about how much Ren would be suffering with Willow gone, how she would be as well, being parted from him like this, especially after how hard Ren had to fight to find his way back to her.

Ren's gaze slid away. "Yeah, all good. Wills is safe, that's all I care about."

He was in pain, but there was a wall around him so thick and sure, I knew better than to try and comfort him. He didn't want it. I got the feeling Ren was more at home in his pain now, that the old Ren was buried so deep after what he went through two years ago, there was no pulling him back—that he was gone for good.

Several hours later, Bram lay on my bed, feet crossed, one hand behind his head, scrolling through Nightscape for any information he could find on the victims. The social media app used mainly by witches and shifters was a good place to start. The victims' own pages could have information that might be useful.

I'd been searching on my laptop for the last two hours and hadn't found one fucking thing. No, I wasn't expecting to find a big red glowing arrow pointing to the killer, but I wasn't expecting a giant brick wall in front of me either. People were dying, horrifically, and I didn't know why, or where to even start.

Calvin's tortured body flashed through my mind, and I gripped the edge of the desk as a shudder moved through me. I'd barely slept last night. I'd been on Nightscape almost constantly since we got home, waiting for Calvin's death to be mentioned, but there still hadn't been a report that he'd been found. The comment section of posts about the other three victims, however, was full of speculation and gossip about who did it and the condition of the bodies.

I'd seriously considered sending in an anonymous tip about Calvin, several times, because I couldn't stand the thought of him there like that, all alone. He was dead, the pain was over, but I didn't care. If it were someone I loved in that room? I shuddered again.

His family had to be worried.

In the end, I hadn't, because all fingers would point to Willow and Isaac would leak it to the press making everything worse for her, because that's the kind of asshole he was. It'd be splashed all over Nightscape within hours.

I forced the images from my mind and looked at Bram again, and the inferno died down to embers. Calm instantly moving through me.

I'd had him home with me almost another full day, and I was too scared to mention it in case I jinxed it. I let my gaze slide over his long, lean body. Though lately he'd filled out. His biceps and thighs were thicker, the skin on his hands rougher. My gaze slid up to the side of his head, to the markings inked there. "Did Rook do the new ink?" Rook was a talented tattoo artist and usually did all the work for their people.

"Yeah," he said without looking up, but I didn't miss how his entire body kind of paused at my question.

"Do you ever think you'll be able to tell me what those lines mean?" I shouldn't push, but this was my best friend. We shared basically everything, or at least we used to.

He lowered his phone, his obsidian gaze moving over me. "I don't know."

Not a definite no. "Are there any circumstances at all, where you would be able to tell me?"

He stared at me for long seconds, a look in his eyes that made my belly feel weird, warm. "Yeah," he finally said.

My mind raced. I really wasn't expecting him to say yes. "About the new ink, or everything?"

His gaze dipped to my mouth, then back, and he licked his lips. It was unconscious, I was sure, but something about it, about the look in his eyes made the warmth in my belly swirl. "Everything."

My pulse sped up as I stared down at him. Goddess, that tension was back, and it was growing thicker by the second. My gaze went to his perfect lips all on their own, and the swirls intensified. This was Bram, my best friend, my belly shouldn't be swirling. But it was, and it wasn't the first time. It also wasn't the first time I'd thought about his lips, or how they'd feel against mine —what he'd taste like.

Other things...

I shoved those thoughts back down as deep as I could. I'd never risk ruining what we had by going there. I'd never risk losing my best friend because I wanted to appease my curiosity. And even if in some alternate reality he'd want me that way as well, it was pointless because I was broken. The idea of being intimate with anyone, even Bram, sent actual terror through me.

I cleared my throat. "But you can't tell me what those circumstances are?"

His gaze didn't leave mine. "No."

The finality of it wasn't just in the word itself, but his tone.

And right then he was impossible to read. "How do you feel about that?" I asked.

"How I feel is irrelevant. The situation is what it is," he said, purposely keeping his expression blank.

Frustration filled me. Fine, anger. "That's a fucking cop-out. I'm starting to get the feeling you're glad you can't tell me your secrets, and that even if you could, you wouldn't want to."

He said nothing.

"How do you feel about it, Bram?" I asked again.

His gaze slid from mine to the window, out to the late-afternoon sky. He was quiet so long I didn't think he was going to answer my question. But then he looked at me again, and the weight in his gaze had me freezing in place.

"It's not an easy question to answer for a lot reasons," he said. "But you're right, there are things...things I'm glad you don't know." He licked his lips again and released a ragged breath. "But if it were possible, if things were...different. If there were certain guarantees, I would want you to know. I'd want you to know all of it."

Certain guarantees? What did that even mean? But there was no point asking because he couldn't tell me, and now I felt even more frustrated than before. I tore my gaze from his and turned back to my laptop. His gaze stayed on me. I felt it. He was waiting for me to say more, but there was nothing else to be said.

Not sure what else to do, I typed all four of the victims' names into the search bar and hit enter. Links to social media popped up, a website for one of Calvin's businesses. An article here and there. I clicked to the next page of results and saw a hit for Roxburgh High School. I clicked on it and scanned an article from the school paper. It was from twelve years ago, naming the prom committee, and three of the victims were named in the article. Calvin Adler and his cousin Katana and the first victim, Clara Hope. "I might've found something." The other members were Chase Golden, Jenna Barlow, and Robert Hazark. Robert was now married to Jenna—and he was also Margot's stepbrother.

Bram got up and read the article over my shoulder. "Can you find anything else?"

I tried, but nothing more came up. "Do you think we'd have better luck at the school?"

"Only one way to find out. We'll go when it gets dark."

"Nothing like a little breaking and entering to top off the day," I said and yawned.

Bram took my hand. "First, you need sleep."

I protested but then gave up and let him tug me from my chair and lead me to the bed. "I have too much to do."

"You won't be any use if you're exhausted," he said, then pulled me down onto the bed with him.

He tucked me in close. "Sleep. I'll wake you when it's time to go."

He was right. I needed sleep or I'd be a liability if something went wrong tonight. "Promise you'll wake me?"

His hand slid up and down my back. "Promise."

Bram

Mags threw her leg over my hip, her hand sliding low on my stomach.

I squeezed my eyes closed.

Fuck. This was agony. The kind that hurt but you craved it anyway.

I looked down at her. She was still asleep, and I couldn't bring myself to wake her. Thankfully, there was still plenty of time before we'd have to leave. I brushed her hair back from her face. Better to go in the middle of the night, anyway.

I'd always preferred the night—not a crow thing, a me thing. I liked the quiet and calm during those hours. I never used to talk much, still didn't, unless it was with Magnolia. I didn't like people looking at me, didn't like being the center of attention.

The only person I wanted noticing me was her.

Mags made a breathy little sound, and my cock grew harder. This wasn't new. When Mags slept beside me, I wanted her. I always wanted her. Usually, though, I could control my shit. I could will my dick down. The last thing I wanted was to make things even weirder between us. And Mags waking up and accidentally brushing up against my hard cock would definitely make things weirder. The way she'd looked at me earlier, yeah, she definitely felt the growing tension between us. I just didn't know what she thought it meant or what would happen when it grew more intense, because it would, it had to. There would be a breaking point.

And I was terrified that when that day came, the truth would come out, and we'd never be the same again—or worse, Mags would withdraw, that she'd pull away from me. My fucking chest hurt even thinking about it.

She curled into me more firmly, and the warmth of her little body, the press of her full curves plastered to my front, had me gasping for fucking air. There was no willing my erection away, not this time.

Fuck. I needed a minute.

Carefully, I slid a pillow between us, so she was resting on it and not me, then eased from the bed. My gaze moved over her. So fucking gorgeous. Every inch of her, inside and out. The grip in my lower gut tightened and my hands fucking shook from how much I wanted to get back in that bed, how much I wanted to touch her.

How much I wanted her to touch me in return.

"Fuck," I muttered and forced myself to leave the room. I

needed to get out of there, just for a minute, just to get myself under control.

The house was silent, everyone asleep, so I took the stairs, walked out the back door and across to my tree house, then flew up to the deck. I kept walking, through the living room, past the bed, and into the bathroom. I needed to cool the fuck off before I went back into her bedroom.

Stripping off, I turned on the shower and stepped in. It was hot tonight, and the cool water felt good on my overheated skin, but it did nothing to ease the ache burning through me. I tried to stop myself from going there, from letting thoughts of Mags and me, of us, doing things that we never could, from filling my mind. It was dangerous, those thoughts, but tonight I was weak, my control for shit. Especially when her warm curves were still imprinted on my flesh, as if she were right there with me.

I slapped my hands against the tiled wall and let the water run down my back as images flooded my mind. When I was younger, I'd been shy, quiet. I'd always been that way. I met Mags when I was sixteen, the freaky, skinny kid with the scary, black eyes. She hadn't been scared, though, she hadn't shied away or flinched when she met my gaze like everyone else, like other girls who weren't from our village. Not that I'd been interested in chasing females back then. I'd never touched a girl, never kissed one, never fucked one, and I still hadn't because Magnolia was it for me, whether she was mine in truth or not. And she always would be. No matter what happened between us, that was a truth that would never change.

Images of Mags and me in her bed filled my head, of her waking beside me, her big amber eyes sleepy and soft like they always were in the morning. And instead of smiling up at me, then resting her head on my chest like she usually did, I cupped the side of her beautiful face with one hand and fisted her hair with the other, then tilting her head back, I took her mouth, owning it. Because it was mine, she was mine. Kissing her deep and hard, washing away Clayton's hateful kiss and Relic's fucking kiss as well, making her taste all the hunger inside me, all the longing and pain and heat that blazed hot inside me, the fire for her that had never gone out since the day I met her.

Squeezing my eyes tight, I ran a hand down my chest, imagining it was hers, over my abs, then curled my fingers around my cock, gripping it tight.

~

Magnolia

I blinked into the dark room. The only sound was rain hitting the roof. My hand shot out, searching for Bram, but the bed was empty.

Panic filled me instantly, and I threw back the covers, shoved on my shoes, snatched up my phone, and rushed down the stairs to the kitchen.

It was 1:00 a.m. He wouldn't leave without saying goodbye. He wouldn't. Still, the panicky feeling grew as I grabbed one of the raincoats by the door, then slipped out to the backyard.

I jogged across the soggy grass to the tree house and quickly scaled the ladder.

"Bram?" I called as I shoved open the door.

The rain was coming down harder now, loud against the tin roof, and if he'd replied, I hadn't heard him. I strode through the living room and into the dark bedroom. The bed was empty, but the bathroom door was open and light spilled out. I didn't hear the shower running until it was too late.

A low moan echoed off the tiles, and I spun around.

And froze.

Get out of there, now, my mind screamed, but I couldn't move.

My feet were cemented in place, and I couldn't look away. My mouth went dry, and my heart hammered in my chest.

Bram stood behind the glass, one forearm braced against the tiles, his head pressed against it, his eyes screwed shut. Muted light danced over his naked body, highlighting the intricate tattoos that covered his back and arms, and showcased every muscle, every ridge, every vein and tendon—his other big, rough-skinned hand was wrapped around the impossibly hard length of his cock.

He bit his lip, as though he was trying to hold back, but another groan escaped as he stroked himself hard and fast.

My breasts felt tight all of a sudden, my nipples hardening. *Walk away. Get the hell out of here!*

"Baby," he said hungrily yet tenderly, voice full of grit. "Fuck me."

A throb started between my thighs, the muscles deep inside contracting with a violent pulse of need at the rawness of his words. My response was so strong and unexpected, I had to bite back a moan of my own.

I retreated several steps, deeper into the shadowed room, because I still couldn't make myself leave.

His breathing was choppy, broken, and as he continued to stroke, each breath turned into a desperate, gasping sound, low and pained, almost like a sob.

The sound had my heart clenching behind my ribs. Who was he imagining behind those tightly closed eyes? Who was he calling baby in that hungry voice? Did he wish she were here? Did he wish he was fucking her in that shower right now? This was so wrong, but jealously wrapped its boney fingers around my throat, the choke hold so tight I barely stopped myself from storming into the bathroom and demanding answers.

Bram hissed through gritted teeth, then with a growl, he came. And, oh god, the sounds he made lifted goose bumps all over my skin.

He slumped against the tiles, panting hard.

I backed up before he opened his eyes, running silently across the living room and out the door, closing it as quietly as I could, then rushed down the ladder so fast I almost slipped and fell but somehow managed to not land on my ass, and sprinted back to the house. I quickly hung up the jacket inside the door and raced back to my room, kicked off my shoes, and dove into bed, slamming my eyes closed.

I lay there, heart racing, mind spinning, waiting for him to come back, and I'd barely calmed myself down when I heard the door open and close, followed by his light tread on the stairs.

He tapped on the door. "Mags?"

I yawned, stretching as the door opened, giving my best impression of someone still sleepy when I was so freaking wide awake it wasn't funny. "Hey." I looked around, trying to appear confused. "Did you go somewhere?" I was not a good actor, but this was the performance of my life and I had to deliver, because he could never know I saw him. Never.

His hair was damp, and he'd tied it back again. His gaze moved over me, an odd look on his face. "We still had time, and you needed the sleep, so I took a shower."

Images of what he'd done in that shower slammed into my mind. Christ, it was burned into the back of my eyes for all eternity. "Oh, right." My mouth was dry, and I had to swallow several times. "I guess we should get going, then."

"Yeah." He frowned a little, still with that odd look on his face.

I shoved back the covers and grabbed my shoes. They were muddy and wet. I quickly shoved them on before he could see.

"You'll need a jacket, it's raining out," he said, his voice going deeper, rougher.

I tucked my hair behind my ear, my very damp hair, then inwardly cringed. I couldn't meet his stare that I felt burning into the top of my head as I did up my laces, then grabbed a jacket from my closet. "Ready."

He didn't say anything about the hair or the shoes, but he had to have noticed. How could he not? Why did I go looking for him? Why couldn't I have just stayed in my damn bed?

And how the hell would I get through the rest of the night after what I saw?

I wasn't sure I'd ever be the same again.

Magnolia

The school loomed ahead. The main building and the dilapidated chapel behind it were *old*. Both were made from large slabs of gray stone and had this whole gothic vibe going on, and at night, shrouded in shadow, the campus looked seriously foreboding.

"I never thought I'd come back here," I said as we got out of the car. There was a big sign on the side of the building announcing the upcoming prom, the theme was Starry Night. I snorted.

Bram walked around and stood beside me, slinging an arm around my shoulders. "Do you wish you'd gone to yours?"

"Not even a little bit."

He scowled at the huge building. "This place is a fucking shithole."

"That it is." I gave him a nudge. "I know you, Talon, and Rook went to the village school, what about Payne?"

"Yeah, him too."

"Why? I know your people like to keep to themselves, but that can't be the only reason?"

He glanced down at me. "Crows can be volatile when they're young. There are few things more dangerous than an adolescent crow pumped up on hormones and ruled by their hunting instincts. Safer to keep us home where we can be kept in line." He took my hand and started toward the building.

"Hunting?"

He didn't answer.

The lightbulb went on. "Oh...like that, was it?" I said and chuckled, even as that unwanted jealousy rushed back.

"Like what?"

"Hormonal and on the hunt? You're kept home so you don't break hearts and knock up half the city," I said and was glad it was dark when my face heated for some stupid reason. *You just saw him jerk off, that's the freaking reason.* "I can see your brothers doing that as teenagers...you, not so much."

I smiled, joking around, trying to keep things light, but he didn't laugh or even smile.

"I was never really interested in any of that, and once I found my best friend, nothing and no one else mattered," he said.

I swallowed hard. He had to be joking. "And before we found each other? Did you go out with anyone at your village?" What the hell was I doing? We had an unspoken rule that we didn't ask each other about this stuff. Everything else, yes. Sex and romantic relationships, never. I didn't know why or when we both decided that was how it would be, but we'd been avoiding this conversation for six years, and *now* I decide to bring it up and break all the rules?

But then so much between us had already changed. Maybe that rule didn't apply anymore. Maybe it shouldn't. Neither of us were kids anymore.

His expression told me he was thinking the same thing, and he waited, I assumed for me to take it back or change the subject. I didn't.

"No one at the village," he finally said, surprising me as he led me around the side of the main building.

An image of him in the shower flashed unbidden through my mind. *Baby.* His throaty voice igniting invisible sparks across my skin.

That swirly sensation curled low in my belly again. "Are you dating anyone?" I blurted, unable to hold it in. We spent enough time apart, it was definitely possible.

His step faltered, then he glanced over at me. "No." He didn't elaborate, and we both went quiet. I thought that was the end of the conversation, then he said, "Are you?"

I shook my head, trying to subtly rub my clammy hands on the front of my jeans. "No. Have you...ever dated anyone?" My heart was racing. Yes, we'd always been in each other's pockets, but we'd had hours apart while I was at school. The idea of sharing him with someone else, anyone else—honestly, I hated it. It was selfish, but I wanted him all to myself.

I couldn't expect him to be alone forever, though, and like Payne had so bluntly said, eventually, Bram would meet someone.

"No," he said, startling me.

"No?" He couldn't mean it. "No one at all?"

He shook his head as he walked to one of the side doors. It was darker around here, but we both had the hoods of our jackets up in case anyone saw us, or if there were security cameras around.

"You?" he asked as he quickly picked the lock.

I swallowed several times. "No."

We walked into the dark building, and Bram pulled a small flashlight from his pocket, shining it up at the alarm system. We only had a few minutes. I quickly sliced an X into my palm and held it up in front of the control panel. I'd learned the spell from Iris, who'd learned it from a witch who frequented a bar she used to work in. It was a simple but seriously effective bit of blood magic.

The alarm instantly shut down, along with any cameras inside the building.

Bram produced a small jar of Else's balm and grabbed my hand. He swiped some over it, then covered it with a large Band-Aid. He carried them with him, always. "Thanks."

He took my other hand and led the way down the wide hall. "Where are we going? Office?"

"Library. This way." I took the next right.

"Where was your locker?" Bram asked.

"A couple corridors over. Why?"

He shrugged. "Trying to imagine you here, walking these halls." We passed a group of pictures. Sports teams. Pride of place, of course. His jaw tightened. "Being ogled by all these asshole jocks, no doubt."

I laughed. "Ah, nope. No one was looking at me."

His nostrils flared, and he shook his head. "The little goth girl, so fucking untouchable, putting out all those come-closer-and-die vibes? All they wanted to do was get closer." He scowled harder. "They were looking at you, all right."

His words stunned me. "You're wrong. They hated me. Pretty much everyone hated me when I went here."

"You scared them because you never have and never will play by the rules. And you never conformed or tried to fit in. They wanted you, they just didn't have the balls to take their shot."

Where was this coming from? "You're wrong," I said again. "I was invisible." And that's the way I liked it.

"I'm not, and you weren't. I guarantee, every boy here was one hundred percent aware of your presence in this school."

My heart did a little flip. "How can you be so sure?"

Bram glanced at me as we approached the library door. "Because you are fucking gorgeous, Magnolia."

He pushed the library door open, leading the way, while I tried to freaking breathe again. He'd never said that to me before. Not ever. "Are you actually trying to say that every male in existence wants me?"

"Yes."

Our eyes locked for a moment, and we both went still...and utterly silent. He was a male who existed, right? Was he including himself in that bold statement? He didn't look away, didn't say a damn thing.

My heart kicked in my chest, and I forced a laugh. "Well, you're my best friend, so you're biased." I pointed to the other side of the room. "The yearbooks are over here." I tried to get my racing heart back under control as we strode over.

Bram didn't respond but kept his fingers firmly wrapped around mine. There was no reason for us to be holding hands, but we always did. If we were together, we were touching or sitting or standing close. I'd never thought too hard about it. I'd assumed all witches and familiars were like that, were as close as us, but over the years, I learned that wasn't the case. It was an *us* thing. Why was I thinking about this now? And why was I so aware of the way the rough skin of his palm felt against mine.

"Where did you sit when you came in here?" he asked.

I'd loved the library. I liked books, and it was always peaceful in here. No one bothered you. "Over there," I said, pointing to a table on the other side of the room, an area that no one liked but me because the lighting wasn't as good and you couldn't see who came and went from my little dark corner. I hadn't cared who came and went.

"Yeah, this scent is familiar. You used to smell like this place when I'd meet you after school."

I laughed. "What can I say...I spent a lot of time here."

He flashed me a grin. "While I waited outside, counting down the seconds for you to finish."

"That was the worst part, being away from you." We'd texted

constantly, but I'd felt like a part of me was missing for six hours a day.

"It was fucking torture," he said as I led him between the shelves.

The tone of his voice lifted goose bumps all over me. "You were always right outside the gates waiting, and I was always desperate to get out of here to see you." I chuckled. "Like we'd been away from each other for weeks not hours." I glanced at him. "All the girls thought you were my boyfriend." Why the hell had I told him that?

His throat worked as he stared up at the row of yearbooks in front of us. "The boys as well," he said with certainty.

I lifted our linked hands. "Not surprising. No wonder no one asked me to prom," I said, laughing again, but it sounded strained.

His lips curled, but it wasn't a smile—there was no humor, the look on his face was menacing as fuck, the same grin I'd seen when we were in the demon neighborhood. "Probably a good thing," he said, obsidian eyes somehow darkening.

"Oh?" Again, I was trying to inject lightness into the conversation, because something dark and heavy had fallen around us, and it was definitely coming from Bram. "I'm guessing, if any of them had hurt me, you would've kicked their asses?"

He shook his head. "If anyone hurts you, or even thinks about it, I'll kill them."

Like he had two and a half years ago, when Brody held a knife to my throat. Bram had shifted into his shadow form, materialized behind Brody, and viciously broken his neck. I shoved the memory of that awful fucking day from my mind. "Well, lucky for you, you don't have to anymore. Thanks to Asher's excellent tutelage, I can do it myself."

He turned back to the shelf. He didn't like that.

"I'll always need you, B, you know that, right?"

He nodded, but it wasn't very convincing, and slid a couple

books from the shelf. "You check these." He passed them to me and grabbed more for himself.

We sat on the floor and started flipping through the books.

I got through the first one, shoved it aside and grabbed the next. I stopped at a picture of the kids who'd written for the school newspaper. Willow stood in the back. I'd forgotten she'd done that. She'd worked on the paper for a few years. Her story ideas were regularly shot down because, more often than not, they were way too controversial. It used to piss her off.

Bram slid his book my way and pointed at a picture. "Prom committee."

I looked over the picture. "All the victims are either in that picture or related to one of them." I pointed to Robert Hazark standing to the side, his arm around Jenna's shoulders. They'd married seven years ago. "Margot's stepbrother. Clara Hope is the one holding Chase Golden's hand." All of them were the rich kids, the ones with influential families. "Calvin and Katana Adler." They stood beside each other in the back. I looked at Bram. "Could this really be what links them? There has to be something else."

"What's your gut telling you?" he asked, surprising me. "Close your eyes."

I didn't do this as much anymore. I'd stopped listening to my inner voice, to my instincts. But I did as he said and quieted my mind, letting my instincts guide me. Encouraging them to rise from below all the other noise, all the crap floating around in my head. I opened my eyes and stared down at the picture again. "My gut is telling me this is definitely a lead." I studied their faces. "Do you think one of them is the killer?"

Bram looked down as well. "Possibly."

I felt nauseous.

"But then why would they try to pin the murders on Willow?" he said.

I had no clue, and I didn't know how much time I had left to find out. There was only one person I could think of who'd want to frame Willow. Who hated her beyond reason.

"What is it?" Bram asked.

"What about Isaac?"

His expression darkened. "You think he could have something to do with this?"

"At this stage, it's just a wild hunch." I pulled my phone out. "But the way he hates Wills... He'd love to destroy her. And they've had recent issues with him trying to buy the stores along her block." I did a quick search. "The real estate company he heads is called Dark Star Investments." The website popped up, and I clicked the "our team" section. There was a picture of Isaac, the founder and CEO, and at the bottom of the page was a list of the company's directors/shareholders. Robert Hazark, Chase Golden, Clara Hope, Calvin Adler, and Maria Watson were listed. All but Isaac and Maria had been on the prom committee. "Look at this." Isaac was a very busy boy. The council wasn't a full-time position and most of the councilors had other employment, businesses or whatever, but it did take up a lot of their time and energy—looked like Isaac had some friends to help him out.

Bram looked down at it. "What are you thinking?"

"Something insane," I said.

"Like Isaac killing off his own shareholders to make it look like Willow? Like she's going after them for coming for her?" he said.

That's exactly what I was thinking. "Come on." I put away all the books except the two with the pictures we'd found. Those I shoved in my bag. Then I strode to the librarian's desk and jiggled the mouse, waking up the computer.

Bram moved to stand behind me. "What're you looking for?"

"Copies of the school newspaper during the time Wills was working on it. They must have it all on file." A space to enter a password popped up on the screen. "Dammit." I turned to Bram. "You think Talon could hack into the school system?"

"Yeah, easily."

"Do you think he would if I asked?" Talon wasn't outwardly hostile to me, but I wasn't sure he'd be willing to do me any favors.

"He'll do it," Bram said, the "I'll make sure of it" went unsaid.

We left the way we came, taking the long halls back to the exit. I reactivated the security system, Bram locked the door after us, and I tugged up my hood before we jogged across the grounds and back to the car.

When we got home, I was too wired to sleep, and the nap I'd had earlier wasn't helping. We strode across the yard to the tree house, and Bram dragged off his shirt, scooped me into his arms, then flew us up to the deck. I plonked down on the couch when we got inside, pulling a yearbook out of my bag to flick through it.

Bram turned on music. It was low and moody, the way he liked it, then he grabbed a couple drinks from the kitchenette and put one down in front of me. "How much time do you think we have to solve this thing?" he asked.

Nerves darted through me. "I don't know." I lifted my shirt, angling my body so he could see the vines created by the mother. "Any change?" I'd looked at them several times a day since she'd impaled my torso with her monster-sized serpent fangs, and so far, so good.

He reached out, brushing my skin with his fingertips, and I barely suppressed my shiver.

"I don't think so," he said, studying them intently.

I dropped my shirt. "At least that's something."

Bram sat and quietly sipped his drink while I got back to flipping through the yearbook. The same people had been on the prom committee for two years in a row, going by the pictures in both books, and there were other pictures of them together as well. "They were friends outside the committee," I said and flipped the page. There were pictures from the prom itself, and several members of the group were together, laughing, dancing, and a few other candid pics around the school as well.

I sat forward. "Check this out." Isaac and Maria Watson had

gone to prom at Roxburgh High. Isaac was beside Clara, and Maria had her head on Chase's shoulder. I studied their faces. "They've all been friends since they were teenagers."

Bram slid his arm along the back of the couch behind me and took a look. "And somewhere along the line they pissed off the wrong person?"

"Yeah, or they already had a complete psycho in their midst." I studied their faces. They looked close, really close. Isaac was a prick, but would he murder people who were so obviously his good friends to get back at my sister? I wasn't so sure—but then people were capable of a lot of horrible things with the right motivation.

Willow defeating his brother, Elmer, and causing their coven to lose the mothers gifts was enough to send someone like Isaac over the edge, but then Warrick killing Elmer defending Willow—that was some seriously strong motivation right there.

Bram studied the prom pictures. "You sure you weren't disappointed you didn't go?" he asked, surprising me. I'd asked Bram if he'd go with me my last year of school, and the look on his face had been answer enough.

"I honestly don't think about it, like at all." We hadn't talked like this for so long, and these last couple of days, having him here, had been awesome, but different—definitely not how things had been before. It was like we were trying to establish our new normal, because there was no going back to the way we used to be. We'd both been through some things, had been forced to grow up a lot, and had too many secrets.

"I should have taken you," he said, glancing over at me.

"Neither of us like people. We would've hated it." I took his hand, linking our fingers. "I don't feel like I missed out. If I remember correctly, we had our own prom. We hung out up here, eating pizza and listening to music."

The song changed, and he stood suddenly, tugging me to my feet.

"What are you doing?" I said, laughing as he pulled me into his arms.

"What I should've done that night. If we were having our own prom, we should've danced," he said, holding me close.

I chuckled and wrapped my arms around him as well, resting my head against his chest. "I much prefer this prom."

"Me too," he said low, his voice rumbling through his chest.

Suddenly I became highly aware of the way he felt pressed up against me. We stood close, slept close, but we'd never done this. "Have you ever danced like this before?" Today was the day I asked *all* the questions apparently. He said he hadn't dated, but it didn't mean he'd never danced with anyone. He went to The Bank...and The Vault, it was highly probable he had.

"No," he said.

I lifted my head, looking up at him, and grinned. "Is it everything you hoped it would be?"

His lips curled up. "And so much more."

We were just being Bram and Mags, but there was something else between us, something new—that tension was back. I forced myself to ignore it and hung on tight.

Goddess, he was everything to me. *Everything*. What would I ever do without him? "What happens when you meet someone?" I said, the words, Payne's words, yanked from me by an invisible force. They were pulled from a place of fear, so much fear that one day I would eventually lose him, that what we had couldn't last forever. Over time things changed for everyone, and that included the relationship between a witch and their familiar. We were proof of that.

His expression was utterly unreadable. "Meet someone?"

"Your mate," I choked out, each word a spike in my throat.

Something that looked a lot like pain filled his eyes. "I'm not leaving you, Mags. Not ever."

"You deserve to be happy." My throat grew tight. "When I went to Clayton...when I fucked everything up...I didn't just hurt my family, I hurt you. I kept what I was doing a secret, and when you found out, you stuck by me, you never tried to make me feel shame or guilt, you were there, like you always have been."

"You did nothing to be ashamed of. Fuck, Mags, you were trying to help your sister. We all fuck up. We all make mistakes." His expression hardened. "You've more than paid the price for it."

"I just... I want you to know when I was with him..." Bile churned in my gut, and my forearm burned, the phantom ache there flaring up. "While I was being held by him—"

"You don't need to talk about it," he said, his eyes dancing with undiluted fury.

If Warrick hadn't killed Clayton that day at the cemetery, Bram would have hunted him down and torn him to pieces. I knew that with complete certainty.

I'd tried to talk to him about it several times, what happened while I was with that monster, but it'd always been too hard, the memories too painful. He knew about the emotional torture, the images Clayton had projected into my mind that had almost driven me insane, but not the rest. My sisters did, I'd recently shared it with them one night when we were all together, but talking to Bram about this stuff had been way too hard.

I swallowed several times. The conversation was well overdue. "I knew I'd made a mistake the moment I got to his place." My mind took me back there now. "I'd tried to make the same deal as Willow, a marriage of convenience, one where he'd gain access to our cemetery, and in return, he'd help find a cure for Rose." I shook my head, remembering the moment I realized I was in trouble. "I'd been so fucking naïve. I'd thought he was handsome. I'd followed him on Nightscape like all the other starry-eyed little idiots. I knew it was Willow he truly wanted, and I was okay with that. I just wanted to help Rose, to be the hero, and sacrificing myself to some handsome rich guy didn't seem such a hardship. It wasn't real, it'd be for show. I could marry Clayton and go back to my life. But he insisted on a proper marriage, and when I refused, everything went...wrong."

"Mags..." Bram growled out, his expression stark.

I pushed on. "He grabbed me, he put his mouth on me. I tried to fight him off, but he...he was too strong."

Bram flinched.

"He didn't rape me," I said quickly. "But he...he touched me. He stripped me naked and made me stand in front of him, then he told me how ugly I was. How my scars were hideous and no male would ever want me. He used his magic to make me, to make me feel every word, every insult like it was a physical touch, a physical blow, until it was so bad I...I begged him to kill me—"

Bram snarled in rage. "If I'd had the chance, what you saw in that garage last night would be fucking child's play to what I would've done to that piece of shit. I would have made him scream until his vocal cords gave out, until they bled."

I stared up at him, but not in shock. I knew Bram was capable of it, I'd always known it. Yes, a darkness surrounded my crow, I'd felt it the day we met. I hadn't needed Agatheena to tell me.

His black eyes burned down at me. "Does that scare you?"

"No." Nothing Bram could do or say could ever scare me.

"Because I'd do it, I'd fucking destroy anyone who hurt you. I know you can fight. I know how fucking strong you are, but I still would, because I was born to protect you, because I need that. I'd need to do that for both of us."

His words were a vow, and I believed every one of them. If I'd known what I did now, if I'd had my spell book and my potions, Clayton wouldn't have gotten the chance to lay a hand on me. "I didn't tell you that to hurt you or upset you. I told you that because, as time goes by, you might want to move on. You might find a female, and I don't want you to miss your chance for happiness. I don't want you to stay here with me out of duty or pity."

He searched my gaze, his eyes filled with so much rage and pain. "What if it's you who finds someone else?"

"That's the thing, that's what I'm trying to tell you...that will never happen. Clayton, he...broke something inside me that day. The magic he used, the things he did and said, he shattered something inside me. I don't want to be touched that way, not ever again. I don't want to be claimed. I don't want to have to explain my ugly scars to someone else, or have them look at me with disgust. I don't want a mate." I gave him a shaky smile, because this night had taken a turn I hadn't expected it to. I rubbed at my forearm again, trying to wipe Clayton's touch away, then forced a grin. "I'm going to die a virgin, and I'm okay with that."

Bram covered my hand still rubbing at the phantom pain under my skin and gently lifted it away, not missing it. Never missing anything. "He's not here, Mags," he said fiercely. "He can't fucking hurt you anymore."

My lips trembled. "Bram..."

He took my face in his hands, and they were trembling. "You need to listen to me, and you need to hear what I'm saying. You, Magnolia Thornheart, are so fucking beautiful, inside and out. There is not one part of you that's ugly. Any male would be lucky to have you, even if none will ever deserve you." He swiped his thumb over my cheek, and I realized I was crying. "I don't know what will happen in the future, but I do know nothing and no one will ever be more important, will ever mean more to me than you. And if you want to stay right here, you and me hanging out in this tree house for the rest of our lives, and that's all you want, I'm here. We can sit in this room, listening to music until we're old as fuck." He pressed his lips to my forehead. "Maggie, if that's what you want, I'll happily die a virgin right alongside you."

Chapter Fourteen

Bram

Magnolia had finally passed out exhausted, and I'd sat beside her, so full of rage—rage with nowhere to go, and no one to work it out on—that I was close to losing my fucking mind.

I knew that piece-of-shit Clayton had touched her. I'd known more had happened than what she'd told me, and now that she'd shared the truth? I didn't know what to do with it because that motherfucker was already a corpse.

I don't want to be touched that way, not ever again. I don't want to be claimed.

I don't want a mate.

Her words sliced me down the middle a second time. She meant what she'd said, but she'd also said them standing in my arms, pressed so tight against me, nothing separated us.

How could she not see it? How could she not feel this thing between us? Every day our connection grew stronger, more volatile. I shoved my fingers through my hair and tried to calm the hell down. How could she think I'd ever leave? That anything on this earth could tempt me away from her? I could handle a lifetime of wanting her, of never having her the way I desperately needed her—as long as she was right here, with me.

But something had to give, and it would, whether I fought the truth of what we were to each other or not, and I was terrified of what would happen when that day came.

The living room door opened, and Payne walked in without knocking.

I scowled at him.

His gaze slid to Mags tucked against me, her head on my chest, and his jaw tightened.

"You ever knock?" I said low.

"Not like there's anything to walk in on, baby bro," he said, eyes hard. "So what? You just sit there awake and play mattress while the princess sleeps?"

"What do you want?" I asked, trying to keep my voice down.

Payne crossed his arms. "Fun time's over. You're needed."

"I'm needed here."

"That's not a choice you get to make, and you know it."

My fingers curled into a fist. Not now. I couldn't go now. "She needs me."

"I don't give one single fuck. You'll be no good to her if you don't take care of yourself. You need this. I can tell just looking at you."

I hated that he was right, especially after what Magnolia told me, but I couldn't leave her. "I'm not going anywhere."

Mags stirred and groggily opened her eyes. "What's going on?" She lifted her head, then she spotted Payne.

"Bram's needed elsewhere," my brother said to her.

"And I said I'm not going," I fired back.

Her fingers curled around my bicep, drawing my attention back to her. "You need to go."

"Mags—"

"It's okay. I'll be okay." She looked back at Payne. "He'll get in trouble if he doesn't go, right?"

Payne's gaze slid from her to me and back, and he nodded. I would, but not the kind of trouble she thought.

She gave my arm another squeeze. "You have to go."

I stared down at her, and the look in her eyes was a gut punch. She wanted me here, needed me, but she was letting me go anyway, putting me first. The darkness swirled inside me, a wild storm that needed release. I wanted to stay, but Payne was right, I needed this as well, badly. I tucked her hair behind her ear. "I'm sorry."

"It's okay, B. Go do what you have to, then come home," she said, her voice still husky from sleep.

I couldn't bring myself to let her go. "I'll be back as fast as I can."

She nodded and eased off my chest, sitting back, doing the hard part for me. "I'll see you when you get back."

I stood and followed Payne to the door, then turned before I walked through. My stomach was in knots, but I couldn't work out what I was feeling. All I knew was something about this moment felt...final. I couldn't explain it. There was a voice in my head saying that once I walked out this door, for better or worse, everything would change, that nothing would ever be the same again.

I took her in, the way she looked in that moment, locking it away in my mind. "Promise me you'll stay safe while I'm gone."

She pulled her knees up, wrapping her arms around herself. "I promise. Now I want the same from you."

"Promise," I rasped.

I shut the door and shifted, then flew into the night sky.

And even though I wanted to go back to her as soon as I'd left—there was also no stopping the dark excitement that filled me.

Time to hunt.

~

Magnolia

I tapped the steering wheel and checked out the massive house in front of me.

It'd been thirty-six hours since Bram left. Thirty-six long freaking hours. He'd texted once this morning to check on me, but nothing since.

I couldn't just wait around and do nothing, so I'd spent the day doing more research on the prom committee. They still had a tight connection socially and in business, and not just Dark Star Investments. I looked down at the open yearbook on my passenger seat, at their smiling faces in their prom picture, and back up at the massive house in front of me.

It belonged to Robert and Jenna Hazark.

I didn't know if one of the witches in that picture, the ones still breathing at least, had anything to do with the killings, but if I were one of them, and I was innocent, you better believe I'd be on high alert after several people I knew had shown up savagely murdered. My wards would be rock solid, and my place would be locked the hell down tight.

The Hazarks obviously didn't think the way I did. The gates to the house were thrown open and several cars were parked out front. Were they having some kind of party? Fucking odd thing to do after what happened. Calvin still hadn't been found, but if they were as tight as I thought, they had to know he was missing.

Another car rolled in. I couldn't see who was driving, but I recognized the female in the passenger seat. Maria Watson, shareholder in Dark Star and Chase's date for prom back in the day. Like the others, she was a witch from a prominent family. Maria also owned a bunch of high-end clothing stores. Emmaline and

Marcel was the name of her boutique chain. The stores stocked designer labels and were named after her sister and brother who both died when they were just teenagers. In the article I found, it said they'd died in a tragic accident of some kind.

Shoving my door open, I jogged across the street to get a better look at what was going on. She parked beside a Lamborghini Miura. Its license plate was GLDNBOY. Not hard to guess who that belonged to. Chase Golden was a manwhore who'd inherited his wealth and never worked a day in his life. He had several businesses that he had nothing to do with, and according to gossip on Nightscape, was the biggest player around. He'd been nicknamed golden boy in high school because he had the looks to match. Perfect chiseled features, golden-brown eyes and thick, blond hair that had a slight wave that all his followers were "desperate to run their fingers through."

I'd only ever had a couple of encounters with him, both times at The Cauldron, when he'd come in for supplies, and both times he'd been a slimy douche canoe.

Maria got out and headed for the house as a Holden's Catering van pulled up on the other side of the Lamborghini. The door opened, and Jamie Graves got out. Jamie was my age, a fellow loner from Roxburgh High and my occasional science partner and study buddy. He'd gotten a job at Holden's straight out of high school.

Looked like I'd just found my way into this shindig.

I waved when he spotted me, and there was no missing his surprise.

"It's been a long time," he said, giving me a wary smile when I strode over, his confusion at seeing me there, obvious.

"Too long. You heard about Margot?"

He nodded. "I was gonna call…"

"I was too." It was bullshit, and we both knew it. We might have thought about it, but the actual calling, that wasn't something either of us actively did unless we totally had to. "I thought I'd see you at the funeral, but then they made it family only…"

"Yeah." He shut the van door, and his gaze darted from mine. "Though, I'm not sure you would've been welcome there."

The rumor mill had been busy. "Willow didn't do it, Jamie. She's innocent."

His head tilted to the side. "I hear they have evidence."

"They're wrong. Someone's setting her up."

He was quiet a couple beats. "So why are you here?"

"I'm trying to clear my sister's name."

"And you think they know something?" He motioned to the Hazarks' mansion.

"I'm sure of it."

Genuine concern filled Jamie's eyes. "If you're right, and Willow was framed, then there's a psycho out there who won't like anyone poking around in their business."

I scanned the parking lot, making sure no one was watching us. "Maybe not, but I don't really have much choice."

"Christ, Mags. It's too dangerous."

"It's not exactly voluntary." I shoved my hands in my pockets. "The mother called, and I had no choice but to answer."

"Fuck...yeah, of course. I heard about your sisters." Disbelief filled his eyes. "So this is your task? Finding a fucking psychotic murderer?"

"Yep. I'm not sure the mother likes me all that much."

"No shit," he said, looking furious on my behalf. "And that's really why you're here?"

"It is, but I need you to keep all of this to yourself, no one can know." I trusted him. No, we'd never been besties, but he, Margot, and I, we'd been there for each other when we'd needed to be. We'd only had each other in that shitty school, and the loyalty between us had always been rock solid. I glanced at the house and back. "So how big is this party?"

"It's not really a party. Jenna Hazark called and wanted catering for an intimate dinner. I'm not sure on the number of people. I'm just setting up, then getting lost."

So not a party, which meant I couldn't just blend in with the other guests. "I need to get inside. You think you can help?"

He blew out a breath. "I mean, yeah, I can get you in...but I can't lose this job, Mags. I just got a promotion—"

"If I get caught, your name won't be mentioned."

He contemplated for only a second. "I've been instructed to set up, then lock the door on my way out. There's a separate door into the kitchen that locks when it's closed. The best I can do is text you when I'm finished. I'll make sure you can slip in when I leave."

"Perfect," I said, ignoring the nerves in my belly.

"They've lowered their wards for me to get in, but they'll put them back up once I'm gone. If they catch you, if you do something crazy, I'm not sure I can help you—"

"They won't and I won't." I squeezed his hand. "This is amazing, Jamie. I owe you." The ward could definitely be an issue, but I'd worry about one thing at a time.

"I'll text when the coast's clear." He started toward the house, then turned back. "And I hope you catch the asshole who hurt Margot. I really do. Call me if you need anything else."

I nodded my thanks. I'd catch the monster who tortured and murdered our friend, who was trying to frame Willow, no matter what. I would find out who this sick fuck was, and I'd expose them. I'd make them pay.

Jamie's text came through thirty minutes later. A thumbs-up.

I watched him drive out, then pulling up the hood on my sweatshirt and making sure to avoid the security cameras, I rushed around the side of the house. He'd wedged something in the door, so it hadn't closed properly, and I slipped inside.

The kitchen was quiet, empty when I walked in. I assumed the Hazarks had staff, they'd have to for a house this size, but it didn't look like anyone was here right now. They'd opted for a caterer instead of their own chef, and with a kitchen like this, I'd be surprised if they didn't have one. Odd. You'd think they'd want all hands on deck tonight since they had guests.

I eased the swinging door open and slipped into the hall. The clink of glasses and the low murmur of voices came from deeper in the house.

The halls of the grand house were still, silent. I followed the voices, rounding a few more corners. Definitely no staff wandering around.

Stopping at the end of the hall, I peeked around the edge. There was a room on the other side of the main foyer. The door was open, and I could see Jenna playing hostess and Robert, her husband, beside her. They were talking to someone, but I couldn't see who.

"I'm starving," someone said.

"Once Ryan gets here, we'll move through to the living room." They had to be talking about Ryan Alway. He was a witch, younger than the Hazarks and the other prom committee members, and he was all over their social media profiles. From what I could ascertain, he worked for several of them, a "guy Friday" if you will, for the group. "I had the caterer set up in there."

The living room? Okay, also weird.

Jenna sipped at the amber liquid in her glass. She looked pale, her eyes red and puffy. She was in pain, they all were, and I felt like a total jerk for eavesdropping on their grief, but I had no choice if I was going to find the killer.

Somehow, I needed to listen in, and I didn't have much time to get situated. I didn't know my way around this place, so I followed my nose, which wasn't hard, their meal smelled amazing. I rushed back the way I came, turning left instead of right this time, and found the living room a few doors down. There was a table set up. The food was laid out buffet-style, a stack of plates and silverware at one end. This was most definitely a casual get-together, but then these guys were besties, so there'd be no need for airs and graces.

The room was decorated in dark tones. There was dark wood furniture, and two large cozy couches, one by the door, the other opposite it. Across from me was a wide window covered by long, navy-blue curtains, and by the looks my only option for a hiding place. I rushed over and peered behind them. There was a low window seat covered in throw pillows. Perfect.

The sound of chatter reached me.

They were coming. I dove in behind the curtains and quickly made myself comfortable. I could be in for a long night, and there was no escape, not until the room cleared out.

My heart raced. This was probably a terrible idea, but my spidey senses weren't wailing at me to get the hell out of there, so that was something.

They walked in, their conversation subdued. I felt the dark cloud of their grief instantly, and wrapped my arms around myself. I really wished Bram was here. I always felt more in control when he was with me. Always.

Promise me you'll be safe while I'm gone.

This might be breaking that promise, in his eyes at least, but it was too late to back out now. I wasn't leaving until I found out what the prom committee knew, and I'd never get the chance again.

There was a small gap in the curtain, and I leaned forward to watch.

Robert grabbed a plate and immediately started loading it with food. Jenna picked up a cherry tomato and popped it in her mouth, then sat on the couch furthest away.

"Any word from Calvin yet?" Maria asked, hugging herself.

"No, and I've been by his house. His housekeeper was there. He hasn't been home for several days."

Isaac.

Both he and Maria weren't part of the original prom committee, but if the pictures in the yearbook were anything to go by, they'd been friends for years. Maria leaned into him, burying her face against his chest, and Isaac curled his arm around her.

"He's dead, isn't he?" Jenna said.

Ryan sat on the couch beside her. "We don't know that."

"He'd never do this, just vanish and not tell us where he was," Chase said, sitting on the floor at Jenna's feet. He looked a mess—his hair was all over the place and his eyes were bloodshot. Jenna threaded her fingers through his hair, and he leaned into her touch. "First Clara, then Margot and Katana...now Calvin—"

"Don't even say it," Robert bit out.

"Why not? It's fucking obvious someone's targeting us!" Chase cried.

"Not someone. Willow fucking Thornheart," Isaac growled.

"I don't understand," Maria said, visibly shaking. "Why would she do that?"

"The Thornhearts are power-hungry bitches. Having that cemetery isn't enough for them," Isaac all but snarled. "She used her connections to stop our development. We made a move against her, and she didn't like it. So she's doing to us what she did by setting her dog of a mate onto my brother, she's eliminating us."

The guy truly hated us, more than hated, but he was insane if he thought Willow would go on a killing spree over that.

"She'll pay for this. I'll make sure of it," Isaac said, actually shaking.

Robert threw his plate suddenly, with a roar. It smashed against the wall, mashed potatoes and beans sliding to the floor. "How? No one knows where she is and she's picking us off one by one. The twisted bitch is too powerful for us to stop. Willow Thornheart's turned into a monster like the hellhound she's fucking," Robert said viciously.

I had to bite my lip hard, my fingernails digging into my palms as fury filled me.

Maria rushed to Robert, wrapping her arms around him, tears rolling down her face. "I'm so scared."

Isaac clenched and unclenched his fists. "I have every enforcer on the council's payroll searching for her. I promise, we will get her."

They truly believed it was Willow. This was utter madness.

"You're doing everything you can, Isaac," Jenna said, still playing with Chase's hair like he was a puppy at her feet. "As long as we look out for each other, like we always have, we'll be okay. We know she's coming, and we can prepare for it." She smiled at Isaac and held out her hand. He went to her instantly and took it. "I'm so glad you found your way back to us. You're one of us and always have been."

"You know what a fucking monster my mother is. I hate that I let her control me for so long, and stayed away because of her. And now Elmer's gone...that bitch got her mate to kill him..." He shook his head and took an angry breath. "You, all of you, you're the only family I have left." He leaned in and kissed Jenna...*on the lips*. "I used to hate going back to school after the summer." He pressed his forehead to hers. "It fucking killed me."

"I hated it as well," Maria said, lips quivering. "Being sent away felt like a punishment after I met all of you."

Jenna smiled sadly, a tear sliding down her cheek. "Those summers, we had so much fun. All of us together."

Ryan ran his hand down her leg, and she reached over and grabbed his dick through the front of his pants. Then Isaac pressed his lips to hers, kissing her again. Only this time, he didn't pull back.

What the actual fuck was going on here?

Robert took Maria's hand, and they sat down as well. Maria climbed onto his lap, then they were kissing as well. Chase crawled closer, and Maria pulled away from Robert, then kissed him, while something similar was happening between Jenna, Isaac, and Ryan.

Holy fuck.

Okay, I wanted to get the hell out, right the fuck now, but I was stuck.

"Shall we go to the playroom?" Chase asked.

Playroom? Jesus.

Jenna shook her head. "Not tonight. I just want to be close to you all. I just want this."

Things progressed from there. People switched partners, and somewhere along the line, most of them ended up on the floor. Maria yanked up her dress, climbing on top of Isaac. "Oh fuck," she groaned.

Isaac arched beneath her, his moans making me feel nauseous. Robert climbed off the couch and moved in behind her, undoing his pants, and joined the fray. All three groaned. Then they were moving, fucking.

Chase sat on the couch, and Jenna slid down between his spread thighs, unzipped his pants, and sucked his cock into her mouth. Ryan moved in behind her, eyes wild, excited, and shoved her dress up, then jerked open his pants. Jenna made a muffled cry when he slammed into her, then started fucking her almost brutally.

I was trapped in a room while a bunch of witches had an orgy—and one, or more of them, could be a serial killer. This sure as hell hadn't been what I thought I'd find when I came here tonight.

This was bad, really bad. My skin crawled as their moans and cries grew louder, the sloppy sounds, the scent turning my stomach.

Maria moved faster, both Robert and Isaac fucking her at the same time. Chase had Jenna's hair fisted, and Ryan looked almost angry as he savagely fucked her from behind. Jenna seemed to love it, though, and her screams for more made my stomach rebel.

A panicky feeling filled me, and I squeezed my eyes closed, doing my best not to hyperventilate.

I had to get the hell out of there before I had a panic attack. I had no idea how long this would go on for, but I couldn't be in this room a moment longer. The door was close. So damn close. No one was looking my way. They were all fully occupied.

Easing out from behind the curtain, I dropped to my hands and knees and quickly crawled behind the couch closest to me.

There was no way they heard my panicked breathing over Jenna's screams and Ryan's obscene grunts and groans, but I held my breath as I rushed for the door.

As soon as I made it out, I clambered to my feet, then ran like hell back the way I'd come. Slipping out the kitchen door, I pulled it quietly closed behind me, dragged fresh night air into my lungs, and rushed for the gate.

I felt for a ward, but there wasn't one. They'd forgotten to put it back up. Thank fuck.

Chapter Fifteen

Magnolia

Gripping the steering wheel, I headed for home, my mind in a whirl. There was so much to unpack from all I saw and heard at the Hazarks', and I wasn't sure where to begin. The witches who started off on the prom committee had stayed tight. No, they weren't just close, they were *close*, and I had to assume that'd been going on for a while now.

There was more, though, there had to be. I growled in frustration, and again wished Bram was with me. We were like two halves of the same person, mind, body and soul, and I was lost without him.

A weird pain swirled in my gut, spreading to my chest, and I rubbed at it. I took the next turn, but the sensation kept growing, twisting into a feeling of...intense wrongness the farther away from the city I got—it was like the call to my task, like last time, when we found Calvin, but also...different, and it was screaming at me to turn around and go the other way.

I had to follow it, right? To let the intense feeling guide me.

Last time, when I was led to that garage, the feeling had come from within. This time it was an outside force. Someone was guiding me, and they were insistent. It didn't feel malevolent exactly, but there was a sense of darkness.

I felt...I felt the way I had when I was in Agatheena's cottage.

It was Agatheena, she was guiding me, I was sure of it. She wanted to show me something. I wasn't sure why, but I didn't think she meant to hurt me. Maybe she was actually trying to help me? I could also be wrong and she was sending me straight into a trap. But the sense of urgency inside me, the dread when I tried to ignore it, was so fierce and all-consuming that all I could do was let her lead me where she will.

I drove along dark streets in a part of the city I'd only ventured to a handful of times. It was near the demon neighborhood, but I felt the urge to stop before I got that far. Strapping my knife to my thigh, I pushed the car door open, got out, and scanned the streets. There were a couple dive bars nearby. Across the street was a diner, closed for the night, and between it and the thrift store next door was a dark alleyway.

And, of course, *that* was where I was being urged to go.

Awesome.

Muttering a protection spell, I pulled my knife free, letting it hang loose at my side, and strode across the street. I treaded as light as possible into the shadows, searching the dingy, narrow space. It carried on ahead to another older building behind the diner. The place was crumbling, and at some point most of the windows had been smashed.

The door hung on its hinges, black nothingness yawning behind it. I really didn't want to go in there, but my senses screamed louder for me to do just that.

Fuck.

My senses on high alert, I gripped my knife tighter and stepped over the threshold. Broken glass crunched under my boots as I moved deeper into the building. The hair on the back of my neck stood on end the deeper I went. Something was in here, something evil.

Why the hell would Agatheena send me to this place? I was starting to think that perhaps her motives hadn't been so wonderful after all.

A roar echoed through the building somewhere in the distance. It was unhinged and full of rage—and still the force driving me forward persisted. The sense of rightness, that this was where I needed to be, was so strong, my flight instincts were completely overridden. This was the part in a horror movie where everyone screamed at their TVs while some moron left their nice safe house to go "check out" the scary noise outside. I was the moron in this situation, I knew this, yet I kept walking because I *had* to.

My breath shook as I stepped through another doorway, my pulse thundering in my ears. A murmured voice came from nearby. I couldn't hear what they said, but I had no trouble hearing the harsh, loud reply. "You think you can stop me?" a male voice said. "Others have tried and failed."

Some of the wall had crumbled away, and a florescent sign close by cast the room in a wash of blue. Taking a deep breath, I eased closer to the door and peered around the edge, because something else was pulling me closer now, something—familiar.

It took me a moment to register what I was seeing. Stunned, I watched the scene playing out in front of me.

A male stood there, panting, fists clenched, legs braced apart. He had a busted nose and a split lip. Fury lined his face, and his twisted, hate-filled eyes were laser focused on his opponent.

I turned to the second male, my gaze sliding over him, tall and muscled, a look etched on his face I'd never seen. Familiar, all of him—but also a complete stranger.

Bram's eyes danced as he beckoned the other male forward, a

low rough sound falling from his lips that had goose bumps lifting across my arms.

The male roared and ran at Bram. He laughed darkly when the other male swung at him, the menacing sound setting off a flurry of swirls in my lower belly. Bram dodged the incoming blow and returned one of his own, so hard his opponent dropped to his knees.

The deranged grin stayed on the other male's face, though, even as he staggered to his feet. "Have you ever heard a female beg for her life?"

Bram said nothing.

"It's beautiful," the other male said. "Do you have a female? A mate?"

Bram still said nothing.

"I'll take that as a yes." The creep laughed. "When I'm done with you, I'll find her, and while I kill her, slowly, I'll tell her you were too weak to save her."

One moment Bram stood across from the creep, the next he was in his shadow form. I tracked his movement as he shot across the room, wrapped an arm around the male and threw him back against the wall. Bram solidified in front of him, his long fingers wrapped around the shorter male's neck, his talon's punching through, sharp and deadly. He made a grating, rattling sound that came straight from his chest, his crow right there in his eyes. He dragged a knife from the sheath at his hip, then pressed it against the other male's throat.

"You're not gonna do it," the other male rasped, that grin still on his smug face.

"No?" Bram leaned in.

"If you kill me, then you'll be no better than me."

That menacing smile tilted up Bram's lips. "That's right," he said. "Only my victims deserve it."

The other male's eyes widened. "Please, don't. Please, I beg you."

Without hesitation, Bram slashed through the begging male's throat. Blood sprayed his shirt and neck as he sliced deeper, his eyes locked on the gasping male staring up at him with obvious shock in his eyes. Then not done, Bram pulled back the knife, and slid it deep into his chest.

My heart was hammering so hard I felt dizzy from it, my stomach churning.

Bram sneered back, not looking away until the guy slumped, until his last breath gurgled from his sliced throat.

My feet finally unfroze, and I stepped into the room.

Bram's head jerked up, and our eyes clashed. Neither of us moved or said a word for several heart-stopping seconds. Bram's nostrils were flared, his breathing heavy. The blood painting his shirt and skin looked black under the glowing blue sign shining from outside.

Finally, and without looking away from me, he yanked his blade free and straightened, letting the dead male crumple to the floor. He wiped the blood off on his thigh, then slid the knife back in its leather sheath, a look in his eyes I had no hope of reading. I didn't know this Bram. In this moment, he was someone else. Someone he'd never introduced me to.

"How did you find me?" he asked, his voice low and rougher than I'd ever heard it.

Electricity zapped between us like a current firing from both of us and clashing in the middle, drawing us closer and pushing us apart at the same time. "Agatheena. I think she led me here."

He nodded, his gaze sliding the length of me and back. "Are you afraid?" His head dipped for a split second, giving me a glimpse of the Bram I knew and loved, then his dark gaze slid back to mine and my lower belly trembled. "Of me?" he finished.

I shook my head, though honestly, I wasn't sure what I was feeling. "You just killed a man while he begged you not to," I said. "Why?"

"Because he deserved it."

"And you get to decide that?"

Bram took a step closer, and I took one back, not because I was afraid, but because I was overwhelmed, by this, by him. Goddess, every part of me felt oversensitized, raw.

He watched me do it. "You are afraid."

I shook my head again. "How do you know him? Why did you do it? Does this have anything to do with my task?"

"I don't know him, and because he enjoys killing females. Does unspeakable things, then he kills them. And no, this has nothing to do with your task."

Agatheena had wanted me to see this. To see Bram like this. To see the truth. I looked down at the male slumped on the floor. He was the evil I felt when I walked in here. I didn't feel it anymore, the feeling left the moment he'd died.

"Is this your job, the thing that takes you away?"

The muscle in Bram's jaw jumped. "Yes," he finally said.

I could tell he was testing it out, testing to see if he could talk. He'd made an oath, but I'd just walked in and seen his secret for myself. Maybe that voided it? "You kill people?"

"Yes," he said.

"So you're some kind of...assassin?"

He nodded. "I hunt bad people and I kill them."

"Why you?"

"Because I'm a crow, it's what we're born to do."

My head was in a whirl. "And your brothers?"

He held his body unnaturally still, watching me closely, and he nodded again.

"And you...you enjoy it, don't you? You enjoy the kill," I rasped.

He didn't look away, didn't flinch or try to hide. "Yes," he said.

I felt as if I were spinning out of control. "Is that why you didn't want me to know?"

"Yes."

I swallowed hard. "And this part of you—"

"It's always there. I'm a shifter, Magnolia. I'm not human. My animal side has always been dominant. I think you know that."

I did. I knew it. It was one of the many things I'd loved about him.

"Crows enjoy the hunt, the kill," he said. "Not to do it is ignoring the very core of our nature." He took several more steps toward me, and this time I didn't retreat, I stayed where I was. Because no matter what I'd just witnessed, this was Bram. My Bram. "And I do it because if I don't, I could become one of the monsters I put down." He took another step toward me, his chest heaving. "We are as dark as our feathers, as the shadows we shift into. I kill because I have to, but also because it's what I am. Because I need it, and yes, because I enjoy it."

He took the last two steps, closing the space between us.

"The oath... Why can you talk to me about it now? Because I saw you?"

"Yes."

"And that's how it is with everyone?"

"Yes."

"Because they don't usually live long enough to tell anyone what they saw?"

His chest heaved, and he tucked a loose strand of my hair behind my ear. "Yes."

I stared up at him. He was splattered with blood and had a strange look in his eyes. I was the exception to that rule. He'd never hurt me, not for any reason. I stared back, looking at a stranger. Goddess, I hated so much that he'd kept this from me, that he'd held a part of himself back from me. "Now I know all your secrets," I said, my voice husky, my heart racing, belly swirling.

He took another of those heaved breaths, gripped my chin in his bloodstained fingers and shook his head. "There's one more."

His eyes were fathomless, intense, and my heart thundered harder. I'd seen this expression before, but only when he thought I wasn't looking. Like the times I woke and found him watching me, or the times we watched a movie and I'd turn to him, only to find his eyes locked on me. Every time, the urge to retreat had slammed through me, and it did now. "Bram—"

"Why do you think I'm the only one who can touch you, Magnolia? Why we need to touch? Why do you think the moment we met, we were so intensely drawn together? It wasn't just because I was your familiar—"

I pressed my fingers to his lips, stopping him. My pulse was racing so hard I felt close to passing out. What was he doing? What the hell was he doing?

His fingers curled around my wrist, and he gently pulled my hand away, shaking his head. "You know, Mags. You know."

"No." I shook my head. "You're not thinking...this situation, it's..."

His fingers slid around the back of my head, into my hair, his gaze dipping to my mouth.

"Bram," I choked out.

He pressed his forehead to mine. "Maggie," he whispered on a shuddering breath and leaned in, his lips a breath from mine.

I jerked back, but he held me fast, not giving me an inch. "Please," he rasped.

My heart exploded in my chest, cold sweat breaking out all over me and I reacted, as if my hands were being controlled my someone else. I shoved at him, pulling from his hold. "No."

We stayed locked like that for long seconds, his gaze searching mine.

Neither of us moved, then finally, pain sliced through his obsidian eyes, and his hand dropped away, releasing me.

As soon as he did, my world cracked down the middle. Terror like never before filled me from the top of my head to the tips of my toes. He couldn't do this. I couldn't do this. He was ruining everything. "Bram..."

He turned away, striding for the door. I rushed after him, but I didn't know what to do, what to say. So many thoughts and feelings stormed inside me. We walked out of the building and down the alley, back to the street.

"Where's your car?" he asked, voice devoid of emotion.

"Bram."

He spotted it and strode over. I expected him to get in with me.

He didn't.

Bram wouldn't meet my gaze. "I need to...go away for a while."

"Hang on. No, you can't do that. You can't leave me—"

"I promised I wouldn't do that, remember?" He was trembling, his entire body vibrating. "And I won't."

"When will you be back?"

His fingers curled and uncurled at his sides. "I don't know. I won't be gone long. I just...I need some time."

He needed time...away from me.

My best friend just tried to kiss me, and I'd pulled away. I said no. I wanted to scream. This wasn't happening. It couldn't be happening. "My task...I need you," I said in desperation, trying to keep him with me.

His hand lifted as though he was going to touch my face, but then he dropped it. Fuck, that hurt so damn badly. "Asher's more than capable of having your back while I'm gone."

"I don't want Asher...I want..." I let the rest fall away.

His lips curled in a broken smile before he leaned in, pressing a kiss to my forehead. Then he shifted into his crow, retreating completely, the way he used to, and exploded into the night sky.

My shattered heart splintered into so many pieces there was no chance of ever putting it back together.

"I don't want Asher... I want you," I choked out.

Chapter Sixteen

Bram

Talon was fucking bouncing with anticipation. Rook looked the way he always did, sinister as fuck, but tonight excitement made his onyx eyes glitter. I'd always been more like Payne, able to keep a tight hold on my control. Not now, though, and definitely not tonight.

Tonight, the blood would flow, and there was no hiding how much I craved it or the thrill of the hunt pumping through my veins.

I wanted to take all the pain and anger and helplessness I was feeling, then listen as it echoed into the night, in the screams of fuckers we'd been sent to kill.

We watched our prey laugh and drink and fuck. The smell of death surrounded their camp, so much of it that it coated the back of my throat. The hyenas were rogue and had been on another killing spree, snatching humans from the city and bringing them back here to torment and eat. Their clan had lost control of them, and other shifters in the area were getting nervous. The last thing any of us needed was the attention of the human authorities.

One of the hyenas laughed, the sound high and deranged, before he tore a piece of thigh meat from a dead male and shoved it into his wide mouth, while another two, covered in human blood, fucked on the ground beside the body.

The human part of me retreated and the predator came to the fore, taking over, dominating. I let it, relished it. It was less painful that way.

I studied my prey. I'd kill the laughing one first, the sound was grating my last nerve. His smile was pissing me off as well.

I'll tear his tongue out before I slit his throat. Yeah, that's what I'll do.

On the other side of the campfire, it was much the same, but my brothers could take care of them. I had dibs on the fucker stuffing his face.

"What are you thinking?" Payne asked beside me.

"Chuckles is mine." We didn't often hunt all together, only when there was a group like this one.

Payne nodded. "He's yours, but that's not what I meant."

I didn't look at him, my big brother was way too perceptive. "Not sure what you're asking."

"Something's bothering you."

Yeah, I wasn't hiding shit. But then the love of my life had just shoved me away when I'd finally worked up the courage to kiss her, after six years of wanting her and fighting it. And my favorite part? When she'd looked at me like I'd lost my fucking mind for even thinking we could go there.

Mags had seen the real me. She'd seen what I truly was, and she'd pulled away so fast my fucking head spun. Her resounding "no" still rang through my mind, hammering me in the skull over and over again. I didn't know if the outcome would have been the same if I'd tried to kiss her at a different time or place, like not right after murdering someone in front of her. I guess I'd never know.

But the realization that swiftly followed had been brutal and undeniable—the female I lived and breathed for, my witch, my mate, my Magnolia, didn't want me the way I did her.

So yeah, it was kind of hard to keep that shit locked down. Honestly? I felt like I was dying. Or maybe I wished I were dead? It was a toss-up.

"Magnolia," Payne said. "She's the only one capable of fucking you up like this."

I dragged in a harsh breath. "I tried to kiss her," I said, because they'd find out eventually. Why hide it?

He was quiet a beat. "What happened?"

"She didn't want to be kissed...by me."

I still didn't turn his way, but I saw his surprise in my peripheral vision. "She turned you down?"

"Yes." There went another one of those daggers thrusting into my chest.

After another pause, his hand came down on my shoulder. "At least now you know and can finally let her go."

My brothers didn't like Mags and couldn't fathom the connection between us. "I'm her familiar, she's my mate, whether or not she wants me is irrelevant. I can never let her go." I'd tried to explain how it was between a witch and their familiar, and they'd struggled to grasp it, mainly because the idea of having no control over a situation freaked them the fuck out.

Payne's gaze burned into me for several seconds as the enormity of what I just said and what it meant for me sunk in. "Mate?"

"Yes, mate." And my mate had rejected me. I would live beside the only female I wanted for the rest of my life, but she would never be mine. Anger filled me, no, fucking rage. Maybe things would've been different if Clayton hadn't hurt her, if she hadn't withdrawn so deeply into herself, maybe...

I scrubbed my hands over my face. No. That was all bullshit. I didn't know why she didn't feel the mating bond between us, but she obviously didn't because if she did, she would have welcomed my kiss, she would've wrapped her arms around me and fucking held on, she would have…

Stop.

I gripped the sides of my head. My mind needed to shut the fuck up.

It was done. Over.

The hope I'd been clinging to for six years needed to fucking die.

"I'm sorry," Payne said. "I know you don't want to hear this, but mate or not, she wasn't right for you. Others at the village have taken lovers after the loss of a mate and so could you. She was self-ish, like all witches. They can't be fucking trusted. You don't have to stay tethered to her—you're a warrior, the son of a chieftain, you deserve a female who would do anything to prove her worth to you."

"Don't," I bit out. "Magnolia isn't Farah. You don't fucking talk shit about her. Not ever. You say one more thing against her and you and I will have a problem we won't ever come back from. There will be no other female, not for me, not ever. Understand?"

Payne's lips peeled back and a throaty *caw* rose from his chest. We didn't mention his ex, Maeve's mom, ever. Payne refused to talk about her, but I didn't give a fuck. Instead of losing his shit like usual, though, that steely control kicked in and he bit back whatever he wanted to say and turned to our brothers. "Ready?"

Talon grinned evilly and Rook dipped his chin, his eyes sliding to his prey.

Payne's wings burst from his back. "Let's go."

We took flight, dropping from the sky, right in the middle of the hyena camp. They shot to their feet, and the moment they got a good look at us, fear filled their eyes. They knew exactly who we were and what it meant when my brothers and I dropped in.

We were the boogeymen. Monsters whispered about but never out loud, afraid if they did, we'd come for them as well—and we would.

I strode toward my target as Talon laughed. Payne moved with purpose, killing with precision, and Rook, like me, was playing with his prey. These twisted fucks deserved to suffer for what they'd done, and they would.

But when I shadowed out, surprising the fucker who had human blood smeared on his face and soaked into his clothes, there was no excitement, not for me, not anymore, not even as I watched the life bleed from his eyes—only a moment of relief.

When we left a while later, the ground was soaked with their blood. I was bitten and clawed, and I relished in the pain. This was the part where I'd go home to Mags, and I could admit that sometimes I let myself get hurt just so she could tend my wounds. A kind of twisted foreplay in anticipation of having her hands on my bare skin.

The urge to go to her, to go to my tree house in her backyard and pretend nothing was wrong, that nothing had happened between us just so she could touch me now was so damn tempting. But I couldn't do it. If I went back now, I'd fucking beg her to want me. I'd crawl on my knees in front of her. I'd fall at her feet and fucking beg for her to take this pain away.

Because without hope, I was lost. Magnolia was my sky and earth, my moon and stars. She was my reason. My everything. She was my fucking oxygen.

And without her, I wasn't sure how to breathe anymore.

Chapter Seventeen

Magnolia

My world had been ripped out from under my feet. I didn't know anything anymore, not even my own feelings. I was confused and felt sick to my stomach. I missed Bram so badly it hurt, and I'd spent the night in his bed alone, crying so fucking hard my throat was raw this morning.

I'd tried calling him multiple times—he hadn't answered.

He hadn't come home. I knew he wouldn't but still I'd hoped he'd change his mind, that I'd wake up in his arms and everything would go back to the way it was.

I shoved my mug away, the coffee only making my stomach worse.

"We got a corpse," Asher said across from me.

I'd called her early this morning, filled her in on everything that was happening, well, everything except what happened with Bram, and she'd agreed to come with me today. Ash also had a way of forcing me out of my own head, and I needed that more than ever.

I took her phone, scanning the post on Nightscape. Calvin's body had been found last night by some teenagers. They'd broken in to hang out and get drunk and found a decomposing, mutilated body instead. I quickly read the rest of the article and scanned the comment section, then wished I hadn't. There were a lot of familiar names taking potshots at Willow, accusing her of all kinds of fucked-up shit.

I slid the phone back to Ash. "Now they'll be even more convinced it was Willow. I'm not even sure the council's looking elsewhere. They're staying quiet right now, and it's not fucking helping." I tapped the table. "Isaac is involved in this somehow, beyond being fuck buddies with the prom committee."

"You think he's our killer?"

"After what I saw at the Hazarks', your guess is as good as mine. Do I think he's capable of doing some seriously fucked-up shit? Definitely. But torture and murder his friends to get his revenge on Willow? I don't know. But I don't trust him. He's up to something."

"Jenna said she was glad he came back to them, right? They haven't been tight this whole time. He weaseled his way back in. Are you sure the closeness you saw between him and the others, and I'm not talking about the orgy, was real?"

I slumped back in my seat. "I don't know."

Asher eyed me over her mug. "Okay, feisty, what's up with you? I mean, besides the whole hunting-a-psycho thing?" Her brow arched. "You're acting all...I don't know, emo."

"I'm not."

"Does it have anything to do with the fact that I'm here instead of your shadow man?" She made a show of looking over my shoulder to the vacant space behind me. "When Bram's here, he's hovering behind you like Lurch, only a hot, goth version. What did you do?"

"I don't want to talk about it."

She shrugged. "Honestly, neither do I. Just thought I should check, since that's the kind of shit Iris makes me do now." She stood, the chair scraping on the wooden floor, then winked. "But you're all good, right? So let's get the fuck on the road before you change your mind."

I swiped my keys and phone from the table, and we headed out of the house. Asher strode right past my car, where I was opening the driver's door, and over to her truck. "I don't do passenger princess, princess."

I snorted. "Maybe not, but you do an excellent impression of an asshole, asshole," I said and walked to her truck instead of arguing. I didn't have the energy after crying for hours and zero sleep.

"Aww, look at you, throwing attitude." She grinned, flashing her sharp canines. "It's cute the way you try so hard to be like me. Maybe someday, but you've still got a long way to go, pup."

I opened the door. "We're nothing alike."

"Loves to fight, has an attitude, angry most of the time, will cut a bitch." She ticked off each description on her fingers. "Sound familiar? We could've come from the same litter...except you'd be the runt."

"And you'd be the cun—"

"Cunning one?" She smirked. "Why, yes, how insightful of you, Magnolia. Now get in and stop bitching."

I flipped her off and got in.

She started the truck and turned to me. "So where to?"

"Council chambers." I needed to talk to Councilor Trotman. He was a good male. He'd also taken our side and treated us fairly in the past. I needed to know if they were looking at anyone else for these murders, or if they were content to pin it on my sister.

Ash nodded as she scrolled through the music app on her phone. A moment later metal filled her truck. She cranked it up and roared along with the lyrics in a deep, demonic voice like the guy blasting through the speakers. Then she planted her foot on the gas, and we sped off.

I let the music crash through me, welcoming the chaotic beat because it made it impossible to think. I'd done enough of that last night, replaying what happened in that run-down building over and over again.

Several songs later, Asher sped into the council's parking lot. We got out and strode up to the main doors.

I pulled my ID from my wallet, showing the guard. All witches had one. It allowed us access to the building, identifying us and the coven we were from. I signed Asher in as my guest, then we were scanned, the magical kind. It checked us for spells or incantations that a witch could use on themselves or others to cause harm. The guard gave us the all-clear and let us in.

Heads turned as we walked in. On my own, I wasn't overly intimidating, though I often got second looks and wide berths. I guess when you exuded a whole lot of anger, people felt it. Add Asher into the mix, both of us dressed in black and more than likely wearing matching resting bitch faces, and we weren't the most approachable-looking people in the building.

And yes, though I tried to deny it, she was right, we did have similarities, and right now, we were both putting out some serious stay-the-fuck-back vibes. Mine weren't intentional, it was just how I was these days, and I assumed it was the same for Asher. She was an alpha female and a warrior, and no one could mistake her for anything else. Most people felt it and steered clear of her path.

A male strode around the corner almost crashing into us. He actually cried out in alarm as he threw himself back so fast that he almost fell on his ass, proving my point.

"Sorry," I muttered, and we carried on down the hall.

"I think his balls just retreated back inside his abdomen," Asher said.

They totally had.

She nudged me. "So, when are you coming out to train? You haven't been to the keep in a while."

"Are you going to let me go on patrol with you?"

"Maybe," she muttered.

"I met the mother in Oldwood Forest on my own. You think I managed that without spilling some demon blood?" I said, feeling frustrated all over again.

"Well, that was a fucking foolish thing to do, feisty," she said, her tawny eyes slicing my way.

"I didn't exactly have much choice. Bram was gone and..." A wave of pain rolled through me.

"I assumed he'd been with you. You didn't think to call me?"

I glanced at her. "I didn't want anyone knowing. You and Iris are besties. I couldn't trust you'd keep it to yourself. My family would've freaked out if I told them. You know how protective my sisters are, and if they knew, they would've tried to get around the rules to help me. I couldn't let that happen. And even if they didn't, what was the point of them sitting around all night worried out of their minds?"

She scowled. "You couldn't trust me? Are you fucking serious?"

Asher was pissed, for real, and I kind of felt like an asshole. "Would you have told Iris?"

Her jaw tightened. "Maybe."

"Exactly. Can we just drop it now?"

"Fine, but if you need to do something else like that, something on your own, at least let me know where you are."

I glanced her way again. "You are literally here with me now. And are you seriously telling me you let Draven know where you are at all times?"

"If I'm doing something that could get me killed, you fucking bet I do." Her eyes narrowed. "And FYI, you do anything else that dumb, I'll kick your ass."

I bumped her with my elbow, trying to lighten the mood. "You could try."

Asher scoffed. "You took me down once. I was having a bad day."

I'd taken her down more than once, but keeping her down was

another story. I wasn't even close to her level. I wasn't sure it was possible. "Nice rewriting of history you did there."

She bumped me back. "Shut up."

We stopped in front of Nathan Trotman's office.

"So what's this guy like? Does he have a stick up his ass, or what?" Ash asked.

I knocked. "Nah, he's actually a good male."

"Come in," Trotman called.

I opened the door, and we strode in. Trotman was about Mom's age. He had dark brown skin and kind eyes, and always wore nice suits. He took us in, and sat back. "Magnolia." He looked around. "I'm not sure you should be here."

"Why? Am I a suspect as well?"

He straightened his glasses. "Of course not, but if people see you here with me, it'll make it harder to help your sister."

"And you want to help her?"

He held my gaze. "I'm a friend of your family." He pointed to the door, to the offices beyond it. "And they know it. I'm already being left out of important discussions where this case is concerned."

Shit. "Look, I just want to know who else the council's looking at. Who are your other suspects?"

He looked pained. "There are no other suspects, Magnolia, and things aren't looking good for Willow. She had a public altercation with Calvin Adler, and now he's been found brutally murdered, and that's on top of all the other evidence we found at The Caldron when we found Katana's body." He glanced at the door behind us, then back again. "There's also the way the victims' mouths were all sewn shut...they're saying it's her calling card."

Fuck.

"No one's forgotten how Willow used that spell during her trial," he added.

These were all things I'd considered but hoped had slipped by everyone else. "Do you think she did it?" We needed Trotman on our side because the rest of the council seemed to have already made up their minds.

"I can't talk about this with you—"

"Do you?" I asked again more forcefully.

He sat back. "She told me she was working for us during Rose's trial, helping us when the demonology department was robbed and that guard went missing. She lied to me, putting her own interests, and that of Coven Thornheart above everything else. She's changed—"

"You think she did it, don't you?"

"I think she's lost her way. I think being mated to a hellhound hasn't helped the situation," Trotman said.

I couldn't believe what I was hearing. I nodded, fury firing through me. "You actually think she did it." I folded my arms so I didn't flip his damn desk. "I will find whoever's responsible for these murders and clear my sister's name. You're wrong about her. So fucking wrong."

He stood. "I want to help her. If you know where she is—"

"I wouldn't tell you. And I promise you, the council's enforcers don't have a chance in hell of getting anywhere near her. No one can, not even me." I ground my teeth. "There's someone else you should be looking at, someone who hates Willow and would love to see her ruined."

Trotman frowned. "Who?"

Was he serious? "Isaac. You know their history. He'd love nothing more than to take Willow down. I honestly think he's involved in this somehow and using his position at the council to his own advantage."

"That's a serious accusation."

He didn't look convinced, like at all. "And I don't make it lightly."

He said nothing for several seconds, his gaze devoid of all its usual warmth. "If that's all, Magnolia, I need to get back to work."

I wasn't getting through to him, and I wasn't going to.

We walked out and I struggled to control the fire burning in my gut.

"Not so sure he's such a good guy anymore," Asher said. "Seems to me he's sold his soul to this place and the rest of the power-hungry assholes here."

I didn't want to believe it, but Asher might be right.

A door opened ahead of us and Asuka walked out. Her gaze darted our way, and as soon as she saw me, her already pale skin, grew even more so, and she reversed so fast I was surprised she didn't leave skid marks as she shut her office door. The sounds of the lock clicking into place was loud in the quiet hall.

"I guess we know where she stands as well," Ash said.

I guess we did. "Nothing's making sense. Trotman, Asuka, they *know* Willow. That they both think she's capable of this...I feel like I'm in the fucking twilight zone."

We spent the rest of the day chasing our tails. Nothing new, nothing that could help me or Willow. We drove by the Hazarks' place, then the Golden mansion after that, then Maria's. They were all locked down, not surprising after the discovery of Calvin's body.

My phone chimed and I snatched it from my pocket so fast I almost dropped it.

Brutal disappointment quickly followed.

Not Bram.

Tears instantly sprang to my eyes. You'd think I'd be all cried out, but apparently not. I swallowed them down, and Asher arched a brow at me when I glanced her way. "Mom wants to know if we'll be there for dinner." Goddess, this was killing me. What was I going to do? How could I make this right?

Ash gave me a hopeful look.

"I'll tell her to save us a plate."

"Nice." She grinned, then her gaze slid over my face and her grin vanished. "What the fuck is up with you?"

"Nothing. I'm fine."

"Don't give me that shit, you're on the verge of tears. You didn't even cry when I dislocated your shoulder that time. Something's fucking with you, and despite what I said back at your place, I am a good sounding board, so fucking talk, feisty. Or I'll pull this car over and we won't move until you do."

I stared out the windshield, my fingers curling and twining together. The look in Bram's eyes, the way he held my chin with his blood-stained fingers, the way he'd leaned in... "Bram almost...he almost kissed me." My breath hitched just saying it out loud.

Ash was quiet several beats, her gaze going from me to the road, then back. "Okay...so what's the problem?"

I curled my fingers into tight fists because my hands were shaking. "Bram's my best friend. He's my familiar."

"Right."

"I knew you wouldn't understand," I said, wishing I hadn't said anything. Talking about this was too damn painful.

"What did you do when he tried to kiss you?" she asked.

Squeezing my eyes closed, I tried to flush the memory from my mind. "I pushed him away. I said...I said, no."

She nodded. "And you said no because?"

"Because he's my best friend."

"You said that already. Tell me what you were feeling in that moment?"

I rubbed my now sweaty palms on my thighs. "I don't know."

"Yes, you do. Was your heart racing?"

My mouth went dry. "Well, yes—"

"Belly all flippy?"

Yes, it had been. There were serious flips. I didn't reply, but the look on her face said I didn't need to.

She glanced at me again. "You ever thought about kissing him?

Looked at him and thought, damn, he's fine? You ever imagined what it would be like to get naked and let loose on each other?"

Yes, yes, and yes. Suddenly, I was struggling to breathe. "Don't...I can't...I can't do this—"

Ash pulled the truck off the road suddenly, stopping in the middle of nowhere. "Look at me."

"Ash—"

"Look at me, feisty."

I turned in my seat and forced myself to look at her, because I knew that tone. We were staying right here until I did what she wanted.

"You're scared. I get that," she said. "Fear is a powerful thing. It makes us think we can't have the things we desperately fucking want. It lies to us, it makes us think we *can't*, when we sure as fuck *can*." She took my hand in a tight grip, forcing me to keep looking at her when I tried to look away. "He's in love with you, Mags. We all see it. He's so in love with you that being close to you is Heaven and Hell for him, all rolled into one."

My mouth opened, closed. I tried to pull my hand from hers, to retreat, to not freak the fuck out at her words.

She held tight, but her gaze softened, something I'd never seen before. "You had to know that."

Yeah, I was definitely struggling to breathe normally now. Because, goddess, I did. Didn't I? I'd tried to tell myself that wasn't what I saw in his eyes. I tried to pretend that wasn't what I felt from him when we were together, that the tension between us wasn't so thick sometimes, I found it hard to draw breath. A couple of years ago, things between us had started to change. I'd started seeing him...differently. There'd been several times when I thought he was going to kiss me.

Then Clayton happened, and I'd shoved it down. I'd pretended I'd never felt the thing inside me slowly unfurling, desperate to bloom.

"I'm scared," I choked out. "I'm so fucking scared, Ash."

"You won't lose him, you have to know that. Whatever happens from this moment on, he'll still be there for you. And you know why, don't you?"

I licked my dry lips, my pulse racing all over again. "How did I miss it, how—"

"You weren't ready to see it, and maybe you aren't totally ready now, but you have to decide if you want to be. Don't let this slip through your fingers." Her voice changed, becoming more forceful. "Don't you fucking dare do that. Nothing will ever compare to what you could have with him...with your mate." Shockingly, her throat worked, emotion filling her eyes. "The years I had with Boone were the best of my life. You're scared, I get that. But you know what's scarier? A lifetime never knowing a love like that, happiness like that. Never sharing a connection with someone, a connection that even if I tried, I couldn't explain the enormity of it. I could never describe the way it feels." She shook her head.

"Ash...I had no idea." She'd been mated.

She shrugged. "I don't talk about it, because it's mine, and because he still lives with me in here." She pressed a hand to her chest. "I try to make the best of the time I have left on this earth, because Boone would want me to. But I'm just killing time until I'm with him again. He was it for me. There will never be anyone else who could take his place. You need to think about that when you make your decision. There is no one either of you will ever want the way you want each other."

My lips trembled and I growled, shutting it down, refusing to cry again. "But I'm...I'm fucking broken. I don't know if I can give him all of me, I don't know if I can...if we could ever..."

Her hand tightened on mine, the other gripping my shoulder, and she jolted me, roughly. "Snap the fuck out of it."

I blinked up at her.

"You're not fucking getting it, feisty. Bram is your mate. *Your mate*. There isn't one thing you can't figure out together. Not one.

He knows you like no one else, he knows what you can and can't handle. *He knows.*"

He did.

He'd always known what I was feeling, thinking at least—until recently, when we'd both closed ourselves off to it. Ignored it.

"I can guarantee no matter how long it takes, he'll wait," Ash said. "He'll wait, because making you happy, pleasing you, caring for you, is all he'll ever want and need." She gave me a sad smile. "Mags, he's already been waiting, and he'll keep on doing it. He'll wait an eternity for you."

Chapter Eighteen

Magnolia

Asher was fully focused on eating the plate of food Mom had put down in front of her, but I couldn't even choke down a bite.

"Eat, then rest. You look exhausted," Mom said and kissed the top of my head before walking out of the room.

There was no way I could rest, not when everything Asher had said to me earlier was on repeat in my head.

I scrubbed my hands over my face, feeling utterly lost. I missed Bram so fucking much.

I couldn't do this, not without him. Not any of it.

I couldn't sleep.

I couldn't think.

I couldn't fucking breathe.

I missed him so much, I ached. I ached for him. Goddess, it hurt.

Asher cleared her throat, and I looked up.

"What are you thinking?" she asked, looking at me as if she could see everything.

"That I need Bram, and that I'm going to get him."

She smiled.

"Will you help me?"

She lowered her fork. "What do you need?"

"A ride. But first I need to get a few things together."

She slid my plate her way. "I'll be right here when you're ready."

I double-checked the spell book, making sure I'd added everything. Satisfied, I started filling the glass vials with the potion.

What I was about to do, it'd be even more difficult than my trip into Oldwood and my visit with the mother, so I'd taken what Agatheena said to heart. The only way to succeed was by embracing who I was, by walking the path between dark and light, and thanks to the ingredients I'd gotten from the demon store, I was more than ready to do it.

"What are you making there, pumpkin?" Else said from the door, startling me.

I slammed the spell book closed and dragged a rag over the vials.

Else limped closer and sat on the wooden rocking chair she used by the fire when she needed to take a load off. "You know there's nothing you can't tell me, don't you, Mags?"

Guilt filled me. "I know."

She nodded. "There's nothing that you could do or say that would change how much I love you, how much we all love you."

I nodded.

She nodded as well. "Iris let slip the mother called you, and about your trial. I wish you'd trusted me enough to tell me yourself. I know I can't help you, but anything you need, anything at all, in here or in the library, anything, you help yourself, okay?"

"I do trust you. I should've told you. I'm sorry." I let out a shaky breath. "Does Mom know?" I was closer to Else than almost anyone, and she was right, I should have been the one to tell her.

"Nope."

Mom was a different story. Else would know the right things to say, the best way to break it to her. Mom worried about me so much, and she'd already had to watch my sisters go through this, feeling terrified and helpless. I wasn't sure how she'd handle it this time. "I know I should do it myself, but would you tell her for me? I can't bear to see the worry in her eyes."

"I'll tell Daisy." She studied me for several seconds. "I don't know what you're about to do, or what you've got under that rag, pumpkin, but whatever it is, whatever you have to do during this trial—it's the right thing. Trust your gut, what's in your heart, and it will lead you right, understand?"

I nodded.

Then she stood, but before she left, she turned back. "I'd feel a lot better if you had Bram with you, though." Her lips quivered. "You're the toughest witch I know, Magnolia Thornheart, strong and unstoppable, like your grandmother. Goddess, so much like her. I don't know how the hell you got to the mother and back on your own that night, sheer stubbornness no doubt." She smiled shakily, then sniffed. "But we need our familiars at times like these, and if you're lucky enough to still have one, you hold them close. Promise me no more going it alone, that you'll take Bram with you."

"I will," I said and gave her a shaky smile of my own. "As a matter of fact, I'm on my way to get him right now."

~

An hour later, Ash and I were deep in Oldwood Forest. It was a different part than where I'd met the mother, and Ash had driven me in as far as she could go. I took in the dense forest that lay ahead. I had to go it alone from here if I was going to do this right, and I was determined to do just that.

"You sure about this?" Ash asked.

I grabbed my pack and checked my knife. "Yes. I've never been more sure of anything in my life." I looked at her across the cab of her truck. "I need to do this."

She nodded, her gaze growing intense. "I respect that, and I won't get in your way, but you need to keep your head on straight. Focus at all times, control your emotions, don't let your anger take hold."

I thought she'd stop me. I thought she'd go to Draven and rat me out. She hadn't. "I'm focused. I'm in control." For the first time in a very long time, I wasn't confused. I had a better handle on my anger now than I had for a long time. I knew exactly what I wanted. The other stuff was there—the fear, the memories, the pain—but I wasn't going to let them stop me, not this time.

We got out of the truck, and I pulled on my pack and strapped my knife to my thigh.

"You want me to keep an eye on the prom committee while you're gone?" Ash asked.

I shouldn't be going. It was reckless, time I didn't have to spare, but I couldn't not. Without Bram, I would fail this task—because I was only half alive, half a soul, without him. "Thanks, but I'll be quick. There and back in a flash."

She nodded and leaned into the truck, taking something from under the seat, and tossed it to me.

I grabbed it. "What's this?" I unrolled the canvas. A dozen small throwing knives shone up at me from their harness.

"Strap them to your chest," she said.

I did as she said as she walked around the truck and undid the massive hunting knife strapped to her thigh. She held it out to me. "Take this as well."

"Ash—"

"Take it. A couple good whacks and you'll just about take a head clean off, even those thick-necked fucks."

She wasn't going to take no for an answer, and I wanted to hug her for it. I resisted. Asher wasn't the hugging type. "Thanks." I strapped it on as well.

"I know I've given you shit in the past about going on patrol, but you've been ready for a while. Draven was nervous, being protective. I should have forced the issue. I didn't and I'm sorry." She gripped my shoulders. "But you're a fucking warrior, Mags. I'd trust you to have my back any day of the week."

I swallowed thickly.

"And don't forget, if you even think you're about to be outnumbered, run like fuck. Demon blood's your best camouflage. Go high when you need to rest, but only if you really have to. Staying in one spot for any length of time's the worst thing you can do. If you don't have time to remove their heads, incapacitate and keep moving. It's a better option for conserving your energy anyway, and a wounded demon's easy eating and will distract the others in the vicinity while you get the fuck out of there."

I nodded as she went over all the things she'd taught me the last six months.

She tapped the side of my head. "You control what's going on in here, and you can do anything, Mags, yeah?" She released me and stood back.

"Thanks, for everything, Ash."

Her jaw tightened, then she held out her fist. I pounded it, and she strode around the truck and opened the door. "Don't die, or I'll never hear the end of it from Iris."

"Not planning on it," I said, refusing to let her see the nerves rioting inside me. "See you in a couple days."

"See you in a couple days." Her gaze grew intense. "Now go get your male."

Then she got in her truck, turned around, and drove away.

I pulled my phone from my pocket and scrolled down to the number I needed.

It rang twice. "Yeah?"

"Payne, it's Magnolia. Is Bram with you?"

"If he's not answering your calls, then take the fucking hint. Don't call again."

"Wait!" I said before he hung up. "This is important. And it's you I want to talk to."

"We have nothing to say to each other."

He was the most arrogant asshole I'd ever met. "I'm going to tell you something, and I want you to keep it to yourself, for now, anyway."

A beat of silence. "And why would I do that?"

"Because if you give Bram my message now, he'll come for me, and he can't do that."

A low growl. "Cut to the chase, witch."

"In thirty-six hours, I need you to tell Bram to stand behind your family's tree house and face the clearing."

More silence, and this time it was heavy as hell.

"Payne?"

He laughed darkly.

"Will you do that?" I asked, refusing to let his reaction piss me off.

"You're not fooling me. First, if you think you're strong enough to do the demon run in thirty-six hours, you're even more fucking clueless than I thought. Witch, you aren't capable of making it in the forty-eight allowed. I see through you, though. You think I'll tell him and he'll come running to stop you. But I won't let you use him anymore. Bram's a warrior, not your fucking lapdog. You are selfish and self-centered, and I won't let you twist him up in knots only to cast him aside again. It won't fucking work."

Each of his words left a bruise. It fucking killed me to think about the pain I'd caused Bram. "I will be there in thirty-six hours. I love Bram, and I'm going to prove it to him."

"It's your funeral," he said, then he disconnected.

I didn't know if he'd pass on my message, but either way, I was doing it, and I hoped like hell Bram was waiting for me at the other end.

Agatheena's words filtered through my mind. *Your task, it'll be a test of strength—magical, physical, but mostly…"* She'd tapped the side of her head. *"But mostly a test of what's in here. Are you mentally strong, Magnolia? Because you'll need to be."* Her finger had pressed against the center of my chest. *"And in here. Your heart will need to be sure, true."*

I hadn't known what she meant at the time, but I did now. My heart was sure, and it was true. I knew what my heart wanted now, what it needed. I needed Bram in my life, not just for this task but for all my days and all my nights. For forever.

I'd always needed him, and not just as my familiar—I needed my mate.

Shoving my phone in my pocket, I started running.

Chapter Nineteen

Magnolia

Planting my foot on the demon's chest, I yanked Asher's knife from its throat. Blood sprayed me, and I dragged my forearm over my eyes so I could see, then scooped up more of its blood and smeared it over any exposed skin to cover my scent. I'd been doing it regularly, but still some of the creatures in these woods scented me.

I hadn't slept in thirty-five hours. I was cut and clawed, there were several bites on my arm and one on my side that I was pretty sure was getting infected, and I had one hour to reach Bram, and a lot of ground still to cover.

Shoving the knife back in its sheath, I spun from the flailing, bleeding demon and ran like hell. Roars and hisses echoed behind me, from breeds of demons, from creatures I'd never encountered before I'd walked into this forest. I shuddered, but now knew more about than I'd ever wanted to.

Hopefully, the demon thrashing about back there would keep

them busy for a short time and give me the chance to put some distance between me and them.

A snarl came from my right several seconds before a demon ran at me. They tended to do that, gave themselves away before they attacked. It was all the time I needed. Spinning, I kicked it in the head. It stumbled back, then came at me again. I tumbled into a roll as it lunged, jumping up and kicking it in the back. It face-planted, and I quickly slashed the tendons above each knee and ankle. The demon screamed, and I jumped to my feet and kept running.

I was fueled by adrenaline and desperation at this point. I'd finished the last of my water a few hours ago. I was hungry as hell, but without water I wasn't sure I'd be able to choke down my last energy bar.

A group of four...not demons, but *creatures*, appeared out of nowhere. Their hideous faces were wide, noses pointed and bony, bloodshot eyes protruding. I cringed. If my belly wasn't so empty, I'd be dry heaving from their smell alone. I yanked a glass vile from my pocket and threw it with force at the rock by one of the fugly fuckers' hairy feet. It smashed, and my potion did its thing, the vapor exploding around them and sending them deep into a hallu-cination haze, blinding them to me.

I only had two vials left. One like the potion I'd just used, inducing confusion and causing hallucinations, and the other, well, that one caused a little more damage.

I yanked my knife free, using it on the next demon who ran at me, somehow taking him out of commission with my frenzied hacking. Yeah, I was running out of steam, and fast. Digging deep, I thought of Bram, of how much pain I'd caused him, of how much I missed him, needed him, of how much I wanted to show him what he meant to me, and gritted my teeth, pushing harder.

I only had twenty minutes left.

Light broke through the trees ahead. I was almost at the edge of the forest. So close. Almost at the clearing between this forest and the crows' village. I just had to get there. I just had to find the strength to run that clearing.

The excited calls and whoops, the growls, grew in volume behind me. I focused ahead, about to pick up the pace, but was forced to slam on the brakes instead.

Demons.

They hadn't seen me yet, but ahead of me were more demons than I had a single hope of getting by.

Fuck.

The hungry sounds grew louder behind me, more of them closing in from all directions.

I needed to make a move. Now. I looked up at the massive tree beside me, its thick branches reaching out to the one beside it. With no time to waste, I gathered every bit of strength I could muster and scrambled up the wide trunk, somehow finding foothold after foothold, like I was being guided by someone else.

The demons crashed through the forest beneath, searching for me. I'd never seen so many demons or hideous creatures in my life. If I fell now, I'd be torn to shreds in seconds.

Taking a deep breath to steady my nerves, I stepped out onto one of the thick branches, using the one above to steady me, then onto another that touched the tree beside it. I focused on my balance, making my way to the next tree, then the next, slowly working my way to the edge of the forest.

What I planned to do when I got there? I had no fucking clue, but I had to think of something fast, because time was almost up.

If I was going to prove to Bram that I was worthy of being his mate, I had to finish this.

Failure wasn't an option.

Bram

I gripped the railing, refusing to rub at the ache in my chest. No, I let it sink deeper. I'd done this to myself. I'd known she wasn't ready, and I'd pushed for more anyway. I'd ruined everything.

Gritting my teeth, I dragged in a breath, then another, trying to calm the fuck down. It didn't work. Nothing worked.

I didn't know what to do with this feeling inside me. This violent twisting behind my ribs, the knives in my gut, the hammering in my skull—it was unbearable.

Magnolia was my everything, but right now, being with her was as painful as being parted from her.

The thud of boots on the deck came a moment before Payne grunted, then growled something under his breath. I turned to find him pacing, lips peeled back, fists clenched.

He'd been acting weird since yesterday. He glanced at his watch, again, something he'd been doing all day.

"What the hell is up with you?"

"Fuck." He growled and planted his hands on his hips. "Fuck," he said again. "Let's go."

"Where?"

"Just fucking follow me." He looked at Talon and Rook. "You two as well."

The three of us looked at each other, then at Payne's retreating back.

Talon rolled his eyes. "Guess we're following."

I pushed away from the railing, strode the edge of the deck, and jumped to the ground after my brothers. Payne walked to the chain-link fence between us and the wide clearing that bordered the forest beyond it.

"Okay, we're here," I said to Payne, then stilled and tilted my head. Roars and howls, a fucking lot of them, echoed from the forest beyond the clearing.

"Something's riled them up," Talon said, walking up to the fence as well. He shaded his eyes and searched the tree line.

Payne's jaw tightened, and he looked antsy as fuck. "You." He pointed at me. "Stand here."

"You having some kind of episode?" Talon asked our older brother.

Payne ignored him. "Here, Bram, now."

I frowned and walked up to the spot my control-freak brother was pointing out, confused as hell.

The demons and other creatures in the forest grew louder, their howls and snarls filled with excitement, with hunger and rage. "What the hell's making them lose their shit like that?"

Rook shifted, a look suddenly crossing his face like a lightbulb just switched on before his gaze sliced to Payne, then back at me.

"Why the fuck are we standing here?" Talon asked, sounding pissed and just as confused as I was.

The roars from the forest grew in volume. I'd never heard anything like it. I felt it in my chest, in my gut. Why the fuck was my heart racing?

Payne looked down at his watch.

"Payne?" Rook growled out.

Payne looked up and grabbed my shoulder in a bruising grip, then pointed to the edge of the forest. "Watch."

There was a strange note to his voice that had every muscle in my body locking tight, that lifted goose bumps all over me. I turned, searching in the direction he pointed, when the creatures in the forest lost their shit to a whole new fucking level.

Something small dropped from one of the tree branches along the edge. I squinted, trying to see what it was—

A dark figure shot up from the ground and started running— fucking sprinting.

Demons, creatures of all shapes and sizes, burst from the forest edge, making chase.

I gripped the fence, my heart hammering harder.

The small figure was dressed in black.

Short.

Curvy.

They turned to look behind them, and a long, black ponytail whipped out.

My entire body jolted.

Magnolia.

Oh fuck.

I gripped the fence about to jump it, to get to her—

Three pairs of strong hands grabbed me, yanking me back down, stopping me from getting to her, from helping her. I fought harder.

"Let me fucking go!" I snarled, losing my shit completely.

Payne gripped me harder. "You know what this is," he growled into my ear. "Fucking look. Look at her."

My heart was beating so hard that black spots were dancing in front of my eyes, not hearing him, not really. "Get the fuck off me."

My brothers held me tighter, not giving me an inch.

"Your little witch has spent the last thirty-six hours fighting her way through a forest full of monsters to get to you," Payne said. "To show you how much you matter to her. Don't take that from her. Let her finish this."

I gripped the fence so tight the wire cut into my fingers. No, that's not what this was. It couldn't be.

"She knows what you are, Bram," Rook said, his voice low. "And still she's running to you. She's not scared, she doesn't want you to rescue her, she's on a fucking mission," my usually quiet brother growled out. "Fucking look at her."

He didn't need to say it, she was all I could see. My wings exploded from my back, every part of me wanting to jump this fence, to snatch her from danger, to protect her.

A demon charged her from the left. Mags pulled something from her pocket and tossed it hard at the fucker. It screamed, grabbing at his now *melting* face. Several more came from the right. Her hands moved so fucking fast, grabbing and tossing throwing knives that were strapped to her chest, taking them down one after the other. Another one came from the left. Her hand shot out, and she slammed a knife into its throat, wrenched it out, then head down, arms pumping, she kept sprinting toward me.

"Holy fuck," Talon muttered.

She was covered in mud and so much blood, I could smell it all the way from here—demon blood and her own—and my crow shrieked, its talons clawing at my subconscious to get to her. To get to my female.

She was close now, and when her eyes came to me, locking on, my fucking knees went weak.

There was a roar and a huge fucking creature broke from the pack, barreling after her on all fours. Fuck, it was gaining on her. My wings started beating.

"Wait," Payne growled beside me. "She got this far without you. Trust her."

The creature pounced, and Mags flipped into a seamless tumble, rolling to her back. The fucker was taken by surprise and couldn't stop. Mags thrust her knife into its chest as the creature ran right over her, its own forward momentum dragging her blade down its belly, gutting it as it ran over the top of her.

Without missing a beat, she rolled, jumped to her feet, and kept sprinting.

Thirty yards.

Twenty.

Ten.

My heart smashed into my ribs. "Come on, baby."

She was almost to me.

My brothers released me, and I took several steps back as she closed the last few yards between us, as she threw herself at the fence, scrambling up it. The demons making chase slammed on the brakes as soon as they saw us, quickly falling back, not dumb enough to come any closer to our territory.

Blood pumped through my veins so hard and fast, I felt fucking dizzy as I watched her.

Mags jumped down, her boots thudding against the hard-packed earth. Then she straightened, demon blood dripping down her face and coating her clothes, her hands.

I tried to speak, but nothing would come. I was in shock. In fucking awe.

"You forgot something when you left," she said, chest heaving.

"What's that?" I choked out.

"Me," she said and ran at me.

I caught her up, lifting her into my arms. She wrapped herself around me, and I buried my face against the side of her throat, my skin to hers, breathing her in.

Uma and Maeve, the rest of the village had come to see what was going on, congregating behind us, and they hooted and cheered now.

Several seconds ticked by, both of us clinging to the other, then she cupped my jaw. "Look at me," she whispered against my ear.

Trembling, I lifted my head, afraid to believe what this meant, what was happening here, but hoping like fuck this was what I thought it was.

Her fingers slid over the shaved sides of my head, her amber eyes searching mine. "I made a mistake," she said.

I swallowed. "What was that?" My voice was so fucking deep and broken, I didn't recognize it.

The pulse in her throat fluttered wildly. "When you tried to kiss me... Instead of listening to the fear, I should have listened to my heart."

I brushed my thumb over her jaw. "And what was your heart telling you?"

She licked her lips. "This." Then her gorgeous mouth came down on mine.

My fucking pulse went haywire, my knees nearly buckled, and my body went up in flames. Wrapping my arms around her tighter,

I groaned, fucking positive this had to be a fever dream, or maybe I'd died and this was Heaven.

"I love you," she said against my lips, then parted hers, sliding her tongue over mine.

I fucking short-circuited, gripping her tighter, taking everything she was giving me, afraid she'd change her mind and take it back, that she'd stop—that I'd fucking wake up in bed alone.

Then she whimpered into my mouth, her scent, the heat of her body, the tang of blood coating her skin and clothes...hit me, lit me up, and I knew it was real. This was no dream.

I wrapped my arms around her tighter, and beating my wings, I lifted off the ground.

I finally had my Magnolia in my arms.

Where she belonged.

Chapter Twenty

Bram shot into the sky, and I hung on tight, lifting my head to look down as we flew over tree houses. Bram's hand gripped the back of my head and he pulled me down again, to take my mouth. He kissed me deep, hard, his body shaking as soft rattles and growls resonated through his chest, vibrating against mine, his crow coming through loud and clear.

I couldn't believe this was happening.

This was Bram. My Bram. And we were *kissing*. I fisted his shirt, holding him close, kissing him back, and it felt so incredibly fucking right.

But it had always felt right when I was in his arms. My body, my heart, had known this was where I belonged, but after what happened with Clayton, my mind had shut it down, it had denied and resisted what was right there all along.

Bram dropped from the sky, landing with a thud on the wooden deck outside his tree house, the one he'd built with his brothers when he was a kid, the one he used when he came to the village.

I clung to him as he strode through the door and kicked it shut behind us. I couldn't take my eyes off his as he lowered me to my feet. His hands were low on my sides as he walked me backward through the living room and into the bedroom.

His glossy obsidian eyes smoldered down at me. "You're so fucking beautiful," he said in that deep yet quiet voice of his.

The rough velvet of it had goose bumps pebbling across my skin. "So are you," I said, eating up the sight of him. I knew his face better than my own, but I'd never seen the expression he currently wore, or the look in his eyes. It was desire, only now he wasn't trying to conceal it. He wasn't hiding anything, any part of him. I knew it all, had seen it all. First in that run-down building with blood on his hands, and now standing in his arms, the full force of his need etched into his handsome face.

His hands slid up to my waist, his grip tightening as he tugged me closer...squeezing a whimper of pain from me.

Bram hissed, pulling back instantly. "Your injuries." He scanned my body. "They need tending."

"I'm okay," I said and lifted to my tiptoes, going after his mouth.

Bram gave me what I wanted, pressing another kiss to my lips before he ended it too damn quickly.

I whimpered again, not in pain this time. "Don't stop."

He pressed his forehead to mine, the tremor still moving through his big body. "I don't ever want to stop, but I need to check your injuries. The scent of your blood is making me want to storm the forest and kill everything in it. So let's do that first, yeah?"

I didn't want to. I wanted to stay where I was, I wanted him to keep kissing me, but I knew he was right. So I let him lead me into the bathroom. He crouched down, helping me out of my boots, then tugged my blood-soaked pants carefully down my legs. His hair was loose and falling to one side, and I slid my fingers through the thick, black strands, needing to touch him, to never stop touching him.

He tilted his head back, looking up at me. "Okay?"

I nodded. "Are you in any doubt now about how much I love you?"

His eyes flared and hands slid up the outside of my thighs to my waist. His fingers gripped me there, lightly this time. His throat worked, then he wrapped his arms around my waist, shaking harder as he pressed his face against my belly and breathed deep. I kept my hands in the soft warmth of his hair, my own emotions rushing through me.

When he looked up at me again, his eyes glistened. "I thought I'd lost you. I never thought you'd... Fuck, seeing you running across that clearing..." His throat worked.

I shook my head. "You will never lose me." I brushed my fingers over the shaved sides of his head. "I lost my way for a little while, but I've found my way back...back to you."

He rose to his feet and took my chin in his hand, tilting my head back before he kissed me again, wild and deep, stealing my breath once more. "You know what we are, don't you, Mags?" he said against my lips, then lifted his head and took my chin again, holding it, demanding without words that I look into his eyes, that I don't shy away or retreat. "What we are to each other?"

I did, and the dominance in his gaze, his voice, the way he held me, sent a delicious shiver through me. "Yes." I thought he'd shown me all of him, but this was another part of Bram I'd never seen, not really, not like this.

"You are my mate, Magnolia. I felt it from the moment I met you. I've waited so fucking long for you to feel it, too, to see it. So make no mistake, you are mine." He pressed another kiss to my lips. "And I want to devour every fucking part of you, own every inch of you, I need you to know that, but we're not going to rush this. I can wait. I'll make you mine in truth, but not until you're ready for it, okay?"

My heart thundered wildly in my chest, and I nodded.

I wanted him, I did, in every way, but I was also scarred, inside and out, in more ways than a person should be, and Bram knew that better than anyone.

He stared down at me, a look of...of wonder on his face as he tucked my hair behind my ear, then leaned in and kissed me gently, as though he couldn't bear not to touch his lips to mine just one more time. "Now, we're going to clean all that demon blood off you before I lose my shit. Your wounds badly need tending, and you need to eat and rest."

I fisted the front of his shirt and tugged him closer. "You think we can fit some more kissing in there somewhere as well?"

He grinned, his abs tightening against my fist. "We fucking better."

Goddess, he was handsome.

He stepped back and tugged off his shirt, then shoved down his jeans. Stripping so he was just in boxer briefs, he reached in and turned on the shower.

"We need to get these clothes off," he said as he gently peeled my shirt up and off, flinging it aside. When he turned back and took in the state of my upper body, he hissed again, his hand trembling as it skimmed carefully over the cuts and bites, the bruises marring my skin, adding to the scars already covering my body.

He shook harder, but with rage this time, as he took in the rest of me. I stood in front of him in only my underwear. He'd seen me like this before—he'd seen me completely naked, more than once—but for the first time, I knew he was looking at me as his female, his mate, and one day soon, his lover.

What did he see when he looked at me? All I saw when I looked in the mirror were imperfections. All the ugliness of my past, immortalized on my skin. I shoved that down, locking it away, refusing to let it ruin this moment.

Bram helped me into the shower, and lathering soap in his hands, he slowly, methodically, ran them over my body, washing the blood and dirt from my skin. As his hand drifted over my chest, he paused, looking down at me, checking I was okay with it. I nodded and bit my lips when his palm grazed my nipples.

His nostrils flared as I ate up the sight of him, tall and lean and muscled. His stomach muscles were tight as hell, and my gaze trailed over the warrior tattoos decorating his body, then down to the V at his hips that led my gaze even lower...

My belly heated, clenching tight. He was hard, straining behind the soaked fabric of his underwear, but Bram seemed content to ignore it, laser focused on getting the smell of demon off me.

His hand slid over my stomach, and he leaned in and kissed me again. My body fired to life in a way that it hadn't for so very long. My nipples tightened, heat flooding me. I squeezed my thighs together, moaning against his lips. "Touch me."

I was weak, hungry, my mind spinning, fuzzy for once, not letting anything else in except for my desperation for Bram's touch.

His hand didn't stop moving over my skin. "You sure?"

"Yes, please. I need you to touch me."

"Tell me where."

I took his wrist, leading him where I needed him, pushing the tips of his fingers under the elastic of my underwear. "Please," I said.

His gaze was locked on mine, searching for any sign that I didn't want this as he slid his fingers down the front of my underwear.

"Fuck," he growled, the sound bouncing off the tiles.

He hooked one strong arm around me, holding me up, and pressed his lips to my forehead. "I need you to tell me if you don't like it, if you want me to stop, okay?"

I nodded as he curled his fingers around my pussy, the middle one pressing deeper. I shoved my forehead against his chest, digging my fingernails into his biceps.

"You're so hot. So fucking slick." Bram groaned as he slid his fingers up and back. "Good?"

"Yes, don't...don't stop."

He fisted my wet hair with his other hand and tilted my head back. "Eyes on me, Magnolia."

The rough, possessiveness in his voice sent a shiver through me. I blinked up at him through the spray and steam, licking the water from my lips.

His gaze dropped to my mouth, then back, and his eyes darkened. "I want to make you come, Maggie, so fucking badly. I want to make you feel good."

The use of that nickname—the one he used so sparingly, the one that I loved so much—and the vulnerability I saw in his eyes had me moving closer, holding him tighter. "It d-does. It feels so good."

His fingers slid higher, circling my clit, and my legs tried to buckle under me again.

"Yeah, right there," he muttered. "Faster?"

I nodded, digging my nails deeper. "P-please."

His chest heaved with his panted breaths as he focused solely on getting me off. His fingers didn't let up, demanding my surrender. I cried out and bit my lip harder when the pleasure started to grow.

He pressed on my lower lip with his thumb, pulling it free, and shook his head. "No hiding from me. We've hidden enough from each other. Not this, never this." He dipped his head, sliding his tongue over my abused lip. "I want to hear it, how good I make you feel, I need to hear it. Give it to me, Mags."

At his words, the feeling growing inside me intensified, its grip on me tightening even more. I panted, sharp sobs bursting from me the closer I got to my breaking point. I squeezed my eyes closed.

"Eyes on me," he said again. "Now."

I forced my eyes open, and when they met his, a sound vibrated through his chest, soft yet deep, rumbling through him. It was almost melodic, a mix of growls and rattles, along with something that could only be described as cooing. I'd never heard it from him before. He nuzzled the side of my face, my neck, sucking the skin there.

At the next swipe of his fingers, I gasped, a cry bursting from me, then I shattered, calling out his name as I came for him, gasping for breath.

Black dots filled my vision, and this time when my knees buckled, there was no stopping it.

Bram scooped me up. "I've got you," he said.

Then everything went dark.

~

Bram

I worked my way across Magnolia's body, liberally using Else's healing balm and some of the other concoctions Mags had made and used on me many times. There was a bite on her side that was starting to look puffy and pink around the edges. Infection would have set in if it'd been left any longer.

It was a good thing she was out cold, it meant she wouldn't feel it when I cleaned it out. I rinsed it a second time with herb-infused warm water. There was a clear outline of a vicious set of teeth deep in her skin.

My hand shook as I dabbed the area clean. Only now that things had quieted down was the shock setting in.

I would never forget the image of Magnolia running across that field, a forest full of monsters right behind her. She'd been powerful, god, magnificent. My Mags was a fucking warrior, but I'd never been as terrified as I was in that moment.

There'd been so many other emotions there as well. Fuck. Pride, possessiveness, hope, love—lust.

My gaze trailed up to her face. Her eyes were closed, her chest rising and falling slow and even. Her lips were puffy and darker from our kisses, and I wanted to taste her again so badly. I wanted to taste every part of her. My need was so great and my gut was in constant knots, but I meant what I said, I'd wait. Yes, I wanted Magnolia in a way that, if she could feel it, see it, would probably scare the hell out of her, but I'd wait another lifetime for her if I had to.

She needed to be ready for me, which meant the ball was in her court. I'd lived with the aftermath of what Clayton fucking Whitlock did to her. I knew how much she'd struggled to live with it, to get past it. It'd been the hardest thing she'd ever done, and I wouldn't undo all that work by pushing for something she wasn't ready for.

The way she'd asked me to touch her, pleaded for it, the way she'd called out my name in the shower, the sounds of her coming for me, kept running through my mind now, and I sucked in a sharp breath when my cock grew heavier.

It's not like I wasn't used to it when I was around her, but it was different than before. Before I had no hope of ever making her mine. Before, I hadn't touched her pussy or felt how slick and hot she was *for me*. I'd resigned myself to never having her, to never knowing these things. Now it wasn't a matter of if, but when.

I dragged in another fortifying breath and willed my dick down as I smeared more balm on her side, rubbing it into the wound as best as I could, then adding another layer before I dressed it with a thick bandage. I'd stripped Mags out of her wet bra and panties while she was out cold and tugged the shirt I'd put on her down to cover her nakedness.

It was late, had grown dark outside, and I climbed into bed

beside her, getting as close as I could so her body was plastered against mine. Wrapping my arms around her curvy, little body, I closed my eyes and breathed her in.

A sense of peace I hadn't felt in a long time, not since the day I found her, filled me. Mags made a breathy little noise, wriggling against me, finally regaining consciousness. I didn't move behind her, still afraid she'd wake up and change her mind, that she'd pull away, that she'd say this was all a huge mistake.

She didn't, instead, her hand covered mine, threading our fingers together. "Night, B," she whispered.

"Night, Mags," I said, and kissed her jaw.

How the fuck was I supposed to sleep now? It felt like Christmas, all my birthdays, every good fucking thing all rolled into one.

Mags was here with me. She was finally mine.

And I was never letting her go.

Chapter Twenty-One

Sun filtered into the room.

I blinked several times, letting my sleepy brain clear, then remembered where I was. With Bram, at his village.

In his bed.

I'd shared a bed with him more times than I could count, pressed against him, draped over him, but this...this was different. We'd kissed, he'd touched me. He'd made me come.

We'd admitted to feelings we'd both hidden from each other, and in my case, from myself, for far too long.

He was plastered against my back, his hand up under the shirt he must have put on me while I was out cold. His palm was flat against my stomach, hot against my skin. I could tell without looking, he'd tended my wounds while I'd been out. I could smell the balm. There was half a glass of water by the bed. He'd given me water, but I had no recollection of it. I shifted, reaching for it now, my wounds smarting as I carefully moved while trying not to wake him.

He muttered something as I lay back, the hand on my belly pressing me into him more firmly and one of his knees lifting, sliding between mine. Heat spiraled through me, and I tried to keep my breathing even, but it was impossible, because all I could think about was the way he'd touched me in the shower. The sounds he'd made when he'd looked into my eyes, the dominant way he'd quietly asked—no, demanded—submission from me. How desperately I'd wanted to give it to him. I'd asked him to touch me, but he'd run with it. He'd taken control, and he'd made it so I didn't have to think, so I could just let go.

I'd never experienced anything like it, but I wasn't surprised it was Bram who'd given it to me.

His fingers flexed against my stomach, and he growled as his arm curled around me more tightly, his thigh lifting higher, until it was pressed firmly against the bare flesh between my legs.

His mouth went to my ear. "Morning."

Somehow, I managed to suppress the shiver that danced up my spine at those roughly spoken words. I really wanted to squeeze my thighs together, but it was impossible. "Morning."

Bram's thigh applied more pressure while the hand on my stomach started to slide up and back, getting a little higher each time.

"You sleep okay?" he asked in that same gritty-as-hell morning voice.

It did things to me, it always had, I'd just been in denial about it. But there was no hiding what it did to me now, not this time. He had to feel it. "Yeah...you?"

He nuzzled my throat. "No." His lips trailed along my skin. "I lay awake all night, too scared to close my eyes in case I woke up this morning and it turned out yesterday was all a dream."

His hand slipped higher, and I sucked in a breath, a sensation moving through me that was full of contradiction. My scars were so incredibly sensitive. I wanted more, but at the same time, it was almost too much. I wanted to arch against his touch and shove his hand away at the same time. I was in sensory overload, and my subconscious was pulling up images of the only other person who had ever touched my bare skin...

I quickly rolled to my back so I could see Bram, so every part of me knew this was him, because he was safe. He was my safe place.

He looked down at me, eyes sleepy, hair mussed, and I hated that my body was still in flight mode; that even now I had to fight against the need to flee when I was touched. My scars burned under his hand and, as he slid it higher, I sucked in another breath and covered it with my own, halting him.

Worry filled his eyes, and I quickly reached up, hooked him around the back of the neck and pulled him down for a kiss before he could speak, before he could apologize or freak out that he'd done something wrong. Because it wasn't Bram, it was me.

He came to me instantly, his kiss soft, gentle, exploring, knowing I needed him to slow down and giving that to me. I hated that I needed time. Bram would never hurt me. Never. I knew that to my very soul. He'd give up everything for me in a heartbeat. He'd give me the world if he could.

My scars burned hotter, and I moaned against his lips, the mix of pleasure and pain saturating my body, making me gasp against his lips. I pulled him closer, fighting it, willing the pain overwhelming me away. But it didn't leave, it heightened.

Then it was too much. Oh, goddess, it was as if every scar had been torn open again. I shoved at Bram's shoulder with a scream of pain. He lifted off me immediately, and I looked down at myself, expecting to see blood, to see knife wounds appearing all over my body like they had that day.

"What is it?" he barked, his gaze slicing over me, fear stark in his eyes as if he expected to see the same. As if he were reliving that awful day as well.

Panting, I shook my head, sweating, body trembling. "I—I don't know. It felt like...like it was happening again."

His chest rose and fell with his labored breaths, and his jaw tightened. "I pushed too hard, too fast."

"No, that's not it. You touch me all the time—"

"This is different. I'm touching you differently, Mags. The only other person to touch you that way..." A look of pure hatred filled his eyes. He was imagining what he'd do to Clayton if he had the chance, I could see it on his face. He shook it off, his eyes softening when they came back to me. "I promised I'd take it slow, then I rushed you. It won't happen again."

I wanted to scream in frustration. I didn't want that monster getting between us. I wanted him wiped from my mind, from my skin. "What if..." I sat up and pushed on his shoulder.

Bram let me, dropping to his back. "You don't need to—"

"I know I don't, but I want to. I want to be close to you. If we have to go slow because I'm so fucking messed up, fine, but I want to keep trying..." I moved over him slowly, ignoring the way the bite at my side throbbed, along with all the other aches and pains all over my body, and rested my hands on the mattress on either side of his head. "We can't stop, okay? We can't stop trying. We need to push, because I want you...I do. I just...I just..." I didn't know what to say, how to make him understand.

He brushed my hair away from my face, and held it against the back of my neck. "You're not messed up, you're perfect—in every conceivable fucking way. You think I'm going to get frustrated with you? That I'll change my mind because we can't have sex? That I'll lose interest?" His thumb swiped over my cheek. "Just knowing you want to be with me is enough. Being with you, just near you, is *enough*. I need you to let that sink in. I need you to believe it, because it's the truth. If it takes a week or a month, or a year, before you're cool with me touching you, I'm fucking cool with that. If it takes a year before you're ready to have sex, more, fucking never, I am cool with that. I'm crazy, insanely, obsessively in love with you, Magnolia, and that will never ever change no matter what we do, or don't do. Not fucking ever, understand?"

I swallowed and nodded. Goddess, everything he'd just said hit hard, so hard I had to fight back tears. I had no idea what to say to that, so I leaned in and kissed him. When our lips met, he lay still, letting me lead, his hands at his sides. I explored his mouth loving the way his chest rose and fell faster as I did. He was right, I was scared he'd give up on me if I couldn't be everything he needed, even though I knew better than that. I knew Bram better than that. "You're obsessively in love with me?" I said against his mouth.

"Are you really in any doubt?" he said. "I have been since you hugged me outside your family's cemetery." He blinked up at me. "You became my entire world that day, Maggie."

"You became mine as well," I said and pressed my face against the side of his throat before I lost the fight and started crying. He rubbed my back, his touch light, cautious, as I breathed heavily.

We stayed like that for a long time, and soaked it in, breathed him in. Reminding my stupid brain every now and then that I was with Bram, and that Bram was crazy, insanely, obsessively in love with me.

For a minute, I thought he'd gone to sleep, then his hand slid up my back and into my hair, fisting it gently. "Baby?"

Baby. "Yeah?"

"Look at me."

I lifted my head.

"Do you have any questions about what you saw the other night," he asked, his gaze searching mine.

I did. Several.

I slid my hand up his chest and lightly wrapped my fingers around his throat, like I'd be able to feel it, stop it if his oath kicked in and tried to choke him again. "How do you decide who to kill?"

"We don't, we're given targets," he said, thankfully without any trouble.

"By who?"

"Pack heads, the witches council, others of all kinds. They call us when one of their own goes rogue and humans are involved. Maybe they can't deal with it themselves, for some reason, or it's too risky or dangerous. That's when they hire us to do the job."

"If the council didn't know about our connection, do you think they would've called you and your brothers in to hunt for Willow?" I asked. "In their eyes, she's a murderous witch out of control."

"I don't know. If humans were involved, then probably. But we don't just kill because someone wants us to. We make sure they deserve to die before we end a life."

"Do the people that hire you take the silencing oath as well?"

"Yes."

"And you...you wanted to do it? Go after your targets?"

"Not at first, I tried to resist, but like I said, we're more animal than human. Payne made sure I had no choice but to join the family business, because hunting is something we need and ignoring our animal instincts can be detrimental, it could turn us rogue or worse."

"You could lose your mind if you don't kill?"

"Yes."

"And all crows are like that?"

"To an extent. Most are satisfied to hunt in the woods every now and then—animals, occasionally demons. Those of us who grow into the warriors of our race, the protectors of our people, are closer to our crows, to that base part of ourselves and we need the... outlet. This work gives us what we need to stay sane and healthy, provides our people with the money we need to thrive, and the humans stay safe."

"But you could get hurt, worse."

A dangerous-as-fuck look transformed his face. "Hunting and killing, we're made for it, Mags. You don't have to worry about me."

What he'd said should probably worry or frighten me. It didn't. Maybe it made me twisted, but instead heat bloomed low in my belly, a throb humming to life between my thighs.

Bram's nostrils flared, and he made a low grunting growl sound, one that was totally animalistic.

"That sound, it's your crow, yes?"

He nodded and licked his lips.

"What does it mean?" All the sounds they made had their own meaning. He'd explained that to me a long time ago. I thought I'd heard all his sounds until now.

"It means I can smell how wet you are right now, and my crow is pleased," he rasped.

I wasn't embarrassed. I wanted him to know how much I wanted him. I couldn't give him all of me, not yet, but I at least wanted him to know my body did even if my mind was fucking with me. I pressed my mouth to his. "And the sound you made in the shower?"

"When I made you come?" he asked, voice gritty as hell.

"Yes." I lifted my head, looking down at him.

"It's the sound...the song, we sing to our mates. It comes from within us, pure instinct. Wild crows obviously can't kiss, so they nuzzle each other, and our people, being closer to our crow, do both, we sing and nuzzle our females to show affection and to let them know how much they're loved." Bram had always done it, pressed his face to my neck, nuzzled me. I hadn't known the significance. He tucked my hair behind my ear. "Our songs, they're incredibly intimate and something we don't do in front of others. No two songs are the same. It's something just for the two of us."

My heart clenched. "Was last night the first time you've done it?"

"It's the first time I've allowed myself to do it. I've wanted to, more times than I can count, when I was alone with you, but I wanted you feeling what I was when I finally allowed it to happen."

My eyes drifted shut as I fought back more goddamn tears. Just thinking about the last six years, the pain he must have suffered thinking I'd never want him the way he did me, it hurt to think about it. The guilt was unbearable. He was my familiar, my best friend, my everything, and I'd hurt him.

His warm palm pressed against the side of my throat, his rough-skinned fingers curling around the back before he drew me down. His forehead touched mine. "Mags, look at me."

I did as he asked, blinking down at him.

"Don't," he said roughly.

"But I—"

"You have nothing to feel guilty about."

Like he always had, he was able to see what was in my heart. "I hurt you."

He shook his head. "We hurt each other."

He gave my throat a light squeeze, and the heat between my thighs intensified.

"How can we have a moment's regret when it all led to now? To this moment."

He was right, regrets were pointless. "We may have taken the long route, and yeah, there are a few more hurdles to jump, but the happily ever after is right there on the horizon," I said and gave him a wobbly smile.

"It's right fucking here, right now."

The door banged open in the living room. "Rook's inking, get your ass up," Payne called through the door. There was a pause. "Morning, Magnolia."

For once there wasn't even a hint of resentment in his tone. Even when he'd tried to hide it for Bram's sake, I'd heard it, or seen it in his eyes.

"You've got five minutes," he added, then the door closed behind him.

It took some serious convincing, but I eventually managed to drag Bram out of bed. Yes, I wanted to stay right there, but I also didn't want to piss off his brothers. They'd pretty much despised me since Bram found me. I thought I might finally have their respect, and I didn't want to mess that up again.

Bram grumbled as he pulled on jeans. He didn't bother with a shirt. I'd seen him bare chested more often than not over the years, but now, it was hard for me to keep my hands off him. I guess that wasn't new either. But now it was heightened, like to the millionth degree.

My jeans were ruined, so I had on a pair of Bram's track pants. I was swimming in them, they looked ridiculous, but the sexy, smoldering smile Bram gave me when I tugged them on, yeah, I'd wear them every day to get that smile.

We walked out, and Rook was bent over Payne, who sat with his elbows resting on his knees while his brother inked another marker on the side of his head.

I glanced up at Bram. "Why do you do that?"

"To count our kills. It's always been done among our warrior ranks. Originally, it was to show our enemies we were not to be fucked with. Now it's mainly to uphold traditions."

My gaze automatically went to Bram's head. He'd collected more than a few. "And I guess it still warns off your enemies?"

He bared his teeth in a wicked smile. "We don't have any, Mags, we killed them all."

Talon laughed, the sound lifting the hair on the back of my neck. "The ink's also laced with their blood. We carry in our skin a part of every soul we send to the afterlife. It's the price we pay for embracing what we are."

Okay, that was intense. I turned to Bram, and he was watching me closely. Did he think I'd judge him for it, judge his people for something they'd been doing for probably thousands of years? I felt the opposite. Taking a life meant something to them, and they carried it with them the rest of their lives. I gave his hand a squeeze.

Payne stood, drawing my attention back to the scene in front of me. Bram's oldest brother gave me a chin lift. "You're looking better this morning, and you don't stink of demon."

"Why, thank you. I feel a lot better." That was as much of the touchy-feely stuff as I was gonna get from that particular male. Talon was grinning at us, and Rook said nothing, which was standard for him.

Maeve came running out of Payne's tree house. "Let me see," she said, tugging on her father's hand.

He immediately crouched so his daughter could see his new ink. She traced it with her little finger. "Are you winning?"

"It's not about winning. You know that." Then he grinned wide, surprising the hell out of me. "But yes, baby, your daddy is winning."

Rook chuckled low, and I was stunned a second time. I'd never heard anything other than the odd word and the occasional grunt from him.

"Now that you and Bram have stopped pining and started boning, you gonna be a good wifey and follow our traditions?" Talon asked, motioning to the chair Payne had just been sitting in.

Bram growled. "For once, how about you keep your mouth shut."

He took a step toward his brother, and I planted my hand on his stomach, stopping him. We weren't "boning" as Talon so charmingly put it, but just because we hadn't been able to mate in truth yet didn't mean I didn't want to do other things a mate would do for her male. "What traditions?"

"Dinner on the table at six on the dot and always ready and willing to submit to your male and fulfill all his needs—"

"What does submit mean?" Maeve asked her father.

Payne's gaze sliced to Talon, and if looks could kill, he'd be shredded on the floor.

"It means to do as you're told," he said to her.

She screwed up her face. "Why would Uncle Bram want that—"

"We'll talk about it later," Payne said, and I got the feeling later would never come.

"There's only one way our females submit," Rook said, low and gritty. "And it's not in the fucking kitchen."

Talon laughed, and Payne's lips twitched.

My belly did that heat-and-swirl combo again, and I looked up at Bram.

His jaw was tight. "Ignore my fuckwit brothers. Considering Rook and Talon have never had females of their own, I wouldn't consider them experts on the subject."

Talon flipped Bram off. "Not sure why you're acting all coy," he said to Bram, then looked at me. "Okay, I was messing with you. Our females do what the fuck they like. We only have one tradition. If a warrior has a female, she usually hangs with him when he gets a new marker, you know, to show everyone she's proud of him, that she's proud to be his—"

"Talon," Bram bit out.

"What? It's one of my top fucking fantasies. Only when I do it, we'll both be naked," he said.

"You're naked, you can ink your fucking self," Rook muttered.

"What do I do?" I asked, warily.

Talon grinned. "Don't worry, it's nothing kinky. All you gotta do is sit on his lap and distract him from the pain."

Bram cursed under his breath, shoved Talon out of the way, and sat on the chair.

"Is that what usually happens?" I asked Rook, who seemed the least likely to make shit up.

Rook's cold, black eyes slid to me, like he was surprised I'd asked him, but then he nodded.

Okay, then that's what I'd do.

"Hair outta the way," Rook said to Bram.

Bram searched his pockets for a hair tie.

"Let me." I took the one from my own hair, and Bram faced forward again, sitting back while I threaded my fingers through his hair, gathering it up. His brothers went silent, and I felt their eyes on me while I tied his hair in a knot the way I knew he liked it, getting it out of the way so Rook could do what he needed to.

Then I walked around him to get on his lap. If my job was to distract him, I'd need to be able to look into his eyes, so I straddled his spread thighs, and he looked at me in a way that sent a tremor of pleasure down my spine. His brothers were still silent and not even trying to pretend they weren't watching us.

I took his strong jaw in my hands. "Ready?"

His hands slid lightly up my thighs and rested on my hips, careful of my scars. "Yeah."

Payne grunted, the sound one of approval, but I didn't look his way or at Rook when he stepped up with the tattoo gun. I kept my eyes on Bram. He'd trusted me with the truth, with all of him, and I didn't want him to regret it. I wanted him to see that I loved all of him, even the part of him that was a predator who needed to hunt and kill.

"Say his name," Payne said.

Bram said the name of the male he killed, then the buzz of the gun started. Bram held my eyes as Rook pressed it to the side of his head. The only sign that he felt it was his lashes fluttering a couple times. I ran my fingers over his stubbled jaw, then leaned in and pressed a kiss to his lips. His hands squeezed my hips, and he kissed me back, slow and easy, and I kept on kissing him as Rook inked his new marker.

Someone cleared their throat a little while later, and I realized the buzzing had stopped and Rook had stepped back. I smiled against his lips. "I'm proud of you," I said. "Proud to be yours. I love every bloodthirsty inch of you."

He grinned.

"Never seen anyone covered in more blood than you, little witch," Payne said.

"Truth," Talon said and laughed, and Rook actually smiled, well, kind of. His lips twitched.

"I'm no crow, but if I was, I'd probably have more markers than you," I said to Payne.

He smirked. "Sure you would, short ass."

Was Bram's surly brother actually teasing me?

I took Bram's jaw and angled his head to the side so I could see the new marker. "Do you remember them all?"

"Yes," he said.

I traced one above his ear. "Was this the first?"

He nodded.

"Who was it?"

He took my hand away and cupped my jaw. "Brody."

I stared into the dark depths of his eyes.

"I collected some of his blood before his body was taken away, because I knew I wanted to carry him on me. I wanted to look at it and remember the way it felt to snap his fucking neck. The way his body looked crumpled and lifeless on the ground. He was the first marker I got Rook to do. He's the kill I'm most proud of. I'm only sorry that Clayton isn't beside him."

I was breathing heavy, my heart pounding. Everything he said, I felt it, deeply. It didn't scare me, it turned me on. I squirmed on his lap. "Bram..."

"Hang on tight," he said and stood. His wings unfurled and I quickly locked my arms around his neck before he shot upward, higher, right up to the crows' lookout, high in the trees.

We landed and I released him, looking out at the view. I turned back, and Bram advanced. He backed me up against the railing, grabbed it each side of me, so he wasn't touching me, but caging me in. I looked up at him, and my breath caught.

"Don't want to push, Mags, and I'm not asking for more than this, but I need to own that mouth," he growled. "I need it. Right the fuck now."

I needed it too. I rested my hands on his chest and lifted to my toes. "Take it."

With a snarl, he kissed me hard, his tongue delving deep. Still, he didn't touch me, even lost in his hunger. What he'd just done, getting the new marker, my acceptance, my pride in the male he was, had affected him, deeply. But he wasn't the only one. His body trembled and he was hard, straining against the front of his jeans, I felt it when he brushed against my stomach.

He'd made me feel good last night, he'd made me come, and I wanted to do that for him as well. I wanted to show him how much he mattered, how much I wanted him. I tugged open the button of his jeans, then slid down the zipper.

His hand covered mine, and panting, he lifted his head. "You don't need to—"

"I want to. I want to touch you," I said and shoved his jeans lower. I pushed my hand down the front of his underwear, and a shuddering breath burst from him when I lightly gripped his cock.

Hunger filled his gaze, his chest pumping hard as I explored. He was like hot iron in my hand, his skin silky smooth.

"Tell me what to do," I said, unsure and desperate to make him feel good. "Tell me how you like to be touched?"

His Adam's apple slid up and down his throat. "Just having your hands on me is enough. Anything you do feels fucking amazing."

I curled my fingers around him more firmly and stroked from root to tip. Hips rocked forward instantly, and his head dropped forward on a groan. "Like that?"

He nodded, breathing hard. His hair had fallen forward, hiding his face from me, and when I did it again, his biceps bulged, the veins in his forearms standing out as he gripped the railing tighter.

Fluid leaked from the slit at the head of his cock and I spread it with my thumb, using it to ease my way. I dragged my hand down and back once more and Bram hissed through clenched teeth.

His head lifted, and dominance rolled off him. His dark eyes were intense, utterly gorgeous. The transformation sent a delicious shiver through me. "Hold me tighter, baby," he said. "Both hands."

I did, stroking him again.

He held my eyes and started thrusting his hips, rolling them. He stood over me, still gripping the railing either side of me and I couldn't look away. He was so beautiful. His tattooed arms and bare chest glistened with sweat, his muscles straining as he worked himself in my grip.

"Dreamed about this, Mags, kissing you, your hands on me." He took my mouth in another hard kiss, wet and deep, hungry. He sucked my tongue and nipped my lips, making me dizzy from how good it was. "Fuck, I can't get enough of you," he said against my lips. "Tighter, faster," he groaned.

His thrusts grew wild, brutal and I imagined how it would feel if he was inside me. Heat pooled between my thighs. I was panting as well, watching him like this was so incredibly hot.

Then he jerked, his cock pulsing in my hands as he came for me, his entire body jolting with each thrust.

Finally, he dropped his head to my shoulder, shaking, breathing hard.

I kissed his neck, working my way to his ear. "Goddess, Bram, you are so fucking hot," I said, throat tight, body electric.

He lifted his head, fisted my hair and kissed me hard and deep and wild. I never wanted him to stop.

But then his fingers grazed my back, right over the vines stretching out from the center, reminding me that I had somewhere I needed to be, that this little pause from my task was over.

I didn't want to go back, I wanted to stay right here forever, but I couldn't do that.

I needed to get back to the city.

Chapter Twenty-Two

I jogged down the stairs after a quick change of clothes, and there was an unmistakable tingling along the markings on my back and stomach. It'd started a few minutes ago.

Bram stood at the bottom.

"We have somewhere to be," I said.

He frowned. "Yeah?"

Mom walked out of the kitchen. "Mags?"

The fear in her eyes said it all. Else had told her about my task.

She didn't ask me about it, she just closed the space between us and pulled me into her arms, trembling. I let her hold me. My scars ached, but I grit my teeth and gave her what she needed, because there was nothing I could do to ease her fears.

Her smile was strained. "You must be hungry. I made you sandwiches. Let me get them." She rushed off, and I let her do that as well, forcing myself to ignore the sense of urgency filling me, because feeding the people she loved was what she did, especially when she was feeling helpless and it was all she could do.

She handed us both wrapped sandwiches.

"Thanks, Mom."

"Promise me you'll be careful," she said, eyes glistening.

"Promise."

We strode out to the car a few minutes later. "We need to head to the city," I said.

Bram took the car keys I held out for him. "Your task?"

I nodded.

The sense of urgency grew as we drove. It definitely wasn't Agatheena meddling this time, and the feeling was so strong that I had to grab for the door handle, sucking in a startled breath.

Bram shot me a look. "Okay?"

I nodded and gripped the door tighter. "Turn right, then take the next left," I said, when we hit the city, letting my instincts guide me.

I directed him down street after street until we reached one of the oldest parts of the city. The buildings were ornate, solid. Most of this street had been developed a few years back, new bars, clubs, and restaurants. A couple of the hotels had been refurbished. This was where the wealthy locals or visitors came to play.

"There," I said, pointing to a parking spot ahead of us.

Bram parked, and I shoved the door open and followed the persistent feeling pulsing through my veins. Bram jogged to catch up as we strode past shops and clubs. It was late enough that most of the shops were closed, and early enough that the bars were still pretty quiet and the clubs hadn't opened yet.

I stopped in front of a cobbled walkway between two buildings. The stones were black, but every so often there was a red one, like a trail leading you somewhere. There were vintage lanterns on either side that provided dim lighting and a small bronze plaque set into the brick wall to the right with "Red" etched into it. "Down here," I said.

Bram grabbed my arm, stopping me. "Careful, we don't know where that leads." He slid his knife free.

I nodded, and pulled mine as well as we walked up to a massive, glossy red door. I tried the handle. Locked. "Keep watch."

I picked the lock, opening the door, then quickly sliced an X in my palm before the alarm went off, about to use the same spell I had at the school, then paused, when I didn't feel the usual vibrations. "The alarm, the cameras, they're already off."

I bunched my shirt in my hand, applying pressure to stop the bleeding. Bram's nostrils flared, gaze darting to my hand. But we didn't have time for him to treat it, not when we didn't know what was behind the set of double red doors ahead of us.

We walked into a foyer and each of us took a side, knives gripped in our hands, and grabbed a door handle.

Bram nodded, and we opened them together—

Then froze.

Bram scented the air. His eyes flared, and he cursed before he grabbed my hand, yanking me closer.

I'd filled Bram in on everything that had happened while he was away on our way back from the village, including what I'd witnessed hiding behind the curtains in the Hazarks' living room. A week ago, I would've been surprised that this was where I'd been called, but not now, not after what I saw. It was a BDSM club. Thankfully, it was currently closed.

The walls were painted black, and there were racks and benches and all kinds of contraptions I'd never seen before dotted around the room. There were also couches, a couple beds, and a small stage.

"You think this is one of the prom committee's hangouts?" Bram asked, taking in the room.

"I don't know, but it would make sense, right? Chase mentioned a playroom. So I guess, this is what they're into." I tried to imagine this place full of people, and my belly swirled. Was I intrigued? Yes. Was it my scene? Oh, hell no. "I guess we should look around."

We checked out the rest of the large main room, then headed down a hall in the back, where there were smaller ones. All different themes, with different devices. I assumed they were for people who wanted to play in private.

The last door was ajar. My instincts skyrocketed. I motioned to it and Bram pushed it open. He stopped abruptly and I bumped into him.

"Fuck," he bit out.

I stepped around him.

Chase Golden.

He was all fucked up, but I recognized that hair instantly. His wrists were bound with wire, secured above his head, mouth sewn shut, face swollen and bloody. His shirt was open and "judgment" was carved into his chest—

His body jerked.

"He's still alive," Bram bit out, yanked out his phone, and quickly called for an ambulance. "We need to leave, now," he said when he disconnected. "It's only a couple minutes away."

A door slammed somewhere in the building. I took off, sprinting in the direction of that sound, Bram right behind me.

We'd interrupted the killer.

I ran down the hall, bursting into the main room and sprinting for the exit. The door flew open before I could reach it, and I slammed on the brakes as a tall male in a dark suit filled the doorway, blocking my way.

Demon, or at least half. I sensed it instantly.

He scowled down at us. "What the fuck are you doing in my club?"

That's when I recognized him. "Brent? I mean...Mr. Silva."

His scowl deepened, and I had to stop myself from shrinking under his hard stare. Brent Silva was a powerful sex demon. I'd only met him a couple of times, when I was with Willow, but it was a long time ago. I knew he owned several clubs, I just didn't realize what type of clubs they were.

"Did you see anyone when you came in, did you pass anyone?"

"Answer me," he demanded.

Bram stiffened and took a step forward, and I grabbed his hand, doing my best to hold him back. "I don't know if you remember me? We've met a couple of times. My name's Magnolia. I'm Willow Thornheart's sister," I rushed out. "Did you see anyone?"

Recognition filled his gaze and some of the fury dissipated. "No, I didn't see anyone. Now how about you explain why you broke into my club?"

"It's a long story..." Sirens wailed, they were close. Too damn close. "Look, I don't have time to explain. Someone tried to kill a guy in one of your private rooms. His pulse is weak, but he's still breathing. The ambulance is almost here and it'd be a lot better for us, and for Willow, if no one knew we'd been here."

His dark eyes burned into me. "Did you do it?"

"No."

"I'm gonna need an explanation."

"And I'll give you one, but the witches council can't know I was here."

Someone banged on the main door. We were trapped.

Brent's gaze slid to Bram and back to me, his jaw like granite. He pulled something from his pocket, keys, and tossed them to me. "Behind the bar, up the stairs. Wait up there."

I nodded, and Bram and I ran across the room, in behind the bar and out the back. There was a door on the left. We rushed through, and up a set of stars. I unlocked the door at the top and we shut ourselves in.

It was a small apartment. It didn't look like anyone used it, just the bare minimum of furniture. I strode to the window and peered around the edge of the curtain.

Witches, shifters, others, we had our own ambulance and

hospital, and when the medics down there realized Golden was a witch, they'd contact the council. If they knew I was connected with the crime scene in any way, well, it wouldn't be good for me or Willow.

I turned back to Bram. "If we hadn't gotten there when we did, Chase would be dead now." My hands balled into fists. "They were here. Whoever's behind all of this, they were right fucking there, and I let them get away."

"We had no idea what we were walking into. Chase is alive. He might know something. I fucking hope so, because whoever did that, they need to be put the fuck down."

He wasn't wrong. Whoever hurt Chase and tortured and killed the others was a twisted monster.

The kind only death could stop.

The council descended on the club like I knew they would. Hours passed and somehow, while we waited, I fell asleep.

The phone in the apartment rang, startling me awake. I lifted my head from Bram's chest. The room was dark. I had no idea how long we'd been up here, but it was late, the moon high in the sky.

Bram grabbed the phone, because there was only one person it could be. "Yeah?" he listened. "On our way." He hung up, then turned to me, tucking my hair behind my ear. "He wants to see us."

Shit.

We took the stairs back down, and slipped out from behind the bar. A low, throbbing beat filled the room. The club was in full swing, business as usual, like nothing had happened.

Bram's jaw worked as he looked around.

Some people were dressed seductively, some barely dressed at all, and some were straight-up naked. There was a couple on the low stage, a mostly naked male was strapped down, his back and ass streaked red, while a female in leather walked around him. Others in the room watched or were engaged in their own...scenes.

Bram's chest expanded. "Can I touch you? I need...I need everyone to know you're mine."

He needed it, and right then, I could thankfully tolerate it. "Yeah."

"He let go of my hand and gripped the back of my neck possessively, pulling me into his side. "Stay beside me, and don't talk to anyone."

"No one's going to hurt me or touch me. Places like this have rules. Brent wouldn't let his members harass one another." Bram looked ready to tear someone to pieces. "It's going to be fine," I said, and hoped I was right.

He didn't look reassured.

We walked around a big male sitting at one of the tables, a female wearing a collar, kneeling at his side. Her head was dipped, and his big hand was threaded in her hair, stroking her like she was his pet.

Bram's grip on my neck tightened, and he snarled when several people looked our way. They weren't just looking at me, but Bram didn't seem to notice that. No, he only saw the eyes that came my way, and he seemed to puff up like a cobra ready to strike.

I leaned into his side, wrapping my arm around his waist, trying to reassure him. Brent was already pissed at us for breaking into his place, the last thing I needed was Bram going full predator and killing a bunch of people for looking at me the wrong way.

"Down here," he said and led me toward the hall where we'd found Chase.

Most of the doors along it were closed, but I could hear the moans and cries of pleasure and pain coming through them. We turned left at the end of the hall and walked up to another set of glossy red doors. Bram tensed beside me.

"What do you know about this guy?" Bram asked.

"Brent's half sex demon and owns several clubs, I assume, like this one."

Bram bared his teeth.

"B, you gotta calm down," I said, looking up at him. "What's gotten into you?"

He took my chin between his thumb and finger. "You ran for almost two days through a demon-infested forest to show me you want me. I watched you run from a bloodthirsty hoard, fight and kill to get to me. Baby, my crow didn't miss it, the male who knows he has his mate at his side, didn't miss it. I was already protective of you, possessive as fuck, and overnight that shit has reached an entirely new level. Anyone even looks at you, at *my* female, the wrong way, and I will fucking end them...that's what's gotten into me."

I blinked up at him several times, my heart in my throat. What the hell did you say to that? I touched his arm, trying to calm him down, when I was far from calm myself. "I've been around my sisters and their mates enough to understand this is something you have to work through, just please, no matter how strong the compulsion is, do not kill Brent. He's a good guy, by all accounts, and a friend of Willow."

"He won't die if he shows the proper respect. If he's a good guy, like you say, then we shouldn't have a problem." He turned back to the door.

Shit. I knocked.

"Come in," a deep voice called.

I opened the door and walked in. Brent stood from behind his desk. He wore dark trousers, his jacket was off and draped over the back of his chair, his shirt unbuttoned at the throat and his sleeves were rolled up. His hair looked like he'd been thrusting his fingers through it, and there was a heavy silver chain around his neck, glinting against his lightly tanned skin, a metal ring hanging at the base—a collar.

"Hey, we're really sorry about earlier. That was kind of...

fucked up. Thanks for giving us somewhere to wait it out." I motioned to Bram. "I uh...didn't get to properly introduce you before. This is my—"

"Mate," Bram finished and pulled me a little closer.

Brent studied us a moment, his lips twitching. "Take a seat."

We both sat, then Bram's hand shot out and grabbed the arm of my chair, dragging it right up against his, and gripped the back of my neck again.

"Bram," I bit out. "Take a freaking breath."

Brent grinned. "Newly mated?"

"Um...not yet."

He nodded. "It's hard to control at the beginning. Wait until you actually mate," he said and gave me a pitying look.

Surely Bram couldn't get worse than this?

Brent sat back. "Brother, you can relax. I'm mated. I'm not looking to take your female or hurt her."

Bram did seem to relax a little then, at least the death grip he had on my neck loosened.

"Did you have any trouble from the witches council?" I asked.

Brent shook his head, a tight smile curling his lips. "No. They came in, cleaned up and left."

I assumed the council would move in. But for them not to be able to see who did this or the previous murders, with their access to a whole lot of powerful witches, made it obvious there was dark magic involved, or they would have brought a seer in and Willow would be off the hook already. Whoever was behind this was wiping their tracks clean with the kinds of spells that had been forbidden for centuries. "Any camera footage? The cameras were already off inside when we got here, but what about the ones outside the club?"

"Disabled as well." Brent's chair creaked as he sat forward, his dark eyes on me. "Tell me, Magnolia. How easy was it for you to break into this place?"

My face heated. "Honestly? Even if someone hadn't already disabled your alarm and cameras, it would've been a piece of cake."

Brent's jaw tightened. "Fuck."

The door opened and a curvy brunette about my height and wearing a black leather corset and short pleated red skirt, walked in. "What's got you cursing?" she said.

She rounded the desk and sat on the arm of her husband's chair. Brent wrapped his arm around her waist, and when he looked up at her, his face softened. "Our security's for shit."

"Hey, Chaya," I said.

Chaya ran her fingers through Brent's disheveled hair, then turned to me. "Hey, Mags, it's been a while."

Thankfully, right now neither Brent nor Chaya seemed overly upset with me, but still, I'd broken into their place. "I really am sorry for breaking in like I did. If I'd known it was your club, or there'd been another way—"

"I'm not pissed about it anymore," Brent said. "But I am pissed that you, and whoever got in before you, were able to do it so easily in the first place, and I'd like you to help me stop it from happening again."

"You want me to ward the club?"

"Yes."

Maybe I could use this to my advantage.

"And what does Magnolia get out of it?" Bram said before I could open my mouth. "She was able to break in, yeah. But like you say, someone did that before her, or they'd been able to hide out until everyone left. She found that guy before the attack turned into a murder. Honestly, you should be thanking her."

Chaya's lips twitched.

"Don't push it," Brent said to him.

"My wards are exceptional. No one will get past it," I said before Bram and Brent started a pissing contest.

Brent's eyes narrowed. "Fine, what do you want?"

"I need access to your client list and who was here last night. I wouldn't ask if it wasn't important."

He shook his head. "My clients come here expecting privacy. It gets out that my security is that weak and I share private information, I lose my business."

I leaned forward, resting my forearms on my knees. "I would never repeat or share any of the names on your list, but I need it. Willow's in trouble. She's been forced into hiding. The council wants to convict her for a bunch of murders she didn't commit. My entire coven could lose everything, including our magic, if I don't catch this fucker. And odds are good, you have a sadistic murderer on that list."

They both stared at me for several long seconds, then Chaya pressed her mouth to Brent's ear and said something I had no hope of hearing.

Brent nodded, then opened his laptop. "I signed a confidentiality agreement, along with my clients." He tapped a few keys. "I'm sorry, I can't tell you anything, Magnolia."

Chaya stood, taking Brent's hand. "We need to step out of the office for a few minutes to check on something," she said. "Will you excuse us?"

They walked out and shut the door firmly behind them. I frowned. "What the hell was that?"

Bram was already up and around the desk.

"What are you doing?"

Bram looked up and grinned. "He couldn't tell us, but what if it's on the screen and we happen to see it?"

I rushed around the desk, and the members list was right there, along with another list, members who'd signed in the night before Chance's attack. Brent had left it open for us. I quickly did a search for the obvious names.

They were all members, and they were all here last night.

"We'll need a copy of that and the full list of members as well," Bram said and tapped a few keys.

The printer started up a second later, spitting them out. I snatched everything up, folded it and stuffed it in my pocket.

The door to the office opened a minute after we sat back down. They were probably watching us on their security cameras.

I stood again, and placed the keys to the apartment on his desk. "We need to head off, but I'll be in touch, and we'll make a time for me to come and ward the club."

"Make sure you do," Brent said, holding my gaze before he stepped aside.

Bram and I strode out, through the club, out the door and down the alleyway.

"Where do we start with these? There has to be a couple hundred names on the members list," I said as we walked toward the car.

"We start with anyone who's remotely connected to the prom committee. Business associates, friends, family, anyone who went to Roxburgh High, especially if they were at Red the night of Chase's attack."

Chapter Twenty-Three

Magnolia

We got out of the car and looked up at Maria Watson's apartment building. She lived in the penthouse, thanks to her family and their money.

"She hung up on me," I said, shoving my phone in my pocket. As soon as I gave Maria my name, the line went dead.

"Surprised?" Bram asked as he shut the car door.

"Not at all." I shielded my eyes and looked up at the wide balcony jutting out from the top floor. "We just won't give her a choice."

Robert and Jenna had locked down their home and weren't answering calls, at least from numbers they didn't recognize. Ryan had snarled down the line for me to fuck off, and there was no way Isaac would talk to me.

Another person had almost died, and I had nothing, no leads. They hadn't released his name to the public, but I'd seen on

Nightscape that the latest victim was alive and had been put into an induced coma.

They'd also thrown in that Willow was still "at large."

There was no way to question Chase, no way to find out if he knew who tried to kill him. Isaac's smug face kept popping into my head, his gleeful expression when they came for Willow at the clubhouse, the way he was with Calvin that night, oily, manipulative. He'd treated Calvin like his attack dog. Calvin had lost it, then one command from Isaac, and he'd backed away snarling.

Then Calvin had turned up dead as well.

Isaac had to be involved in this somehow, and the more I thought about him and his actions in the past, the last couple of weeks, the more convinced I became that he was capable of almost anything.

With no other leads, we'd spent most of the night looking up names on Brent's list. There'd been a few surprises, one of them being Rook's name. I'd shown Bram, and he'd raised a brow but hadn't seemed overly shocked that his brother would frequent a place like that.

Besides the prom committee members, and Maria and Isaac, there were three other people who were linked to at least one of them, all via business of some kind, and who had been at the club the night of Chase's attempted murder. Chloe Chan, a wolf shifter, was the first. She was the Hazarks' realtor and had been a member of Red for several years. Ryan Alway had only been a member of the club for the last four months. I shuddered, and I knew firsthand he was deep in the inner circle. And the last was a shifter named Luke Donaghy. The male was rich and powerful and, since moving back to Roxburgh, had made a name for himself as someone not to mess with, but he'd also formed strong alliances with not only several powerful witches but shifters and demons as well.

He seemed to have gained their trust, not an easy thing to do in this city. People tended to shoot first and ask questions later. He'd been a member of Red for five months.

The connections were tenuous at best, but it wasn't like I had much else to go on. Whoever hurt Chase, they'd chosen Red for a reason. The only one I could come up with was to expose the prom committee. They wanted everyone to know what they were into, to ruin them, and to humiliate them, and a member of their tight inner circle murdered in a BDSM club would most definitely cause a stir. Bram and me showing up had ruined that plan. And not only had Chase lived, but he'd been taken away by the witches council before any Nightscape reporters could descend.

"Ready?" Bram asked.

I nodded.

"Will you be okay? I'm gonna have to hold you close," he said.

"I'm okay right now." And I hoped like fuck I stayed that way, for a little while at least, for both our sakes. Bram needed to be able to touch me, and I needed to be touched. This increase in my scar sensitivity, especially when it came to him, was honestly starting to scare me.

"You'll tell me if it gets too much?" he said as he tugged off his shirt. He tucked it in the waistband of his jeans, and his wings sprouted from his back.

"I will."

He scooped me up, and I wrapped my arms around his neck. There was a low vibration fluttering across my skin, and I wasn't sure if my scars were waking up and taking notice or it was just my body's reaction to being so close to Bram. His hold was firm but not tight, his muscles rock solid. Then he pressed his nose against my throat and breathed deep. A quiver rolled through him and he groaned in a way I knew was involuntary.

"Jesus," he muttered.

I bit my lip. Just being this close had my pulse fluttering like mad. "You okay?"

He cleared his throat. "Yeah, you just…you smell really fucking good."

I fought my own shiver. "You smell pretty good yourself." And he did, so good. I thought about the way he'd looked while we were up in the lookout, the sounds he'd made, the way he'd watched me. I moistened my lips, my belly flipping about.

His gaze slid to my mouth and back, and his nostrils flared. "Fuck," he muttered, then his jaw tightened and we shot up, his wings beating hard. We soared higher, looping around the side of the building, up to the top floor. He hovered above.

Maria sat below us, relaxing on the balcony, reading.

This was probably a terrible idea, but I was running out of time and options.

Bram tucked in his wings and dropped, landing on the penthouse balcony with a thud.

Maria screamed and jumped off her banana lounger, tossing her book at us. Bram caught it.

I lifted my hands. "We're not here to hurt you, Maria. We just want to talk."

Her eyes were wide as she stumbled back. "I told you I don't want to talk to you."

"I just have a couple of questions, then we'll leave, okay?"

She started shrieking, uncontrollably.

Bram shadowed out and popped up behind her. He clamped his hand over her mouth, and she started struggling, completely freaking out.

"We're not going to hurt you," I said again. "We just want to talk. Calm down." I looked up at Bram. "If you promise not to scream, he'll take his hand away."

Her wild eyes were locked on me.

"Okay?"

She jerkily nodded, and Bram eased his hand from her mouth.

"W-what do you want?" she said.

"We just want to ask you a few questions. That's all."

She nodded again.

"I promise, we're not here to hurt you," I said a third time, because she still looked terrified. "I'm trying to clear my sister's name. She didn't do the things people are saying. Someone's hurting your friends, and I know it's not her. The real killer is out there, and I want to find them and stop them." I kept my hands out at my sides. "Will you answer my questions?"

She took several shaky steps away from Bram, and her expression changed from fear to disbelief. "This is so weird, and intrusive...you know that, right?"

I did. "I'm sorry we scared you, but this is important."

Maria crossed her arms. "You really are just like her, aren't you? Just as self-righteous and self-important as your sister. You think you can just come here like this? That even if it isn't your sister butchering my friends, which it is, that *you* have the skills to find the killer when the witches council hasn't been able to? The arrogance of your family is astounding."

She seemed to have gotten over her fear quickly. I bit back what I wanted to say because that wouldn't help right then. "Has Chase's condition improved?"

"That's none of your business," she bit out.

"Do you have any enemies? Can you think of anyone who'd want to hurt you or your friends?"

The outrage left her eyes and was replaced with a look that sent a shiver down my spine. "Yes, your psycho sister."

My fingers curled into a fist, and I had to work really hard at controlling my anger. "Why would Willow want to hurt you, Maria? You've had literally nothing to do with each other."

"There's no one else. And your sister has had it in for us since high school. She's hell-bent on sabotaging all of us."

I was starting to think this was a complete waste of time. "You went away to school. She doesn't know you. And why on earth would she risk everything to go on a killing spree targeting your friends?"

Maria planted her hands on her thin hips. "She wrote that awful piece for the high school newspaper her senior year, showing everyone how spiteful and jealous of us she was, and no, I wasn't at the same high school as her, but her attack on my friends was spiteful and cruel. She's held on to that grudge all these years, going out of her way to mess with them. I mean, she set her attack mutt on Isaac's brother! She got her mate to kill for her. How can you be so blind?"

"That was self-defense. *Elmer* tried to kill her. I was there, Warrick did what he had to."

Maria shrugged. "That's what she wanted you to see. What she wanted everyone to see. Maybe she made him attack her? Did you ever think of that? Maybe she hexed him somehow so her mate would kill him? All I know is your sister hates us, and she's made it her life's mission to hurt us at every turn."

She was delusional. "She never talks about any of you, Maria. She doesn't waste time thinking about you, any of you. You said she was holding on to a grudge? Are you saying the article she wrote was some kind of retaliation?"

She colored. "There was this...harmless prank, and she got all bent out of shape."

"What prank?"

She jerked her chin up. "Just kids' stuff. Peroxide in her shampoo."

I remembered that. Willow's hair had ended up with green streaks through it. She'd been allergic to peroxide as well, and she'd been covered in an awful rash. She'd never said what happened, and I assumed she'd tried to dye it herself. I was still pretty young, so no one filled me in on the facts. No wonder Wills wanted revenge back then.

"What your friends did was shitty, but I know my sister and she wouldn't go on a killing spree over something like that, something that happened so long ago. And why now? Why all of a sudden would she come after you and your friends? You have to see how insane that is."

"If she doesn't care about us or what we do, then why did she stop us from buying the property we wanted? She could move her store anywhere, but no. Instead, she rejected our generous offer, then made sure everyone else on the street rejected our offers as well."

"She was protecting her store and the others around her." Wills knew everyone on that street. We all did. The other stores were mainly owned by witches or shifters, and they knew what happened during Willow's trial. One look at Isaac's name and they would have shut him down even without her saying a thing. "She has friends there. Loyal ones. They wouldn't want Isaac there any more than Willow would."

"You think you know your sister, the Keeper, the big deal, but you don't. Isaac was kicked out of an...an exclusive club because of your sister, without explanation, I might add." Her hands shook, her eyes filling with fury. "That was Willow's doing as well."

She was talking about Red, it had to be. "I'd say that probably had more to do with Isaac being a dick than Willow stepping in." I was seriously starting to lose my patience with this nonsense.

"Wrong, Isaac did some digging. Your sister is a friend of the owner—"

"That doesn't mean she had anything to do with him being kicked out."

Her face colored again, with anger this time. "Isaac just wants your awful family to leave him alone, but Willow won't stop. And then there was all the stuff during Iris's task as well. We just want her to leave us alone." A tear streaked down her face. "No, she killed our friends, and she won't stop until we're all dead."

I ground my molars. Maybe I was just a horrible person, but I was struggling to find sympathy for her. "You're wrong."

Her eyes flashed. "She has all this power, and she lords it over everyone. She's selfish and conceited."

What the actual hell was she talking about? "You don't even know her."

Her eyes narrowed. "I know all I need to. She's let power go to her head, then she mated a monster and turned into one. She's as vicious and deranged as the dog she lies down with. Now get the hell out of here before I call the witches council and report you."

Isaac had poisoned her. He'd poisoned all of them against my sister. The guy was a master manipulator, that much was obvious, and Maria had fallen for his bullshit.

There was no talking her around—she clearly couldn't think for herself, and the last thing I needed was the council breathing down my neck. Though, I wouldn't be surprised if she called them, anyway.

Bram scooped me up and dove off the balcony.

"Well, that was a waste of time," I said when he landed.

He gave the back of my neck a gentle squeeze, then released me. "Where to now?" he asked when we got back to the car.

"Let's go to the Golden mansion." I'd tried calling the hospital, but they weren't giving out information on Chase's condition, not unless you were family. I'd lied and said I was Leah, his bitch of a cousin, but then they'd asked for a password. Not surprising since reporters from several Nightscape news and gossip pages had apparently been hounding the hospital staff for details.

So far, Chase was the only one to survive one of these attacks, and people wanted to know all the gory details.

We rolled up to the mansion a short time later, and the gates opened immediately.

I glanced at Bram. "Maria had to have warned everyone about us."

"Without doubt." I'd expected the gates to stay firmly closed and locked, honestly. I'd planned to try to pay off one of their staff members to get the intel. This was definitely a surprise.

Bram parked the car, and we got out as the main door to the

house opened and Leah Golden walked out. *Great. Just freaking wonderful.*

Chase and his cousin weren't all that close from what I'd understood. She certainly didn't look upset as she skipped down the stairs in her short, floaty sundress. She also didn't look my way once. Her eyes were firmly on Bram.

That explains why we were let in so easily.

"Hey," she said as she strode toward us. "Maria called." She glanced at me and screwed up her face. "You scared the hell out of her, and if anyone else was here, they wouldn't have let you in. You're lucky it's just me." She turned to Bram. "I volunteered to house-sit. Chase has a couple dogs that need feeding and..." She motioned to the huge house and grinned. "Staying here is no great hardship." She honest to god batted her lashes at him. "It does get kind of lonely, though, all on my own—"

"How is Chase?" I said, cutting off whatever was about to come out of her mouth next. It didn't take a genius to work out what she was hinting at.

Her gaze sliced back to me. "Why do you want to know? How is it any of your business, Magnolia?"

"I'm sure Maria filled you in. I'm trying to clear my sister's name."

"Good luck with that." She rolled her eyes and dismissed me, turning back to Bram, and the hungry look she gave him lifted my hackles. "How've you been, Bram? I haven't seen you around in a while."

Heat rose from my gut, filling me with instant fire. I didn't like her looking at Bram, let alone talking to him.

His eyes narrowed. "Is Chase still in a coma?" he asked, voice low, clipped, and ignoring her question.

She clasped her hands in front of her, squeezing her boobs together so they bulged out of her dress, and licked her lips. "If you say please, I'll tell you."

Bram's eyes darkened dangerously.

Her eyes went wide, but not from fear, from excitement. She giggled nervously and lightly hit his arm. "I'm just kidding around." She looked at me. "And not that it's any of your business, but yes, he is. The doctors say he'll be like that for a while. He was pretty fucked up when they brought him in, even the best healers said it could take weeks before he's ready to be woken up."

Shit.

She turned back to Bram. "So, um...did Magnolia tell you I was going to call? I tried a few times, but you didn't pick up. I assumed you didn't know it was me." She held out her hand. "Give me your phone and I'll add my number to your contacts, so you know who's calling next time."

"No," Bram said.

She blinked up at him, a confounded look on her face. "No?"

He curled his arm around me, and I leaned into him.

Fury filled her eyes. "You said you weren't together!"

I shrugged. "We weren't, now we are."

"You did that on purpose!" she fired at me.

I laughed, I couldn't help it. "Are you serious?"

"I told you I was interested in him, and you moved in. You couldn't stand that Bram might want me—"

"He doesn't and never did, and I can assure you, Leah, neither of us spared you a thought when we finally got together." I shook my head. "He's my mate. You never stood a chance."

A low laugh rumbled from Bram, dark and sexy, and my belly quivered.

Her mouth pinched up. "Get in your car and get lost, and if you come back, I'll set the dogs on you."

"Thanks for your help," I said, and we got back in and drove away.

Chase had been my best bet.

What the hell was I going to do now?

Chapter Twenty-Four

I scrolled through the articles from the school newspaper. Talon had worked his computer-hacking magic and gotten us access to the high school server.

Most Likely To... by Willow Thornheart.

I clicked the file open and quickly scanned it, and bit back a laugh. "Well, this would've definitely pissed off the prom committee."

Bram read it over my shoulder and grinned. "Yeah, that'd do it."

Robert Hazark: Most likely to get turned on by his own reflection.

Jenna Barlow: Most likely to marry a complete and utter loser.

Chase Golden: Most likely to catch something and have his dick rot and fall off.

Clara Hope: Most likely to live off Daddy's ill-gotten gains.

Calvin Adler: Most likely to marry his cousin.

Katana Adler: See above.

I had no idea how she'd managed to sneak that one into the school paper, but I knew without a doubt that's what happened. No editor would have let that run. "Willow isn't cruel, but she was obviously pissed off. I'd bet anything the peroxide prank wasn't the first either." I turned in my seat to face Bram and sighed. "What does any of this mean? We're not getting anywhere with this. So they hated each other in high school, big freaking deal. Everyone hated me, but you don't see me running around torturing and murdering a bunch of people. They can't seriously believe Willow is doing this because of what happened back then?"

"We know she's innocent, but the evidence is there. The murder at The Cauldron and all the DNA planted there. Her lip-sewing spell being replicated, at least something like it, and Calvin's murder after their altercation at the clubhouse," Bram said from my bed.

He was right, of course, but still. "None of this is making any sense." I rubbed my temples, then covered my face with my hands, trying to keep the out-of-control feeling inside me at bay.

"Hey," he said and came to me, kneeling down beside me. "It's gonna be okay. We'll figure this out."

"What if we can't?" I thought about my sisters and how scared they must've felt, how heavily the burden their own trials must have weighed on them. Rose's was only six months ago, and we were still reeling from the aftermath of it, especially with the sacrifice Zinnia had made for her and the coven.

And before that, Death had come to Rose in her dreams repeatedly, tormenting her, blackmailing her. We'd almost lost her—

An idea struck. "What if...what if I could get inside Chase's head while he's still in a coma?"

"And what? Dig through his memories?"

"I don't know. Maybe I can talk to him, or see what he saw? It has to be there, right? All of it. Including who hurt him."

Bram straightened. "Okay, but how?"

I chewed my lip. It was risky, but it was all I had. "I've heard of a spell, it's...it's forbidden, but—"

"No," Bram said.

"We don't have any real leads, B, we're coming up against brick wall after brick wall. I'm just saying we get our hands on the spell. I don't have to use it, right? It can be a last resort, an insurance policy, if all else fails."

He gripped the side of my chair. "And what happens if you get caught?"

"I won't, and I'm pretty sure I can use it like a blueprint, use the bare bones but change the spell to suit me. I can make it my own, then I wouldn't be breaking any rules, right?" It was a technicality and we both knew it. But I wouldn't let my coven suffer because I failed to do my task, not after all my sisters had been through to get us this far. I'd do whatever it took, they'd done the same, and I wouldn't let all the risks and sacrifices they made be for nothing.

Bram's fingers brushed my arm. "Where's the spell?"

He wasn't going to like this. "It's in an ancient book. It's dark, so dark it can't be kept at the library or the council chambers..." I took a steadying breath. "It's at Shadow Falls."

Bram cursed viciously. "You meddle with that kind of darkness, and the council will come after you."

He was right, of course, but it was a risk I was willing to take. "I'll cover my tracks. I can do it, you know I can. I need you to trust me."

"I fucking do, and you know it. But this?" He shook his head. "It's too dangerous. If they come for you, you'll either end up in Umbra Sanitarium...or worse."

"Agatheena said I can straddle darkness and light, and if I can do that—"

"I don't give a fuck what Agatheena said. It's not her head on the chopping block." He stood and moved to the bed.

I followed and pressed my hands to his chest and pushed. He sat, and I moved in between his thighs, threading my fingers in his hair. "What can I do to ease your worries?" Because I needed to do this, and I needed Bram with me.

He pushed his fingers through the belt loops of my jeans and pulled me closer. "Nothing, and I won't get in your way, as long as you make me a promise."

"What promise?"

His obsidian eyes held mine. "You only use that spell as a last resort, like you said."

"I promise."

He shook his head. "That's not all of it." He tugged me closer. "If you're forced to use it, and for some reason it doesn't go our way...if the council comes for you? You have to let me keep you safe, even if that means I get you the hell out of Roxburgh and we never come back."

I dragged in a breath, but he was right, if the council came for me, we'd have to run. If we didn't, I'd be locked up, or worse. I'd be put to death and my body placed at Shadow Falls with all the other dark witches.

I wouldn't use the spell lightly, and I'd use every precaution. I wouldn't tip the scales into darkness, I was sure of it, but if Bram needed my promise, he had it. "I promise."

~

Bram

We flew over the barren forest, the trees brown and sick or dead. The evil from the falls was so potent it poisoned everything around it. This place had been used as a burial ground by witches for centuries. It was where they put the witches who'd gone dark. Their covens didn't want them in their cemeteries, tainting the earth and their magic. So they brought them here.

Both Willow and Iris came here during their trials, and both nearly didn't make it back out. I wanted to tell Magnolia no. I wanted to fly away from here and not let her walk into that cave. But that wasn't how we did things, or at least it hadn't been before I'd fucked everything up. Mags and I had always been either all in or all out, together, and I was more than familiar with the determined look in her eyes—she'd do anything to save her coven, which meant, like it or not, we were here at this fucking twisted place, because she would come here, with or without me.

We landed on the stone path, and the roar of the falls left no room for anything else, not that there was anything. No wildlife, not even demons came here.

"This way," Mags said and straightened the bag she'd slung over her shoulder. She walked ahead, her lips moving rapidly, chanting a protection spell over and over again. We both knew it wasn't going to do much, but she was hoping it bought us at least a few extra minutes when we walked in there.

The crones who haunted this place couldn't be stopped, not easily. We'd need to be on our guard, and we'd need to move fast.

The path led us behind the falls itself, a furious wall of water on one side and stone on the other. The spray of water hit my over-heated skin and the stone beneath our feet was slippery as hell. I grabbed the back of Magnolia's shirt, terrified she'd fall as we carefully made our way to the cave opening.

The temperature inside was frigid, the air musty. Mags rubbed her arms and looked around the open cavern. The cave went deep into the rock, and I stared into the darkness. I couldn't see a damn thing, but still the hair lifted on the back of my neck.

There was a dais to one side with dried, rusty-colored blood staining its rough stone surface. Mags froze in place as she looked at it, her eyes wide. Willow had almost died right there, and I could see the horror of that in Magnolia's eyes.

"Where's the book?" I said low, trying to pull her from whatever living nightmare was filling her mind.

Mags jolted and turned to me. Her teeth were chattering. "I—I can feel them, the crones. They were at rest here, for so long, but not anymore, and they're...they're so angry," she whispered.

I went for my knife on instinct, even though I knew it was utterly useless. "What do we need to do? We need to move, baby."

Mags turned to the cave wall, where linen-wrapped corpses were tucked into gruesome stone bunk beds. "The book is with a crone named Frances. She was one of the first brought here a really long time ago." She strode to the wall. "Which means she should be at this end somewhere." She slid her hands under one of the bodies, wincing as she felt around, then pulled her arms free before lifting back the linen covering the witch's skull. Shaking her head, she re-covered the bones, then moved to the next.

I tried the one beside her. Nothing. Then lifted back the linen. "What am I looking for?"

"This book is powerful, dangerous. They would've concealed it. Look for unusual markings on the skull." She moved to the next and cursed. "Where the hell is it?" She tilted her head to the side and all color drained from her face.

"What is it?"

Her gaze sliced to me. "They're coming."

Fuck. I moved to the next corpse, jostling it to check underneath. The linen draped across its face fell away. Hollow skeletal eye sockets stared blindly ahead, its jaw hanging open—and there was a symbol carved into the bone. "Here."

Mags rushed over. "This has to be Frances. That's a concealment rune, not one I've ever seen before, but I'm sure that's what it is."

It was the darkest kind of magic, and witches who adhered to their rules and laws wouldn't ever have occasion to see anything like that. Magnolia was walking a dangerous road right now, and I had no idea how to help her. How to keep her safe from what might come of this.

"It's here, it has to be," she said.

Whispers echoed from the shadows, rising from the dark caves beyond the cavern. I couldn't hear what was being said, but the voices were clearly angry. I heard it, felt it. "What do we do?"

She pulled something from her bag and handed it to me. "Surround us with this."

It was a mix of salt, herbs, and cemetery dirt. I quickly did as she instructed as Mags pulled her blade from her pocket and sliced her finger, then traced the rune carved into the skull with her blood.

The scent of my female's blood had the predator in me screeching, clawing to be released. There was nothing my crow could do, though, no physical form to attack, no body to claw. Nothing to kill. I was used to the feeling, the drive to protect when Mags cut herself, but that roar inside me was at a whole new level now. It was so fierce that it was almost impossible to control.

She started chanting.

"Reveal your secrets to me, I command you, show me what I cannot see." Her eyes were wild as she again traced the rune etched into the skull. "Reveal your secrets to me, I command you, show me what I cannot see," she said again, her voice rising, her body shaking harder. "Show me what I cannot see. Show me what I cannot see," she cried as wind whipped around us. The whispers turned to screeches as the spirits of the crones exploded into the cavern. They flew at us, screaming louder when they reached the salt line protecting us, battering it over and over again.

The rune smoldered, then short flames ran along the lines etched into the bone, scorching it.

Magnolia thrust her hands under the body, and this time when she pulled her hands back, she held the book.

"How did you know to do that?"

She glanced at me. "I didn't."

Shit. "How the fuck are we gonna get out of here?" I roared over the crones' furious screaming.

"Overlapping salt circles," she said, quickly and carefully turning the pages of the ancient book.

"Take the book and let's go."

She shook her head. "We can't take it. It's too dangerous." She turned another page, then another.

The salt beside me was slowly being eaten away by the crones' constant attacks.

"Got it," Mags said and pulled out her phone and snapped a picture, shoved the book back where it came from, and covered Frances's skull with linen. Then she held out her hand for the bag of salt.

I handed it to her, and she poured another circle, overlapping the edge of the one we were in. But the crones were working together and the wind they'd created had become a wild storm in the cavern, whipping around us, not letting the salt settle in a thick line. The one surrounding us was thinning with every passing second.

"Fuck," Mags said and reached for something in her bag.

The circle broke—

Cold, grasping hands grabbed me, wrenching me away and tossing me across the cave. My body slammed against the hard stone wall, jarring every bone in my body.

"Bram!" Mags screamed a moment before she was tossed across the cavern as well and pinned to the opposite wall.

I roared, fighting, but the crones were too strong.

A force slammed my head back, and light danced across my vision.

She is ours, a distorted voice whispered in my ear.

Chapter Twenty-Five

Magnolia

The crones' laughter echoed through the room as they attacked Bram. His shirt was torn off and scratches were appearing across his skin, then bruises, slices.

"Let him go!" I screamed, fighting. "Please, let him go!"

The crones hissed with fury, ignoring my pleas, holding me fast.

You're staying with us, little witch.

You are ours.

We're going to make you bleed.

Tear you limb from limb.

Their whispers filled my head, their cold breath brushing my skin and chilling me to the bone. Bram roared, fighting, blood dripping from his body and down his face.

This wasn't happening. I wouldn't let it. No one I loved was getting hurt, not again, not because of me.

I screamed in fear, in rage, and words filled my head. A spell swirled, coming from deep inside me. Again, somehow, I just knew what I needed to do.

My hands were being forced against the wall. I fought, managing to get my knife from my pocket, and carved a hexagon into my palm, one inside the other, then sliced across them from point to point until the lines crisscrossed my palm, and I repeated the words filling my head. "Hear me, darkness, crawl from your slumber deep in the shadows and leash these restless souls, bind the evil in their bones, and thrust them back from where they came." Hissing through my teeth, I lifted my hand. "Eyes blinded with blood. Hands, feet, mouths bound with skin," I yelled, then slammed my palm against the stone wall with a cry.

Fire burned through my hand, blasting, exploding inside me. I screamed as a force flowed from me, a wall of magic pouring from my body, so heavy and wild that it threw the souls back, dragging them screaming back down into the caves they'd come from. I dropped to the floor, and silence filled the cavern again.

Bram hit the ground, and I scrambled to my feet, running for him. "Bram? Oh, goddess, what did they do to you?"

He coughed, then staggered to his feet. "I'm okay. Let's just get the fuck out of here."

I wrapped my arm around his waist, and we stumbled across the cavern and out through the wide entrance, then ran along the path under the falls. I stopped as soon as we were far enough away. "Let me see you?"

He leaned against the trunk of a dead tree, and I cupped his face, taking in the scratches just below his eyes, letting my hands hover an inch above his chest, using my magic to search for any serious injuries. There was nothing life threatening, but he was cut up badly. "You're okay, you're going to be okay."

He fisted my shirt at my belly, pulling me closer. "What the fuck happened back there?"

"I don't know, they were...so much stronger than I thought

they'd be. I'm sorry. I almost got us killed." I rested my hands against his chest, then I pulled the one I'd cut back with a hiss.

Bram grabbed my wrist.

"What the fuck did you do to yourself?" He uncurled my fingers.

"I don't know." The design I'd carved into my hand had welted, now puffy like badly healed scar tissue. "They were attacking you, and a spell...it just...it came to me. It flowed through me and forced them back."

"It just came to you?"

"Yes." I didn't want to think about what that meant. Not yet.

I quickly checked the photo I'd taken on my phone, worried that somehow the crones had wiped it clean or somehow messed with it, but thankfully, it was still there.

"That ever happen before?" he asked as he pulled a small jar of healing balm from his pocket and smeared it across my palm.

"Kind of." I quickly scanned the spell.

"Should we be worried about that?"

I didn't look up. I didn't want him to see the worry in my own eyes.

"Magnolia? Should we be worried about it?"

I forced myself to look at him. "Honestly? I don't know. There's no one I can ask." I looked back down at the spell, not wanting to talk about it anymore. I'd worry about that later, after I'd found the killer. "So this isn't just a spell...there's a potion as well. These ingredients, some of them I've never used before."

"You don't need to worry about it yet, though, right?" Bram said, letting me change the subject.

"Right." But something told me it was only a matter of when, not if I was going to need it. That was why I'd come here today, that feeling was too strong to ignore. Yes, I'd try to pass this task without it, but this spell, it might be the only way to save my coven.

Bram tugged on my shirt again. "Ready?"

I nodded, and he lifted me into his arms. His blood instantly soaked through my shirt, and I felt enraged all over again. "I need to look after your wounds."

"They're superficial," he said as we lifted off.

Bram flew fast, and I could hear his heart pounding hard against me. I held on to him, even though I felt impossibly raw right then.

As the minutes ticked by, my scars began to tingle, itch, they started to burn hot, painful.

Not now. I wanted to fucking scream in frustration.

The urge to pull away, to escape Bram's touch, hit me hard, but that was impossible while we were in the air. My anger rose because I fucking hated that right then, being in Bram's arms was close to actual torture.

Goddess, it hurt. So bad.

When we finally landed, I was breathing heavily, ready to scratch my own skin off.

"Mags?" Bram asked when I pulled away, stumbling back.

"My scars," I said, fighting back all I was feeling. I didn't want him to see the truth of just how bad it'd gotten. I didn't want him to see that his touch had hurt me because that would hurt him, and I couldn't bear it.

He stepped forward, reaching for me, and I stepped back, cringing away from him.

Bram froze, his dark eyes missing none of it. "You're in pain."

"I'll be okay."

He lifted his hands. "I'm not gonna touch you, I promise."

"I'll be okay in a minute. Just give me a minute." I motioned to the bedroom door. "Let me look after you, please. That's what I need right now. Let me take care of your wounds."

He watched me closely, then nodded and did as I asked, walking into the room and sitting on the edge of the bed for me, like we'd done so many times before. I rushed to the bathroom on shaky legs and grabbed my basket.

Bram's gaze didn't leave me as I took out my mortar and pestle and several bags of herbs, dropping a small spoon of each into the stone bowl. "We need to cleanse as well as heal. I don't know what those twisted bitches did to you, but they were able to cut you, and I don't want their evil anywhere on you." I added some lavender oil and worked it and the herbs into a paste, followed by a scoop of healing balm. I mixed it all together, then, holding my hand over the potion, I let my magic pulse through me and into it, whispering a spell to increase its power.

"Put that on your hand first," he said, watching me.

"I will, I just need to—"

"No. You first," he said. "Now. I would, but..."

But right then, I'd pull away if he even tried. I quickly did as he asked, smearing some over the angry new scar on my hand, then grabbed a cotton pad and started on Bram, smearing it over all the cuts and scratches, the bruises they'd given him. "Bitches," I muttered.

Bram was quiet for several seconds. "One of them spoke to me."

"What did they say?"

"That you were theirs."

A shiver moved through me. "Well, they were wrong. And I won't ever be going back to that place, so they're shit out of luck." At least while I was alive. If this mark on my hand meant what I thought it did, my family might have no choice but to put me there one day, anyway. The darkness in me might be too great.

"No," Bram growled out. "You won't ever go back, and if you even think about it, I'll fucking tie you down and never let you out of my sight."

Instead of being irritated at his order, my body heated, my belly doing that swirling thing it did around him. "Is that so?"

"Yes."

"Did I tell you how bossy you've gotten lately?" I said and

swiped some of the healing oil over another scratch on his chest. Bram was silent again, and I looked up.

His gaze locked with mine, then he shook his head. "No, but I'm not too worried."

My heart raced faster. "Oh? And why is that?"

His nostrils flared and he breathed deep. "Because you love it."

My face heated, but I didn't look away. "Caught that, did you?"

"Yeah, I fucking did," he said, his voice gravelly as hell.

I carried on, cleaning and treating the wounds on his chest, while his gaze burned into me. I felt the hunger rolling off him, but he didn't move, didn't attempt to touch me or kiss me or pull me closer. I loved him for it and wanted to cry at the same time.

"It's okay," he said.

I kept my head down. "No...it's not."

"We talked about this, Mags. I want you, of course I do, but this is enough. You think I lied about that?"

I shook my head.

"Good."

"But Wills and Warrick and Iris and Daven, Rose and Ronan—"

"Aren't us. We'll work out our own thing, yeah? And who says we have to touch each other to give pleasure. There are other things we can do," he said roughly.

"There is?"

He nodded. "But right now, we're going to talk through what we know about this task," he said, changing the subject, trying to distract me. "Okay? So tell me what you know so far."

I wanted him to elaborate on the "things we can do," but I felt too raw to go there right then, and Bram knew it, hence the change of subject. "We know a group of friends and the people close to them are being targeted, tortured, and killed. Body parts, skin, and other organs have been taken from each scene for reasons unknown, and all have had judgment carved into their skin."

Bram nodded. "What else?"

"We know the prom committee's relationships aren't platonic. They partake in group sex, they frequent Brent Silva's club, Red. And after what I saw at the Hazarks', we know they sometimes bring others into their circle. Like Isaac, Maria, and Ryan. All of whom are also members of Red, well, except for Isaac who was kicked out. They're in each other's pockets, and they've been that way since they were teenagers."

"They're convinced Willow is the one hunting them," Bram said. "Someone planted evidence at The Cauldron, and they're using some old high school resentment, and Isaac's investment company, trying to buy Willow's store, as well as the death of his brother and Willow's supposed grudge against his family as a motive. And they pranked Willow, right? I doubt she's the only one they did that shit to. They're entitled assholes, all of them. We've seen them in action. I have no doubt they were the bullies in high school. We've been searching for someone they fucked with recently, but maybe we need to go back farther than that."

"Like another high school prank gone wrong?"

Bram shrugged. "They were dicks to Wills; it's easy to assume they were dicks to a lot of other people as well."

"You think someone could hold a grudge that long?"

"If the damage they'd caused was bad enough? Yeah, I do."

Chapter Twenty-Six

Magnolia

"Do you think Chloe knows anything?" I asked Bram as we walked out of her office.

Chloe Chan was all about money, and the prom committee had that in spades. The wolf shifter made a killing off them, no pun intended, as their sole realtor.

"It doesn't make sense to kill them off," Bram said.

This was true. I couldn't see her cooking the geese that laid all the golden eggs.

We'd started with the two members of Red who were in business with or worked for the group, then narrowed it down to those who were also Roxburgh High School alumni. If that didn't bear fruit, we'd have to cast a wider net.

Thankfully, Chloe was several years older than me and had left school before I started, so didn't recognize me when we showed up. She bought my fake name and our ruse as organizers of the next RHS reunion and that we were after stories to include in a reunion yearbook. High school was hard for a lot of people, and those people tended to remember the assholes, the kids they'd been forced to avoid in the halls or the cafeteria.

But Chloe hadn't fallen for my attempt to draw her into any "off the record" gossip. No, she wasn't going to say a bad word about any of them, not when the prom committee funded her very nice lifestyle.

We got in the car as another pulled up across the street. "Is that Ryan Alway?" He got out of his car, and Chloe strutted out of her office.

"Yep."

She smiled wide and strode over to him. They kissed, deeply, then she got in his car and they drove away.

"Ryan sure likes mixing business with pleasure."

"I guess they work closely. Ryan and Chloe most likely scout out potential investment properties before they take it to Isaac and the other shareholders."

I locked this new bit of info away with everything else, and we headed for Luke Donaghy's office next. Going by the yearbook we'd taken from the library, Luke hadn't been one of the cool kids. He'd been awkward, kind of nerdy, the skinny mathlete with glasses and braces.

And a far cry from the male who'd rolled back into Roxburgh six months ago, quickly making a name for himself as the kind of guy you did not want to fuck with—and not just in business—and he'd most definitely grown out of his awkward phase.

"Do you think the rumors about Luke are true?" I asked Bram. Luke had been the same year as Willow. They hadn't been friends, as far as I knew, but they'd shared several classes together.

Bram stared ahead, but his fingers tightened on the wheel. "I know they are."

"You think he's capable of murder?"

"Yes."

I turned in my seat. "So you know him?"

He shook his head. "I know of him, because that's the world I'm part of and because he likes people to know. He also introduced himself to Payne not long after he moved back."

"What did Payne think of him?"

"He said he'd prefer to work with him than against him," Bram said. "Payne couldn't work out what he was, though. Shifter, most likely, at least that's what he puts out there. Luke wasn't forthcoming, but he's powerful."

"So he could totally be our killer?" I said, beginning to feel a little edgy meeting this guy.

"It's possible."

"Oh goody." We'd called and made an appointment to see him, using the same school reunion bullshit and, surprisingly, he'd agreed to see us.

Bram parked the car, and I looked out the window and up at the building where Luke had his offices. It was architecturally designed by an award-winning architect, twenty stories high and made of black iron with tinted windows. It looked like some dark lair, or the fortress of some evil, maniacal supervillain. "What's his line of business?"

"He calls himself an entrepreneur and has his fingers in all sorts of pies," Bram said.

"Sounds messy."

"Oh yeah, from what I hear, he's more than happy to get his hands dirty." Bram glanced my way. "I'm not sure going to see this guy is a good idea."

It was probably a terrible idea, but we needed to do this. Not only was I feeling the call from my task but my inner spidey senses were definitely telling me I needed to speak to this guy. "I feel drawn to this place, Bram. We need to do this."

The muscle in his jaw jumped. "Fine, but if I decide we need to leave, we're getting the fuck out of there, yeah?"

I nodded my agreement and reached for the door handle. Bram tugged the sleeve of my shirt, stopping me.

I turned back and he leaned forward, his eyes dark and hot as they held mine before they dipped to my mouth and back up. "But first, I want you to kiss me."

The gravel in his voice had tingles dancing all over me. He was being careful, not touching me, not even brushing his fingers over my skin, but still letting me know that he wanted me. A kiss I could handle, and I instantly gave him what he asked for, resting my hand on his chest, I leaned forward and pressed my mouth against his. Heat spiraled through me, and I cupped his jaw, my thumb brushing across the corner of his mouth. Bram groaned and licked the seam of my lips, and I opened for him immediately.

"Can I touch your hair?" he said roughly against my lips.

"Yes."

He instantly gripped a handful in his fist and tilted my head to the side so he could kiss me harder, deeper, his hunger for me unmistakable. I didn't want to stop, there was no way I could pull away, but eventually, he slowed things down and lifted his head.

"That was...nice," I said and grinned up at him.

"Nice?"

"Okay, stupidly hot."

He licked his lips. "Definitely a more accurate description."

I hadn't been able to stop thinking about what he said last night, and that kiss had his words flying around my head again.

"What is it?" he said, seeing right through me.

My cheeks warmed. "It's nothing."

He grabbed my shirt at my belly, fisting it, stopping my retreat, but again being careful not to touch me. "It's not nothing. Talk to me."

"Bram...honestly, it's nothing."

He studied me for several seconds, and I thought he'd drop it. Instead, he leaned closer. "I'm your male, Magnolia. We may not have mated yet, but we should be able to talk about anything, no matter how hard, or"—he swiped his fingers over my hot cheek, allowing himself that brief contact—"embarrassed we are."

"I'm not embarrassed," I said, and I wasn't totally lying.

"Good, so tell me what you're thinking."

I blew out a breath, attempting to steady the butterflies in my belly. "I've been thinking about what you said...last night."

"What did I say?" he said, but judging by the way his gaze had heated, he knew exactly what I was talking about.

"Don't play with me, B. You know exactly what I'm talking about," I said.

"I haven't even begun to play with you, Mags," he said, his voice so impossibly deep I barely suppressed a shiver. "I've had a long time to think about it, what I want to do to you. I tried not to, I did, but there was no stopping my mind conjuring up all kinds of dirty shit. All the things I'd do if you were mine."

Guilt and frustration filled me. "But my scars, I'm not sure I can—"

"You saw me, didn't you?" he said, tugging on my shirt again. "That night I left your room while you slept. When I came back, you were in bed, but you were faking it, weren't you, baby?"

Oh goddess. I swallowed, audibly. "Yes."

"I woke up beside you, and I was so fucking hard, wanting you, I had to go to the tree house and get in the shower. I told myself I just needed the cold water to cool me down, that I had to stop thinking about you like that, but there was no stopping it, and I closed my eyes and let the fantasies play out. After that, I had no choice but to stroke my cock while thinking of you, and it wasn't the first time, Mags." He tucked my hair behind my ear. "You saw me, didn't you?" he asked again.

I nodded, struggling to breathe. "Yes." I gripped the side of his neck. "And you were...goddess, so beautiful."

His nostrils flared. "You liked it. You liked watching me?"

I nodded again.

"Have you ever thought about me like that? Have you ever touched yourself while you did?" he rasped.

I blew out a shaky breath. "Yes."

Bram's chest was rising and falling rapidly, and a husky *caw* rose in his throat. "You have?"

"Yes."

"Fuck," he snarled.

"That's what you were talking about? When you said there were other things we could do? You were talking about us doing that...together?" I said.

His mouth was so close now, his breath brushing my lips when he spoke. "Would you? Would you do that? Touch yourself and let me watch?"

His black eyes were locked on mine, the heat of him, his scent filling my head, making me freaking dizzy. "Yes. Will you?"

"Yes," he said without hesitation.

I wanted him, really, really badly.

A shudder moved through him, and his nostrils flared. "How the fuck am I going to think about anything else now?"

A car horn blasted somewhere nearby, jolting us from the intimacy of the moment. I cleared my throat. "I ah...I guess we better go in."

"I guess so," he said and tugged on my shirt one more time before releasing it.

"You think you can manage to hold my hand?" he asked.

I took his. "Yeah." My hands had the least amount of damage, and holding hands was usually fine, but with the way my scars had been lately, I wasn't sure how much longer that would last. There was no pain now, though, no burning when his skin touched mine. I'd been trying not to think about it, why the pain was getting worse, but something was very wrong, and we both knew it. It wasn't just because of what Clayton did to me. There was something else, something inside me, and it was growing in strength.

We walked into the building, got in the elevator, and I hit the button for the fifth floor.

"You should probably take your hair down. If he's a shifter and he sees your markers, he'll know what you are," I said.

Bram gripped my hand tighter. "I don't think putting my hair down will hide it, not with this guy." He pulled the hair tie out anyway, letting his hair fall around his face. "But no reason to broadcast it."

The doors slid open, and we strode up to the reception desk.

"We have an appointment with Luke Donaghy," I said to the receptionist. He asked for our names. "Brad and Magda. We're here about the Roxburgh High School reunion."

The guy smiled. "Ah, yes. He's expecting you. Go through."

"Thanks."

"Brad and Magda?" Bram said, lips twitching as we headed for the office door.

"I thought they were the closest to our own names, less chance to mess up." I grinned up at him.

"After today, if you ever call me Brad again, we'll have a serious problem," he said, an expression on his face that had me biting back a grin.

"Hey, you could totally be a Brad. You've got those big shoulders now. You could be the quarterback of the football team, Brad." If quarterbacks were dark goths with murderous tendencies. Bram was so far from a Brad it wasn't funny.

"Would a Brad sit you in a chair, strap your legs wide, and make you play with yourself until you come so many times you passed the fuck out?" he said.

I sucked in a sharp breath, my gaze flying to him. Bram laughed, and it was dark and dirty. A throb started between my thighs. "That wasn't fair."

"Oh, I'm definitely not planning on playing fair," he said, then knocked on the door before I could reply.

A deep, masculine voice called for us to come in.

Bram opened the door and walked in, and I followed, trying to focus on why we were here and not the images now filling my head.

Luke sat behind a massive desk. The wall behind him was all glass and the view utterly breathtaking. "Brad and Magda?" he said and stood.

Bram stepped forward and shook his hand. Luke looked at me, and I waved instead. I could hold Bram's hand, but the idea of touching anyone else sent more dread through me.

He frowned, but then motioned to the chairs opposite him. "Please, take a seat."

I pulled a notepad and a pen from my bag and we both sat. "Thanks so much for agreeing to speak with us, Mr. Donaghy."

"Call me Luke." His sharp gaze moved over me before sliding to Bram.

"We're gathering stories from past students of Roxburgh High School, for a reunion yearbook. And as a successful Roxburgh High alum we thought you might have some fun stories to share? We'll include a brief bio as well, just a few details about you alongside it. What you're doing now, that sort of thing," I said, spouting the bullshit I'd come up with.

He sat back. "I don't really have many fond memories from my time at RHS, if you want the truth. I was a bit of a loner."

I grinned. "You and me both. I spent most of my time in the library."

"So did I." His gaze darkened. "I'm positive I'd remember you, Magda. How old are you, sweetheart?"

Bram froze beside me a moment before his hand came down on my knee, in a tight possessive grip. Pain instantly fired through me, my scars burning under my skin. I jolted, and he immediately pulled his hand back with a hiss.

"You okay?" he asked, alarm in his voice.

He'd felt territorial and his instincts had taken over completely. "Of course." I smiled at Luke and forced a chuckle. "I fell over this morning and grazed my knee. Don't mind us."

Luke tilted his head back...then breathed deep. His lids fluttered. "*Mmm*, you smell good. Very good, but I don't smell blood, Magda." His gaze was hot when he refocused on me. "I wonder why you're lying to me?"

Bram shot to his feet. "You smell my female again and I'll tear your fucking face off."

Luke slowly rose from his chair, buttoning his suit jacket as he did. "Finally, a little honesty. And you can try it, boy."

Bram took a step forward, and I jumped to my feet, getting between them. "Let's all just calm down, okay?"

"Why are you here?" Luke demanded. "Because you're sure as fuck not working on some nonexistent high school reunion." His gaze slid to Bram over my head. "And I can smell the death all over you, crow. You can hide your markers, but I see right through you."

"He's not here for you," I said to Luke. "He's helping me."

"Oh, I know he's not here for me," the other male said. "If I thought he was, he'd already be dead."

Bram laughed; it was cold and nasty. "I'm sure my other kills thought the same thing, unfortunately I can't ask them, since they're all rotting in the ground."

Luke snarled and leaned forward, planting his hands on his desk.

"We're sorry we lied about our reason for being here," I said quickly, before he bounded over that wide desk and all hell broke loose. "Bram definitely isn't here to...kill you." I couldn't believe those words just came out of my mouth, like it was a reasonable clarification. "But I do need to ask you some questions."

"I'm not sure why you think I'd answer," he said, his expression now stoic, even though fury still burned in his eyes.

"I know we went about this the wrong way, but I would really appreciate it." He was about to tell us to get lost, I could see it all over his face. "You might remember my sister Willow? Willow

Thornheart. She was the same year as you. I think you shared a few classes?"

He stilled, then straightened. "You're Willow's sister?"

I didn't know if he and Willow knew each other well, but I knew my sister was a good person. She sure as hell hadn't been cruel or a bully in high school. "Yes, and I'm sure you've heard the accusations being made against her."

"I have. They're utter bullshit, of course," he said, surprising me.

"You don't think she's guilty?"

His glaze flicked to Bram, then he slowly sat back in his chair, so I did the same. Then I grabbed Bram's hand and tugged him down as well when he continued to loom.

"No," Luke said. "I don't."

Was that because he knew my sister wasn't the murdering kind or because he was the one doing the murdering? "So you remember her from school?"

"She was one of the few people who were kind to me back then." He smiled and it was...terrifying. "She spoke up more than once when I was outnumbered and getting the shit kicked out of me."

"Why did they pick on you?" I asked, genuinely interested but also trying to get him to open up.

He tapped a finger on his desk. "Because they didn't know what I was. They sensed something...something wasn't right. I scared them, I guess, so they attacked first."

I wanted to ask what he was, but I didn't think he'd like that, especially since he seemed to have gone to a lot of trouble to hide it. "Did you ever have any trouble with Robert and Jenna Hazark, or Chase Golden, Clara Hope or Calvin Adler and his cousin Katana? I know you do business with them now, and move in the same...um, circles, but they were a tight group even back then, and I get the feeling they weren't the nicest in high school."

He studied me for several seconds. "They were bullies then and now. Narcissists, all of them. I've enjoyed coming back and... repaying them for their treatment of me and a few others from back then."

"Does repayment include torture and disembowelment?" Bram asked.

Luke smiled, but it didn't reach his eyes.

Bram stared back. "How about removing and collecting limbs?"

"You think I'm killing them off?" Luke asked.

"Are you?" Bram asked without looking away.

"Do I look like a vicious killer, sweetheart?" Luke asked, turning back to me.

Well, yeah, he kind of did.

"I mean, you'd know," he said and tilted his head toward Bram.

Bram bared his teeth.

Okay, testosterone was flying all over the damn place. We needed to move this along. "Can you remember anyone else they bullied back then?"

"You're grasping at straws, you know that, don't you?" Luke said.

"Maybe. Humor me."

A small smile curled his lips, and this time it did reach his cool blue eyes. They actually sparkled. It was unsettling as hell. "I like you, sweetheart, you're tenacious."

"She's not your sweetheart. Say it again and I'll slit your fucking throat," Bram said.

Luke didn't spare him a glance, but the muscle in his jaw pulsed. "The only reason you're still sitting in my office and not out on your asses is because I liked Willow. She was a good person, and I haven't encountered many of them over the years. Yes, they fucked with other kids. Mainly those younger than them. There was a group of kids that hung out at the library, a poetry group. They were their number one targets."

"Can you give us names?"

"No. As I said, I was a loner."

"Is there anything else you can tell us?" I said.

"No." Luke stood. "Now get the fuck out of my office."

"Thank you for your time." I grabbed Bram's hand, tugging him from his seat and dragged him from the room and into the elevator.

I blew out a frustrated breath and turned to him as the doors slid shut in front of us. "Well, you were in fine form back there."

"He was looking at you like he wanted to fuck you," Bram said by way of explanation.

I thought he looked at me like he wanted to take a bite out of me, and not the good kind. "Do you think he's our killer?"

"He's capable of it," Bram said, then shook his head. "But I don't think so."

Shit.

I didn't think so either. "The yearbook, the one with Willow's piece in it, there were several poems scattered through it as well, I'm sure of it."

Maybe one of them was our killer? Or maybe it was time to cast that wider net? I wasn't sure. I wasn't sure of any fucking thing.

Chapter Twenty-Seven

I flicked through the yearbook. I'd showered while Bram had heated us up the dinner Mom left for us, and now we were back to scouring for clues.

"You find any?" Bram asked, sitting on the couch opposite me.

"Two. The first was by Maria's brother, Marcel, the one who passed away in some accident with his younger sister, and it's seriously dark." It was called "In the Dead of the Night." "If the guy hadn't been dead for years, this would put him at the top of my serial killer suspect list."

I leaned forward on my wooden kitchen chair, and turned the book so Bram could read it. He scanned the poem, and I knew when he screwed up his face that he'd gotten to the bit about stabbing his broken heart and letting it bleed into the mouth of the person who broke it, so they could taste his pain. "Fucking hell," he muttered.

"My thoughts exactly. There's another one." I flipped the page. "By a guy named Thomas Alway."

Bram looked over at me. "A relative of Ryan's?"

"That'd be my guess." I crossed my legs, and his dark gaze slid over my bare skin. My belly swirled.

"Any good?"

"It's about a flower."

"Sounds riveting." Bram flipped a few more pages. "There any pictures of the poetry group in here?"

"None." I was guessing they were lucky to get their poems in the yearbook, let alone a photo as well.

He nodded, then looked back up at me. His stare was intense. "Love it when you wear my shirts," he said.

"Yeah?" There was another swirl, this one dipping lower. I'd put one on after my shower.

He nodded and moistened his lips. "Nearly every one I own, you've worn. I used to think about how they'd been against your bare skin." His gaze grew darker still. "You ever notice that I always wore whatever shirt you'd slept in the night before?"

I hadn't thought too much about it. I usually tossed the one I'd worn on his bed after I dressed, I'd assumed he'd just grabbed the first one he saw. "You did it on purpose?"

"Fuck yeah. Your scent was all over it, and knowing your bare skin had been right up against it and was now right up against mine, it helped satisfy the possessive male in me."

I'd had no idea. None. "And how does it make you feel now?" I asked, my heart racing faster, an ache building between my thighs.

"Like a fucking caveman." His gaze dipped to my legs again. "I can smell how wet you're getting, Mags, and every time you cross and uncross your legs, I'm tipping closer and closer to the edge."

"What do you want to do?" I asked, the pounding of my heart making my voice quiver.

His nostrils flared. "I want you to spread your legs wide for me and let me taste you." He shook his head. "The last fucking thing I want is to hurt you, baby. I know your scars are causing you pain, but knowing you need me, that you're aching for me, my crow is growing restless. No pressure, okay? You don't want it, we wait until you do. But know the only part of me that would touch you, is my mouth against your hot, little pussy."

His chest was rising and falling fast, watching, waiting for what I'd say. I was breathing hard as well now, my skin burning up, but for once it was in a good way. I placed the yearbook on the floor, and slowly uncrossed my legs. "I want it."

"You sure? I don't want to make you—"

"You're not making me do anything. I want it. Please," I whispered.

He bared his teeth and it was wicked and sexy as hell. "Panties off, baby."

I stood and slid them down my legs, kicking them aside.

"Sit back in the chair, ass on the edge."

I did as he asked, excited, wanting what he said so bad.

He got off the couch and sat on the floor, then positioned his legs between the wooden legs of the chair I was on, before gripping them and dragging, it and me, right up to him. My legs had nowhere to go and I automatically spread them wide.

Bram's face was level with my bare pussy.

"Legs on the couch either side of me, and lean back," he rasped.

I did, bending my knees, and bracing my legs either side of him, before leaning back. I was already wet, the ache inside growing unbearable. "Bram," I whimpered.

"Lift the shirt and show me how wet you are."

My hand trembled as I did as he asked. I was hot and flushed, and needy as hell.

Bram groaned. "Fuck. Look at you." He looked up at me. "Fucking dreamed of this. You have no idea how long I've thought about how you'd taste, Magnolia. I thought it was a craving that I'd never get to satisfy, a secret you'd never share with me." His biceps bunched and he tugged the chair closer and breathed deep, and his eyes drifted shut on a full-body shudder. "Fist my hair, move me how you want me, take what you want, rub, grind, do whatever the fuck feels good."

I slid my fingers into his hair and whimpered again at the picture he painted, at the feel of his hot breath against my bare, damp flesh.

Then he leaned in, closing the small space between us and covered my pussy with his mouth, then dragging his tongue through my slick flesh with a deep groan. I pushed back against the chair, fisted his hair tighter, and spread wider for him.

Bram's eyes were closed, lashes fluttering as he feasted on me. Sucking and licking me, exploring every inch. He opened his eyes as he swirled his tongue around my clit, then sucked on it gently. I cried out, my stomach quivering, my legs shaking. He worked me until I couldn't stop myself from grinding against his mouth.

"Can you take one of my fingers?" he growled.

"D-do it."

Bram flicked his tongue over my clit as he slid a long, thick finger inside me. I arched against the seat with a groan and rocked against his hand. He started fucking me with his finger then, and working my clit, sucking and licking it so good.

My orgasm roared up on me, slamming through me and I cried out, coming hard, my inner muscles clutching and gripping around his finger.

Finally, I collapsed back and Bram lapped at me gently setting off delicious aftershocks, before sliding out his finger. I looked down at him, watching as he slid it into his mouth and sucked it clean.

"Good?" I asked.

"What do you think?" he said, his voice little more than a snarl.

"Fuck, Mags, I want to live right fucking there, between your thighs."

I stood on shaky legs and shoved the chair out of the way, then dropped to my knees, reaching for the front of his pants, and yanked them open.

"Mags?"

"Now it's my turn," I said, tugging down his jeans and underwear. His hard cock sprang free.

"I don't expect you—"

I sucked his long, thick cock deep into my mouth as deep as I could. I wasn't ready for everything, not yet, but I wanted to give him this. I could do this for him. I wanted to, badly.

Bram barked out a curse, his hips lifting.

I had no idea what I was doing, I just knew I wanted to make him feel as good as he'd made me feel. I wanted to know his taste. I wanted to know everything. He was too long to take all of him, so I stroked the base the way I had at the lookout, while I sucked and licked the rest.

His fingers thrust into my hair and the sounds that came from him made me hot and bothered all over again.

I sucked him harder, faster, over and over again.

He hissed through clenched teeth. "I can't...I can't hold back, baby. I can't..." His cock pulsed in my hand a moment before his come flooded my mouth. He called out my name, fisting my hair, his hips thrusting and twisting beneath me.

I swallowed him down, and kept sucking him until he was done. When I released his cock, he loosened his grip on my hair and brushed it away from my face, before tilting my head back. His gaze was full of a dark possessiveness I'd never seen before. I loved it.

He swiped his thumb over my swollen lips. "Maggie," he rasped.

That's all he said, all he needed to say. It was all there in my name. I was his, and he was mine, no matter what.

He pulled me in for a gentle kiss and I wanted to curl up in his lap and stay there forever, but I couldn't, the scars on my body wouldn't let me have that.

A thump came from outside the tree house, followed by a bang on the door. I lifted my head, my stomach sinking because I instantly knew who it was and what it meant.

Bram cursed as he stood, and helped me up. He tugged down my shirt and wrapped the blanket on the back of the couch around my shoulders.

Tucking himself back in his jeans and doing them up, Bram strode to the door, that he'd thankfully started locking, and opened it.

Rook stood there, his expression almost violent, but then that was how he always looked. "You're needed," he said and didn't elaborate, he didn't need to.

"No one else can handle it?" Bram asked.

Rook shook his head.

"Payne and Talon?"

"Another hunt," he said and ducked back out.

Bram's jaw tightened.

"Go." I hadn't missed how aggressive Bram had become the last few days. He needed this.

The muscles and tendons in his forearms bunched. "You sure?" he asked, and I could see the conflict in his eyes.

I curled my fingers around his. "You'll be back as soon as you can, and I'll be careful."

"You'll call Ash?"

"I will."

Bram closed the space between us. "I'll be as quick as I can."

"I know." I dropped the blanket when Bram gripped either side of my shirt at my waist. Holding the fabric tight, he pulled me close without actually touching my skin, then leaned in and kissed me. I could taste myself on his lips.

"I don't wanna leave you," he said against my mouth, a growl in his voice.

"You'll be back before we know it."

He held my shirt more firmly, the fabric tightening around my waist, almost having the same effect as a hug, before he released me and stepped back. The lack of contact was killing me, and I could see Bram was struggling as badly as I was without it. We'd gotten each other off, and it was amazing, but what would have made it even better? Lying in his arms afterwards. We both still needed more.

"Be safe," he said, then with one last quick press of his lips to mine, he walked out and closed the door behind him.

I stood there and stared at that door for far longer than was sane. Shaking myself out of it, I finally sat and jotted down everything I knew. Isaac's name glared up at me. On a whim, I pulled out my phone and hit Brent's number.

He answered on the third ring. "Yeah?"

"Hey, it's Magnolia. I know you have a whole confidentiality thing, but I wanted to ask you something."

There was a beat of silence. "You can ask."

"Why did you end Isaac Eldridge's membership?"

Another beat. "Usually, I wouldn't tell you shit, but I think we've already crossed that bridge. I kicked his ass out because he was getting too rough with females who weren't into pain. He crossed the line. And I would have kicked him out sooner, but the females in question only came forward after I saw it myself."

I recoiled. "So you're saying he has an aggressive streak?"

"Yes. And there's something else, something I hadn't really thought too much about until now. They were all redheads. I just assumed that was his type, but the level of violence he was dishing out, it was more than that."

Fuck. "Thanks, Brent."

We ended the call, and I instantly hit Asher's number.

She answered on the second ring. "What's doing, feisty?"

"You free?"

"Yep. Where are we going?"

It was dark by the time I pulled up outside Ryan Alway's apartment. Clouds had gathered, rain was brewing, and it was muggy as hell. But this was where I was supposed to be. I had planned to go to Isaac's place, but the moment I got in the car, the vines had started tingling in the middle of my back and I'd been led here. What part Ryan played in all this, I had no idea, but going by the alarm bells wailing through my head, there was definitely a link between him and my task.

It was hot, and I yanked up my sleeves as I looked up at the second floor. The lights were on at Ryan's place, and I could see a shadow moving behind the curtains. He was home, thank fuck. As soon as Asher got here, we'd head up.

Ryan knew something, that much was obvious, and I wasn't leaving until I'd extracted every bit of information I could from the little creep. That night at the Hazarks', the way he'd been with Jenna, the look in his eyes—I shuddered—Isaac wasn't the only one with a violent streak. The guy had given me the major icks.

The door to the building opened and Ryan strode out, heading down the street, hands in pockets, whistling while he walked. *Shit.* My internal alarm wailed again, screaming at me to follow.

I had no choice. I followed my instincts. I quickly texted Ash, letting her know the direction I was headed. Ryan walked faster, carrying on for a couple blocks, and I was forced to pick up the pace to keep up with him. He turned down the next street, and I jogged after him, rounding the corner—

Fuck.

I slammed on the brakes.

He was leaning against the building, arms crossed, waiting for me with a smirk on his face. "You're not very good at the whole stealth thing, are you, Magnolia?" he said, gaze burning into me.

My heart kicked to life in my chest, and I forced a chuckle. "Obviously not. When did you make me?"

"I saw you sitting in your piece-of-shit car outside my very nice apartment. What the fuck do you want?" he said, the amused expression falling away.

"To talk to you, that's all."

He tilted his head to the side. "Aren't you persistent. And what would we have to talk about?"

I got the feeling this guy wouldn't believe anything less than the truth. Besides, I knew without a doubt that Maria and Leah Golden would have filled the whole prom committee in after we'd stopped by to talk to them. "I'm trying to clear my sister's name, and I was hoping you'd help me."

"You really believe she's innocent?" he asked with what appeared to be genuine surprise on his face.

"I know she is."

He studied me for several seconds. "Fine. Honestly, I'm curious how you think I can help." He motioned ahead. "I was on my way to a wine bar. You have a drink with me, we'll talk."

I pulled my phone from my pocket. "Sounds good. What's the name of the bar? I was meeting my friend, and I need to tell her where we're going."

"What friend? Your familiar?" he asked.

"Nope, Bram's busy tonight."

He smirked. "Oh dear, trouble in paradise already, huh?"

Dick. "Not at all. The name?"

He chuckled, amused with himself for some reason. "Angelo's."

We walked the block to the bar in silence. He glanced my way at regular intervals, his lips curled in what I'm sure he thought looked like a congenial smile, but I couldn't work out what was behind it. I was usually a pretty good judge of character, but I wasn't getting a read from him right then. Nothing but dead air.

He opened the door to the wine bar and led me to a table in the back. We sat, and he smiled again. It was...friendly. "How far away is your friend? Are we ordering for them as well?"

"She prefers to order for herself," I said.

"Just us, then." He stood, then strode to the bar, even though I hadn't actually told him what I wanted.

I shifted in my seat, taking in my surroundings. The place was quiet. The people that were here mainly sat at the front near the large windows. Bram wouldn't like this, not one bit, but we were in a public place and Ash was on her way.

Ryan was laughing and chatting with the barman like they were old friends. Finally, he walked back with two glasses of red wine. He put one down in front of me. "This is one of my favorites." Then he rounded the table and took his seat again. "Try it." He lifted his glass, swirling it, then breathed it in deeply, then grinned, about to take a sip.

I leaned across the table, wrapped my fingers around his glass and took it, then slid mine across the table toward him. "A girl can never be too careful."

His eyes narrowed. "You think I'm going to drug you? Do I look like the kind of guy who needs to drug his dates?"

"I wouldn't know. And this isn't a date," I said.

"We're two young, attractive people enjoying a nice glass of wine, seems like a date to me. Try your wine."

Such a fucking creep. I forced myself to take a sip while he watched me intently. It was nice, I guess. I wasn't much of a drinker, wine or otherwise. It was hard, but I managed not to screw up my face.

"Well?" he said. "Do you like it? It's stunning, isn't it?"

Stunning? What a dick. I pitied Chloe or any other female he dated. I'm sure he thought he was impressing them with his apparent knowledge of fine wines, but he just sounded like a douche bag. "It's okay, I guess. I don't know much about wine."

He sat back, his frustration clear. "But you must know if something tastes good or not?"

"Of course."

"Take another sip."

He was offended, and that sounded more like an order than a request, but you caught more bees with honey, right? I wanted him to talk, and a few drinks might actually loosen his tongue. I forced myself to take another sip.

"Well?" he demanded, watching me closely.

"It's good." Still tasted like vinegar to me.

He smiled. "Don't feel bad, not everyone has the kind of refined palate to really appreciate a truly superior wine."

"Oh, I don't feel bad," I said.

His smile widened, giving me an indulgent look, like he thought I was an adorable little moron. "You're one of those tough girls, aren't you, Magnolia?" he said, the smile turning into a smirk. "All bluster. You talk a big game but can't actually deliver. Under all the black clothes and eyeliner, you're scared out of your mind."

"What do I have to be scared of, Ryan?" I asked, doing my best to keep my temper in check. It wasn't easy. I wanted to throat punch this asshole, badly.

"You tell me?"

That smirk was still front and center, and my fingers curled into a fist at my side. I shook my head. "I have no idea what you're talking about. I just want to ask you a couple questions."

"Then ask," he said, taking another sip of his drink.

The tips of my fingers felt a little tingly. "How long have you worked for the Hazarks, Chase Golden and Maria Watson?" I shook my hand out, trying to get the blood flowing again.

"Seven months, and I work for Dark Star."

"So you work for Isaac as well?"

"Yes," he said.

A dull thump started behind my temples. "What do you do for them?"

He sat forward. "Anything they ask of me. I'm their assistant. I'm there to assist in any way they see fit."

A cold sweat coated my skin, and my hands felt kind of numb. "Do you know Thomas Alway?"

"Yes."

"How?" My head spun.

He took his wallet from his pocket, pulled out his license, and slid it to me. "Thomas Ryan Alway" was printed on it. "I dropped Thomas years ago. It's kind of old and stodgy sounding."

He was Thomas Alway. One of the kids the prom committee relentlessly bullied.

My head did another loop. Something was seriously wrong. I tried to stand, but my legs gave out. *Fuck.*

Ryan leaned in and slid his fingers under my chin, tilting my head back. "I also use Ryan because I didn't want anyone to know who I was, not right away. I'm a lot hotter now than I was in high school, you know. I've lost a lot of weight. No one guessed I was the sad boy from the poetry group that no one would look twice at...unless they were about to spit on me, that is—or kick the shit out of me."

My eyes grew heavy, and Ryan stood, laughing like I'd told some amazing joke. He pulled me out of my chair and tucked me under his arm. "I think you've had enough to drink, honey."

I tried to open my mouth, to call for help, to tell him to back the fuck off, but he was already leading me through the bar and out the back, and no matter how hard I fought, my limbs were utterly useless. His hand delved into my pocket, and he took out my phone, switched it off and tossed it in the dumpster, then looked down at me. "You're wondering how I knew you'd switch drinks? I didn't, but I added a little insurance just in case you did," he said and smiled. "I'm immune to it. I'm sure you're wondering that as well. I ingested small quantities, slowly over time, increasing the amount until I built a tolerance to it."

He was completely insane.

He all but carried me out the back and through an alleyway, then back out onto the street behind the bar and lifted his hand. A cab pulled up beside us, and Ryan stuffed me in, got in beside me, and rattled off an address I didn't recognize.

"The wife and I...celebrated our anniversary a little too hard," he said, slurring his words, pretending to be drunk. I guess so that the driver didn't think he was taking advantage of some poor drunk girl. So he didn't try to help me or ask if I was okay.

"Ready to have a little fun, Magnolia? I know I am," he said low against my ear.

Inside I was screaming, but the words wouldn't come. My entire body was paralyzed. I could hear everything, feel everything, but my body wouldn't work. I was in serious trouble. Asher wouldn't know where I was, and with my phone back there, she had no way of tracking me.

We didn't drive for very long, and when the car pulled over, I willed my limbs to move and my mouth to work, but nothing. Ryan lifted me from the car, laughing and pretending we were having a grand old time as he dragged me away.

There was a big for sale sign at the front of the house, with a picture of Chloe Chan's face on it. He pulled a key from his pocket and opened the door to the house. A new build, like he'd taken Margot.

He unlocked the door. "Chloe's a decent fuck, but she really is as dumb as a post," he said and slid the key in his pocket.

It was big and empty. There was plastic sheeting still on the floor, cans of paint, tools scattered here and there. He was using Chloe's real estate business to help find places he could take his kills. I tried to talk again, and all I managed was a moan.

Ryan set me on the floor, but I couldn't hold my head up. He crouched in front of me, taking my chin in his hand, and shoved my head back roughly before swiping the drool from my chin. "Messy girl. Look at the state of you." He tutted. "Not so tough now, are you, Magnolia?" He laughed. "Are you cursing me out in your head? Attempting some gruesome spell? I like to think so, better than pleading for your life, that'd just be pathetic. Now, I'm going to set up, so you wait right here, okay?"

He released me and stood, and I fell to my side, hitting the ground hard.

Unfortunately, it didn't take long before he was back, yanking me off the floor and dragging my limp body to the wall in some-one's freshly painted living room. He'd drilled a hole through the wall, into one of the studs, and attached a piece of thick wire, then using his body, he pressed me against the wall, gripped my wrists tight in one hand, and twisted the wire around both of them, so tightly it cut in. Agony shot through my forearms when he released me, the wire the only thing supporting the dead weight of my body. The wire cut deeper, and warm blood trickled down my arms.

I tried to speak again, to use the power of my blood to spell, but still no words would come out.

Ryan walked to a bag in the corner, took something out, and strode back. He held up a needle and thread. "We need to make sure you can't talk when the drug starts to wear off. And, of course, use your sister's calling card, right? Since she likes to sew people's mouths closed."

Then he pressed my lips together and started sewing.

I screamed, the sound exploded through my mind, but again nothing passed my lips. The pain was unbearable, but I couldn't fight, couldn't move. I thought about all the people he'd killed before me. How they must have suffered. Still conscious while he tortured them, while he removed organs and hacked off limbs.

Ryan was a monster, and the way he was breathing heavily, the excitement in his eyes—he got off on this. He was enjoying every moment.

Ryan wanted people to think it was Willow, but he couldn't even replicate the spell she'd used during her trial with Elmer Eldridge when she sewed his mouth closed and the one the witches council was using as evidence of her guilt. It wasn't a spell; it was a psycho with a needle and thread and no magic at all. The council was either somehow blinded to the truth or more interested in hurting Willow, hurting our coven, than finding the real killer.

I knew who was framing her, finally, but I didn't know why, and unless I thought of a way to get the hell down from here, I'd never get the chance to tell anyone.

Chapter Twenty-Eight

Bram

My heart pounded, excitement filling me as I watched the life drain from the vampire's bloodshot eyes. It wasn't often we were hired to take out a vamp, but there were things going on among their leaders, things that put chasing a rogue deep in bloodlust low on their list of priorities.

This one had been snacking on humans in the basement of an abandoned theater for days. I tossed his limp body to the floor, then removed his head with my axe. I straightened and screwed up my nose. The stench of rotting corpses was strong as hell in the confined space. He'd been too lost to his thirst to be careful, and if anyone found these bodies full of fang marks, well, it might lead to questions. Questions we didn't want the humans asking.

Removing a vamp's head, then burning them was the best way to ensure they stayed dead, which meant there was only one thing to be done.

Rook poured gasoline over the bodies, dropped the can, and I flicked open my lighter and tossed it. Rook climbed out the window and I followed, the room going up in flames behind us.

"I'll text Nero and tell him it's done," I said.

Rook dipped his chin, shifted and flew away.

I strode across the parking lot, smoke billowing from the building behind me, and pulled out my phone. I'd had it on silent while we'd hunted and froze when I got a look at the screen. I'd had multiple calls from Asher.

My gut fucking knotted, followed by an adrenaline spike as I hit her number.

Something was wrong.

Something had happened to Magnolia.

I fucking felt it, the dread in every part of my body.

"Where the hell have you been?" Ash hissed down the line.

"Where is she?"

"No fucking clue. I was supposed to meet her at a wine bar. Found her car but no sign of her."

I swallowed down my roar. "Where are you?"

"Downtown, on Grant Street, outside The Crest apartments."

I disconnected, yanked off my shirt, my wings bursting from my back, and exploded into the sky. That was Alway's apartment building. She'd gone to talk to him on her own. *Fuck.*

An image of Calvin's body after we'd found it in that garage slammed into my head, and fear like nothing I'd ever experienced gripped me by the throat. Ryan. He had her. It had to be him.

He'd just marked himself for death.

Ryan was going to die today, screaming.

~

Magnolia

Ryan was toying with me.

And no one was going to stop him.

No one was coming to save me. No one knew where I was.

He had all the time in the world, and he was making the most of it.

He sliced down the front of my shirt, yanking it open, then stood back and stared at my mostly naked body. He tutted. "Not much I can use here. You're scarred almost everywhere, not a fan of the ink either. Not very appealing, are you, Magnolia?" He rubbed his chin. "Your organs will be useful, maybe your legs?" He shook his head, his gaze lifting to mine. "Don't get me wrong, I mean, I'd fuck you...I just wouldn't tell anyone about it. You know, because you look like...that."

He stepped closer. My body was still utterly useless, but I refused to let him see my fear and hoped he saw all the hatred I felt burning through my eyes.

I let that hatred swell and curl inside me, let the anger build higher. That anger, it felt safe. I'd used it to protect myself for so long, and it was wild and dangerous. Recently I'd been able to control it, contain it, but right then, I needed it. I needed that wild rage inside me more than ever.

Agatheena's words filtered through my mind. I was light, but I was also darkness. Like Gran, like so many other witches who were forced to hide the power their darkness gave them.

Ryan pressed the tip of his knife to the underside of one breast and slid it around the curve, not hard enough to cause real damage but enough to cause pain, to slice skin, to create a new scar. He carried on up to a point in the center of my chest, then back down and around the other breast. Warm blood slid down my ribs.

All I could do was take it—but instead of drowning in the pain and horror, I embraced it, all of it, and let the darkness grow inside me, let it feed on the surge of power that spilling more of my blood gave me.

Then the words came like they had at Shadow Falls, a spell

derived purely from darkness, one that was all my own. It was dangerous, but it was either go dark or do nothing and let this evil little fuck cut me up and kill me. Let him walk free to do the same to others.

"Your lungs could be of use. Your ribs as well," he was saying.

I shut out his voice and focused inward. I'd never spelled this way before. I wasn't even sure it could be done. Ryan obviously didn't think so. I'd only ever spoken the words of my spells out loud, but this time it wasn't my corporeal body that was casting the spell, no, this time it was my spirit. I repeated words over and over in my head, words that would sever the tether between my physical form and my soul. I needed to release it from my body.

I'd read about astral projection, but I'd never attempted it. I wasn't even sure it was possible while you were still conscious, but I continued to repeat the spell filtering through my mind.

Something wrenched inside me.

I looked down at my hand, and when I tried to lift it this time, it moved. My soul lifting from my physical body.

The tether snapped and I stepped away, away from Ryan and his knife slicing my body.

I wasn't dead or alive, I was in the in-between.

The darkness inside me grew.

Aiming my hands at Ryan's back, I yelled one of the spells I'd created, a spell I'd written in my book when I'd been filled with hatred and vengeance after Clayton hurt me. Ryan froze in place, a horrified look on his face, as I used my powers to control the knife in his hand. He cried out in terror, watching his own hand lift. Screaming when I forced him to angle the blade downward, then bring it down hard, sinking it into his own thigh.

The scar on my palm tingled and burned as I forced him to bend to my will, to pull the knife back out, to raise it high again, ignoring his screams and begging me to stop.

But before I could bring it back down, I staggered back. My head spun wildly.

What was happening?

My soul was ripped away from the room, the house. I was dragged at an unnatural speed through the city, the forest, deep among the trees—and right up to Limbo's gates.

I threw up my hands. *No.* But the boulders rolled, reforming into an arch, the door opening, and I was pulled through, dragged along a path made of skulls, past souls wandering aimlessly through a dark forest, and through the door of a stone fortress.

My mind spun again. I fought for consciousness but blacked out. I don't know how much time passed, but consciousness came and went.

"She entered my world. She chose this," a monstrous voice said, so horrifying it sent terror through every part of me.

"Send her back."

Zinnia.

It was Zinnia. She was here as well, and she was angry.

I tried to open my eyes, but I couldn't. I felt a hand take mine. Zinny was right there, right beside me. "I've asked for nothing," she said, fury in her voice. "I've lived by your rules. You owe me this."

Silence, and it was deafening. "I owe you nothing, wife. We made a deal. By being here you are merely holding up your end of our bargain. If you want me to send her back, there will be a price, for her...and for you."

"What kind of price? What will happen to her?"

I tried to speak, but I was fighting not to be pulled back under.

"You ask only of her price. Do you have no concern for you own?" he said.

"You already know I'd do anything for my family, and the worst has already happened. I'm here, living this nightmare with you," Zinnia fired at him, then squeezed my hand. "Tell me what her goddamn price is?"

"That is not your concern," he snarled. "She either lives or she dies. Choose."

"You're a fucking monster," Zinnia snarled back.

"Are you only coming to that realization now?" He chuckled, and the sound lifted painful goose bumps all over me.

"I hate you."

"Choose," he said.

Zinnia growled under her breath. "For once, can you just do something because it's the right thing to do? Just send her back, no deals, no payment...please."

There was a heavy pause, the tension growing impossibly thick, so thick I could feel it even in my semiconscious state.

"Mors...please," Zinnia said, using Death's true name.

There was a snarl. "I told you what would happen if you spoke my name again, wife."

"I remember," she said.

Another pause. "And you will come willingly?" Death asked.

I had no idea what they were talking about, but it didn't sound good.

Zinnia didn't reply, not quickly enough, anyway.

The tension snapped, and a jarring crash came next, followed by stone hitting the floor. "She lives or she dies. Choose," he growled, his rage rolling over me.

"Hang on a minute—"

"Choose," he said again, the word deadly calm this time. "Or I will choose for you."

"She lives." Zinnia squeezed my hand again. "Now send Magnolia back."

Her hand was torn from mine, and I was dragged back the way I came, past the lost souls wandering the dark forest, along the path made of skulls, and through the stone archway.

Then I was flying through the forest, the city, through the door of the house—and slammed back into my body, the force knocking the wind from me.

I searched the darkness. Something moved, a shadow. It filled my vision standing in front of me, looming. No, not a shadow, Death, draped in his hooded cloak. I was still uncon-scious, that was the only way he could be here, away from his realm.

His frigid blue eyes glowed from under his hood. "Magnolia Thornheart, you live because I allow it. You entered my realm without my permission, now you must pay a price."

"What price?"

"You are now my reaper. When I request it, you will collect souls and escort them to me."

The darkness around us was heavy. In here, in my mind, it was just him and me. "Do I get a choice?"

"No," he said, and the world around me shook from the violence in his voice.

"What will happen to me?"

"You will become an extension of me. My reapers are my right hand. I am Death, you deliver it."

"I won't kill for you. I won't do it."

He slammed the twisted wooden staff in his hand on the floor. "You will do whatever I say, or I will rip your soul from your body and take you back." Then he held a large, scarred hand in front of his hood, palm up, and blew across it.

Black smoke flowed from under his hood and into my face. I coughed, choking as it crawled inside me, taking hold, gripping on to my own darkness with unrelenting claws.

"Until you learn to control it, your touch is death," he said.

What? "I can't touch anyone?"

He shook his head.

"How do I control it?"

"No two reapers are the same."

And if I didn't learn to control it, I'd never be able to touch Bram again. I'd never be able to hug my mom, or Else or my sisters, or hold Willow's baby.

"You think this is a punishment, witch," he said, his soul-shaking voice slicing through me. "But I feel the darkness inside you, so vast it would have eventually taken over. I've given you a way of channeling it."

He made it sound like a good thing. It didn't feel that way to me.

Death took a step back. "You will hear from me, reaper."

He lifted his staff, about to pound it on the floor, to make his exit.

"Please, don't hurt Zinnia," I said quickly. "Don't hurt my cousin." I didn't know if a being such as him was capable of kindness or mercy, but I knew without a doubt he was capable of cruelty.

He froze, his glowing eyes boring into me, and I wanted to shrivel up and die under that frigid stare, to vanish from the face of the earth. Looking into them was like staring into a nightmare come to life.

He said nothing, then finally, he slammed his staff on the ground.

Then he was gone.

Consciousness returned with a harsh jolt.

I was back in that room with Ryan, and it was as if time had stopped. He was still screeching, blood pouring from his leg. I tried to move, and this time I was able to. I wasn't paralyzed anymore, the numbness completely gone.

Ryan looked up at me, murder in his eyes as he stumbled toward me. I kicked out, slamming my foot into his chest, hard. He stumbled back, falling on his ass.

I didn't have time to waste. With a scream, I forced my mouth open, tearing the stitches, ripping through flesh so I could speak, and yelled my spell. This one most definitely came from a place of hatred, and now that I was Death's reaper, I didn't need to hold back. My voice was strong, cold, pure venom as the words fell from my torn lips.

Ryan was thrown back, and his body slammed into the wall. He yelled and thrashed, but the hold I had on him was strong. It was his turn to feel powerless. Goddess, it was easy, so easy for me when I allowed my anger to fuel me.

The next spell I called, the words came to me without even thinking, in a language so old I didn't understand it. The wire around my wrist moved, untwisting, loosening as I spoke.

The door crashed open, and I turned to see Bram and Asher run in.

Bram took one look at me and roared.

He ran for Ryan as Asher rushed for me.

The wire released, and I fell to the floor. "Stay back," I yelled at Ash.

Then my power collapsed, my magic drained. Ryan fell to the floor as well, then instantly jumped to his feet and ran at me. Pain overwhelmed me, every bit of strength I had, I'd used up. Ryan got to me first, dragging me off the floor, holding me in front of him, a knife to my throat.

"Stay back or I'll slice her throat," Ryan screamed.

"You're already dead," Bram snarled, about to shift, to turn into a shadow.

My mouth and the tips of my fingers were burning, I assumed from my injuries, but then the dark thing that Death had given me reared up, coming to life, and snapped its teeth, taking a bite. Ryan made a choking sound, then his hands loosened and released me. We both fell, hitting the ground hard.

He was dead, I could tell without looking. His soul...I *felt* it leave his body. Time stilled. Then Ryan's soul stood, looking down at his body in horror, then at me, and I could see it all. His face twisted, and he took a step toward me—

A male...no, a monster, appeared out of nowhere. He grabbed Ryan. Ryan screamed and fought, but the hellish male subdued him easily. The monster paused then, looking at me. I couldn't make out his face—I knew he had one, but no matter how hard I tried, I couldn't see it. His head tilted to the side. A demon.

Then he gave me a nod and vanished, taking Ryan with him.

Lucifer's own reaper, and he'd dragged Ryan to Hell. Somehow, I just knew that as well.

Then the room exploded back into action and Bram and Asher rushed for me.

I lifted my hands, scrambling back. "No, you have to stay back. You can't touch me. No one can touch me."

Chapter Twenty-Nine

Magnolia scrambled backward. "I mean it, stay away."

Blood dripped from her torn mouth, her clothes had been cut off her body, more blood dripped from under her breasts, covering her ribs and stomach. She was huddled against the fucking wall, and she wanted me to stay back? She had to be confused? Or seeing things that weren't there.

"It's okay, Mags," I said, my voice cracking. I took another step closer. "It's me. You're safe now."

She shook her head. "Y-you need to listen to me." She lifted her hands as if to ward me off. "Don't come any closer."

I froze in place. "What's wrong with your hands, baby?" The tips of her fingers were black. "What the fuck did he do?"

She shook her head again. "N-not him. Not Ryan. Death. He...he made me a reaper." More blood ran from her ruined lips. "Oh goddess, I'm a reaper."

"You're hallucinating or confused—"

"No." She struggled to her feet, swaying in place and grabbing for the wall to hold herself up. "If you t-touch me, you will d-die, just like Ryan did." Her entire body was trembling from pain, from shock. "I'm Death's servant."

~

Getting her out of that place and back to the tree house was fucking torture. Mags kept passing out, and I was forced to stand there and do fucking nothing. I was jumping out of my skin, my entire body aching to pick her up and hold her to me.

She'd wake, struggle a little farther across the room, then black out and fall again. She managed to pull my shirt on to cover herself, and Ash and I laid out a drop cloth. Mags finally crawled into it, and we carried her outside and got her in the car—then she passed the fuck out again.

When we got to the house, she insisted on climbing the fucking ladder to the tree house, terrified her mom or Else or one of her sisters would accidentally touch her.

Now she was in my bed, still out cold.

She'd been asleep for two days, and the longer she took to wake, the more out of control I felt. I didn't exist without her. I was fucking nothing. I needed her to open her eyes and look at me.

Thank fuck Talon was able to hack into Ryan's phone and track it.

My gaze traveled over her, down to her pale hand and black-tipped fingers. I wanted to take it in mine, to feel the warmth of her skin so fucking badly. But I couldn't do that. Before she'd passed out again, she'd managed to fill me in on everything that had happened. Ryan had nearly killed her; he'd nearly taken her from me.

Then fucking Death had made her one of his reapers.

Whenever I left her, something bad happened. I should never

have left her alone. No matter what, we were always stronger when we were together. Always.

My mind filled with images of Magnolia in that fucking house, bleeding. It was the second time someone had used their knife on her, had cut her. If Mags hadn't killed him, I would have torn Ryan to pieces. I wished I had.

Magnolia's family was freaking out and Daisy had literally collapsed when she'd seen Mags lying here. The reality of how close we'd all come to losing her to that piece of shit had hit her hard. Rose and Jazzy had clung to each other, and Iris had called the council and told them where to find Ryan's body and what he'd done to Magnolia. They couldn't doubt Willow's innocence now, the evidence of Ryan's guilt was right fucking there, sliced into Magnolia's flesh for fuck's sake.

I lifted the small jar of balm from the bedside table as I took in Magnolia's face. My fucking chest ached just looking at her. Her mouth was looking a lot better, thanks to some new and improved heavy-duty balm Else had come up with, but the thought of what almost happened to her...I couldn't bear it.

I opened the lid and swiped a cotton ball through it, making sure my skin didn't touch hers, and carefully dabbed it on her lips.

Her lips had changed as well, and not from her wounds. The color was brighter, candy-apple red. Like all poisonous things, they were colorful and enticing. One touch and I'd be dead. God, I felt the poison flowing through her.

I'd searched for information on reapers while I waited for her to wake, and the red lips and the black-tipped fingers came with the job.

The fates had made her for me, and me for her, yet they seemed to be throwing every fucking thing they could think of at us to keep us apart. I wanted to tear down the fucking walls.

"Wake up, Maggie," I choked out. "I need you. Come on, baby. Please, come back to me." She didn't move. Her eyes firmly closed.

Someone knocked on the door, and I dragged myself away to see who it was.

Rose held up two plates of food. "I brought dinner. She awake yet?"

"Not yet." I took the food from her and put it on the counter.

Her eyes softened. "She will wake, Bram. Her body just needs time to heal."

"Then what happens? When she wakes, will Death call her away?" I paced across the room and back. "I've been reading everything I can on reapers, but there isn't much."

"We've been looking as well. Reapers have always been elusive; their job is kept secret for obvious reasons. If we knew how they worked, we'd try to avoid them or kill them. It's not for us to know." All pretense of calm evaporated, and Rose cursed viciously, shaking with fury. "Why would Death do this? Hasn't he taken enough from us? He got what he wanted, he forced Zinny to be with him in Limbo, he can't have Magnolia as well."

My fingers curled into tight fists, and it was only because Rose was there that I didn't tear everything in my small living room to pieces. "Mags said if she can figure out how to control it—"

"But how long will that take?" Rose said. "What if she never learns? Me and Iris are hitting the books again today. There has to be something. If there's a loophole or a way out of this, we'll find it."

I nodded my thanks.

"I'm just glad her task is over. Ryan's dead. She found the killer, at least that's something."

Yeah, thank fuck for that. I didn't want her leaving my side. I wanted her safe in my tree house, with me. She'd been through so fucking much. Magnolia needed time to heal.

"Let me know when she wakes, okay?" Rose said, then headed back to the house.

My phone dinged. Payne. My brothers had been calling, texting, checking on Mags regularly, but Payne was especially feeling it. The way he'd treated her in the past, the fact he'd insisted on me going on that vampire hunt—yeah, he was struggling with the guilt. But not as much as me. The fact that once again, I hadn't been here for her when she needed me most was fucking killing me.

I strode back to the bedroom.

Magnolia was awake, and staring back at me.

I rushed for her, and she jerked away, her hands flying up.

Fuck. I stopped in my tracks. "It's okay, I'm not gonna touch you, baby."

She blinked up at me, once, twice, and a tear streaked down her cheek. Then another. I wanted to pull her into my arms so fucking badly, but all I could do was stand there and watch her cry.

Right then, I was willing to die just to hold her one more fucking time.

"I was hoping it was all just some fucked-up dream," she said and lifted her hands, looking at her fingers. "But it's true. It actually happened. How long was I out?"

"Two days. And we'll work it out," I said, because there was no other option.

She touched her healing lips. "How?" She fisted the covers. "We can't do this. It's impossible, Bram."

I took another step closer, unable to stay so far away. "Nothing's impossible."

"I'm a reaper. I'm literally poisonous. One touch and you die." She shook her head. "I can't stay here. I can't be around you or my family. I'd never forgive myself if I... I could kill one of you. It would be so easy, one accidental touch, just one."

"You're not going anywhere, you hear me?" I growled out.

She looked up at me, her eyes filled with despair. "I can never be your true mate, we can never touch, or even kiss anymore, we can't...sleep together. This is it. Looking at each other from across the room. I won't do that to you, I won't—"

A roar exploded from me. "Stop!" I snarled. "Stop trying to fucking leave me or send me away. I'm not going anywhere, and neither are you, do you hear me? Death said you can learn to control it, so you'll fucking learn. This is not the end for you and me. It can't be because there is nothing else. There is only this. There is only us." I strode from the room, grabbed her plate of food, brought it back and set it beside her. "Now eat your fucking dinner, because you need your strength for whatever is thrown at us next."

She looked a little shocked, not something I saw on Magnolia very often. "B—"

"You need anything else?" I said, gentling my voice, but I was not having this fucking conversation.

"No," she said and licked her still-healing lips. "I'm sorry I freaked out."

"I hope you're sorry, because I don't want you saying that shit to me ever again." I blew out a frustrated breath and planted my hands on my hips. "Female, you are mine, no matter what. I've told you, more than once. I thought you understood. I see now I was wrong."

A small smile curved her lips. "I think I'm starting to get it now."

"Fucking finally," I said, then I sat on the end of the bed. "Now eat."

"Yes, sir," she said.

"Still managing to be a smart-ass I see? You must be feeling better."

Her lips twitched, and she picked up the fork and ate a piece of potato, then another. She looked up at me. "Are you just going to sit there and watch me eat?"

"Yes." She wasn't leaving my damn sight, not until I was positive she wasn't going to try a disappearing act.

"You get more and more like your brothers every day," she said. "So bossy and surly."

I growled under my breath. "You're fucking lucky I can't touch you right now."

Her gaze flicked up. "And why's that?"

"Because I'd take you over my knee and spank your round ass until it glowed." It wasn't the first time I'd wanted to do it, and it wouldn't be the last. But then I wanted to do a lot of things to Magnolia.

Her cheeks colored, then she snorted and rolled her eyes, trying to lighten the moment, to deflect. "So Rook was right, then, huh? What he said about your males being dominant? I mean, he is a member of Red."

She wanted me to joke around with her, to make me forget she'd just tried to leave me. But I couldn't, not then and not about this. "Yes, we are. We're dominant, we crave control, and that spills over into all aspects of our lives."

She lowered her fork. "Jesus, Bram." She blew out a breath. "You're being serious?"

"Yes."

"So you do...want to spank me?"

"For what you said about leaving me? Yes, badly." I stood because I needed to cool off. I was scared and I wanted to kiss her so fucking much I ached. "I need a shower. Finish your dinner, then we can watch a movie, okay?"

"Okay," she said.

I turned back before I closed the bathroom door. "And if you're gone when I come out, I'll come after you and drag your ass back, so do us both a favor and keep your ass in my bed." Then I shut myself in the bathroom, turned on the shower and prayed the cold water would help calm me the fuck down.

❧

Magnolia

. . .

I stepped out of the shower and wrapped a towel around myself. Bram had walked out of the bathroom half an hour ago in only a pair of track pants, his hair wet and hanging over his face. His dark gaze had slid to me in the bed instantly, and I'd seen his relief.

He'd expected me to run.

I won't lie, I had thought about it. I didn't know if I'd ever get a handle on this thing Death had forced on me, and keeping everyone I loved safe was more important than anything else, but I couldn't do it to Bram—or to me. So I stayed.

I dried off, my body still a bit sore and bruised, but with the help of Else's balm and tonics, I felt better than I should. I turned to the mirror, my gaze trailing over my bare skin again, my new scars.

Then froze.

The vine markings the mother had given me were still reaching for each other, still a few inches between them, and they were black. Ryan was the killer, and he was dead. If my trial was over, the vines should have changed color, right?

Which meant, it wasn't fucking over.

I pulled on my underwear and tugged on a clean shirt I'd taken from Bram's dresser and walked out. Bram was sitting on the couch in the living room.

He turned when I walked in, and his gaze darkened as it moved over me. "How do you feel?"

"Physically? Pretty good, actually." I gripped the bottom of my shirt and lifted the side, showing him the vine markings from the mother. "But we have a serious problem."

His gaze instantly dipped to what I was showing him, and he stood, stalking closer. I took a step back, and he pulled up short. "Fuck." He looked from the vine markings and back up, then shoved his fingers through his hair, his biceps bulging, abs tightening. "How can that be?"

"I don't know. Someone else has to be in on it with him. Isaac. It has to be him." Bram's chest was pumping, the veins in his forearms bulging. He was furious on my behalf. I wasn't that freaking happy, either, to put it mildly, but for once anger didn't come, because I didn't want to think about it, any of it. I was struggling to do anything but watch Bram. Goddess, I couldn't take my eyes off him. He was beautiful like that.

I took in every raw, furious, wild inch of him, and my body heated.

Bram stilled and his nostrils flared before his eyes locked with mine. "You sure you're not in any pain."

"I'm not in any pain," I said.

He straightened. "But you've got an ache you need to ease, haven't you, Magnolia?"

"Yes." The word slipped from my damaged lips all on its own.

He watched me for several long seconds, his abs tightening with every one of his labored breaths. "Take the shirt off, baby," he finally said.

At his rough command, a throb started deep inside me. I did what he said, lifting his shirt over my head and tossing it aside. Clayton and Ryan had both tried to make me feel ugly, unworthy, but what those monsters thought of me didn't matter. I only needed to look into Bram's eyes to see he thought the complete opposite.

"So fucking beautiful," he said, making sure I knew it. "Cup your tits for me, Mags, give them a squeeze."

I did, and a shuddering breath escaped when my palms pressed against my hard nipples and I squeezed lightly. I did it again.

"Good?" he asked, watching me closely.

"Yeah."

"Play with your nipples. Gently squeeze them."

I did as he said, imagining it was his hands on me, that the warmth of my skin was his.

"I'd lick them and suck them deep into my mouth," he said,

raw need on his face. "Lick your fingers for me, Mags, and do it again. Make them slippery for me, show me."

I was so turned on now that I struggled to catch my breath. My fingers slipped over my hard nipples, and Bram reached down and squeezed the obvious hardness behind the front of his track pants. He groaned, then shoved the pants down, kicking them off.

He was only in his boxer briefs now, and the outline of his erection made my heart pound. I could see how thick and long he was, the ridge below the fat swollen head, all perfectly outlined, and remembered how he felt in my hands, in my mouth.

"Slide your fingers down your stomach, nice and slow," he said roughly. "That's it, now down the front of your panties."

As he watched me do it, he shoved his hand down the front of his underwear, and I could see him grip his length and squeeze. Liquid heat trickled over my fingers.

"Tell me how wet you are," he demanded, the dominance rolling from him now.

"So wet," I said. "My panties are soaked."

"Show me your fingers."

I slid my hand free and showed him.

"Fuck," he growled. "Put them in your mouth, lick them clean for me. Tell me how good you taste, Mags."

Again, I did as he said, slipping my fingers into my mouth, tasting my own arousal for him. A moan slipped free, because having him watching me, wanting me, was so goddamn hot.

"You're making me fucking jealous, Magnolia, tasting your pussy for me. Panties off, baby," he bit out. "Toss them to me."

Sliding my fingers down the sides of my underwear, I pushed them down and stepped out. He held out his hand, and I threw them to him. He snatched them and pressed them to his face, breathing deep with a rough growl. "Fuck."

His hand was stroking faster inside his boxer briefs, and I couldn't take my eyes off him.

"Spread your legs for me," he rasped. "That's it. Now show

me. Show me how you get yourself off thinking about me, imagining me fucking you. Show me exactly what you do."

My knees quivered and my face heated, but I did what he asked, needing to please him, desperate to get off, to show him what he did to me. I ran a finger over my slick clit, then circled it.

"Spread your pussy for me, so I can see," he said, every muscle in his body tight and straining.

I did, then repeated the move, circling my clit, and a whimper broke free. Having Bram's hot gaze on me was exciting as hell. I'd never been this turned on. "I—I want you naked," I said. "I want to see you."

He shoved his underwear down instantly, kicking them aside, and his heavy cock jutted from his strong, lean body, thick and so impossibly hard. He gripped it immediately and started stroking again. The head glistened, leaking with every stroke.

I wanted to squeeze my legs together, the ache was so bad.

"You hurting, baby?"

"Yes."

"Do you push your fingers inside when you get yourself off?" he asked through gritted teeth, his black eyes utterly wild now.

I nodded, another moan escaping.

"Do it," he ordered.

I'd been waiting, needing him to tell me what to do, craving it, and as soon as he did, I felt a deep pulse inside me, another rush of arousal. I slid my fingers lower, pushing one inside me, just the tip, in and out, teasing Bram and myself.

"More," he demanded. "Push it in, Magnolia. Fuck yourself for me."

I did it, helpless to do anything else. I slid in and out, and his gaze was locked on what I was doing.

"You're so fucking wet, baby. It's all over your hand. Fuck. Add another finger, that's it, can you feel the stretch?"

"Yes, I feel it." I worked myself with two fingers, pushing deep, seeking out that spot inside me that made me come hard every time.

"Faster, deeper, Mags," he said.

The wet sounds of me finger-fucking myself and Bram stroking his cock, along with our labored breaths, filled the room.

"Now rub your clit with the other hand," he said, panting.

As soon as my fingers grazed my clit, the pleasure shot higher. I rubbed once, twice—and tipped over the edge, coming hard and calling Bram's name. My inner muscles pulsed around my fingers, and I couldn't stay on my feet. I dropped to my knees while I carried on working my clit, wringing out every last bit of pleasure I could while Bram watched.

Panting, I looked up at him. "Please," I rasped, not sure what I was asking for but needing something more.

But Bram did, he knew what I needed. He walked toward me, his hard cock still in his hand. He was stroking hard and fast, his face a mask of wild hunger. "Sit on your heels, hands on your knees," he said.

I did as he asked, and he moved closer, too close, but I was so lost to this moment, all I wanted was to see Bram come for me. Then he looked into my eyes and groaned, stroking himself hard and fast.

With a shout, he came, pumping furiously and angling his cock so he spurted across my breasts, emptying himself on me as he called my name.

It was beautiful. He was beautiful.

"Rub it in," he said, still breathing hard, trying to catch his breath. "Do it." He stared down at me with bright eyes.

I did. I lifted my hands to my chest and rubbed his come over my skin.

He watched me, a fierce expression on his face. "I don't need to touch you to make you mine, Mags. Do you doubt it now?"

I shook my head. I was his, no matter what happened next.

I would always and forever belong to him.

Chapter Thirty

Magnolia

We kept our heads down as we strode through the foyer of the council building. They'd let Bram and me through without issue, which meant Maria hadn't called to rat me out after we dropped in on her.

Though it wasn't like they had a leg to stand on, not after the prom committee's assistant-slash-sex toy attempted to mutilate and murder me.

It was lunchtime, and after we'd watched Isaac drive away from the building, Bram and I had made our way inside.

We strode down the hall to where the councilors' offices were located and stopped at the end, in front of the door with Isaac's name on it. Bram quickly picked the lock and we let ourselves in.

"You search the shelves, I'll get his desk," I said and started riffling through his drawers. Nothing of importance jumped out at me. I yanked open the next drawer and was hit with the scent of vervain, a common herb among witches and one that held great importance. It was used during our wedding ceremonies and was the first herb a witch planted in her own garden when she left to live with her mate. On its own it was harmless. I picked up a lone juniper berry that had rolled to the back of the drawer beside a small square of brown leather—mixed with a few different things, however...

"This anything?" Bram said.

I looked up, and he was holding a vial.

"Where was it?" I stood.

"In the box."

There was a small decorative wooden box on the shelf. He handed it to me, and I popped the cork and took a sniff. "It's lavender oil." I sniffed again, and there was a bitter undertone that was easily recognizable. "And snake venom." It was rare and expensive, so not often used, unless you were wealthy.

"What do you use if for?"

"On its own, nothing too nefarious. Add vervain, juniper berries, and a few other things, like the skull of a rodent, and a few drops of blood, put it in a leather pouch, and you have a fairly powerful enchantment charm. You can bend people to your way of thinking." The spell was most definitely forbidden.

"You think that's what he's done here?"

"You can't spell at the council chambers, but I think at some point this is where he'd stored his ingredients. I'd guarantee he's used it on the other council members. Trotman and Asuka haven't been themselves through this whole thing. They'd never believe Willow was capable of the things they've been accusing her of. Maybe even the prom committee as well."

We quickly left, making sure everything was where we'd found it, and got the hell out of there. Trotman and Asuka weren't in their offices, so I called and left them messages to call me back. I had to be careful how I approached this. Right now they were under Isaac's thrall, and the longer a person was under a spell like that, the stronger it became. They might not believe me even if I told them what we found.

We walked out and got in the car. "Let's try Trotman's house. Maybe he's at home."

Bram started the car and we headed out.

That's when it hit me, that tight grip in my gut, the feeling of wrongness.

"What is it?" Bram said, glancing at me, instantly sensing something was wrong.

"I'm being called somewhere. It's strong, Bram. Something's happened."

I let the feeling inside guide me.

It led us to the edge of the city, then into an affluent part of Roxburgh. "Turn right," I said, and we drove for a little bit more. "Take the next left." As soon as Bram turned, I knew exactly where we were going. "Pull over here."

"Fuck," Bram said beside me when he looked through the window at Chase Golden's mansion looming ahead of us.

A sick feeling filled me. "I have to go in."

When we reached the security gate, the ward sent tiny shocks over my skin. It was a strong one, which was not surprising. I wasn't on the council, so there was only one way I was getting through this ward—I had to prove good intent. If your motives were honest and you had no intention of causing harm, the spell would let me through. It could literally see into your heart and was the impartial judge that would grant you entrance or not. Which was why blood was required. You gave the spell life, and for a short time, its own beating heart.

I pulled my knife from my pocket, and Bram made a growly sound. I looked up at him, surprised.

"You've bled enough."

"I don't have any other choice," I said as I sliced an X into my palm.

Bram actually flinched, something he'd never done before, but he said nothing more. I quickly held my palm against the gate. Time was ticking. I felt it. I recited the spell, repeating it over and over, faster and faster.

Pins and needles flowed across my chest and down my arm, then through my hand still pressed against the gate. A surge of power pulsed through me, and I had to plant my feet when it tried to shoved me back. The force of it was so incredibly strong that I wasn't sure I'd be able to hold my ground. Usually, someone needed to stand behind you, to hold you in place, but Bram couldn't help me, and I cried out as I gripped on to the iron bars of the gate with everything I had, fighting not to let it throw me back.

Bram stepped closer. "Magnolia?"

"I've got it," I ground out.

Then finally, the ward dropped and the gate unlocked.

I stumbled back as the power receded and the gate swung open. Quickly righting myself, I ran through, and we rushed up the stairs. I pounded on the door. "Leah? Open up!"

Nothing. Not a sound came from inside.

I banged on the door again, still nothing.

Bram quickly picked the lock, and we burst inside. Biscuit ran around in circles barking, then tore off down a hall. We followed, down a flight of stairs and through the kitchen. The feeling inside me was unbearable now. "Whatever it is, it's through there," I said, pointing to the door in front of us.

But I already knew, didn't I? There was a body behind that door. Ryan was dead, but my task wasn't over. Someone else was working with him or helping him. Isaac, it had to be.

Leah's familiar was losing his mind, shaking and barking. I scooped him up and shut him in the kitchen, then watched as Bram turned the handle and pushed the door open.

It was oppressively dark, and he felt around for the light.

It was a garage. I could tell by the smell.

He flicked on the lights.

Oh, goddess.

Leah.

She was naked, propped up against one of the pillars, blood soaking the concrete floor around her. Bram and I rushed over. She was dead. There was no need to check for a pulse. Goddess, both of her legs had been taken.

I touched her cheek. "She's already cool."

I tried to remain emotionless as I studied the scene.

It was different than the others, like someone had tried to make it the same but hadn't quite pulled it off. Her wrists were bound with wire, the wire wrapped around the pillar to hold them up. The stitches through her lips were wider apart than the others, than the ones Ryan had given me, and they'd used different string. This was thicker.

The word "judgment" was carved into her forearm, but again, it looked different than the others.

"It's messier, done in haste," I said.

Bram walked around her. "They didn't take quite as much pleasure as Ryan did."

"No, they wanted to get it over with quickly." Her chest had been opened up and her ribs were missing, her insides spilling out.

I crouched down. "They didn't take as much time to torture her." I checked the pockets of her discarded clothes for her phone, but it wasn't there. The ward had been active when we arrived, which meant whoever did this either used dark magic to get in or Leah knew them. "Check if her phone's somewhere in the house. There might be something important on it."

Bram nodded and strode back into the house.

Leah hadn't been my friend. We hadn't liked each other, but she sure as hell didn't deserve this. I stared down at her. "I'm so sorry, Leah."

"Don't move." A voice echoed through the garage behind me. "Keep your hands at your sides so I can see them. If you even attempt to spell, I'll take you down. Now turn around...slowly."

I recognized the voice. Asuka. I turned, and she stood with her hands held out in front of her, magic swirling, ready to spell. Peter Lewis, another council member, stood beside her. Two more witches watched me on either side of them. Both were extremely powerful and worked as enforcers for the witches council.

"I didn't do this," I said.

The enforcers fired up their magic as well. It snapped out and wrapped around me, tight, binding me and my magic.

"Magnolia Thornheart, we're taking you into custody for the murders of Katana Adler, Calvin Adler, Margot Huxley, Ryan Alway, Leah Golden, and the attempted murder of Chase Golden," Asuka said.

"What? You can't be serious? You're making a mistake. I'm telling you I didn't do this. I didn't do any of it."

"We just heard you apologize to that girl for killing her," Peter said. "Her blood is still on your hands."

I looked down and realized I'd gotten blood on my hands when I'd touched her. This wasn't looking good, not at all, not with all of them under Isaac's enchantment spell. "I found her like that. I touched her to see if she was still warm, to work out how long she's been like this."

Peter Lewis strode forward. "Look at her palm and her fingers. She's been practicing dark magic." He turned back to me. "We're taking you in, you twisted little bitch."

He reached for me.

"No! Don't touch me!" I tried to move back, but I was bound too tight.

He grabbed my arm in a tight grip, then he froze for a split second, his eyes widening before they rolled back in his head. He dropped like a stone, falling to the floor. Instantly and unmistakably dead. I watched his soul rise from his body, and a beam of light shot down, surrounding him, then he was gone.

The room snapped back into focus, time returning to normal, and everyone exploded into action. Asuka cried out in shock. The witches fired more of their magic at me, binding me so tight I could barely breathe. Bram banged on the door, roaring my name. They knew what Bram was, and they were using magic to lock him out, the kind that even his shadow form couldn't get past.

"How the fuck did she do that? She's bound?" one of the enforcers said.

Asuka shook her head. "The foulest of dark magic. Nobody touch her."

"What about her familiar?" one of them said.

"Leave him."

Because they knew if they tried to take him, if they let him through that door, they'd all be dead.

Using magic, they dragged me from the room and out to a waiting van. They forced me in, the enforcers keeping plenty of space between us, and we sped off. As we drove away, I spotted several other witches standing in the yard, their hands aimed at the house. They were keeping Bram locked inside so he couldn't follow me.

"This was a setup," I said, trying to fight the bindings, but it was too strong and I couldn't reach my knife. "Someone told you to come here, yes?"

"Someone saw you breaking into the Golden mansion and called it in," Asuka said. "Are you really going to sit there and profess your innocence when I just watched you kill Peter right in front of me?" She shook with fury. "You killed and tortured all those witches. You tried to pin it on Ryan Alway, killing him and hurting yourself. It's even starting to look like you tried to frame your own sister, unless she's in on it with you." Hatred burned in her eyes. "You disgust me."

"You know Willow. You know she's not capable of this, and neither am I."

"I thought I knew her, but after seeing this? I'm not sure about anything anymore. Only that death and pain follows your family everywhere you go," she said.

There was no getting through to her. She wasn't going to listen. "Where are you taking me?"

"Where monsters belong. Umbra Sanitarium, to await judgment," she said, then slid up the soundproof glass barrier between us, shutting me out.

My blood ran cold. There was no getting out of that place. If a witch went where I was going, she never came back out.

Twenty minutes later, we pulled up outside Umbra. The enforcers opened the door, then used magic to force me out onto a gurney, like I was their own personal marionette puppet. Thick leather straps snapped around me, securing me tight.

The wards were heavy, and I tried to flex my magic, but it was useless. I was being fully suppressed. All the witches here, with the exception of those working at this place, were as powerless as humans.

They wheeled me down a hall to an elevator, and one of the enforcers hit the button for the basement after I was wheeled inside. I tried to stay calm, but it was impossible. My family, Bram, they'd sort this out. I wasn't guilty, the truth would come to the surface. It had to. Innocent until proven guilty, right? That was how it was supposed to work.

Except, they'd just caught me with Leah's body, her blood on my hands—and then watched me kill a male in cold blood right in front of them, and with Isaac's enchantment spell holding them hostage, there was no way they'd listen to reason.

I wasn't getting out of this, was I? How could I? Isaac had turned everyone against our family.

The elevator doors slid open, and they wheeled me out.

There were cells on either side, and as they pushed me along, witches screamed and called for help from behind thick glass walls. They hissed and laughed and called out spells that couldn't work. If they hadn't been mad when they were brought in down here, they would be now. Having your magic suppressed like this was mental and physical torture. I'd only been in the building for a matter of minutes and already I felt as if I was being scraped raw from the inside out, from my magic trying to fight against it.

We reached the end of the hallway, and they opened a cell door. The straps released and invisible hands shoved me off it.

Magic tugged at my clothes next, tearing the fabric from my body, yanking the shoes from my feet, leaving me naked on the ground. One of the witches tossed a gown at me, then they shut the door, locking me in.

Their footsteps echoed off the walls as they walked away.

Then the lights went out.

Bram

I couldn't find her, couldn't feel her. The council had dragged Magnolia away, and I didn't know where they'd taken her. I paced the kitchen. When all else had failed, I'd come home to Magnolia's family, my family.

Daisy walked in, pale, her phone in her hand.

"You know where they took her?" I asked.

"Oh, goddess, they took her to Umbra. Trotman said they're keeping her there until judgment is passed, but after what happened when they found her? He said there's no way they'll let her back out."

"She's a reaper, for fuck's sake," Iris said, gripping the back of a chair. "That position has to trump any of those fuckwits at the council."

Else limped in, carrying a thick book. "We have no way of proving it. She has the markings, but at this point they're going to believe it's dark magic over her being one of Death's little helpers."

"They said there's a symbol on her hand, and not a good one,"

Daisy said shaking. "They say she used dark magic, that it's the only way she could've gotten it." She shook her head. "But Mags wouldn't do that, would she, Else? She'd never do that."

Else sighed and sat at the table. "She would and she did, just like your mother before her."

Rose rocked back. "What?"

Else shrugged. "You don't have to be either or, despite what the witches council will have you believe. Mags is like her grandmother, the darkness comes natural. She hasn't gone bad, Daisy, she's just using what she was born with. Your mom thought she might end up at Shadow Falls one day, but that never happened, because she wasn't a dark witch, she just occasionally used dark magic. There's a difference. Pure evil goes to those falls. My sister wasn't evil, and Mags isn't either. Neither of them have an evil bone between them, *that's* the difference."

"She's the same person she always was," I bit out. "Agatheena said she could balance darkness and light, and she has been. Yes, she was struggling with it, but Death told her she won't struggle anymore, now that she's a reaper."

Daisy closed the space between us and rested her hand on my arm. "We know she's still our Mags. Things have just...taken a turn I wasn't expecting." She turned to Else. "I've seen my baby struggling. I wish I'd known." Her lip quivered. "Why didn't you tell me about Mom?"

"She saw what happened to other witches when they even veered toward darkness. She knew the rules and our laws like the rest of us, and she'd never do anything to put this coven at risk. But for Mags, I see now it was stronger, far more powerful. That girl, she must have been fighting so hard for so long."

"We need to get her out of that place," Iris said through gritted teeth. "I won't leave her there. I won't do it."

Else sat back in her seat. "Mags being held there is wrong, we all know it, but if we go charging in there or try to break her out, not only will the mother see it as interference but the council will see it as a declaration of war. We want her out, but we need to be careful how we approach this."

"I think we need to trust Mags."

Everyone turned at the new voice in the room.

Willow stood in the doorway, Warrick behind her. Ren, Relic, and Jagger hovered at the door as well.

Daisy ran to her oldest daughter, pulling her into her arms, Iris, Rose, and Jasmine following.

"I missed you so much," Daisy said, brushing her hair back. "But it's not safe, the council still thinks you could be involved."

Warrick growled. "I tried, but she wouldn't stay the fuck put."

"No one has to know I'm here, and if they do, well, there's a bunch of hellhounds and my familiar to get through first," Wills said. "Lucifer told me what was going on. I couldn't stay away. I won't let Mags rot in that place, but she's not powerless. Give her a chance to figure this out, and if all else fails, we declare war."

Figure it out? "No, we get Mags now," I growled. "She's been in there too fucking long already."

Several heads turned my way at my barked words, surprise on more than one face.

"Didn't know you could speak, crow," Warrick said and snorted, then dismissed me, turning back to Daisy. "Not cool with us making a move if it puts my mate in danger—"

"Then your mate stays out of it," I bit out. I wasn't in the mood for the hounds and their bullshit, not tonight. "Because nothing is getting in the way of me getting to mine, especially not you or your brothers, understand?"

The room went silent.

Warrick straightened and turned my way, his gaze slid over me, then up to the side of my shaved head before his eyes met mine again. "Nice markers. They new?"

Relic chuckled behind him.

"No." My gaze slid to Relic. "And I'm looking to add to them. Just give me a reason."

Relic smiled wide, flashing his long canines.

Warrick moved around Willow to stand in front of me. "You telling me you'd take on the whole pack to get to our Mags, crow?" Warrick said.

"She's my Mags. And I wouldn't need to. You're not the only one with brothers who like tearing shit apart," I said.

Warrick barked out a laugh and thumped me on the arm. The male had more power than one being should have, but I managed to stand my ground and not rock back. "Good to hear, brother," he said and gave me another bone-jarring thump. "But we're not going off half-cocked and risking anyone in this family, not until we know there isn't another way."

"I don't give a fuck what you do. I'm going to bring my female home," I bit out, then strode out of the house.

Chapter Thirty-One

Magnolia

My scars felt as if they were being torn open.

I lay on the floor, my arms locked around my knees, and tried to breathe through the pain. The floor was cold through the thin cotton gown, somehow making it worse. It'd never been this bad. No one was touching me, but I was on fire. I bit my lip harder, drawing blood, then cried out, unable to hold it in another moment.

"Hurts, does it?" a voice called.

A familiar voice.

I ground my teeth, of course those assholes would put me in a cell opposite Cora—the evil bitch who'd tried to kill us all during Willow's trial. I wouldn't be surprised if they were watching our reunion for their own entertainment. It took everything I had, but I managed to crawl to the glass wall and pull myself up.

Cora watched me, several feet back from the glass of her own cell, her expression filled with glee. She'd changed, a lot. The sweet old-lady facade was long gone. In front of me stood a stooped crone with yellowed teeth and bloodshot eyes. Her once soft, gray hair was a tangled mess on her head.

"Still a twisted bitch, then?" I said, staring back at her.

"Apparently, it takes one to know one, Magnolia. I hear you've been a very bad girl." She made a tutting sound. "Torturing and killing all those people like you did. Feels good, though, doesn't it? Making people bleed?"

I gripped the glass wall, hissing as another wave of pain washed through me. "I'm nothing like you," I said through gritted teeth. "You're a monster, and you're exactly where you belong."

She tilted her head to the side. "You really do feel it. You don't know how much that pleases me." She smiled wide. "But it's obvious you do."

The pain shot higher, and I sucked in a breath. "W-what are you talking about?"

"The spell I used to stab you...over and over and over and over again." She threw her head back and laughed like the deranged lunatic she was. "Your screams were so loud, I could hear them from next door. I wanted to watch so badly."

Her words made the blood in my veins turn cold. "My scars? That's what you're talking about?"

"Of course," she said between cackles.

My legs almost collapsed from under me as another wave of pain hit me. "Why do they still hurt, Cora?" I growled out.

"In general, or right now?"

"Both."

Her laughter stopped abruptly. "You haven't worked it out?"

"Tell me!" I screamed, all semblance of self-control shattering under the constant agonizing onslaught of my scars.

She rushed up to the glass wall of her cell, her gaze locking with mine. "It wasn't just a spell to hurt you, Magnolia, it was a hex to corrupt you, to destroy anything good in your life. Your grandmother was dark, did you know that? She tried to hide it, but it was there. I felt it. Dark senses dark, you know. I sensed it in you as well. I just had to give you a little push to bring it out. The rotten apple, that's what you are. The rot in your coven that would spoil the rest. It was my backup plan, in case you lived. Turns out it worked very well. The pain is your body trying to fight it, to get it out, and it gets worse whenever you try to be happy, like one of those science experiments with rats, shocking them to make them avoid something they want again and again until they give up entirely." Her eyes flashed. "And it's even worse now because I'm near. Magic binding this place or not, it senses me, it's part of me and it's working harder for me."

I gasped in agony and horror.

"You really did go above and beyond my wildest expectations, though. I hoped, but I never imagined anything like this. You're a monster." She laughed again as she stared at me, unmoving, just watching and enjoying her triumph.

The fucking bitch had hexed me. I wanted to claw at my skin and tear her out of me. She was the reason the pain grew worse when Bram touched me. I was finally reaching for happiness and her hex had tried to put a stop to it.

The pain hit me again, and I retreated into the corner of my cell, where Cora couldn't see me, where she couldn't take pleasure in the damage she'd done, and dropped to the ground, crawling into a ball and gritting my teeth as pain sliced into me over and over again.

I bit down on my lip. I wouldn't let that bitch hear me cry.

This wasn't how this was supposed to end. I had to get out of here.

Anger filled me, and the darkness inside was a furious storm.

I used it to fight the pain, to fight Cora's poison inside me—then I felt it, a shadow memory of Death's claws, the way they'd felt taking hold on me. It sent dread through me. Everything in me wanted to retreat from it, but something told me to do the opposite and I did, I gripped on to it in return.

Something wrenched inside me, like a dislocated limb being forced to the side and snapping back into place. Finally, the relief came. The sense of wrongness disappeared, replaced by a power that surged through me, not like my magic but something new and exhilarating and terrifying all at once.

There was a knowing that came with it, now that I'd quieted my mind and allowed it in.

I was a reaper.

No doors or bars, no magic, could hold me. I struggled to my feet.

I was Death's servant.

Nothing could stop me.

Bram

Umbra Sanitarium loomed in the darkness.

It was warded. I felt the vibration of magic the closer I got to it.

Still, I felt her.

I felt my Magnolia.

She was in that fucking place, and I was going to get her out. I wasn't sure I could do it alone, though. "What do you think?" I asked my brothers.

Payne studied the building. "I think your plan's sound."

"It could bring heat our way. If you're having second thoughts, I'll understand," I said to them.

Payne smiled. It was vicious as hell. "There won't be any heat, baby brother, I promise you that."

Rook grunted. "There is? Easy fix." He dragged his thumb across his throat.

Talon laughed. "Bring on the fucking heat." Then he bounced on his feet and cracked his neck.

"Magnolia's one of ours now," Payne said. "We look after our own."

"I'll take first shift?" Talon said and exploded into the sky.

The only way to get in was using someone who already had access, someone who worked at Umbra. The cleaning crew, a doctor, a cook, it didn't matter. Talon would see them coming, and we'd stop them and take their place before they were let in.

I paced away and back, near fucking vibrating with the need to get to her.

"Breathe," Payne said. "We've got this."

I opened my mouth to reply when a crack of sound rolled from the building, making the ground shake. "What the fuck?" A shimmering light wavered around the asylum, then the fucking ward dropped. I felt the invisible shield crashing down with a ground-shaking rumble.

"Magnolia." Somehow, she'd done it.

My brothers and I shadowed out and shot across the field behind the building. The world swam around me, spinning and moving as we flew around the side and to the main doors, Talon swooping down to follow.

The massive iron doors wouldn't stop us. Not much could, which was why we were so deadly. With the ward down, I easily slid through the tiniest gap and into the building.

I let my instincts guide me down the hall to the stairs beside the elevator, my brothers following close behind.

I was about to dive down the stairwell when the numbers above the elevator flashed, shooting up from the basement. I stopped, because I felt her so fucking strongly now. Shifting into my human form, my heart hammered in my chest, and I stepped back.

The elevator dinged, reaching our floor.

Then the doors slid open.

Mags stood there, head down, looking so fucking small. Her black, wavy hair was wild covering her face. Her little curvy frame was swamped in a plain cotton gown, her feet bare. Then she lifted her head, and I fucking froze. She stared straight ahead—her eyes white, fingers black tipped—and her fucking bones were glowing, I could see them through her skin, making her face a skeletal mask.

She stumbled forward.

"Mags," I choked out.

She walked out, hugging herself. Then she doubled over with a groan of pain and fell to the floor.

I ground my teeth, wanting to scoop her up in my arms so fucking badly I had to curl my fingers into fists at my side. Because I couldn't. I couldn't touch her. I crouched beside her. "Maggie? Look at me, baby."

She blinked up at me, her skin, her eyes returning to normal. "B-Bram?"

"I'm here." This was fucking torture. "I need you to stand, can you stand?"

She nodded, then spotted my brothers and, gasping in pain, dragged herself to her feet.

"What the fuck did they do to you?" There was no mistaking the pain etched into her beautiful face.

"My scars, they're...bad," she said and grabbed for the wall. "That evil bitch, she's down there. She did this." She gritted her teeth, looking around. "How did you get in here?"

Seeing her in pain again and not being able to touch her was fucking torture. "You took down the ward."

"I thought...I hoped. We need to go." With a hiss, she gave my brothers a wide berth, then headed for the door.

"What evil bitch, Mags?"

"Cora."

I snarled. "Payne, get her out of here. I'll catch up."

"Leave her," Magnolia said. "She doesn't matter."

I shook my head. "She needs to die."

Magnolia stared up at me. "Don't. Don't let her get off that easily. Let her rot in there," she said, eyes locked on mine.

I'd imagined killing that female ever since she used her magic to attack Magnolia. I wanted to break the bitch's neck. I wanted nothing left of her but a marker on the side of my head.

"We need to go," Payne growled.

He was right, of course. Getting Magnolia out of here was more important than my thirst for revenge. It was fucking hard, but I nodded.

Three witches exploded from the stairwell, braced for a fight. Asuka was one of them. My brothers and I closed ranks, standing in front of Magnolia.

"Get out of the way," Asuka said. "You walk away now, we'll forget you were aiding a prisoner."

Like the rest of the council, Asuka knew our value. Losing us and our services would be bad for all of them. Very bad. Making us an enemy? Even worse. "You know what we can do," I growled. "You don't step aside, all three of you will be dead before you open your mouths to spell."

"Magnolia Thornheart is a killer—"

"Are you fucking stupid?" I snarled. "She's been trying to clear her sister's name, who is also fucking innocent. Ryan Alway killed those witches, but he wasn't doing it alone. Someone else is still out there. You didn't see the differences between the previous murders and what was done to Leah Golden?"

Asuka shook with rage. "Magnolia had blood on her hands!"

"She checked if Leah was cold, which she was. If you'd checked yourself, you would've known that. If Magnolia had killed her, she would've still been warm. The witches council has failed, repeatedly, so focused on Coven Thornheart, you blinded yourselves to any other possibilities. Which was why we are now hunting the killer ourselves."

"The mark on her hand!" Asuka cried. "The tips of her fingers. Darkness. She's been corrupted. She killed Peter."

"She's a reaper, appointed by Death. She told Peter not to touch her, and he did, anyway, which makes his death his own damn fault. If you'd stopped to listen to her, we could have explained all of this, and we wouldn't be standing here now."

She looked at the witches on either side of her. They were faltering.

"I don't know why the council is so blind with this," I said. "But something isn't right. We all see it, but for some reason, you and the other council members don't."

Asuka blustered.

"It's Isaac," Magnolia said, stepping out from behind us. "I know you won't believe me right now," she said to the councilor, "but he's enchanted you, and others, I'm sure of it, to make you see what he wants you to. Check his office. Please. I think he killed Leah."

Asuka gave Mags a look as if she thought she was insane.

I was done with this. I wanted Mags out of here. "We're leaving, and you're not going to stop us. If you're stupid enough to try, you will die," I snarled. "Now step the fuck aside."

The others moved and Asuka, seeing she had no other choice, finally wised up and did the same.

"I didn't hurt anyone, Asuka," Magnolia said. "And neither did Willow. Deep down you know it's true. I'll bring you your killer. I'm close. I just need a little more time."

Asuka said nothing, just stared at Magnolia, looking angry and afraid. She didn't believe us. She truly thought Magnolia and Willow had done all those twisted things.

We rushed out of the building, and a car sped up beside us.

I braced for attack, until I saw who was in the driver's seat.

"Get in," Ren barked.

My brothers shifted and exploded into the sky, and Mags and I jumped in the back seat.

Fucking Relic sat in the passenger side, and he glanced back, looking over Mags as Ren planted his foot on the gas, speeding from the parking lot. "You solid?" the hound asked Magnolia.

"Yeah...yeah, I'm okay."

The farther we got from Umbra and Cora, the more the tension in her body and pain on her face eased.

"Thanks," I said to Ren.

"You know I've got you," he said.

I did. Ren was my friend. He was family, though I hadn't been there for him either for a long fucking time, so wrapped up in my own stuff.

Relic tilted his head back, scenting the air, and his jaw tightened before his gaze slid to me in the rearview mirror. "I get you've claimed Magnolia, brother," he said roughly to me, "but if you wanna actually protect her, you need to stop fucking around and figure out a way to mate her."

"Relic," Magnolia bit out. "Mind your own damn business."

Every muscle in my body tightened. I didn't like him talking to her, or fucking looking at her. "Magnolia can look after herself, but I guarantee, no one will be getting anywhere fucking near her from this day on. As for when we mate? Like she said, it's none of your fucking business."

The hound scowled. "Immortality is the only real way to protect her."

"What the fuck are you talking about?"

"Like your sisters?" he said to Mags. "The deal with Lucifer."

Magnolia made a choking sound. "What deal? You're telling me all my sisters are immortal?"

I stared at him in fucking shock.

Relic's chin jerked back. "You didn't know?"

Magnolia sat forward. "No, I sure as fuck didn't."

"My bad," Relic muttered.

She turned to Ren. "Is that true?"

Ren shot Relic a look. "Warrick made the deal for Willow, and included her sisters. Lucifer countered, only if they mated. They each found out when they did."

Well, shit. "You okay?" I asked her.

"Scratch that," Relic said. "Forgot reapers are already immortal. So you're good. No harm no foul."

Her eyes widened in alarm. "Are Ronan and Draven immortal as well?"

"That's how the deal works."

Mags spun to me.

I was a shifter, I was long lived, but I would die. "Mags, it's okay."

She shook her head. "I don't want to be immortal. Not without you."

Fuck. "You don't need to think about this. Not right now."

Ren turned into the driveway of Magnolia's house and shut off the car.

She shoved the door open, then turned back to me. "I need to talk to my sisters. I won't be long. Will you wait for me in the tree house?"

I nodded, and she took off into the house.

Chapter Thirty-Two

Everyone turned to look at me when I walked into the kitchen, jumping to their feet, Mom and Else barely stopping themselves from running at me and hugging me like they were desperate too.

"How?" Mom said.

"I'm a reaper, nothing can hold me. Somehow, I tapped into it," I said to the room, then turned to Willow. "Glad you're back."

Her gaze moved over me, making sure I was in one piece. "Back at ya."

"How's the peanut?"

She grinned. "The peanut's perfect."

"I'm going to make you something to eat, you must be starving," Mom said, trying to feed me since she couldn't show affection the way she usually did, by pulling me in for a tight hug.

"I'll help," Else said. "Then we can sit down and figure this thing out."

I turned to my sisters. "Can I have a word?" They followed me into the living room.

Iris looked worried. "Are you okay, truly?"

Her worry wasn't a surprise since we were all worried. There were so many fucking things to be worried about, but I couldn't let this go. "I am. Now that I'm out of that place." I wanted answers, and I wanted them now. "Are you immortal? All of you?" I said.

They were momentarily stunned by my sudden change of topic, then they looked at each other, something passing between them before they looked back at me. "Yes," they all said together.

"Were you ever going to tell me?"

"Of course, when you mated," Willow said.

"Well, therein lies the problem. I can't touch Bram without killing him, and even before Death made me a reaper, my scars…" I looked up at my sisters. "They hurt… And they've grown more painful the last few months. A hug, a simple goddamn touch causes excruciating pain."

Sadness filled Rose's eyes. "You never said."

"I was handling it, until…I wasn't." I gripped the back of the couch. "They put me in a cell across from Cora—"

"They did what?" Iris said, furious.

"Yeah, and she had a few things to say." I told them about the hex she'd put on me, that it was inside me still, infecting me with her darkness to draw out my own, to stop me from finding happiness. "I want it out," I said to my sisters. "Now."

Willow nodded. "We've got you, Mags. I think if we work together, we can do it."

"What's going on?" Jasmine asked, walking into the room.

"We're going to the cemetery," Willow said. "And we could use your help. Will you come?"

"Of course," she said, taking in all the serious faces in front of her.

"Let's go while Mom and Else are busy," Rose said.

We slipped out the front door and headed down the path to the cemetery. I thought about Bram as we walked, about how much I wanted to be his mate and of how that might never be. An eternity of never being touched by him was not a welcome prospect, but an eternity without him at all wasn't a life I wanted. I didn't want to live forever if I didn't have him with me.

The moon was high when we pushed open the iron gates. "I got out of Umbra, but I still don't have control over this whole reaper thing. I can feel the poison inside me, on my skin. What if I never can? What if I can never touch Bram, never mate with him, and I lose him. He'll eventually grow old, and I'll be stuck here without him," I said, voicing my deepest fear as we weaved through the headstones.

Jasmine frowned. "But if you mate, you're both immortal, right? The reaper thing won't matter if Bram can't die."

"But we can't mate if we can't touch," I said.

Jazzy's cheeks darkened. "Oh, right."

Rose cleared her throat. "I mean, to mate you've just got to, you know, both finish while he's..."

"Inside you," Iris said. "Seems easy enough to me."

Willow nodded. "All you have to do is get yourselves *close* to the finish line, and just before you both, you know...Bram thrusts inside—"

"You think that will work?" I said cutting her off before Jazzy died of mortification. "I won't risk Bram, not on a maybe."

"Give me sec," Rose said, and she sliced her finger and stared into the blade's shiny surface. Her eyes rolled back in her head.

"She's getting good at that," Iris said.

Rose couldn't see into the future, not really. But images came to her, visions. Sometimes she asked for them, sometimes they came on their own.

Her eyes rolled down and she smiled at me. "It'll work."

"You're positive?"

"I mean, I didn't see you *doing it*, thank the goddess, but I did see you and Bram a week from now, and you were cuddled up on the couch together."

That was good enough for me, Rose's visions hadn't been wrong yet.

"We have a plan," Wills said and clapped her hands. "Mate tonight...catch a killer tomorrow."

"As much as we want to, we can't help her," Rose warned, sounding frustrated as hell.

"I know, but I have complete faith in Mags." Willow strode deeper into the cemetery. "And she needs to wrap this up fast. The council won't let what happened tonight go. We have to assume they're rallying the troops as we speak. If we don't come up with the real killer ASAP, they'll come after us, all of us."

"So no pressure," Iris said, giving Willow an exasperated look.

"We can always move to Hell, right?" Rose said with a strained laugh.

"Or Ronan could hide us," Iris said.

Ronan could make us all disappear if we needed him to. Rose and Ronan's place looked like a vacant lot to everyone else, but vanishing into thin air was no way to live, not long term. It was a good thing I knew exactly what I needed to do next. "I have a plan. We're not going to Hell or living in an invisible little world of Ronan's making, not just yet."

"I'm glad to hear it," Willow said. "Now let's break this curse so you can go jump Bram's bones."

Jasmine laughed, her cheeks flaming. It was good to hear. She'd been closed off and quiet for so long.

"So how do we do this?" Rose asked.

Willow smirked. "Well, first, we get naked."

Jasmine groaned at the same time as me.

Of course, we did.

～

I was naked, lying on the ground under the cemetery's ancient oak tree. A wooden bowl containing a little of my blood sat beside me.

The bowl had always fascinated me. It was stained with the blood of our coven from centuries past, from spells and incantations that witches in our family had performed, like the one we were doing now. One of our ancestors made it long ago from a branch that fell from the oak after it was struck by lightning, and it was incredibly powerful.

My sisters and Jazzy stood around me, and one by one they called for the tree and our ancestors to cleanse me of Cora's darkness, to shatter her hex, and each time they called, they dipped a finger in my blood and traced one of my scars.

My entire body felt alive, buzzing. My scars were warm but not burning—instead of stabbing pain, they tingled.

They all called to the tree again as Willow painted the last scar with blood, then she straightened and sliced an X into her palm and began the chant.

Iris joined in, slicing the same mark into her own palm. Rose next, then Jazzy followed, all cutting the same X into their palms before they clasped hands surrounding me.

Their feet bare, toes pushed into the dirt and heads dipped, they repeated the spell one step behind the other, creating an unbreakable wall of words, of sound and magic that echoed around us.

The chanting grew in volume and speed. Magic snapped through the air, lifting the hair on my arms and the back of my neck. They were crying out now, shaking from the force of the magic they were using, giving everything they had to break the hex.

Cora's darkness gathered inside me, steadily building in intensity. The hex was like a serpent in my gut, twisting and writhing, fighting against the magic, fighting to stay where it was. I gritted my teeth, biting back my scream.

They dropped to their knees and placed their hands on my stomach and cried out the final words of the spell. My spine bowed as Cora's darkness, her hex, was dragged from my belly, pulled down through my back and forced into the ground beneath me.

I cried out as it left my body, as her evil was drawn away by the roots of the mighty oak and pushed down into the earth where it couldn't do anymore harm.

I collapsed back, shaking from relief and exhaustion.

It was gone and the change was instant.

It'd been so long since I felt like this, it took me a moment to recognize it—to recognize myself. All this time we hadn't known why I'd changed so much, not entirely. Clayton and what he did to me was a big part of it, but Cora's evil had made it so much harder. She'd been locked away, but her hex had been slowly poisoning me. Now it was gone. It was finally gone.

Willow grinned down at me. "How do you feel?"

I climbed to my feet. "Like me."

Rose, Iris, and Jazzy grinned as well.

"I think we should tell Mom about this later, yeah? She's already freaking out," Iris said.

"Agreed," Rose said, throwing her arm around Willow's shoulders. "We better get back. She'll be wondering where we are."

Everyone got dressed, and I tugged back on the plain cotton Umbra gown, and headed across the cemetery toward the gates.

"We'll pass on your apologies, then, Mags?" Willow called after me, her chuckle reaching me as I broke into a run.

I wouldn't go another night without him.

Not one more.

$\sim$

Bram

I paced from one end of the tree house and back, wearing out a fucking track. I'd been waiting for Magnolia for over two hours. I got her and her sisters had a lot to talk about, but I was climbing the fucking walls.

Shoving the door open, I walked out onto the deck again, searching the backyard.

If the witches council made a move tonight, I needed to be with her so I could stop them, even if that meant killing every single fucking one of them.

The moon was high, lighting up some areas of the yard and casting others in deep shadow. The sensor light at the side of the house flicked on, and a moment later Mags rounded the corner.

My heart smashed against the back of my ribs at the sight of her, like I'd been plugged into an electrical socket. The white cotton gown she wore clung to her as she ran, her black, wavy hair streaming out behind her.

I strode to the ladder as she reached it, and my heart did another of those heavy thumps when she tilted her head back and smiled up at me. It knocked the wind right out of me and made me fucking weak at the knees.

She climbed the ladder, and when she reached the top, I took a step back and kept going, backing into the tree house, unable to take my eyes off her. The scent of her blood hit me, and I snarled. "Why are you bleeding?"

Magnolia shook her head. "I'm okay. We did a ritual, one that needed my blood." Then she gripped the bottom of her gown and lifted it off, tossing it aside.

She stood in front of me completely naked. Streaks of blood had been painted over every one of her scars. "What is this? What did you do?" I was fucking panting, because my female was naked and not only could I smell her blood, but I could smell how much she needed me. Wanted me.

"While I was in Umbra, I found out the pain I was feeling was because of Cora. Every stab of her knife forced some of her evil inside me. She hexed me, but it's gone now."

"It's gone? No more pain?" I choked out.

"No more pain."

"Thank fuck. Knowing you were in pain... It was killing me." My skin felt tight over my bones, and my palms itched to reach for her. Being this close to the female I loved, knowing that if Death hadn't done what he had to her, I'd be pulling her into my arms right now, carrying her to my bed and finally making her mine—I won't lie, it fucking cut me to the core. But I shoved it down. Mags didn't need to feel that from me. It would hurt her, and I'd rather die than do that.

"I found out something else tonight," she said, her voice barely more than a whisper.

I searched her amber eyes but wasn't able to read what I saw. I don't think I'd ever seen that look on her face before. "What did you find out?"

"Do you trust me?" she asked.

"You know I do."

"With your life?"

"I'd fucking die for you," I said, and she knew that as well.

"I want to be your mate, Bram, in truth."

I hauled in a ragged breath. "I want that, too, baby, more than anything. You'll get control over this thing, I know you will, then we can—"

"No, I want to be your mate now. I want you to make me your mate tonight," she said, her voice shaky.

I stared at her, at the way her eyes sparkled, the excitement on her face. "There's a way?" I didn't want to hope, but I couldn't stop it.

"Yeah, there's a way," she said, the pulse at her throat fluttering wildly. "You game?"

"Fuck, yes, I'm game." There was no need to think it over, I'd do anything to make her mine.

I gripped the couch to hold myself back as she explained what we had to do.

"Rose used her powers. She said you'd be okay, and she hasn't been wrong yet." She chewed her lip. "But I guess there could always be a first time, right? Maybe we shouldn't—"

"We're doing it." Magnolia trusted her sister and her gift. If she didn't, she wouldn't be proposing this to me now.

Silence stretched out between us.

Her hands were fisted at her sides, her feet pressed together, her naked body streaked with blood. Her hair was wild around her face, and her eyes were wide and bright. She was the most stunning thing I'd ever laid eyes on.

And she was waiting for me to tell her what to do, like I had the last time we were standing here like this.

"Bedroom, Magnolia," I said, the strength of my need for her deepening my voice. "Get on the bed."

She licked her nearly healed lips and did as I asked.

I followed, watching as Magnolia crawled onto the bed and sat in the middle. Her long hair fell over her shoulder, and she stared up at me. Her deep cherry lips were glossy and full, and I was desperate to taste them again.

Fuck, she was beautiful. I couldn't believe this was finally happening, that I was finally going to claim my Magnolia in truth. I'd waited for this day for so long. I swallowed hard, my mouth dry as hell. There was something I needed to ask first. "Can I mark you? I know you hate your scars, and I'll understand if you don't want more, but crows, when they mate—"

"Do it, whatever it is, I want you to do it," she said, no hesitation, trusting me with her body, trusting me to take care of her, like she always had.

I swallowed again, the sound audible in the small room. "You sure?"

"Positive. I want your mark on me, Bram."

The predator in me spread its wings and flexed its claws. "Lie on your back and spread your legs for me. Show me what I've been missing. Show me what you're gonna give me." Her breasts shook with her labored breaths, nipples taut. She did as I asked, lying back and letting her legs fall wide.

My skin was burning and tight. Reaching back, I gripped my shirt, dragged it over my head and tossed it aside. "More, Magnolia, spread yourself for me. Are you wet, baby?"

Her hand drifted down her belly and, panting, she did as I asked, and slid a finger over her pretty, slick flesh. "I'm...I'm so wet," she said.

"I need you dripping for me, Mags. I don't want you feeling a moment of pain, just pleasure when I push inside you for the first time." I squeezed my hard cock through my jeans.

"Take the jeans off," she said. "I want to see you."

"Not yet. If I start stroking now, watching you like that, I won't last." I dropped to my knees at the end of the bed, my gaze reaching hers between her spread thighs. "Play with your clit, Mags. Make yourself come fast for me, can you do that?"

She nodded and slid her fingers over her clit while her gaze held mine. Her scent filled the room, and it was driving me closer and closer to the edge of sanity. I wanted to taste her again, tease her, make her scream my name over and over.

Magnolia whimpered, the muscles in her thighs tensing and releasing, her belly quivering. Her lids lowered, eyes heavy with lust. She was breathtaking. "You close, baby?"

"Yes."

I growled when she rubbed her slick little clit faster, and I had to press my hard dick against the mattress to ease the ache, barely stopping myself from thrusting against it. She cried out, and I fisted the covers to hold myself back when she arched against the bed. Her pussy clenched and released as she came for me, so wet she glistened from it, soaking the covers beneath her ass.

Standing, I undid my jeans, shoved them down and kicked them off, squeezing my cock again through my underwear, then shoved them down as well because I couldn't hold back now. "Show me your hand, two fingers out." She instantly did what I asked and I bent down and spit on them, needing part of me inside her right the fuck now. "Push them inside for me, Mags, but not all the way in, not yet."

She trembled, breathing hard, still not fully recovered from her first orgasm. Her second would be with me buried deep inside her. She nodded and pushed her slick fingers inside, and her hips lifted instantly. She drew them out, then back in with a whimper.

The color on her cheeks deepened, and she was breathing heavily. "You're already close, aren't you, baby?"

"Yes."

I stroked my cock faster. "Your reaper power kicks in fast, so I need to try not to make any contact with your skin before I slide inside you. I'm gonna need you to roll over for me, baby. Ass in the air, those fingers still in your pussy."

She did as I said, and I had to squeeze my cock hard not to come when her perfect round ass was aimed right at me, pussy spread and ready to be filled.

"Nice and wide, that's it, chest to the bed. I'm gonna get up behind you now, so don't move, the only thing moving are your fingers, okay?"

"Okay," she groaned.

She was so wet, her juices dripped down her fingers.

I moved as close as I dared. "I don't want to hurt you, Mags, but I'm gonna need to shove my cock inside you hard and fast. I can't ease into you, and you're gonna have to push back to take me deep."

"I k-know. It's okay." She moaned into the covers, her fingers still thrusting in and out.

I stroked my cock again and groaned. I was gonna go off as soon as I was inside her. Holding back was the hardest thing I'd ever done. "Deeper now, baby, faster. Get yourself to the edge. Do it. Quickly now."

The sound of Mags fucking herself for me was more than I could take.

"Bram," she moaned. "Oh, I'm...do it. Do it now."

"Brace," I growled, lined my cock up with her wet-as-fuck entrance, and slammed my hips forward. The head of my cock punched inside her. "Take me," I snarled as she shoved back, taking me all the way to the root.

She screamed, and her pussy clamped down on me, clutching and gripping over and over. I roared as I pulsed inside her, coming hard, filling her. My talons exploded from the ends of my fingers, and I grabbed her shoulder, holding her in place as I pulled out and slammed back in.

Then my eyes rolled into the back of my fucking head, pleasure, euphoria, joy filling me. My crow's song bubbled up from my gut, my chest, bursting from my throat—

Then everything went black.

Chapter Thirty-Three

Magnolia

"Bram!" I spun around.

He lay slumped on his side, face gray, chest deathly still. With a cry, I shoved him to his back, pounding my fists against his chest, once, twice. "Bram," I screamed.

He gasped, his eyes flying open, and sat up. He was shaking hard.

I quickly tried to back away, terrified if I touched him he'd stop breathing again, but his hand shot out, locked on to my arm and he hauled me against him.

"No...wait..."

He rolled me to my back and took my face in his hand.

I blinked up at him, afraid to move, to freaking breathe.

A grin curled his lips. "I'm touching you. You're touching me. I'm still breathing." He pressed his forehead to mine, then he kissed me hard, gripping me tight to him. "You're mine, Maggie. For eternity, you're mine."

A tear streaked down my face, relief and happiness over-whelming me.

He pressed his face against my neck and breathed me in as he ran his hands over my body. "Finally," he said against my shoulder, then lifted his head. He swiped the tear from my cheek. "I've missed you, Mags. Fuck, I've missed touching you so much."

"I've missed you too." We held each other for a long time, just running our hands over each other, reveling in it while we breathed in the other's scent.

Finally, Bram lifted his head and tucked my hair behind my ear. "You okay? Did I hurt you? Your scars? Any pain?"

"No, no pain." I shook my head. "Not anywhere."

He released a relieved breath. "Don't move." He got off the bed and strode into the bathroom. When he came back out, he was holding a washcloth. He carefully spread my thighs, wiping me clean, and when he looked up at me again, his expression was impossibly hot. "I know we don't have much time, but if I don't taste you again, Mags, right the fuck now, I think I'll lose whatever grip I have on my sanity."

"Well, we don't want that," I said, as desperate for him to touch me again, to be with me any way he wanted to.

He tossed the cloth aside and came down on top of me, brushing my hair back from my face. "It's gonna be you and me forever, Mags." His body trembled against mine. "An eternity of loving each other, because fuck, I love you, Magnolia, so much," he said, staring into my eyes.

"I love you too." My heart raced wildly.

His eyes grew heavy, and he took my mouth in a deep, hard kiss that literally made my toes curl. Then he was kissing his way down my neck, not caring about the dried blood streaking my skin, and sucked a nipple into his mouth with a moan. I shoved my fingers into his thick hair and squirmed beneath him.

He looked up at me. "I can't take my time like I want to. But fuck, I want to worship every inch of this beautiful body."

He sucked and kissed his way across my breasts, toying with my nipples, then down, over my ribs, my belly. His strong hands slid between my thighs, and he spread them wide as he shifted farther down. Then, holding my gaze, he dragged his tongue through my pussy, wringing a cry from me. His lids fluttered and a deep, rough groan rolled from him.

Wrapping his arms around my thighs, he gripped me tight to him, and I arched against the mattress when he used his tongue and lips, tasting me, pleasuring me while he snarled and groaned. His fingers flexed against my thighs, digging in when he slid his tongue deep inside me, his growl vibrating through my body, and I was so sensitive already, I couldn't hold back.

I fisted his hair harder. "Bram, oh shit, I—I'm going to—"

One moment he was between my thighs, the next he was looming over me. "I want to feel you come while I'm inside you again."

I nodded, rolling my hips against him. "Please."

He kissed me once more, then lifted to his elbows. "Fuck," he said as he looked down between us. We both watched as he gripped his cock and rubbed the head through my slickness before notching himself at my opening. "Ready?" he said, his obsidian gaze smoldering.

"So ready."

He rocked his hips forward, pushing inside me, and we both groaned. He stayed there for long seconds, panting hard. "Fuck, you're so hot and tight." With another moan, he eased out, then thrust back in, all the way this time. His hiss as he ground against me set off tingles all over my body.

He came down on top of me then, and I wrapped my arms and legs around him, nothing between us now, and I held on tight as we rocked and strained against each other.

"You feel so good," I said against his shoulder.

"Fuck, Mags, so do you." He thrust deep inside me, grinding

again, as if he couldn't get deep enough. "I want to stay here for eternity, inside my mate," he rasped, then kissed me.

We moved together, harder, faster, until our harsh breathing and the sounds of our bodies colliding filled my head. Bram's gasping grunts mingled with his crow's song. A husky, growly melody that was just for me. Waves of pleasure built inside me, higher and higher, and there was no holding it back, not anymore.

I arched in his arms, crying out as I came again, shaking and clutching him to me.

Bram groaned before he pulsed hard inside me, filling me again.

We clung tight to each other, sweat, and blood from the ritual, all over us as we slid together, as we finally collapsed in each other's arms.

I lay there listening to his heart pounding.

"Was it how you imagined it'd be?" I asked when I could finally catch my breath.

He lifted his head and smiled down. "My imagination couldn't have come up with anything as fucking beautiful as this."

The night air was warm, moving through my hair as we flew through the sky. I tightened my arms around Bram's neck and could feel the tension rolling through him. He wasn't happy about my plan, but there was no other choice. Not only had the vines on my skin grown even closer, but I'd just broken myself out of Umbra. In the eyes of the council, I was a serial killer on the run, and they would assume my family had aided in my escape or were hiding me. Time had well and truly run out.

Asuka and the rest of the council weren't going to back off, and she hadn't believed what I'd said about Isaac. As soon as they had enough witches to stand behind them, they were coming after us—all of us.

Which was why my house was currently surrounded by wolf shifters and hellhounds and my sisters, Jazzy, Mom, and Else were taking turns to walk the perimeter of our property, spelling to keep our wards strong. No one was getting in and no one except Bram and I were getting out, not until this was over.

I had no choice but to end this thing tonight, and there was only one way that was going to happen. I needed proof. There was no room for a misstep. When I took Isaac down, I wanted to hand the council indisputable evidence.

We landed, and Bram immediately took my hand as we strode down the demon-filled street. I hadn't been back to this place since the last time Bram and I ventured here, but there were things I needed. Ingredients the demon-run store had that I couldn't get anywhere else.

Bram pushed the door open, and the same female as last time stood behind the counter. When she looked up and saw us, she sighed heavily. "You're still alive, then."

"You seem disappointed." I strode up to the counter.

She shrugged. "Just surprised." Her gaze moved over me. "But you're different." Her eyes narrowed. "What's changed?"

I pulled my hands from my pockets and wiggled my black-tipped fingers. "I'm a reaper."

She took an abrupt step back. "You're not—"

"Here to collect your soul?" I shook my head. "Nope. But I'm hoping you have some oleander and that vial of vampire blood." I had the spell I'd gotten from Shadow Falls, and if this was going to work, I needed that blood.

Her shoulders relaxed a little. "The oleander I can help you with. Still a no for the vamp blood. You're going to have to source it yourself."

"What about Ronan?" Bram asked.

If only. "It needs to be one hundred percent vampire."

"We'll take the oleander," Bram said, then he turned to me. "I think I know someone who can help us with the blood. He owes me."

We left the demon neighborhood a short time later, and Bram flew us to the other side of the city.

The Bank was packed when we walked in. The vampire-owned club always was on the weekends. I'd been here several times, and it could get wild. I had no idea about The Vault, the separate club in the basement. I'd never been able to get down there since it was only for blood drinkers and those willing to offer themselves up as donors.

Bram kept a tight grip on my hand as we strode through the crowd on the dance floor, then stopped in front of the door on the other side of the room.

The big vampire standing in front of it greeted us. "We got business with you tonight, crow?"

Bram shook his head. "Ender here?"

He jerked his chin up and opened the door, stepping aside.

Bram strode through, pulling me after him, and we made our way down the stairs. "Why were you here that time? The time Leah and the others saw you?"

He stopped in front of a massive, round iron door, made from an old safe.

"We had business with Nero. They lost a couple of their elders and were in the middle of a reshuffle. There's been fighting over who takes their place. They didn't have time to deal with a couple rogues, so we were called in to do if for them."

"Why does Ender owe you?" Pretender or "Ender" to most, worked for Nero. I knew this because Iris had met him during her own trial.

"He fucked up, made a mess he didn't want Nero to know about. We cleaned it for him."

By all accounts, Nero was an utterly terrifying and very old male who would kill you without blinking an eye. "Is there anything else I need to know before we walk in there?"

He curled his fingers around mine. "Just stay close to me, okay? Don't leave my side." Then he turned The Vault's big handles and pushed the door open.

We walked into a large room. Music played, and the scent of blood and sex filled the air. Blood drinkers of every kind were hanging out, some feeding from donors, some fucking for all to see while they did it.

Bram headed across the room, his hand tightly around mine. Unlike the others here, the male we were walking toward wasn't in a suit—or completely naked. He was wearing black jeans and a hooded sweatshirt. The hood was up, and the shadows from it concealed most of his face. He was leaning against a tall table, looking at his phone and ignoring everyone around him, including several people overtly trying to get his attention.

He turned then and watched us from under his hood as we approached.

"Bram," he said when we finally reached him.

"Ender," Bram returned, then smiled, and it wasn't friendly.

Vibrant lilac eyes glowed from under Ender's hood. "You're here to collect."

Bram nodded. "You have somewhere private we can talk?"

Ender jerked his chin up, and we followed him deeper into the club, down a hall, and through a door at the end. We walked into a bedroom—and *wow*. It was a freaking horror show.

"Someone has a major fairy-tale fetish," I said, looking around stunned. "What the hell is this place?"

"A place we don't talk about if we want to live, so keep that in mind," Ender said.

I turned away from the four-poster bed draped in pink and finally got a good look at the male. He was...well, there was no other word for it, beautiful. Like he could give Ren a run for his money in the male model stakes, and that was no easy feat. I blinked up at him, momentarily mesmerized. The guy was so gorgeous, he didn't seem real.

"I know your sister Iris," he said. "And I've seen you upstairs." His gaze slid over me, and there was no mistaking the hunger in his eyes for anything else. Though, I wasn't sure which kind, lust or he was contemplating taking a bite out of me.

Bram stepped closer. "Don't look at my mate, and don't talk to her."

"Let me guess? Touch her and die?" Ender said with a rough laugh.

I pulled my hands from my pockets and flashed my black-tipped fingers. "Literally."

Ender's violet eyes slid to Bram. "You brought a fucking reaper in here?"

"She's not here for your soul, but we would like some of your blood," Bram said.

Ender's eyes narrowed. "I don't have a soul, and I'll take a pass on the blood donation."

Bram and the vampire locked eyes. "You owe me, big. Don't fucking test me on this."

Ender's nostrils flared, and though he was wearing a baggy sweatshirt, I could see him tense for a fight. I quickly stepped forward. "You have my word it won't be used against you or anyone else you know. I need it for a spell, nothing more. And if there's any left, I'll destroy it," I said.

His gaze slid to me. "I want a blood oath."

Bram grabbed the front of his shirt, and they snarled in each other's faces. "Not happening—"

I rested my hand on his forearm. "B, it's okay." Then I looked at Ender. "I'd do it, but I'm not sure how? My blood gets anywhere near you, I'm pretty sure it'll kill you."

Ender flashed his fangs. "We're already dead, sweetheart. You can touch me all you like."

I hadn't thought of that.

I'd broken my last blood vow, and everything had gone to shit afterward. Nerves filled me, but what choice did I have? And there wasn't a chance in hell I'd break this one. I didn't know if vampires had souls or not, but they were the undead. "Fine, let's do it." I pulled my blade from my pocket and made a slice in my palm before I changed my mind.

Bram closed in behind me, his front pressed to my back, and his arm came around me, locking around my middle. I didn't have to turn around to know he was staring Ender down. But I guess if it kept my new, seriously protective mate under control, I wasn't going to argue.

Ender cut his own palm, then held out his hand. "Take it and repeat what you said."

I pressed my palm to his, and he curled his fingers around mine firmly. "You have my word that your blood won't be used against you in any way, and I'll destroy whatever's left."

He nodded his approval and released my hand. "You got something for me to put it in?"

I pulled a vial from my bag. He took it, sliced his wrist and filled it, corked it and handed it back. He covered the cut with his mouth, and when he pulled his hand away, the slice had already sealed. "Use it wisely, little witch."

I carefully put it in my pack, and when I looked up, Ender was swiping his tongue over his palm.

His eyes flashed. "Fuck, you taste good. You ever wanna return the favor, I'll accept a donation from you anytime."

Bram growled, viciously, and slammed his fist into Ender's face. The vampire's head jerked back and blood sprayed from his nose. He laughed, flashing blood-coated teeth and fangs.

Bram grabbed my hand and towed me toward the door.

"We're square now, crow," Ender called after us. "Don't forget that."

Chapter Thirty-Four

Magnolia

The hospital was easy enough to get into, but Chase's room, not so much. He had a guard stationed in front of the door.

Bram eyed me, then the guard, from our current spot down the hall. The nurse's uniform I'd acquired was a little on the tight side.

"Did it work? Do I look different?" I said, holding my bag containing the potion I'd carefully mixed.

He frowned. "Yes. I don't like it."

I had enough of Ender's blood to work another spell. One where I could take on someone else's likeness. I just had to keep a personal item of theirs with me at all times. I'd broken into a few lockers and found a necklace that belonged to one of the nurses and, presto-chango, I was now Nurse McGill.

This was another spell the council didn't approve of. It was outlawed when they first came to be. It was definitely on the dark side of the magic spectrum, and if Death hadn't used his mojo on me and made me one of his minions, this spell alone probably would have tipped my internal scale into the pool of terrors Agatheena spoke of. Using my magic to infiltrate Chase's comatose brain and ferret around in his memories? Yeah, that would've definitely done it.

"Time to go," Bram said.

A nurse had left Chase's room a short time ago, so I'd have some time before another one showed up. I lifted to my tiptoes to give Bram a kiss, and he jerked his head back.

I grinned up at him. "Sorry, forgot."

"I'm sure Nurse McGill's a nice lady, but no kissing until you have your face back, yeah?"

"Roger that." I patted him on the butt, and he jumped. I grinned. "Right, see you in a couple minutes."

Bram shook his head at me, and I strode toward the guard. "Hey," I said when I reached him.

He smiled and instantly stepped aside. I walked into Chase's room and shut the door behind me. Piece of cake.

Chase lay still in his bed. The bruises on his face were gone, but I had no idea what condition the rest of him was in. His other wounds were dressed or under the covers. I hovered my hand over his forehead, using my healing ability to feel out the damage to his mind. What I got was a whole lot of nothing. Well, mostly nothing. He was there, I could feel him, but he'd withdrawn completely. It was like he'd shut down his mind to hide from the horror of what he went through.

I got it, and I didn't blame him, and my evening with Ryan hadn't been half as bad as what Chase had endured. I still understood, though. I'd wanted to check out multiple times a couple of years ago, but I hadn't because of Bram, and I'd used anger to get through it instead. That anger hadn't all been mine, though. Cora's hex had made everything worse.

A tap came from the window. Bram hovered in front of it, his wings steadily beating behind him. I rushed over and opened it for him.

He quickly climbed in and jumped down. "Let's do this." He strode to the door and carefully and quietly turned the lock.

I pulled a vial from my bag and stood beside the bed. "Hey, Chase, I wish I didn't have to do this, but it's our only hope of catching the person who did this to you, okay?"

Bram raised a brow.

"I'm taking invading his privacy to a whole new level. If he can hear me, I'd like to give the guy a little warning." I popped the lid off my potion. I'd used Frances's spell and her ingredients, but I'd also tweaked it a little and made it my own. Her way caused the recipient a lot of pain, intentionally as far as I could see, mine did not.

I held the vial out to Bram, since I couldn't touch Chase, and he dipped his finger into it as I recited my spell and drew the symbol I'd shown him on Chase's forehead. On the second recitation, I dipped my finger in the potion and drew the same symbol on the center of my own hand, then the third time, I hovered my palm above Chase's forehead.

"If my hand gets too close to him, you'll need to hold it up," I said to Bram.

He nodded, and I closed my eyes, uttering the spell a final time.

Oppressive darkness filled my mind's eye immediately, the hospital room, Bram, no longer there.

There was just...nothing.

"Hello?" I called into the darkness, my voice echoing through what had to be Chase's mind.

Something fundamental had fractured the day he was attacked, and instead of just locking away the awful memories of what happened to him, he'd slammed everything behind a door and thrown away the key.

He'd been trying to protect himself, but he'd taken it too far, and now he was lost, stuck in the dark, unable to find his way out.

"Chase? Are you here?" There was a shuffling sound to my right. A figure huddled in the corner, curled in a ball. "Chase?"

His head lifted, and he stared up at me wide-eyed. "What are you...why are you here?" He slowly rose to his feet. "Am I dreaming?"

"It's not a dream. I'm in your room at the hospital, and I don't have much time." I took another step closer to him. "I need you to help me. I need you to show me who hurt you."

He scrambled back into the shadows. "No. I can't. I can't do that."

"I know you're afraid, but they can't hurt you here. In here, they're not real," I said, holding out my hand to him. "If you don't want to wake up yet, that's okay. But I need to see who did this, Chase, so I can stop them."

"I—I don't know," he said. "I can't remember. I don't want to."

"I know, and you don't have to. I can do it for you. I just need you to show me where it is. Where the memory is," I said.

"You won't make me go?"

"You can stay right here."

He sat down on the floor again and wrapped his arms around his knees.

"Chase?"

"You can stop them?" he asked, his voice so childlike now it was unnerving.

"I promise, I'll stop them. They won't hurt you ever again," I said and hoped that was true, for everyone's sake.

He buried his face against one arm and pointed to a door that hadn't been there before on the other side of the room.

The door was tall and wide, and as I got closer I saw that blood dripped from the cracks around it. I gripped the handle, took a deep breath, and turned it.

It flew open, and Chase screamed behind me. I quickly threw myself through and slammed the door behind me—and almost dropped to the floor when everything Chase had been feeling, physical and mental, slammed into me.

The images spun around my head, blood, so much blood. Chase trying to scream but unable to with his lips sewn closed and from the drug he'd been given. The pain was unimaginable, the kind that had you begging for death rather than endure a moment more.

I fell to the floor, shaking, and covered my head with my hands. It was too much. Oh, goddess, it was too awful.

"Magnolia?"

My name echoed around me, coming from a distance.

"Mags...baby?"

Bram.

His voice calling me back snapped me out of the despair, the horror. Time was running out. I needed to get the fuck up. Now.

"Maggie!" Bram's voice was louder, more urgent.

I pushed off the floor and struggled to my feet, then forced myself to open my eyes, looking through Chase's eyes, looking out at that room we'd found him in at Red.

I struggled to breathe through the agony and fear as the door opened across the room, forcing myself to keep watching as someone walked in and shut themselves in with Chase.

Ryan.

If it was only Ryan, if he was there on his own, this was all for nothing. I had nowhere else to go from here, there wasn't enough time.

The door behind Ryan opened again.

I felt myself being pulled back through the one in Chase's mind, the memory fading. I just needed another minute.

The second person closed the door and walked in. They were talking to Ryan. I could hear them, I could hear everything, but I couldn't see them. My eyes wanted to close again when the newcomer stepped closer, but I forced them to stay open, to look into their eyes—

Then I was sucked back through the door and it slammed shut. A moment later I was yanked back to consciousness.

"Magnolia?" Bram said, shaking me.

I blinked, and the hospital room came back into focus.

"I didn't think you were going to wake up," he said hoarsely. "You scared the fuck out of me."

I straightened, feeling sick to my stomach. "I know who it is. Who was working with Ryan."

~

I held the phone tighter. "Where is she?"

Isaac hissed down the line. "I'm a bit busy right now, Magnolia. We're outside your mother's house. If you don't want anyone to get hurt, you better come home."

"Or better yet, you could break the enchantment spells you have over the other council members and your business partners and call them off."

There was a beat of silence. "I don't know what the fuck you're talking about."

"Yes, you do. Did you do it because you truly believed Willow was the killer, or are you in on it with Ryan and Maria?"

"In on what?" I could hear the hesitation in his voice.

"Ryan and Maria are the ones killing your friends. Did you agree to help them so you could get your hands on my sister's store and the other properties, so your development could go through, or just because you hate my family, you sack of shit?"

"You've lost your fucking mind," he snarled.

Chanting started in the background, the council had their army, and they were about to start a fucking war. "I've seen it. I saw Maria hack up Chase. I fucking saw it. Call the council off, now! You start a war with my family, and you will lose. You're not just taking on my coven, you're taking on the hounds, the wolf pack, the bats, the crows, and the knights of Hell as well."

He released a shaky breath. "How did you see it?"

"I looked into Chase's mind. He showed me."

"And you're sure it was Maria?" he asked.

Anger hit me. "Let me guess. She convinced you to enchant everyone?"

A shaky breath rattled down the line. "I was sure it was Willow. Positive. Maria said...she said I should do it so Willow didn't get away with killing our friends like she did Elmer. I thought I was doing the right thing... I thought—"

"You thought it was a fast way to get Willow locked away so you could buy the property you wanted and take down the witch you blame for your brother's death all in one go."

"I didn't know," he said. "I didn't know what Maria and Ryan were doing."

"Then call the council off before you start a war you can't finish, and tell them what happened."

"Stop," he yelled. "Stop the spell!" The chanting in the background stopped.

"Where is she, Isaac? Where's Maria?"

"I don't know." He cursed. "She hasn't been answering my calls."

I cursed and disconnected. "How the hell are we going to find her?"

"You're a reaper," Bram said beside me.

I paced the roof of the hospital. "I don't even know what I can do?" I said to him, feeling fucking helpless.

"Reapers can find their targets anywhere. They have access to any place they want. Nothing can stop them," he said.

He was right. I rubbed my hands over my face. "I'm not even sure how I did it in that cell."

"Those powers are there. They're part of you. You just have to pull them forward again."

He was right, of course. Everything had been so crazy, I hadn't had time to really think about what I could do, apart from the whole touch-me-and-die thing. I needed to slow things down, panicking wasn't going to help me.

Bram strode over and took my hands. "Sit."

I sat and Bram did the same.

"Close your eyes."

I did.

"Breathe deeply. In and out. I want you to focus inward. I want you to remember how you felt, what you did in that cell."

I did, and that same darkness swirled inside me. Cora's darkness was gone, but my own, Death's, they were there, and they were powerful, fierce. I gripped on to it, like I had the day before.

And this time it clicked into place with ease, the power pulsing through me, so strong and wild, violent.

"I haven't been called to collect Maria's soul, so I can't just find her. But I know how I can," I said and opened my eyes.

Bram was watching me intently, a fierce expression on his face. "You're fucking amazing."

"Not without you." I leaned in and kissed him. I wanted to keep on kissing him, but that would have to wait.

"How do we find her?" Bram asked when I lifted my head.

"I need to hold something of hers."

"Easy," Bram said, tugged off his shirt, tucked it in the back of his jeans and scooped me into his arms.

Chapter Thirty-Five

Magnolia

The wind swirled around us. Maria's apartment was dark, empty, not that I expected her to be here. Would have made things a hell of a lot easier, though. Resting my hand on the banana lounger I'd seen Maria sitting on last time I was here, I closed my eyes.

Shadows rushed in at the edges of my mind, a vision flashing in front of me. It felt kind of the same as when Death dragged me to Limbo, but this time my soul was still with me, and I was being shown where to go, rather than actually being taken there. My fingers and lips burned and I knew I'd transformed. I was the reaper.

A massive building filled my mind's eye. "I've got it." Bram's palm was warm against the side of my face, and I blinked up at him.

His expression was fierce, his gaze unfaltering. My bones were literally glowing through my skin and he was looking at me as if I were the most beautiful thing he'd ever seen. "Whatever happens tonight, remember, you're not in this alone. I'm with you every step of the way."

"I know."

He dipped his head and kissed me, not caring that I looked like a monster right then. I released my reaper powers, letting them flow out of me, feeling myself transform back to normal, and kissed him back harder. I never wanted to stop. I wanted this task over with. I wanted my trial in the rearview mirror and for something to be easy for us.

"When this is over, you want to go away on a vacation?" I said.

"Where are we going?"

"I don't care. As long as it's just you and me and no one else, it'll be the best place on earth." He flashed me a grin and my heart went a little crazy in my chest.

"Let's get this the fuck over with, then, baby. We got somewhere to be." His wings unfurled, large and shiny black.

My dark angel.

He scooped me in his arms.

"Where to?"

"Roxburgh High School."

Bram cursed but held me tighter and dove off the side of the building.

He flew fast, and I tucked my face into the side of his neck when my hair whipped around me. I had no idea what we were going to walk in on when we found her. Maria's motives were still a complete mystery. Why would she kill all those people? People that she pretended to be friends with, more than friends. The level of evil for someone to do that, to lock emotion away like that? I mean, I'd watched her in the living room comforting her *friends*, seeking comfort in return while crocodile tears had rolled down her face, grieving for people who she and Ryan had mercilessly and brutally murdered.

Yeah, there was something terribly wrong with her.

We reached the school, and the parking lot lights lit up the area. A couple of cars were parked there—and Isaac's was one of them. Jenna and Robert's was the other.

"Isaac must have gone straight to her after our call." Either he was in on it or he'd stupidly decided to confront her himself.

Bram flew behind the main building, landing in the shadows. I had my knife strapped to my thigh, though, I'd only needed to touch Maria and she'd go down. Killing her wasn't the goal, however. "I need to take her alive. The council needs proof, and I'm going to deliver it to them."

Bram nodded.

Maria hadn't attended this school, yet she seemed fixated with it. We strode to the back entrance, but my instincts told me that wasn't where I needed to go, so I let them guide me. "Around here."

The grounds had numerous smaller buildings, but when we rounded the corner, I knew exactly where I was being led.

The old chapel was one of the original buildings, but it'd been left to crumble after an earthquake a year after I started here. The cost to fix it had been more than the school could afford, but it was also a historical building, and the school and community were trying to raise funds to eventually have it restored.

"The chapel." Sticking to the shadows, we sprinted around the back of the old building. A light flickered through one of the windows.

The building was warded, one that bound magic, similar to the one at Umbra. This one allowed you entry, but strangled your magic. I didn't need it though, not now that I'd tapped in to my reaper powers.

I slid my knife free as Bram gripped the handle, easing the door open.

The chapel itself was quiet, the candlelight dancing over the remaining stained-glass windows that had survived the quake. The pews were jostled from their perfect formation and covered in dust.

"I'll check back here," Bram said quietly.

I nodded, then froze when a muffled cry came from the back of the church. We rushed toward it. Jenna was trussed up on the ground. She looked up at us with huge, terrified eyes. I pressed my finger to my lips, telling her to be quiet, and yanked the gag from her mouth.

"Where is she?"

"Basement. She's got Robert and Isaac," Jenna said. "I d-don't understand what's going on."

Bram quickly untied her. "Go," he said.

She shook her head, lips trembling. "Not without Robert."

I held her terrified gaze. "We'll do our best to get him out of here alive, but you need to go get help. Get the council and tell them what happened."

A tear streaked down her cheek, but she nodded.

"Stay low, stick to the shadows," I said.

She slipped out, and we moved on silent feet down the center aisle and in behind the ornate pulpit. There were heavy, dark wooden doors against the walls on either side of the room. Bram checked the first. "Pastor's office," he whispered.

I nodded and gripped the door handle of the opposite door, opening it as quietly as I could. A terrible but familiar smell hit me almost immediately—rot. Death.

Candlelight flickered at the bottom of the stairs, and we started down. My mind kept throwing scenarios at me, of what this could be, of why Maria and Ryan had done this, but the truth was, I had absolutely no idea.

Someone's voice carried up to us.

Isaac.

We paused on the stairs.

Isaac was trying to reason with Maria, but there was no

missing the tremble of fear in his voice. "Tell me Ryan forced you into it," he was saying. "This isn't you. It can't be."

"You don't know anything about me, Isaac. And you never really bothered to ask, did you? If you weren't fucking me, you were using me for my money. Don't pretend you ever cared about me, when we all know the only person you care about is yourself. You're all the same, every one of you."

Bram took the next step, and switched forms, shadowing out so he could check around the corner. He rematerialized again a moment later and waved me forward. Maria had Robert and Isaac on the far side of the basement, where numerous old bookcases filled with junk created several walled-off sections.

"I don't know what you're talking about," Robert said. "We love you."

"No, Rob, you love yourself, and you and your friends are *fucking monsters.*" Maria screamed the last, then laughed, the switch unnerving, the sound deranged. "Well, it's my turn to be the monster, and it's your turn to feel pain. I want you to feel the kind of loss that breaks you, mind and soul, the kind of pain that drives you to do anything to make it stop."

I eased closer. What the hell was she talking about? How had they hurt her?

"What are you going to do?" Isaac asked.

"I've already done it. I just need a couple things from you, and I'll have everything I want." The sound of another door opening echoed through the room.

"Oh goddess," Isaac rasped. "What the fuck have you done, Maria?"

"Come meet your new friends, my dears," she said, I assumed to whoever had just revealed themselves.

And going by Robert's scream of pure terror, Maria wasn't the only monster in the room.

There was a scrape and a groan, then shuffling sounds. I

stepped closer to the shelves in front of me and peered through. Maria stood in front of Robert. Isaac was beside him, and they were both tied up. Isaac had a pretty bad gash on his head, and blood dripped down the side of his face steadily.

"We still need an arm, Rob, and I thought you'd be the perfect candidate."

Bram looked at me, and he didn't need to say a word. I nodded. We couldn't just stand here while she started chopping limbs, we needed to do something.

Bram and I stepped out from behind the shelf, and Maria's head swung our way. Fury filled her eyes. "Emmaline, Marcel come to me."

They were the names of her brother and sister, the ones who'd died while Maria had been away at boarding school.

Another scrape came from the corner, and what walked out turned my blood cold. Bodies, but not human, not anymore, stitched together like Frankenstein's monster.

"How?" I gasped.

"Dark magic, Magnolia, the kind you're all too familiar with." She ran the backs of her fingers down the side of "Emmaline's" patchwork cheek. "Their spirits were lost, so full of rage they refused to cross over, so I worked out a way for them to be with me all the time." Emmaline seemed to have all her body parts. Marcel, on the other hand, was still missing an arm.

"You cut up your friends and the people they loved to use their organs, their body parts, to turn your brother and sister into zombies?" Because that's what I was looking at. The undead. This wasn't reanimation, this was shoving a couple of lost and angry spirits into vessels and hoping for the best.

But to create them, she would've needed more...*parts* than the ones we knew about. She'd killed others to create these monsters.

"That's not what they are," she spat. "It's Emma and Marcel. I have them back."

"No, you don't. They stopped being your brother and sister a long time ago. Spirits that refuse to pass over become angry." I held her wild stare. "And you know what the undead need to stop their bodies from decomposing." Blood, flesh. Human flesh. And if they hadn't developed a hunger for it yet, they would very soon. "You killed others, you had to have. Where are they?"

She waved a hand. "They're not important."

No, she made sure only the prom committee and their loved ones were found, so they knew they were being targeted.

Emmaline turned to me and I jerked back when I realized whose eyes Maria had used when she'd created Emmaline. They were Margot's. They were dull and lifeless, but they were my friend's eyes. "Why did you do this?" I choked out.

She strode over to Robert, crouching down in front of him, and fisted his hair. "You know, don't you, Rob?"

He shook his head, eyes wide.

"Rob here doesn't understand the word no, do you, Robert? And when you cornered my baby sister in the library one day when no one else was around, and she said no, you didn't listen then either. No, you took what you wanted."

Robert's mouth opened and closed, true horror filling his eyes. "I thought...I didn't know..."

Maria turned to me. "We were going through some of Emmaline's things a few months ago, and I found her old diary. You can imagine my horror, my utter disgust to learn the people I loved and trusted were the reason I no longer had my brother and sister. I'd let them touch me, fuck me. I scrubbed my skin raw that night."

"What happened?" I asked, feeling sick to my stomach.

"It started off with bullying, a lot of it. My brother and sister, the rest of the poetry group as well. First Clara pretended she was interested in Marcel. Her acting skills really paid off, didn't they, Rob? She made him fall in love with her. She said she wanted everyone to know, that they should go on a date, and when he got there, Clara and her friends laughed at him, mocked him, humiliated him."

That explained the poem Marcel wrote. "That's why you chose Red when you attempted to murder Chase, to expose them, to humiliate him, all of them, the way they had Emmaline and Marcel."

Her eyes narrowed on me. She wanted me dead as well, it was written all over her face. I'd gotten in her way, I'd killed Ryan.

"Ryan was Marcel's best friend," Maria said. "And he'd been dating Emmaline for six months. He loved her." She shoved Robert's head back and stood. "Marcel and Emma were close, only a year apart, more like best friends as well, and after Robert forced himself on my sister, she withdrew, stayed in her room. I never knew why, not until I found her diary, but it was all there. Everything they did to both of them."

It was all clicking into place. "What did they do?"

"They made a suicide pact. They came here to this chapel, where no one would find them, and hung themselves from those beams, right there," she said, pointing to a spot above her. "Robert and Jemma, Chase and Clara, and Calvin and his bitch cousin Katana, they tortured my sister, bullied and tormented my brother, until they couldn't take it anymore."

"You showed Ryan the diary, didn't you? And he agreed to help?" I guessed.

Ryan had been in the poetry group as well, another of the prom committee's targets, no doubt.

"He was more than happy to help me, and he relished taking his pound of flesh." I bet it was Ryan's idea to carve judgment into each victim as well. "He wanted Emma back like I did. We wanted them both back, and with Isaac's help, and his little enchantment spell, of course, it wasn't hard convincing everyone it was Willow running around killing everyone."

Which was why Leah's murder had been different. Maria had

been forced to kill Leah herself with Ryan dead. "Why Willow? Why me?"

"I never meant for you to become the prime suspect, that just kind of happened." She strode to Isaac and gripped his jaw. "Isaac wanted to believe it was Willow so badly that he didn't think twice when I suggested he tip the scale and help her get convicted faster." She shoved his head aside. "As for why? Because it was easy, because I had Isaac in my pocket and he hated your sister, and because your family is powerful and hoard that power, keeping it for themselves. Willow was strong, even back then, and she did *nothing*. She let those monsters roam the halls and terrorize people weaker than them, than her, and she did *nothing* to stop them. She's Keeper of her coven—she strolls around this city like she fucking owns it—but she's just the same as the rest of them."

"If Willow had known, she would have stopped it, Maria. She stood up for others at this school. If she'd seen them hurt Emma, she would have stopped it, I know she would."

"Lies!" Maria screamed. "Get them," she said to her brother and sister.

I expected them to move slow, but they were *fast*. Emma came at me, grabbing for me. I tried to shove her back, but she was strong as hell. I touched her, but because she was already dead, nothing happened. I didn't think even hacking off body parts would do much.

Marcel had other ideas completely, and instead of coming for me and Bram, he pounced on Robert, tearing into him and taking a bite out of the side of his throat. Robert screamed as blood pumped out of him.

Maria watched on, stunned.

"Untie Isaac and get Maria out of here," I called to Bram, as Emmaline came at me again, mouth open, lips peeled back, trying to take a bite out of me.

Bram did as I said, slashing the ropes around Isaac's feet and hands, while Marcel chowed down on Robert, who was now unmoving and obviously dead. Isaac sprinted for the exit, while Bram grabbed Maria. She kicked and screamed, hitting and scratching him, trying to get him to let her go.

"Run, Mags," he roared.

I spun with force, kicking Emmaline's legs out from under her. She hit the ground, and I sprinted for the stairs, Bram and a spitting, screaming Maria right behind me. We bolted to the top and I slammed the door shut after Bram, turning the old iron key in the lock, then dragged a heavy wooden seat over and jammed it under the handle.

Bram threw Maria down, and Isaac stepped forward, offering his belt. Bram quickly and efficiently tied her hands together with it, then used his own belt for her ankles.

"That door's not going to hold them long," I said when everything went quiet. "Once they're done with Robert, they'll come looking for more."

"What do you want to do?" Bram asked.

"We need to hand Maria off to the council, then deal with those monsters."

"I'll take her in," Isaac said, still visibly shaken.

"You'll have to excuse me for not trusting you," I said. "You know, since you tried to frame my sister for murder and all."

He shoved his shaking fingers through his hair. "After finding all that evidence at The Cauldron, I truly believed she was doing it. I had no idea... I never would have—"

"Save it."

The door opened and Asuka strode in, Jenna and several other council members behind her.

Bram immediately hauled Maria off the floor and dumped her at Asuka's feet. "You need to get her out of here."

Asuka looked at me, her expression stricken. "I'm so sorry, Magnolia. The council's withdrawn all charges. Willow's included in that, of course." Her gaze slid to Isaac, and she all but bared her teeth. "We found the enchantment charms you hid in our houses. You'll be held at Umbra Sanitarium while you await trial."

The council enforcers moved in, grabbing him and hauled him and Maria away.

A crash came from the basement.

"It's not over yet," I said. "Maria and Ryan weren't just killing for the hell of it. They were collecting body parts to build new bodies for her dead sister and brother." I motioned to the door. "That's them, behind door number one."

Asuka paled. "The undead?"

"Yes." Tingles danced across my back and around my side, swirling around my belly button, the markings the mother had given me heating until they were burning under my skin. I yanked up my shirt. "Bram?"

He rushed over, crouching to check them. His hand covered my side before he looked up at me. "They're touching, but they're colorful."

I'd passed. I'd passed my task.

I didn't get a chance to reply because pain arrowed down my spine, and I staggered back.

Bram grabbed hold of me. "Mags?"

I dropped to the floor like a dead weight, and a silent scream tried to burst from me as power exploded through my body. It built higher and higher, surging in waves; the gifts the mother had given our coven strengthening and solidifying inside me.

Bram cupped my face. "Mags?" he snarled. "What the fuck's going on?"

I tried, but I still couldn't speak, my back arching against the stone floor when another wave crashed over me, through me. The pain increased, until I couldn't take any more—

Another surge of power caused my body to jerk under the strength of it—then it seemed to wash away, taking the pain with it.

"Magnolia," Bram called, shaking me.

"I passed," I choked out. "I passed my task. I-it's okay. I'm okay."

He pressed his lips to my forehead, then scooped me up in his arms. "What the fuck was that?"

"Our coven's powers taking hold. It's done."

"Thank fuck," Bram said, fisting my hair and holding me tight against him.

A crash came from below the church, then another one.

Bram cursed and helped me to my feet as a council enforcer ran into the church, his face white, visibly shaken. "Whatever was in the basement, it got out. Looked like two of them. They ran into the forest."

"They're strong and fast," I said to Asuka. "We don't know how old they are, but they're only going to get stronger with every hour that passes."

Shouts, screams, came from outside.

"Maybe they doubled back?" I pulled my knife free and ran outside. The witches who came with Asuka had backed up, awe and horror on their faces.

Then a rattle echoed through the night—a sound I recognized all too well.

The mother, in her serpent's vessel, was sliding across the school field, heading straight for me. I dropped my knife and braced, not sure what was about to happen.

She stopped in front of me, so close, her hiss blew my hair back. Her massive head swayed as her black eyes locked on me.

You passed your task, young witch, but you are no longer the mother's child alone. You are Death's servant, and you have an unfair advantage.

She stared down at me, and I wasn't sure what she wanted me to say. "I didn't seek Death out, mother."

Did I ask you to speak?

I shut my mouth.

A combat trial is now pointless. You would win, easily. But your touch cannot kill the undead.

She paused, and I didn't know if it was for dramatic pause, but I was close to jumping out of my skin.

One final test for you...and your sisters. Her head shot forward, her tail rattling with the sudden movement. *No mates, no familiars. The four of you, alone, must destroy the undead, and you, reaper, will deliver their souls to Death.*

Chapter Thirty-Six

Magnolia

My sisters were gathered around me, dressed for battle and ready for anything.

"I'm sorry you have to do this," I said.

"Don't." Willow planted her hands on her hips. "This isn't on you, and who's to say this wouldn't have happened anyway? You're the last, this might've always been the mother's endgame."

"Wills is right," Iris said. "It makes sense this is how it ends, all of us fighting together."

Rose took Iris's hand. "We're stronger together." She looked over her shoulder. "I just hope Ronan stayed at the house with the others."

Willow blew out a frustrated breath. "War's being a stubborn ass. I have a feeling they won't do what they're told."

"Oh, I know they won't," Iris said. "But Ash is going to do her best to talk sense into them, or at least stall them. She's an alpha; she knows their language."

I searched the sky and the surrounding trees for Bram. If he was here, he was staying out of sight. "They're worried, and in Bram's case, hopped up on newly-mated-male possessiveness. He won't be stopped. Tell me he'll eventually calm the hell down?"

Iris laughed. "That's a myth they tell us to make sure we mate them. The truth is, it gets worse the longer you're with them, not better."

"Just wait 'til you're pregnant," Willow said. "Relic promised to try and stop Warrick if he loses it and comes after me. Or get a bunch of his brothers to hold him down, whatever works."

It was going to be hard on all of them. Our mates were going to have to fight every one of their instincts to come after us, to protect us, but they also knew what we'd been through to get to this point, and they wouldn't mess that up for us, not unless they absolutely had to.

"How fast do you think Marcel and Emma are moving?" I asked Rose.

She'd gotten back from a reconnaissance flight a few minutes ago.

"They're moving fairly quickly, but we won't have any trouble catching up."

"Probably because they're not hungry yet," Iris said.

No, they'd only eaten Robert a couple of hours ago. "We need to be quick. They won't be satisfied long." I strapped my knife to my thigh. "I think if we send Rose back up, she can keep us updated on their position and can use her powers to knock them back if she absolutely has to, though we don't want you draining too much of your magic." I checked my pack, making sure my vials were easily accessible. It wasn't just Emmaline and Marcel we had to worry about in that forest. "Iris, if you go wolf and run ahead, it'll drive most of the demons back." Since Draven's pack had been culling the demons around their keep ruthlessly for a few years now, they tended to avoid a wolf when they sensed one. "And, Wills, do not engage. Do not get close, not to the demons or the fucking zombies. Peanut comes first. She's more important than this trial, more important than anything, understand?" I pulled on my pack and adjusted the straps. "None of you get close enough for Emmaline or Marcel to touch you. If they get hold of you, they're not letting go and then they're taking a bite out of you. We corner them, then I finish them the way we planned, agreed?"

Silence greeted me, and I looked up from strapping on a set of throwing knives. All three of my sisters were watching me—surprise, but mostly pride on each of their faces.

"You got it," Rose said and bit her lip. I knew it was to stop it from quivering.

"Good plan," Iris said.

Willow grinned. "Well, aren't you the little badass."

"Why yes, yes, I am." I grinned. "Though, obviously, I defer to you. You are the oldest."

Willow shook her head. "You don't need to defer shit to me, Mags. Your plan's perfect."

That felt good, really fucking good. After two years of fucking up, of worrying my sisters, worrying my entire coven—feeling in control, feeling like me, and making my sisters proud, felt amazing. "Okay, let's go catch us a couple bloodthirsty zombies."

Rose's white bat wings unfurled, and her eyes flicked to black. "I'll stay back, but I'll try to slow their progress," she said, then lifted off.

Iris called on her wolf, and her eyes changed from brown to blue. Physically, she stayed the same, no matter what animal she chose to surround her. But you could still see the animal, and a translucent wolf enveloped Iris now. "I'll call the animals when I get close. They'll help drive them back this way."

Then she jogged into the forest, and Wills and I followed. It wasn't like we'd be able to keep up, not when she went wolf.

Fifteen minutes later, we were deep in the forest and our plan was working. The scent of Iris's wolf had the demons scattering, and until now, we hadn't seen any. The one that had just stepped out onto the path ahead of us was tall, gray, and its mouth was wide and full of razor-sharp teeth.

Willow moved fast, firing her blade at it. The magic knife never missed and sunk deep into the demon's throat. It charged at us, and I rolled, sweeping its feet out from under it. It hit the ground hard as Willow's knife dislodged itself and flew back to her hand. I quickly pulled mine from its sheath and finished what Willow started, removing its head. I didn't want her getting anywhere near this demon.

"Nice decapitation, little sister," she said when we kept running.

"Thanks."

We met three more demons a few minutes later. Willow fired her magic at the forest floor and tree roots burst from the ground, wrapping around them, stopping them from running at us. I pulled a vial from my pack and tossed it at them, and we kept running, their screams echoing behind us.

Wills smirked. "Vicious little thing, aren't you?"

"Something we have in common."

She chuckled. "These undead fuckers better not be too much farther. Another couple of hours and my morning sickness will kick in."

"Trust you to get your morning sickness at night." My phone buzzed. Rose. "Your wish has been granted. Rose says they're less than a mile away from here."

"Good, let's get this over with."

We jogged for a little while longer, then spotted Iris just ahead. She was crouched behind a boulder near a cluster of trees, and she pressed her finger to her lips when she saw us. We slowed down and bent low, moving as quietly as we could to join her.

"Rose blocked their way, threw a few obstacles in front of them, sending them off course. The animals helped, but I told them not to get too close," Iris said.

Something heavy hit the ground, and I peered around the

boulder. Rose was in the air, and she was using her power to throw dead trees and rocks at Emmaline and Marcel, driving them back in our direction.

"They're moving quicker," Iris said as Marcel picked up one of the boulders and tossed it aside like it was nothing. "Fuck, and stronger."

She was right. "We need to act now, before they're impossible to stop." We had a plan, we just had to execute it perfectly. So, no pressure at all.

"Promise me you'll stay back," I said to Willow. "No matter what, okay?"

"I don't make promises I can't keep, but I promise to try."

"Stubborn witch," I said.

"Takes one to know one."

I looked up at Rose and gave her a thumbs-up, then turned back to Iris and Wills. "Right, you stay the fuck here," I said to Willow, because it needed to be said again to our headstrong sister. Then I turned to Iris. "Call them."

Iris silently called on her magic, and in minutes the forest went from birdsong and the occasional growl from a distant demon to a low-building thunder as every animal within hearing distance headed our way. Sounds of thousands of small feet, flapping wings, chirping and squawking, squeaks and growls and hisses filled the air.

Rose's little bat familiars joined them. They burst through the trees and, swarming, flew around Emmaline and Marcel, animals, birds, bats dive-bombing them.

They both roared and shrieked, making inhuman sounds that lifted the hair on the back of my neck. Iris and I rushed out from behind the boulder, and despite the animals attacking, both sets of milky but lifeless eyes slid to us. Goddess, Calvin's and Margot's eyes, and the hunger aimed our way sent ice through my veins.

"Fuck," Iris said beside me.

They sprinted for us, moving so fucking fast there was no way we could outrun them. Wills called out a spell from behind us, sending her magic into the ground. Tree roots shot up, trying to latch on to their legs as they ran, but they were moving too fast.

Rose flew in front of them and, gritting her teeth, fired her power at them full force. It slowed them down enough for the tree roots to coil around their legs and arms, stopping their forward momentum. They tore at the roots, snapping them as if they were toothpicks. Rose lowered to the ground and, planting her feet, cried out as her power battered against them, as she fought to hold them back. Iris called out orders to her little animal army, and they dove at them, scratching and biting, disorientating Emmaline and Marcel.

I ran for them.

Marcel suddenly wrenched his only arm free and grabbed Rose. Emmaline snapped her teeth, and before I could get to them, Marcel bit down on Rose's bicep.

She screamed in horror and pain.

I slammed my blade into his skull, and it was as if I'd done nothing. He shook his head, as though my blade was nothing more than an annoying bug, and tore at Rose's flesh. A zombie died when you destroyed the brain, but Emmaline and Marcel weren't actual zombies, they were stitched-together meatsuits controlled by angry and vengeful spirits.

Wrenching my blade free, I sliced through his cheek and twisted the blade downward, into the hinge of his jaw. It dislocated and fell limp, releasing Rose. She stumbled back, and Iris grabbed her, pulling her away and wrapping her belt around Rose's upper arm to stop the blood pouring from her.

Marcel made a throaty gurgling sound as he tore the roots from his limbs, and broke free—then ran straight at me. Emmaline right behind him.

Marcel tackled me to the ground, dragging his upper teeth over me, unable to bite down hard without his jaw. Iris kicked Emmaline's legs out from under her, as I hacked at Marcel's arm, through ligaments as he thrashed on top of me. I dug the tip of my blade into his shoulder joint and smacked the end of the pommel, once, twice, popping the bone out. Rendering it useless.

Shoving him off, I sliced the tendons in his legs and ran for Iris. Rose was shrieking, her claws extended from the ends of her fingers, scratching, trying to get Emmaline off Iris.

I screamed a spell as I ran, one that would render Emmaline blind, but it didn't work. Marcel and Emmaline shouldn't exist, and though we could spell *around* them—Willow's earth magic, Rose's burst of power, and Iris's animals—the magic wasn't working on them, which meant we were in serious trouble.

Iris's struggles suddenly stopped. She went limp, blood everywhere. Willow ran forward, unable to stand back any longer.

"Emmaline!" I yelled to get her attention off Iris.

Her head came up, her eyes slicing to me a moment before she bounded to her feet and sprinted for me. Willow ran for us, her hands outstretched, screaming now, calling on her earth magic. Emmaline collided with me, teeth rabidly biting, tearing at my flesh. I shoved my forearm against her throat, trying to hold her snapping mouth away from my throat, and stabbed and sliced at her patchwork flesh.

Willow tried to drag her off, and Emmaline shoved her back with so much force, she flew across the forest floor and into a tree trunk. Willow crawled back to her feet, blood dripping down her face and her arm, not stopping, still calling on her magic, until the earth shook from it.

Roots again flew at Emmaline, dragging her back, whipping around Marcel as well. Willow kept coming, wrapping vines and roots and branches around and around them both. I dragged myself up, blood pouring from the scratches and bites all over me.

I pulled a handful of vials from my bag. "Get back," I yelled at my sisters and closed in on the struggling, snapping undead monsters Maria had created.

Willow stumbled back and Rose grabbed her, pulling her

down beside her. With a cry of rage, I threw the vials with force, and they smashed against the trunk Emmaline and Marcel were bound to.

Their skin instantly started smoking, sizzling and bubbling, their flesh melting from their bones, the bones corroding and disintegrating, their bodies quickly turning to nothing but pulp at the base of the tree.

I turned back to my sisters. Iris was still unmoving, Rose and Willow clinging to her as they watched Emmaline and Marcel dissolve before their eyes. Until all that remained were two souls, confused and angry and afraid.

Power surged through me, not magic but the power Death gave me. A staff appeared in my hand, a smaller version of Death's. Somehow, I knew what I needed to do. "Come with me now," I said to them. "It's time to go."

"We don't want to," Emmaline said. "We're scared."

They'd resisted and missed their chance to go to Heaven. They didn't belong in Hell. But they couldn't stay here, which meant the only place left for them was Limbo. "It's going to be okay," I said.

"Will we be together?"

I held out my hand. "Yes. You'll be together forever."

Emmaline took it, and Marcel took hers. I lifted my staff and banged it on the forest floor, then I was flying through the trees, not just my soul this time but my physical self, all of me, and taking them both with me.

We flew up to the pile of rocks, and I banged my staff again. The rocks reformed into Limbo's gates. We flew through the gateway, along the path of skulls, but instead of traveling to Death's fortress, I took a worn path to a cottage that appeared in the distance.

Emmaline smiled.

"You know this place?" I asked.

"My grandmother's cottage," she said. "It's our favorite place."

I led them to the door, and my skeletal face was reflected back at me in the glass panes. I don't think I'd ever get used to that. Emmaline let go of my hand, then she and Marcel walked in, shutting the door behind them.

Then I was flying back the way I'd come, back through the gates and the forest, back to my sisters. They hadn't moved. What felt like fifteen minutes to me had been no time for them. I looked down at the staff and willed it away. It vanished.

"It's done. They're in Limbo," I said, rushing over to them.

"Thank fuck," Willow said.

I helped her up. "We need to move. Our wounds need treating."

We were immortal, yes. But I wasn't willing to risk it. I had no idea what would happen to one of us if we were close to death. What if we ended up like Chase Golden, stuck in a coma for eternity? Anything was possible.

Rose stayed in her shifted form, she was stronger that way, and half carried, half dragged Iris back the way we had come. I wrapped my arm around Willow and took her weight as she limped along.

The way back took a hell of a lot longer, and it didn't help that we were weak from blood loss. Several demons came at us, and I took them down, killing each and every one before they could attack. Adrenaline pumped through me, and that was the only thing keeping me standing.

"We're almost there," I said when I spotted the forest opening ahead.

That's when I saw our mates. They were headed toward us, and they were moving fast. With snarls and glowing eyes, they crashed through the forest like the monsters they were to get to us.

Then they were there, snatching us off our feet—and getting us the fuck out of there.

Three months later

The entire coven was here, my brothers, Maeve and Uma as well. Daisy had insisted on a proper mating ceremony, and I wasn't going to argue. Not that I wanted to. I'd take any excuse to show everyone that Magnolia was mine.

My mate laughed at something Rose said while she danced with her sisters. Then they were all laughing, happy, carefree for the first time in a fucking long time. Daisy joined them, twirling around and throwing her arms around her girls, now that Magnolia had learned to control her powers.

It had taken some practice, but her control over it became easier and easier with each passing day. Now she could lock them away until she needed them. She'd also ushered several souls to Limbo for Death. She was handling it a lot better than me. I hated that there was somewhere she could go that I couldn't follow.

She'd also been talking to a counselor, someone that Rose knew. It was helping and I was fucking proud of her.

"When's the bedding?" Talon said beside me.

I shook my head at my brother. "We're not doing that. We're not at the village. They do things differently here. Besides, we are already mated."

"You marked her already?" Rook asked, dark eyes sliding to Mags.

After a crow mated, he had his female display his mark on her skin, to show every male with eyes in their heads that she was taken and to touch her was to sign their own death warrant. "I marked her the first time we mated."

"Uma will be disappointed," Payne said.

"Some of the warriors at the village might think she's still fair game," Talon said and shook his head. "You start slitting throats, we lose good warriors. Best she wear something that shows it off next time you bring her home."

"Fine," I said, and possessiveness filled me because deep down I needed them to see it as well.

Magnolia ran to me then, and I pulled her into my arms, sliding my fingers into her thick hair. "You're fucking beautiful."

She grinned up at me. "Dance with me?"

"I only slow dance," I said.

"Sounds good to me."

She took my hand, dragging me out to where the rest of her family was. War, Draven, and Ronan had all claimed their mates as well. Daisy and Art, and Else and Connor were all dancing.

I pulled Mags close. "Happy?"

"Are you really in any doubt?"

"No." I tilted her back and kissed her candy-apple lips. I wanted to kiss her all the time. I had to restrain myself often, or I'd be permanently attached to her gorgeous fucking mouth.

Payne lifted Maeve in his arms, and they came out to dance as well, swaying beside us.

"I wish my parents were here. I wish they got to meet you, that they saw how fucking happy you make me."

"I think they know," she said.

I smiled down at her, holding her tight to me. "So you think you can handle an eternity with me?"

"I think I'll manage," she said and smiled back. "I can handle anything when I'm with you."

I felt the same way.

I kissed her again then, because I couldn't stop myself, and I didn't have to, not anymore.

Then we danced. We danced the rest of the night.

Jasmine

Ren was looking at me again. I felt his amber eyes burning across my skin.

I glanced up and he looked away. Coward.

"What do you think?" I asked Rome who was checking out the picture I'd drawn for my next tattoo.

"Yeah, Jaz, no problem," Rome said and sipped his beer.

Roman did all the tattoos for the hounds—and me. His skill was second to none, but I guess that's what happened when you'd had a thousand years of practice—and I'd taken full advantage of it the last six months. I'd traded a few of my designs for his services, and it was working out well for both of us.

The party was in full swing around us. Mags and Bram's mating was a good excuse to blow off some steam after a stressful few years, and everyone was here—except Zinnia. Her absence was a constant ache. She'd gone back to Death two weeks ago, and her month at home hadn't been long enough. It was never long enough.

I glanced Ren's way again. *Busted.* Again, the fox shifter was staring at me. He gave me a chin lift this time, then turned back to the wolf shifter he was talking to. She was gorgeous and confident, all the things I wasn't. I focused back on Rome. "Cool. I'm helping Wills with the nursery next week, if you're free?"

"I'm free," he said, then winked at Esmeralda, a third cousin of ours.

She blushed while simultaneously undressing him with her eyes. That was my cue to get the hell out of there. It was getting late, and I'd reached my social integration limit. Time to sneak back to my room.

I spotted Ren walking down the side of the house, and I knew I shouldn't. I really shouldn't. But I couldn't stop myself from following him—and wished I hadn't when I rounded the corner.

The wolf was with him, and he was leading her through the front door.

"Bathroom's through there," he was saying to her. She kissed him, giving his ass a squeeze before she dragged herself away.

I should be used to it, but seeing him with her—I felt sick to my stomach. I was about to retreat and get the hell out of there when Ren turned, spotting me, and I had no choice but to keep walking. He smiled instantly, flashing me his flirty grin, the same grin he'd just given his wolf, the same grin he gave all the females who happened to venture into his orbit.

A smile that meant absolutely nothing.

"Hey, Jazzy." His gaze trailed over me, hot, lingering. "You look pretty."

That smile, that look from him in that moment while I felt so lonely for Zinny and guilty over my jealousy of Mags and Bram's happiness was more than I could take. I snapped.

I usually shied away from him when he did that shit, because it meant nothing. I wanted a genuine interaction, instead I got the player. I wasn't a fan of this iteration of Ren, not at all. Anger shot through me, and ignoring the way my heart pounded, I gave him back what he had me. I let my gaze trail over him slowly, before my eyes met his again.

He looked surprised, momentarily stunned, but then he smirked, turning it back on.

Idiot. "You know, I used to think you were a good guy."

His head tilted to the side, his gaze flat, giving me nothing. "And now?"

"Now I think you're a slimy fucking creep, and you kinda make my skin crawl," I said, angry at myself and taking it out on him. His head jerked back, his eyes widening in surprise, not flat anymore, and I won't lie, it was seriously satisfying. "I mean, you were literally kissing a female five seconds ago, then you have the stones to look at me like that?"

"Hang on a minute, I was just—"

"You were just what? Do you even know?" I was so done with pining after this guy. Why did I care? Why? I had to be missing some fucking brain cells. "Behaving like a slime ball comes so naturally to you now, I don't even think you're aware of it."

Ren's lips curled, and he leaned against the wall, not taking his eyes off me. "You kind of sound like a judgmental bitch, Jasmine."

My heart felt as if he'd gone psycho killer on it, rendering it nothing more than a bloody pulp behind my ribs. "I don't really give a fuck how you think I sound." *Yeah, good cover, Jasmine, your voice is hardly shaking at all.*

"Really? You look like you're about to cry." He straightened from the wall and stepped close, too close.

I could smell the wolf's perfume on his clothes and bourbon on his breath. He was drunk. He dipped his head, his face an inch from mine.

"Or maybe you wish it was you I was kissing, that it was you I was taking home to fuck?" he said low, rough.

Ren was a lot of things, but he wasn't cruel. Apparently only I could bring out that side of him. That invisible dagger stabbed me in the heart one more time, then it was jiggled from side to side, over and over, turning the already damaged organ into mincemeat, making sure it was well and truly dead. He was right, I was close to crying, but I sure as hell wouldn't let him see it.

I shoved him. "I'd sooner fuck a cactus, asshole. Smile at me like that again, look at me the way you did…look at me at all, and I'll knee you in the nuts so hard you'll black the fuck out." Then I stormed off, up the stairs, his laughter following me.

I didn't know him anymore. I wasn't sure he knew himself.

He wasn't the fun-loving male I'd met when I was a little girl, or the wounded creature I'd delivered a message to a few years ago after receiving my very first message from the spirit world. He was someone else, someone I didn't like all that much.

It was a pity my head and my heart weren't in cahoots—instead they were bitter rivals.

One was telling me to forget about him.

The other was telling me to never let go.

Which sucked for me since there was literally nothing to grab hold of.

Also by Sherilee Gray

Blood Moon Brides:

Blood Moon Bound

The Thornheart Trials:

A Curse in Darkness

A Vow of Ruin

A Trial by Blood

An Oath at Midnight

A Promise of Ashes

Knights of Hell:

Knight's Seduction

Knight's Redemption

Knight's Salvation

Demon's Temptation

Knight's Dominion

Knight's Absolution

Knight's Retribution

Rocktown Ink:

Beg For You

Sin For You

Meant For you

Bad For You

All For You

Just for You

The Smith Brothers:

Mountain Man

Wild Man

Solitary Man

Lawless Kings:

Shattered King

Broken Rebel

Beautiful Killer

Ruthless Protector

Glorious Sinner

Merciless King

Boosted Hearts:

Swerve

Spin

Slide

Spark

Axle Alley Vipers:

Crashed

Revved

Wrecked

Black Hills Pack:

Lone Wolf's Captive

A Wolf's Deception

Stand Alone Novels:

Breaking Him

About the Author

Sherilee Gray is a kiwi girl and lives in beautiful New Zealand with her husband and their two children. When she isn't writing sexy contemporary or paranormal romance, searching for her next alpha hero on Pinterest, or fueling her voracious book addiction, she can be found dreaming of far off places with a mug of tea in one hand and a bar of chocolate in the other. Visit her at: www.sherileegray.com